So Deadly Fair
Diamonds Don't Burn

GERTRUDE WALKER

INTRODUCTION BY BILL KELLY

Stark House Press • Eureka California

SO DEADLY FAIR / DIAMONDS DON'T BURN

Published by Stark House Press
1315 H Street
Eureka, CA 95501
griffinskye3@sbcglobal.net
www.starkhousepress.com

SO DEADLY FAIR
Copyright © 1948 by Gertrude Walker and published by G. P. Putnam's Sons, New York. Reprinted in paperback by Popular Library, 1952.

DIAMONDS DON'T BURN
Copyright © 1955 by Gertrude Walker and published by Herbert Jenkins, London.

All rights reserved under International and Pan-American Copyright Conventions.

"Introduction" copyright © 2023 by Bill Kelly

ISBN: 979-8-88601-034-3

Cover design by Jeff Vorzimmer, ¡caliente! design, Austin, Texas
Cover illustration by Harry Barton
Text design by Mark Shepard, shepgraphics.com

PUBLISHER'S NOTE:
This is a work of fiction. Names, characters, places and incidents are either the products of the author's imagination or used fictionally, and any resemblance to actual persons, living or dead, events or locales, is entirely coincidental.

Without limiting the rights under copyright reserved above, no part of this publication may be reproduced, stored, or introduced into a retrieval system or transmitted in any form or by any means (electronic, mechanical, photocopying, recording or otherwise) without the prior written permission of both the copyright owner and the above publisher of the book.

First Stark House Press Edition: July 2023

SO DEADLY FAIR

It was dark and raining when Walter Johnson crawls out of the freight car that night. So when he sees a woman motioning to him from the window of a house across from the tracks, he decides to investigate. What he finds is a bloodied corpse, and the set-up with him as the killer. But Johnson doesn't intend to allow himself to be railroaded into a murder charge. He grabs the woman who tried to frame him, and takes off with her for California. Elizabeth is no victim herself. Sooner or later, she is going to have her way. She settles in with Johnson as a reluctant married couple, but Johnson knows that it's only a matter of time before she makes her break. He just didn't realize that this time he'd be accused of *her* murder.

DIAMONDS DON'T BURN

Clara and her husband John have grown apart. Then John introduces her to his friend Roger, and she feels an immediate attraction. But Clara is torn. She doesn't want to become an unfaithful wife. Still, Roger is persuasive, and Clara finds herself meeting him in a New York hotel room. What neither of them could suspect is that a diamond robbery has been planned for the next room that night. Mike Grant has been working on this plan for some time, and nothing is going to get in his way. But how could he know that the man he has set out to rob would wake up, that he would be forced to shoot him? And that racing to escape he would bump into Clara, also trying to escape her situation? Who could foresee that their bags would get mixed up in the confusion?

Gertrude Walker Bibliography
(1902-1995)

Novels:
So Deadly Fair (Putnam, 1947)
Diamonds Don't Burn (Jenkins, 1955; UK only)
The Suspect (Major, 1978; novelization of screenplay for
 Whispering Footsteps, 1943)

Screenplays / Adaptations / Original Story:
Danger! Women at Work (1943)
Mystery Broadcast (1943)
Whispering Footsteps (1943)
Silent Partner (1944)
End of the Road (1944)
Beyond City Lights (1945)
Crime of the Century (1946)
My Dog Shep (1946)
Railroaded! (1947)
The Damned Don't Cry (1950)
Insurance Investigator (1951)

Television Scripts:
Screen Directors Playhouse (episode: "Want Ad Wedding," 1955)
Front Row Center (episode: "Pretend You Belong to Me," 1956)
The New Adventures of Charlie Chan (episode: "The
 Chippendale Racket," 1958)

7
So Deadly Me: The Enemy in the Mirror
The Novels of Gertrude Walker
By Bill Kelly

17
So Deadly Fair
By Gertrude Walker

159
Diamonds Don't Burn
By Gertrude Walker

So Deadly Me: The Enemy in the Mirror
The Novels of Gertrude Walker

By Bill Kelly

Gertrude Walker (1902-1995) wrote three novels, *So Deadly Fair*, *Diamonds Don't Burn* and *The Suspect*. She has thirteen film and TV writing credits and is credited with a bit role in the 1935 movie *Mary Burns, Fugitive* as a nightclub "hostess.", i.e. taxi dancer. Walker has not been credited with any published short fiction work, although the 1950 movie *The Damned Don't Cry* credits a Walker story "Case History" as its source. Walker's credited film and TV career ran from the mid-1930s to the late 1950s and she did not make a "big splash" in either medium. The most intriguing story related to her film work involves her screenwriting credit for the movie *Whispering Footsteps*, a B programmer issued by Republic Studios in 1943. Walker shares screenwriting credit with Dane Lussier and no mention is made of a specific source work upon which the movie is based. Thirty-five years later her final novel, *The Suspect*, was issued by Manor Books as a paperback original. Anyone who has watched *Whispering Footsteps* and read *The Suspect* will have no trouble seeing the similarities between the two works. The movie is well paced and features some good supporting player performances, but is clearly written to the escapist crime thriller standards of the time, with the obligatory happy ending, which in 1943 would be exactly what the public needed and wanted. There is the possibility, based on a reading of *The Suspect*, that Walker's original concept for the movie may have been more hard-edged, but was "toned down" by the studio. Pure projection. Dissatisfied with *Whispering Footsteps*, Walker may have gunny sacked the story and eventually it emerged as a "true Walker" with *The Suspect*, but this is also projection. There is also the possibility that the original work lay dormant and Walker chose to update it to the 1970s milieu, as the novel clearly is not of the 1940s. We may never know the whys and wherefores, but both the movie and novel are well done, the movie by the "B" standards of the time and the novel as a work where, for the third time around, Walker portrays self-obsessed individuals losing control by being forced out of their all-consuming inner lives.

Walter Johnson, the protagonist and narrator of *So Deadly Fair*, is on the bum and has just alighted from a freight train in Minnesota, with not much more than his philosophy to keep him fed and warm. Elizabeth Frazer, Circe-like, beckons to him from a hotel window and asks a simple favor: do some simple grocery shopping for me. Johnson obliges and begins his journey through hell; he becomes obsessed with a woman he feels is pure evil, and will end up spending years resolving the dilemmas that arise from living with her, her betrayals and his own ambivalence about where his own true nature lies. This is indeed a noir novel: an ordinary man makes decisions that plunge him into a maelstrom of grief—with the suspense inherent in noir: will he be able to extricate himself or will he perish?

In Elizabeth, Johnson faces a formidable opponent. The book opens with a quote from Lord Byron's *Giaour*: "So coldly sweet, so deadly fair, / We start, for soul is wanting there." Elizabeth is an existential type character, seeing only the moment and reacting to it: her "life action" for all threatening situations is to manipulate them to her own advantage, on a moment-to-moment basis if necessary, and take down anyone in her way. A totally amoral (soulless) creature, she nevertheless enchants Walter to the point where he will endure anything to enjoy the occasional moments where she fulfills him, fulfillment in this case consisting solely of sexual satisfaction. He is unable to reach her on any other level. Elizabeth is a femme fatale, but innocent in the sense that she can be nothing else and Walter is a full partner in his own downfall. Walter is aware of his irrational obsession, but seems as concerned about the loss of his own soul as much as he is about the consequences of enabling Elizabeth as he provides her with a fall guy, not once, but twice. When he makes his own decisions, Walter digs his hole deeper and in the beginning it is only through fate, "that little word that can excuse a lifetime of mistakes" that Walter is periodically given some hope of revenging himself on Elizabeth, a reason to live that imprisons Walter in his internal hell. Walter believes that there is a better way to live, but he is as hopelessly tied to his revenge mission as he is to his fascination with evil. He is fully aware of the nature of his inner demon after he spots a look-alike in a bar shortly after being released from prison and believing himself "cured":

The moment I walked out of the door of that dive on Market Street I knew that my old sickness had not returned, but a new one had taken its place. A new sickness of old hate, instead of an old sickness of new love. The relapse was upon me.

Those familiar with the works of Jim Thompson will see some similarities between Walter Johnson as a first-person narrator and some of Thompson's protagonists. At times, not unexpectedly, Walter seems wildly unstable, but unlike many of Thompson's characters, he has not crossed the line where he becomes an unredeemable evil figure. He has not become Elizabeth. The war that is going on inside of Walter Johnson is a war he intends to win and somehow achieve the peace he envisions. Thompson's characters, sometimes gleefully, inflict their destruction on others and themselves, consequences be damned. Johnson, interestingly, is often at his best in dealing with other people, getting what he needs while inflicting as little pain as possible. Johnson is capable of respecting and being grateful to those who lend a hand and on occasion, puts aside his own needs to help others.

Gertrude Walker's novels are characterized by situations where the characters make many mistakes, but are provided with opportunities to extricate themselves from the disasters they have created. Her characters often look to "fate" or a "higher power" to answer their pleas and/or believe that a force other than themselves is playing a role in the outcomes they experience. They are not proponents of "faith" as such, but are believers in unseen, uncontrollable events that override their own attempts at control.

Walker presents one significant challenge to the reader and that is the concept of coincidence and its occurrence at pivotal junctures in the story. The frequency of its use would probably be the principal bone of contention for any negative criticism of this work. The ideas of coincidence and believability are of course linked, so it is up to the reader to decide if the coincidences that unwind during the course of plot are believable and if not, do they "spoil" the story. Walker and her characters are very much aware of this potential conflict and address it directly:

> Coincidence is a screwy thing. Some people don't pay much attention to it. They simply call it coincidence and go on about their and someone else's business. To me coincidence is reason, a reason. In other words, there was a reason for me to pick out this particular garage to work in. There was a reason for the guy to hire me, to be nice to me and find me a room. There was a definite reason for me to back that Oldsmobile out of the garage. Some religious folk would call it divine reason. Some infidels would say evil reason. I just say reason. Because that something beyond us that some of us recognize as God, when we call on It or if we call on It, It usually directs us. I was directed to that garage for a reason.

Obviously, most people have a need and sometimes a desire to understand what is happening to them and it can be argued that Johnson's words are "rationalization", that is, an artificial construct designed to relieve internal doubt and confusion. In any case, where the reader may be more concerned is when coincidence seems to bail the author out of a dead end in the story. Walter is searching for Elizabeth, a search triggered by seeing a look-alike just after being released from prison and he believes the breaks are going his way and most importantly, believes he can free himself of his obsession with Elizabeth. After a final promising lead falls flat, Walter faces up to the reality that Elizabeth could be anywhere in this world and ponders that his quest is doomed to failure. But displaying some of the resiliency that has got him this far, he decides to go to New York: "If you haven't got any brains, a hunch is a good substitute." This time he does actually spot Elizabeth, but loses her in a crowd. He will eventually rediscover her through a "coincidence," an event that Walker has in fact laid the ground work for earlier in the book. These prior events do provide all the links in the chain leading to Walter's final confrontation with Elizabeth. More importantly, Walter's tenacity and the decisions he makes, and his efforts to act on these decisions help facilitate the events that eventually lead him to Elizabeth. Fate/coincidence plays a role, but is not the sole determining factor in resolving the story.

Revenge tales can be pretty grim, but the quirky leaps of the narrator's thoughts and scenes interspersed in the book that are sometimes funny and sometimes heart-warming elevate this tale above the ordinary. The courtroom scene that features Walter acting as his own attorney is bizarre, bordering on the surreal. Walker may be having some fun here as Walter's passionate pleas seeking justice for the downtrodden against a world full of enemies probably helps convict him. Or she may have written the scene with cinema in mind. However, Walter, to his credit, is not a complete ideologue. His observations on his fellows (and himself) are often humorously hardboiled:

> I don't know what Frazer taught Hargraves or Hargraves taught Frazer, but it wouldn't be worth writing down on a piece of toilet paper.

> You have to get close to trouble to destroy it. To kick it out. For good. At least I thought so. But I thought a lot of things were right that were subsequently proven wrong. Wisdom doesn't always come with age. My aunt was old and she died an idiot.

That night I took a walk on the beach. I found a lonely rock overlooking the beautiful Pacific. I sat on top of the rock and pretended it was the world I was sitting on and that I had command of not only the entire universe but myself as well. That didn't last long.

So Deadly Fair also features some socio-economic observations from Walter, some of which are eternal, but mostly serve to place his character in a context where we see him rail against "the enemy" but ironically, the people who provide him with the most support come from the wealthy and/or powerful figures in society. Walter neither fails to see the irony nor is he unappreciative when he gets help from those members of the class he berates.

Gertrude Walker may have been having a go at the reader when she decided to dedicate this novel: "To Walter Johnson—who gave me the facts." The narrator has a take it or leave it attitude to his "audience" and seems at no time apologetic for his actions or attitudes, despite seeing his own flaws so vividly. For Walker, dedicating a fiction book to the narrator she created seems to evoke the same attitude, as if to say, "puzzle that one out folks."

So Deadly Fair is a book rich in characterization, not only of the leads, but also of the "supporting players", who emerge as vivid human beings and are not mere props. The reader will find many well-turned phrases, vivid dramatic scenes and running counterpoint to the basic revenge story: a continual self-preservation effort by the protagonist not to extinguish the good within himself with rage, self-pity and the soulless selfishness of his nemesis, Elizabeth.

Diamonds Don't Burn shares thematic elements with *So Deadly Fair*: alienation, selfishness, quest for self-fulfillment and (for two of the characters) an obsession with fate. Both books also feature relatively simple criminous activities and are more focused on the inner lives of the characters than the resolution of the crimes committed. The books are very different in form however, with *Diamonds Don't Burn* using a third person narrative that moves between the activities and inner lives of four characters. There are minor characters, but they play fleeting, and with one exception, colorless roles—unlike *So Deadly Fair*, where most of the minor characters are distinctly drawn and memorable.

Clara is married to John, but John's overwhelming interest is in his work, so Clara, after a one-night stand, engages in a more serious, ambitious affair with Roger. Added to this love triangle is Mike, a low-level, not too competent criminal who has worked his way up to his big score—a diamond burglary. The characters, at first each a corner in a narrative square, meet in the center when Clara and Roger stumble upon Mike attempting to escape his crime from the same hotel where Clara and Roger are meeting. Clara and Mike literally bump into each other and unwittingly exchange the bags they are carrying, resulting in Clara unknowingly making off with the diamonds. Mike's carefully designed in-and-out burglary plan comes a cropper when fate steps in as a sudden breeze through an open window knocks over a lamp, alerting his victim:

> Why the *hell* had that wind blown up like that so strangely, without the slightest warning? It wasn't blowing now. ... Tonight, he thought, for some evil reason, the wind blew crooked.

He kills the owner of the diamonds to avoid capture and thus begins a spiral downward, which to Mike, seems entirely dictated by fate. Clara, too, perceives herself the victim of "chance": regretting her infidelity, she lays her current circumstances at the feet of an unlucky event, the loss of her lucky piece and the big bad world in general:

> It was the St. Christopher! She shouldn't have lost the St. Christopher. Everything would have been all right if she hadn't lost her good-luck charm. Luck! There was no such thing. One made his own luck. How could everything be all right when, according to society, it was all wrong? Society? What society? Whose society? Society as it is today? Rotten to the core!

Clara is clearly not owning, like Mike, the responsibility for her own actions. This is a common attribute for all four characters: mirrors are used for cosmetic use only. All are very selfish people who plea-bargain with themselves, each other and fate when cornered. Of course, the question for the reader is, "will any of these people evolve or will we be subjected to The Pity Pot Chronicles?" All do, however, work to extricate themselves from their predicaments, so the story moves on. Roger is picked up by the police as he is still at the hotel when the police arrive. At first he resolves to shield Clara, but upon further reflection, decides that if he is arrested for murder, he will give her up: "Martyrdom hurts like hell." The point becomes moot when Roger is released and the balance of the plot involves Mike attempting to track Clara down and recover the diamonds.

John eventually learns of Clara's infidelity and is forced to confront his own role in contributing to the situation:

Now he was an object of self-pity, *hurt*, which is self-pity, which is selfishness in one of its most subtle forms. You can be hurt only if you're thinking constantly of yourself. And he was jealous. ... Someone was taking a person *he* loved, enjoying some good *he* desired. Now he had the delayed opportunity of proving the power and perfectibility of his [professional] theories, his philosophy he'd labored so hard to set down. While giving the pills to others, he had neglected to see if they worked on himself, who needed desperately— a healing. ... Yes! Tolerance. He must make every effort to be tolerant. What was it someone said on the subject? "Intolerance is ignorance matured."

Clara too is seeking peace through reconciliation, and Mike, for far different motivations, is also seeking peace, but peace through wealth. After tracking down Clara he challenges *her* idea of peace:

To live a fairly normal life in this abnormal world perhaps would seem a better way of existing to you. Although it wasn't a better way or you wouldn't have been in New York that night. This is a crazy mixed-up world. Where's its security? It hasn't any. Neither in home nor government. Where's its opportunity? It has none. What we create we tear down again. What we earn we give to crooks ... if you'll excuse the expression crooks, *crooks* and politicians. I don't know where one can go to escape it, but at least I have the dough to search for the place.

The final confrontation between the four characters is of page turner quality with all twists and turns being character-driven. Redemption for two comes from shifting their focus from inward to outward, while the two who continue to focus inward seal their own doom. There is a particularly effective series of psychological encounters between John and Michael directly leading to the story's resolution. This type of confrontation has been done many times and is often tedious and/or unconvincing, but not so here. Their confrontation resembles an evenly matched sword duel, so the deck is not stacked and the outcome once again is helped along but not purely determined by outside forces. Although the principals have crippling weaknesses, they are by no means without strengths, so no outcomes can be seen as foregone conclusions, with an "inevitable" ending.

Walker almost always employs an economical style with her prose, whether it is filling in character backstory in small well-spaced increments or writing dramatic scenes of high tension. Walker is equally facile using first person or third person voices. The narrator of *So Deadly Fair* feels like a companion more than merely someone who is just telling you a story, which adds depth to the reading experience. The characters in *Diamonds Don't Burn* do not speak to the reader directly, but so much of their inner life is exposed that they seem much more accessible as human beings: the reader feels involved beyond being a mere observer looking down from above.

At the beginning of this essay, I mentioned Walker's third and final novel, *The Suspect*, a story similar to the 1943 film, *Whispering Footsteps*. Walker returns to the first-person narrator voice, here a narrator who makes Walter Johnson look mellow by comparison. The suspense hook is whether the narrator is a serial murderer or not—even he doesn't know. Walker themes of self-involvement, the ruthless use of others to achieve goals and the element of fate taking a hand and how the character reacts are all present.

Gertrude Walker was not a prolific novelist; much of her professional time from the mid-thirties onward seems to have been focused on Hollywood. There were significant time intervals (seven and twenty-three years) between her three novels. Thematically, Walker has a relatively narrow focus, but without knowing who the author was, I think it would be difficult to say that the same person wrote all three books. *The Suspect* and *So Deadly Fair* have amped-up first-person narrators, but aside from their energy the characters are very different, separating very early from each other as they react very differently to life threatening circumstances. *Diamonds Don't Burn* saw only a British publication (Jenkins), the why of it being lost in the mists of time, but I suspect the plot may have been deemed to similar to many other works of the time, potential publishers perhaps believing that the book was a hybrid genre/mainstream novel concoction that readers wouldn't go for. Ironically perhaps, the two major action scenes in the book, the hotel burglary with the Clara/Mike confrontation and the final confrontation between the four principals trapped in a house during a raging storm, have a cinematic quality that elevates the book above many thrillers of the time. But contemporary US publication was not to be. Fortunately thanks to Jenkins in 1955 and Stark House today, we do have this intriguing mix of domestic strife and heist-gone-wrong to enjoy.

—Mesa, Arizona
April, 2023

Bill Kelly has proofread many Stark House releases since 2017 and recently has contributed introductions to several volumes, including the recently released *Pulp Champagne* by Lorenz Heller. Bill received a B.A. in English from Columbia University and was a technical writer and illustrator for several corporations. Bill's first exposure to crime fiction was the works of Raymond Chandler, Penguin UK editions, purchased in Singapore.

So Deadly Fair

GERTRUDE WALKER

> So coldly sweet, so deadly fair,
> We start, for soul is wanting there.
> —Lord Byron, *The Giaour*

To Walter Johnson—
who gave me the facts.

Chapter 1

When the Minneapolis-bound freight train pulled out of the small Middletown, Minnesota, freight yards, it left behind it very little of importance: a few rolls of barbed wire, some packing cases, and *me*. And God knows I wasn't important. I wasn't important to anyone. Not even to myself.

I wasn't going any place in particular. As a matter of fact, if anyone had asked me I wouldn't have been able to tell where I'd been or where I was at the moment, because I didn't know and somehow I didn't really care. I'd simply got out of the boxcar because I was tired of riding in it. It was cold in there. I didn't know why it was so cold because I didn't have any matches, but as I jumped out I saw I'd been riding in a cold-storage car.

And that was another reason I had got off—because I wanted a match. I wanted to smoke and I wanted to stretch my legs and I wanted something to eat—I was damned hungry. I'd been riding like that for two days. Not on the same freight, of course.

But when I got off it wasn't much better than when I was still on, because it was raining, and because of the rain it felt colder than the freight car. I crouched down beside the tracks until I heard the last faint whistle, and then I stood up to do that little stretching I had promised myself. I stretched all right, but when I looked around at my surroundings I realized that I didn't need to limber up my bones because I was going to have quite a walk to whatever town I was near. It was a good half mile to the small station ahead. I wondered if the paper-thin soles of my shoes could stand the walk along the railroad ties. To hell with my shoes! I wondered if *I* could stand it.

Well, I had been in a lot of other funny predicaments. This was the life that I had chosen. Not that I had been forced to choose it. That was the trouble. I had never been forced to do anything—that was why I'd never done anything. Nuts. The time for philosophizing was always later. Much later. Right then, at that moment, I had a damn long walk to take, and that was all that was important in my life.

As I started down the tracks toward the station it began to rain harder. Of course it always does. And I began to think of all the walks I had taken in my life. Not the walks that got you anyplace, anyplace good, but the walks you took that you had to take because you'd always been on the wrong path.

I remembered that walk I took to the principal's office, that last walk to the principal's office because that was the day when I quit school. I didn't quit school because I hated the principal or because I hated the school—I just hated the walk. It was so damn far from the eighth-grade schoolroom, down that long hall, past all those dirty toilets, up those stairs, and past those silly faces, especially when you knew you were wrong—then they looked sillier—to that big oak door that said, "Mr. Marquand, Principal."

That last day, of course, I didn't get quite to the oak door and I never went back home again.

And then there was that one other walk I remembered so well. I had to remember it. It was always with me. The consequence was always with me. It had first started in one of those cheap little bars on Eighth Avenue in New York. Well, that's the way it always started—in one of those cheap little bars. I walked in just to get a glass of beer. There it was. I walked in. If I had stumbled in or fallen in, it wouldn't have happened. But I walked in. Sober. And I never could keep out of trouble when I was sober. I didn't believe what they said about a guy thinking straight when he hadn't been drinking. For twenty years in my life I could think straight only when I had been drinking. The night I walked into that cheap little bar was the twenty-first year, the sober year.

She was sitting at the far end. That's where they always sit—the far end. And I saw her even before I ordered the beer. You usually see them the moment you throw your dime down. Somehow they can always hear the jingle of a coin and they make you see them. It's sort of a power of suggestion or maybe just plain concentration, because when they want something, the minute they want it—two minutes later—they get it. After I saw her I didn't care anything about the beer. I didn't care anything about the fact that for the first time in my life I'd decided to do some honest labor the next morning. I didn't care about the guy she was with. I didn't even care about getting drunk, if I had had enough money to get drunk on. I simply got off the bar stool, walked the length of the bar, stopped in front of her, and stood there staring.

She was trying to light a cigarette. Naturally she knew that I'd get to her sooner or later, but the staring made her nervous. I didn't say anything to her. I didn't say, "C'mon, babe." I didn't say, "Can I buy you a drink?" I just stood there staring. She got so nervous she finally dropped the match and burned a hole in her dress. Yes, I remember that dress too well. I bought her another one, but that didn't make up for what I finally lost. I only knew her for three weeks. That's all you ever know any of those women—for three weeks. You don't know them for a length of mind, you know them for a length of time. Sometimes, of course, it's longer than three weeks. That's when it's bad. Only, you see, this was my unlucky night, and it could just as well have been three years because the three weeks were worse than bad.

I'd gone back to the hotel one night after a hot poker game where I had won three hundred dollars to buy her another new dress. She wasn't there to get the three hundred, but some guy was there and he got it. And with it he got part of a human body—part of my body, a part that you use every day when you work, if you want to work. Of course it wasn't much loss to me. I never wanted to work anyway. But it wasn't the loss of part of me, part of the physical me, that mattered. It was that damn long walk again from that crummy hotel room to that big white building that looked like a church and smelled like a butcher shop. I always hated hospitals. I never was born in one and I hoped to God I never died in one. And I never will die in one. I already died in one that night. Nobody carried me in. Nobody helped me in. I walked into the operating room.

Yes, it was a good half mile to the station and the rain hadn't stopped. And I wasn't any happier, because when I got there I saw it would be another good mile to the town where I could bum a meal.

I looked in the window at the complacent stationmaster tapping out messages that would never be sent, and if they were, who the hell cared? The train would be wrecked anyhow. I took another few steps, stopped, and looked in another window. The waiting room wasn't crowded and it didn't look like Grand Central. There was no one in it at all. Not even a poor little gray-haired lady with a lunch basket. And there certainly must be a poor little gray-haired lady in a little town in Minnesota.

Well, I figured I'd stand a few minutes and think more thoughts that didn't get me anyplace, then I'd start out to see a new town with the same faces—Ohio, Indiana, Illinois, Minnesota.

I pulled my coat collar up around my neck. It didn't keep out the cold but it kept the rain from dripping down the back of my neck. I fumbled in my pocket and hoped to God I'd find a match caught in the seam or something. No luck. Well, I wouldn't have any luck if I just kept standing there, so I started to cross the tracks. I looked ahead of me. There was an apartment house across the tracks—a three-story apartment house. That was funny. You know you can stand in one spot and look in one direction, think in one direction, and not even be conscious that if you turned your head ever so slightly you might see something that you didn't even know was there—something that might solve your problem.

So after I turned my head and saw the house I figured I'd go right up to the door, ring somebody's bell, and ask for a crust of bread.

Wait a minute! I stopped. What was that in the window of the third floor? It looked like someone standing, watching me. Watching me—

why? Yes, and a woman! From where I stood, it looked like a young woman. I stared at her and she didn't go away. As a matter of fact, she seemed to be waving—waving her hand. Certainly not at me! I looked around. I looked back at the station. I looked down the tracks. She wasn't waving at the stationmaster. He couldn't see her. If the engineer of the freight train was a friend of hers, she'd certainly missed him. It was even too wet for the dogs to be out. There was no one around. No one but me. She was waving to me and I hadn't met a familiar face since I left Canton, Ohio, days ago.

What should I do? Wave back? Was that the polite thing, or was she a lady? Oh, to hell with it! There was a kitchen in the apartment. Whatever she wanted, it couldn't be as important as what I wanted, and that was to feed my face.

I ran quickly across the train tracks and down the small grade to the apartment house. I started to open the door when I heard the buzzer. Ah, the door had opened before me. The world was an open door that no man could shut. At least not for too long, anyway.

I walked on in and stood in the hall, waiting. There wasn't any elevator. I heard her coming down the steps. Not slow but fast. She was in a damn big hurry, and there were so few people that ever hurried to get to me. I heard her hesitate on that last landing before she came into view. That was a good entrance. I liked her already. Subconsciously, I like to make entrances too. I do them very sloppy, but I know there's a flair about me. I like to think of it as a dramatic flair, although I don't know too much about the unreal part of acting, the part you do behind footlights. But if I had a mind to it, I could know.

But somehow that woman hesitated a little too long. It didn't make me like her any the less, understand? It just made me curious, that funny kind of curiosity that bothers you, that you keep wanting to put your finger on. No matter how long you know people that make you feel that curiosity, as the novelists say, you keep wanting to find out what makes them tick.

I've never read many stories. I never needed to—I was always in the midst of one. And you don't read stories and you don't write stories when you're in the midst of them. And you don't write them at all until you're out of them. And if you're not a writer you don't get out of them. I wasn't a writer because I had taken that walk to the principal's office and hadn't gone in, and because I had taken that walk to the hospital and *had* gone in. And because, hell, I didn't want to write! But I wanted damn badly to find out what that woman looked like.

I took one step toward the landing. She didn't hear it but she sensed it. That's another thing about women—they don't have to hear anything.

That sixth sense always tells them. Then I saw her turn the corner and start down the stairs toward me, smiling. If I'd had that sixth sense instead of she, I would have turned and not walked, but run out of that apartment house. But I stood there staring, and after she smiled that way at me I still stood there. And even after she said, "I suppose you think I've got a nerve calling to you like I did?" I still didn't say anything.

She walked clear down to me, to that first step, close to me, too close to me, before I could get my breath, and then she was too close for me to get a good breath. It wasn't until she said, "I wonder if you'd do me a favor?" that I came back to earth. After all, that kind of question would make anybody come back to earth. It was a very interesting question. Would *I* do *her* a favor?

A woman stands in the window and waves to a stranger. A woman in a soft gray negligee runs down three flights of stairs to ask a stranger to do her a favor. A stranger that's cold and wet and tired and hungry and all those things that strangers usually are stands at the bottom of a warm, well-lighted hall and looks up into the face of one of the most beautiful women he ever saw in his life; blue eyes that were really gray, like your first look at the sea, the sea when it's gray. You imagined it should be blue, like the pictures you'd seen hanging in the hallway in your house, too brightly painted, too unreal, but you didn't know it then. That kind of artist's ideas are just that—ideas. Because when you go to look at what you saw painted, it's never the same, because there aren't many masters in life. At least you don't have those masterpieces hanging in your hall, especially when no one looks at them anyway but you, when you're little.

So that first look at the sea doesn't give you a peaceful feeling; it doesn't exactly give you a feeling of great beauty. Of power, yes; of vastness, yes; and of destruction—oh, yes! The kind of destruction you can't get away from if it suddenly decides to envelop you, and without the slightest warning it might overflow its banks and destroy you. And I guess that thrill of uncertainty that nature gives you I got when I looked into her eyes. I didn't need to look any farther, but of course I did. All I could think was that she didn't belong in Middletown, Minnesota, and I felt she hadn't been there long. I knew she hadn't bought that negligee in Middletown. I knew that she hadn't got her hair fixed that way in a little shop around the corner, or rather that she hadn't learned to fix it that way in Middletown. And the body ... I knew the body didn't belong any place but in bed!

But the voice. The voice didn't belong at all. It didn't belong to her. She should have had one of those voices that sounded like coal sliding down a copper chute, or the kind that wakes you up at five in the morning, and when you got sleep in your eyes, but sex in your heart, the voice says, "You're the only guy I ever met that could make me forget the dawn." But her voice wasn't like that. That's the second time I should have run—when I heard her voice. It was sharp and cold and hateful and it belied the smile on her face. When a smile is warm, the voice should be warm. It should come out all warm and throaty and husky. It shouldn't drip ice, sharp jagged points of ice, the kind of ice you dislike to find in a highball glass. She must have used it for screaming. Yet you'd think if she screamed a lot, it would have got hoarse. It was a funny voice that didn't belong anywhere except on a broken victrola record that you were going to throw away. But even that didn't make you like her any less. She still had that body and those long thin hands that almost touched you when she talked, those hands that made you feel even more because they didn't touch you. They just wanted to or had to and you wished to God they would and yet you hated them when they did.

And what can you say to a face like that and eyes like that, and what can you answer to a voice like that when it asks you, "Will you do me a favor?"

You say, "Sure," and then you wait for her to tell you what it is. She opened her left hand and there was a dollar bill in it, all rolled up, like she'd been holding it very tight on the way downstairs. She unfolded it carefully and handed it to me and in that voice began again, "I know this sounds funny and all that, but you see I haven't been very well and I can't get out, especially since it's been raining. I can't get out and there doesn't seem to be anybody around. I called a friend of mine who lives in the apartment upstairs next to mine, but she wasn't home."

She paused to take a deep breath and I wanted to say, "Go on, lady, get to the point," but I knew she was one of those women who never got to the point unless they had a point to get to, immediately—a very dangerous point. I found all that out later, but if I would have admitted it, I knew it all the time.

So I waited and she went on, "I've got to have some things from the grocery. Of course, I know you're a stranger here and all that." She stopped a moment and looked at me as though she'd said something wrong, and then as though she'd said something wrong she began to explain.

"I mean, I saw you at the station and I knew you had got off a train or something, and so because I was in this predicament—well, I just waved, that's all. So would you mind going to the grocery for me? It's only a block down this street," she pointed toward the door, "and then to your left and around the corner."

She handed me the dollar. I made the old familiar gesture. I took off my hat and scratched my head. "O.K. The grocery's right around the corner," I said. "But what am I supposed to get there? You know you haven't told me."

She looked at me and laughed. I wished she hadn't. The voice was worse when it was in a laugh. "Isn't that silly? Of course. I'd like a loaf of bread and a can of vegetable soup, just any kind, and if they have any cake left now, sometimes they don't when it's late." I nodded as though I knew that they didn't have any cake left when it was late in Middletown. "And let's see. Well, I think that's all." She hesitated, I guess because I hesitated.

"Look," I said. She'd started that old gesture of dropping the eyelashes and then batting the eyes—one, two, three. And that time I read her thoughts. So I said them for her. "Look. You were going to ask me to have some dinner in case I hadn't eaten, weren't you?"

But she didn't pull that other old one about "How did you know?" That's what threw me. She simply nodded her head and smiled. The Mona Lisa wasn't missing.

I turned from her and started for the door and I didn't say anything till I got to it. I like to make an exit too. So when I got to it I made a definite turn. "I'll be back in a minute," I said. "And in case your husband comes home, you'd better explain it to him."

She looked at me for a long time and then she said something else that I didn't expect. "I'll leave the door open and when you come back just put the stuff in the hall and keep the change!" Then she turned and ran back up the stairs. It was a good last speech, and if I had been any other kind of guy I would have taken it as a last speech, but I'd heard too many of them in my life, and besides, I was hungry enough to eat the soup out of the can without bothering to open the can.

When I got back from the grocery the door was open all right, but I didn't leave the stuff in the hall and it didn't take me long to run up those stairs and find her apartment because the apartment door was open and I could smell something cooking and I could feel the heat from the gas grate and I could see the room without walking into it. It was a comfortable room, and although it didn't look like she had decorated it, it still had a big chair by a fake fireplace and there were pictures on the wall.

She didn't want me to come in. She wanted me to leave the stuff in the hall. But there was a pair of men's slippers set by the comfortable chair and there was a smoking jacket, at least I think that's what they call them, thrown over the back of the chair. I knew they couldn't be for anybody but me because they were placed with that carelessness that's planned beforehand. I'd never worn a smoking jacket, but I knew that

I was never going to be able to say that again—that I'd never worn a smoking jacket—because before I took that first step into the room she called, "C'mon in. Make yourself at home. I'll be there in a minute."

I was to find out later that she had eyes in the back of her head. I had a teacher once who had eyes in the back of her head. She could stand at the blackboard and call off the names of the kids in the back of the room who were not in the back of the room as they were supposed to be. She could even see through a door when it was closed. I didn't like her either because I never trusted her. She was always able to make me do things I didn't want to do.

And so when I walked in that room after she called to me from the kitchen I didn't want to walk into it. I didn't want to put those groceries on the table, set them down with—what is it they call it?—"that gesture of finality." I didn't want to take off my wet coat and put on that smoking jacket. I didn't want to watch my tired, dirty, wet feet slide into those new slippers she'd put on the floor. But when she came into the room, there I sat, like I had been sitting for hours, as if I'd come home from a hard day's work to see the little wife and to read the evening paper and to smoke the pipe of peace for a few minutes, until the trouble began.

I had never been married but I could always imagine the few minutes of peace you have before you eat that badly cooked food that lies like a lump in your stomach afterward, because of the lie on your tongue first. You always have to say it's good. And then the arguments come about the petty things. And then the dull conversation about what she did today and what she didn't do, and what she said today and what she didn't say, and what she thought and what she didn't think—mostly what she didn't think. And there I was sitting in that chair as if all those things were about to happen.

There was an unreal feeling about the whole thing. I hate anything planned. All my life when things were planned for me I felt they were unreal. Reality is something that's unpredictable. And yet that damned woman was unpredictable. It all didn't make sense.

She walked in front of me and looked down at me. And when I looked up at her and saw that flicker of a smile, her face and the room and everything went away but that smile, and all I could hear was the beating of the underbrush in the jungle when the big cats walk at night. They stalk and you can't hear their feet because nature has padded them, but you can hear that underbrush beat, beat, beat! You can hear their tails beating the underbrush. That's how you know they're coming. So before I knew it I was on my feet and my arms were around her. It was that jungle rhythm. It was the beating of the underbrush. It was the pounding of those native drums. It was that jive roar that deafens you to everything but the roar.

Even after the dynamite exploded I couldn't let go. Naturally she was the one who pulled away. And I wanted her first words to be the kind that go with just what happened when we kissed. And I waited for those first words. But if you have to wait for them you might as well quit waiting, because they're not going to be said. Instead she walked to the table and like a slut in a house dress she picked up the groceries and started to the kitchen, and the first words she spoke she threw over her shoulder. She said, "Make yourself comfortable. I'll have some dinner ready in a minute."

Make yourself comfortable! I felt like a shipwrecked man with no clothes on in the middle of the Waldorf lobby. I sat down again and reached for a newspaper she had so thoughtfully put on the table beside me, but I didn't even get a chance to look at the headlines and I wanted to look at the headlines because I didn't know what was going on in the world and I wanted to know what was going on, but before my fingers could close over that newspaper I heard that voice and I heard it screaming, like I never wanted to hear it, like I knew it could scream but like I hoped to God I'd never have to hear it—in a scream!

She ran into the room so fast that her dove-gray negligee caught on the edge of the table and she had to stop and pull it away. That was a bad move in the scene. That wasn't rehearsed. And it was all so crazy because that was the thing I remembered afterward, how she had to stop screaming a minute to unfasten that negligee caught on the edge of the table. I remembered it because she stopped screaming quickly, like someone had removed the arm off the victrola record and it got all still and then put it on again and it got all noisy. But when she got on her record again she screamed louder.

I caught hold of her just as she started for the window, but she got away from me like a mad dog gets away from you even after you've got it down and are banging its head against the sidewalk. She got to the window just ahead of me to begin that pounding, that native rhythm, not made with drums this time, but made with those long thin hands, clenched. Clenched until their nails must have been digging into the palms, clenched and beating upon the window. Beat upon beat. Beat upon beat. I couldn't understand what she was screaming until she began that beating, and the noise of it was like more dynamite exploded and then suddenly got clear again, got clear enough for me to understand what she was yelling about.

She was screaming the goddamnedest, most ordinary phrases you could think of if you were going to write a bad play. "Help! Help!

Murder, murder! Help! Help!"

I grabbed hold of her shoulders and swung her around toward me. And in the midst of all the crazy unexpected madness sex was there again. That negligee that was like a costume that she'd picked out to wear for this very show she was putting on, the shoulder of it slipped and slipped far enough for me to see something I hadn't seen before. She didn't have anything on underneath it! I hadn't seen it before because I found out later she'd purposely undressed for this big scene. When she'd left me to go to the kitchen, she hadn't gone to the kitchen. She'd gone in the bedroom to strip for her finale.

And so for the second time she stopped the whole performance and she smiled that flicker of a smile. And like the bitch she was she waited for me to pull the negligee over her shoulder again, but I didn't touch it. I didn't reach out and grab her by that beautiful shoulder that I was to know so much about later, that shoulder that I was to see in so many poses, particularly that pose when it shrugged you off till later.

Instead of touching her then like the way she wanted me to, I began to slap the hell out of her. Not once. Not twice. I must have hit her a dozen times, but the expression on her face never changed. I hit her like you'd hit an epileptic or the mad thing that she really was at the moment, but I could have beaten her well into the next day and that wouldn't have stopped her. She knew what she was doing all right. She just waited until I got tired of hitting her and then she began to scream again. This time she added, "Police!"

I never talk a lot but I usually talk when I should, and that time I should have asked her what the hell she was yelling about. Anybody in the situation I was in would have asked for an explanation. But I couldn't talk. And the only thing I could think about was padded cells and people in them trying to get out, people who never would get out because all their lives they had been in them. And I guess that's how I felt then—I felt doomed. And I didn't know why I felt that way. I didn't know what it was all about and I couldn't make my mouth work long enough to ask. And wouldn't it have sounded silly if I had asked? If in a quiet voice I had said, "Look, lady, what is this all about?"

But I got an answer soon enough anyway. As soon as she heard the people, the people running up the stairs from every place and from no place, she got to the door, fast. I didn't try to stop her because my feet wouldn't work and my mouth wouldn't work. So when she got to the door and opened it, the people were already standing in the doorway.

They didn't come into the room. That wasn't normal either—like everything that was happening around us wasn't normal. Those silly sad-eyed people with curiosity hanging on their faces like a wet shawl, they didn't come into the room.

Once I saw an old lady getting on the subway and it was raining like the devil and she had a gray shawl on her head and the rain had soaked through it and she had lost the safety pins somewhere that held it together so the way it was hanging on her head you couldn't distinguish her face from the shawl. And when you looked at her, it gave you a feeling of curiosity because you wanted to know which was the face and which was the shawl, and you wanted to know how long that blankness could hang that way. And I wanted to know how long those faces in that door could hang that way because when she started to scream at them, the same words she screamed at me, they didn't get excited, those faces, and froth at the mouth and run in the room and out of the room and take steps that got them nowhere because they were excited about something that they didn't know the meaning of.

So I kept wanting to scream at them like she was screaming and ask why they didn't act like people act at the scene of an accident or when they know a body is going to be carried out of an apartment house. I wanted to ask them why they didn't leap into the burning building and try to help the policeman drag out somebody they didn't know. Well, if they didn't have that morbid curiosity, I had it! It was beginning to surge up in me. I was beginning to come alive again.

I ran over to where she was standing like a dreadful sentinel in front of those people. She was pointing toward a door and I pulled that arm, the arm that was pointing, and in a voice that naturally didn't sound like my own I said those silly words, "What is this all about?"

She got very calm. She got calmer than she'd ever been, than I ever saw her. Than she ever was when I ever knew her. And because she got calm maybe for the first time in her life, her voice was a little lower, a little less rasping, and she said, this time pointing to me, "That man killed my husband!"

Then the faces began to move. They came closer and closer, and yet if you'd had a measuring stick you would have found they'd only moved a few inches, just inside the door, because they didn't believe it yet. They wanted to believe it. Suddenly they were eager faces and they wanted to believe it because they were looking around for the blood but they were afraid they might step in it so they didn't come too far in the room.

Before I had time to make one of those speeches in defense of myself, she ran to the door she had pointed to at first and flung it open. And in the room, on the floor, near the ugliest brass bed I'd ever seen, a man lay—a fat, squashy, ugly man, uglier at that particular moment because death was lying beside him. And the ugly man had two knife wounds in his heart, in his big fat, generous heart—for he was the guy who had bought her that dove-gray negligee.

It would have looked better on him right then. It would have covered the blood all over his white shirt, and if it had covered the blood on his white shirt it would have covered the bloat on his blue face, because if she had taken it off and covered him up she would have had to cover that face. I couldn't look at him longer than the minute that I did look at him, and I knew that the people standing in that doorway straining their necks to look at death, I knew they couldn't look at him any longer either, because I heard their shudder. But she could look at him. She must have looked at him every night for weeks, looked at him and gloated and waited till she could play this scene.

I guess after all I should have been an actor, because as soon as I got over feeling sick I turned to our audience and in my new calm actorish voice said, "I never saw that man before in my life!"

And without any more buildup and without any more screaming, without movement even, she said, "He lies! The knife he used is in the pocket of his robe."

I put my hand into the pocket of the robe, *my* robe then, and my hand stuck to the bloody blade!

But that was only the beginning, the beginning for me. It was my turn. I took my hand out slowly. I paused and looked at the people. I looked at her. They were waiting all right. They were waiting to see a bloody hand come out of that pocket. And they got their money's worth. But they got more than they expected when they paid for their tickets. They got a hell of a lot more. My hand didn't come out alone. The knife came out with it and the blade was sticking to my palm! I held it up for everyone to see. I knew if there was a God He was with me. Or if there was a law of gravity or something like that, it was with me, because I knew it was going to work and it did!

The knife stuck to my hand until I got it as high as I wanted it, then I shook my hand and the knife fell off to the floor. It didn't make one of those big sounds that you expect—a crash that isn't a crash. It made hardly any sound at all, so it didn't take away from the rest of my performance. Their eyes were still on my hand, my hand that wasn't my hand, and I held their eyes there because I knew that they almost knew that it wasn't my hand. They almost knew. I would have to tell them. I would have to make it plain for them. So I took my time again and I turned to the bloated face and I made myself look at it until they looked at it and then I looked down at the blood on the white shirt and I smiled and said, "I know a lot about guys that have been stabbed. I've seen a lot of guys stabbed and I know about knife wounds. I had a couple myself. I know pretty damned quick whether they're made by a right-handed person or whether they're made by a left-handed person. Whoever that man is, he was stabbed by someone with a right hand."

It was a long speech, and a shot in the dark, but they were with me. She was with me. The very stillness around about her was with me. She had turned white but she hadn't begun to shake yet. She was waiting for my last speech. The short one. The short speech.

I looked at her when I made it. I looked at her and said, "See, *I* haven't got a right hand. The one you're looking at, with the blood on it, isn't mine. Some guy in Detroit made it. For twenty-five dollars. I never paid him for it but he let me have it. It looks real, doesn't it? But real things move. I can't move one finger on that hand because you can't move wood and you can't stab people with your right hand—not when it's made of wood."

I said it was a short speech. It was. Because the minute I started talking they knew. But I carried it on to the end. I carried it on to think what our next move was going to be. I say our, because when I began that speech I knew what I was going to do. I was going to make her understand how she had lost, but I was going to turn right around and save her for myself.

When the faces began to move again they began to move fast, but I was too quick for them. Even with my wooden hand I was too quick. I got to the door before they got too far into the room and I began shoving them. I began herding them, like you do cattle, but instead of using a horse to herd them I used a bloody hand, so they got out much quicker than they had moved in. When the last one got into the hall I slammed the door shut and turned the key in the lock; then I turned around.

She hadn't moved at all. The bloody hand didn't seem to scare her. I guess she was a couple of paragraphs ahead of me because as I turned around to her she made her first move. She ran to the bedroom where the bloated face was, and that time her negligee didn't catch on anything because his mouth wasn't open and it couldn't catch on his teeth so it didn't catch on anything. It just floated over the ugly blueness of his face and some of the blood from the knife wound, made by the right-handed person, stuck to the bottom of her gown.

I stood watching her long enough to see her step over the body. And when she stepped over it I knew right then that she forgot it was even there. I knew she forgot things were there when their usefulness had gone.

I let her do what she had to do in the bedroom and I knew what it was. She was opening a drawer. I could hear her even as I ran to the closet in the living room with the fake fireplace. I opened the closet door and grabbed an overcoat, one that belonged to the ugly face. And though I didn't hear her take the money out of the drawer, I knew she took it.

By the time I had the overcoat on she had made her final gesture of sympathy to the dead. She had shut the door to the room and was standing waiting for my next decision. I said, "Where's your car?" She looked at me but that flicker of a smile didn't come. She hadn't any time for sex right then. You don't have time for sex when you're trying to save your life.

"The keys are in that coat pocket, the coat you've got on. And there's a back stairway through the kitchen." I started to the kitchen but she had the same idea too and we bumped as we went through the door. I wanted to laugh. I wanted to scream. But I knew the scream would come out like hers. I was on the verge of hysteria—me—a great hulk like me—six feet tall with a brain on top, a brain that was never used quite enough, I was on the verge of feminine hysteria.

But I wouldn't have got a chance to laugh much or rather no one would have heard it because the pounding in the hall began, a pounding that was going to end very soon in a door busting in.

We got through the kitchen and down the back stairs. How I never knew. You go through so many of those damned things and you can always apply the phrase "How I never knew."

As we were going down the stairs I bumped my head several times, and to this day I don't know what I bumped it against. The ceiling was too high and there weren't any rafters. She was too far ahead for me to hit her. Maybe my head was bumping against my conscience. If it was, it was the only way I could tell I had a conscience—when it hurt that way. A real hurt, a physical hurt.

I was going to have my worst hurt later. I was going to die later and forget to bury my body. I was going to walk to my own grave and never find it because I wasn't going to remember where I'd dug it. I was finally going to do what they had all done before me—pin little white notes to despair.

Thank God the car wasn't in the garage because she had parked it in the alley for a quick getaway, alone. You see, plans don't work. She'd never be alone again. Not until that last day, and then she wouldn't know about the aloneness. She wouldn't even know it was the last day.

She got in the car first, but I shoved her out of the driver's seat. And even as I shoved her and did all those mechanical things that you do in a hurry—things that you never did before ... I had never driven a car like that but I put the right key in the ignition and I found the starter ... I found it without a moment's hesitation ... I found the lights too and I even looked at the gas tank and saw it was full—all the time I wasn't thinking about any of those things. I was thinking of that last day. And as I put the key in the ignition, stepped on the starter, switched on the lights, and checked the gas, I could have written the end of our story. And that's what I was thinking about as I drove out of that alley, as she kept telling me which way to go. But I didn't go the way she told me to. I let the car go the way it wanted to.

And when I finally talked to her, I talked through my teeth and I said, "Shut up. Stop yapping! If there's a highway around I'll find it, but let me find it my way. It's my game now."

She shut up all right and I found the highway. I guess it was the right highway for me to find but it was the wrong path again.

As I turned on the highway I saw that she wanted to talk to me but she was scared. I saw her make a gesture as though to say, "This isn't the way I had planned it. I wasn't going this way. Turn around. Turn back."

She didn't say it because she saw the look on my face. That was the strongest moment I ever had with her from that time on.

Chapter 2

I managed her all along that highway—all along that highway my heel was ground in her face and it was a damned long highway because we went clear from Middletown, Minnesota, to some little dump of a town in California.

I traveled once through the states of Kansas and Nebraska—through that stinking dust bowl on a handcar, and I looked like a petrified Okie when I got to where I thought I was going, which wasn't anyplace. I bought a fishing boat once, a dirty busted-up fishing boat, and I sailed clear down the coast of Mexico by myself. I've ridden in trains and planes, in submarines, busses, boxcars, and battleships. I've been alone. I've been with two people, three people, hundreds of people. I've been hungry, tired, well fed, and well heeled. I've slept with bums, chorus boys, and a countess who wasn't a countess because she hadn't been anyplace to be a countess. But that ride to California, that long ride that didn't seem to have any end, that I took with Elizabeth Frazer—yeah, I found out her name—I had to call her something—she didn't tell me it was her name but I had to call her something so I asked her, and I always liked the name Elizabeth; that ride was one of the strangest rides in history if anybody was going to write a history that included strange rides like Ichabod Crane and the Headless Horseman, the Highwayman and "the road, a ribbon of moonlight," and Paul Revere and his goddam lantern. Yeah, I remembered those rides from school, from reading about them. Of course, that was the only thing I did remember. Maybe I screwed them up a little bit when I remembered them with her, but the feeling was there all right.

She didn't have any radio in the car. At first I was mad about that. I was mad at her because she had never bought one. But after a few hundred miles I was glad. I was glad not to hear the reports coming over. I knew they'd be looking for us but it was better we didn't hear about it. It's better when you don't hear about people looking for you. They find you when the time is ripe.

Naturally I did all those things that you read about. I had my wits. I stopped long enough to steal license plates and change them on the car. I avoided big towns, and when we had to eat we ate in white-tiled joints and some of them not so white.

She still had on that bloody, stinking negligee, but she had thought to put a coat, a camel's hair greatcoat, in the back of the car because she knew whichever way she went it was to be a quick getaway. So she kept warm in that and it covered up the ugly spots on the negligee. I guess she pinned the negligee up around her. I wasn't in the mood to be looking at her legs much.

As soon as I could I got rid of the beautiful new maroon smoking jacket with the bloody crust sticking to the sides of the pocket. I burned it in a real fireplace in one of those crummy motels where we made our only overnight stop. I can smell that odor yet and it was such an ordinary odor of burning wool. But when it came out it smelled to me like burning flesh. She didn't smell it. She didn't even watch me burn it. She'd been in the next bed to mine asleep for two hours.

And when they write stories about those women again they should tell about their sleep. They should put in a paragraph about how they sleep—like a child. How they look—like a spent child in sleep. A child that has forgotten about her everyday cares, her broken toys, her dolls. So innocent, so without guile. And that's the way they look because that's the way they have to think. As far as they're concerned, they are without guile. They're without guile all right. They don't even know the meaning of the word.

We drove at nights except for our one stopover. Then one night while we were passing through a little town on the Texas border she got a brilliant idea she wanted to go shopping. It was Saturday night and she felt we'd be safe if we went shopping on Saturday night when the town was crowded. I let her out at Sears, Roebuck. She told me to come back for her in about an hour. I shook my head. "Uh-uh, Elizabeth," I said, "I wouldn't let you out of my sight for more than a minute. You could turn this town upside down in a minute."

I smiled but she wasn't having any of it. She flounced into the store with me at her heels. She still had on the greatcoat. It was a warm night and I saw some of the Western housewives giving her the old one, two, three. We went to the ladies' department and she bought a cheap rayon dress, a pair of slacks, some shoes, and a blouse.

As I waited outside of the dressing room I heard her talking to the clerk, explaining about her negligee. "I been sick," she said, "and there isn't one dress I have that fits me. My husband came down with me to get a few things I needed. I'm not really supposed to be out."

Then I heard the clerk's voice and my hands got clammy. "Are you new here in town?" she asked. The question was bona fide. Elizabeth didn't look like Westbrook, Texas, and the clerk was observant enough to know it. But the answer? I waited. It might be anything. I wasn't so well acquainted with all of Elizabeth's reactions, but I knew enough to expect anything. There was a long pause, then, "I'm staying with friends here," she said. "I've been to a hot springs resort nearby."

I unclenched my fists and took a deep breath to steady my knees. Elizabeth was still talking. "I'll be leaving shortly for Los Angeles," she was saying. "I have friends there and I think I'll stay. Lovely country, California. Have you ever been there?"

The clerk must have shaken her head no. Elizabeth started to tell her about the natural beauties of California when the clerk interrupted her. "Is that your home?" she asked. God, I thought, why doesn't Elizabeth just put that bloody awful Sears, Roebuck special on and shut up and get out? After we'd made the decision to stop for clothes I had a premonition it was a bad idea.

Then I heard Elizabeth answering her, "No, I come from the Middle West, or rather that's where my husband and I have been living lately."

"What state?" The clerk was a curious biddy. I began to wonder why.

I heard Elizabeth clear her throat and that was my last cue. I stuck my head in through the dressing room curtain. "Elizabeth," I barked, "make it snappy. The doctor said you weren't to stand on your feet too long. Your head maybe, but not your feet."

Elizabeth glared at me, then she began to giggle, two pauses behind the point. "Don't worry, Walter dear," she said. "I know what I'm doing."

I pulled my head out of the stuffy dressing room. "I doubt it," I mumbled.

In a few minutes she came out wearing the dress. It was too tight for her and the neck was cut so low she didn't dare lean over. I looked at her and smiled. "You couldn't drink out of a spring," I said.

The clerk laughed. "Your wife's the type that can wear those things. She's so lovely."

While she went to get the change I stood and surveyed Elizabeth. Despite the cheap tightness of the ugly rayon she was lovely. Standing in front of a mirror, daubing herself with powder, she looked like a young matron, fresh and happy and without any sin except the original one of being a woman. She looked like a girl just out of boarding school who'd got herself a new black dress to wear to the spring dance. She looked like a smart career dame, one whose nails were stained only with red polish, not dripping with the blood of a murdered man; a girl who smelled brightly of cologne and good air, not a woman who was wrapped in the odor of death and breathing the dank air of putrefaction. She turned from the mirror and smiled at me. "These are the cheapest clothes I ever wore," she said.

The clerk came back with the change and thanked us. I grabbed Elizabeth's arm. She pulled away from me and looked down at my wooden hand distastefully. I moved on the other side and took hold of her with my good hand. As we walked down the stairs to the first floor I whispered in her ear. "You should be squeamish," I said, "especially about a hand. Remember where you came from."

She glared hate at me and quickened her steps to the door. I had to run to catch up with her.

We had parked the car in the parking lot at the side of the store. When we got in the lot we saw a bunch of people standing around a car. I stopped short and pulled Elizabeth toward me.

"Keep quiet," I said, "but I think that's our car they're looking at. Have you got your driver's license?" She nodded calmly. "Give it to me," I said.

She reached in the pocket of the camel's hair coat she had thrown over her arm, fishing around a few minutes until she found the license. I took it from her and moved into the light to look at it. It was made out to Elizabeth Frazer. A Minnesota state license, issued at Minneapolis. I moved back, close to her. "O.K.," I said, "at least this doesn't say Middletown. Come on, and no matter what happens let me do the talking."

We walked up to the car. I was right. They were standing around her car and it had a honey of a smashed fender. I looked at it a few minutes as though I were a spectator, too. Then she lamped it and I saw the pride of possession in her angry eyes. She ran to the car. I knew she was going to blast her fool head off about her beautiful car and it never had a dent in it before and who the hell was so careless as to bang into it and she'd have them arrested and more of that mad car talk so I beat her to it.

"Who hit the guy's car?" I said.

An old man matted with the good Texas earth spoke up. "Wal, I was jist backin' out when my wife says somethin' to me about stoppin' to let her out. She forgot to git an egg beater. So I went to reach fer the brake and instead I stuck the goldarned thing in gear and backed into this here autymobile. I been waitin' fer the gentleman that owns it so's I could give him my name."

I took hold of the fender that was scraping the tire. "Give me a hand here, fellows." Two young kids were standing by, looking for a little excitement. They moved on either side of me and we pulled the fender away from the tire.

"O.K., that does it." I turned to the old man. "If I was you, pardner, I'd just leave these folks a note with your name and address. They may be on the town and there's no tellin' when they'll get back here."

The old geezer hesitated. "Wal," he said, "I thought maybe I oughter call the sheriff. That'll cost about twenty-five bucks to git fixed. The sheriff's a friend of mine and he'd know I wasn't no hit-and-run driver."

With the mention of the word sheriff I heard Elizabeth gasp.

"That's not necessary," I said. "I'll tell you what." I reached in my pocket. "Here." I handed the old man a card and a pencil. "Write your name here and I'll stick it on the steering wheel. They'll get in touch with you tomorrow, I'm sure."

The old man took the card and examined it carefully, turning it over in his hand a couple of times. I didn't know what the devil was on it. I was so anxious to get the hell out of there without claiming the car in front of the sheriff that I'd handed him the card without looking at it. Finally he nodded his head. "Yep, maybe you're right. I gotta git home anyways. I got a sick calf to see about. Yep." He put on his glasses, held the card against my back, and printed his name and address. It was a laborious process. I looked at Elizabeth's face. She was more nervous than the old man's calf.

He finished writing and handed me the card. I tossed it in the car, then we waited till he got in his Ford and drove away.

The two boys were still standing by our car when Elizabeth and I got in. I started the motor and they looked at me like I was crazy. I saw the card I'd given the old man was advertising a Texas dairy. I tossed it out the window toward the boys. "It's O.K., fellows," I said, "it's my car. I just didn't want the old guy to have to pay for it."

The kids nodded, surprised, and Elizabeth and I beat it out of the parking lot. The kids probably went home and told their parents about the incident and what a great fellow I was, a good human being, a real American, didn't even make a scene about a guy hitting his fender, didn't even ask the poor guy to pay for it. It was an accident. Who pays for accidents?

Yeah, fellows, one of the better human beings, a guy that started across the state of Texas with a murderess, a fine American, an accomplice with his trigger woman.

How many times I wanted to stop, get out of that car, and run you'll never know. Just run anywhere that would take me away from her. And yet anywhere that would take me away from her I didn't want to be. What malignant power evil has! I hated her guts like I hated the villainess in a movie thriller when I was eight years old and a stranger to strong emotion. I hated the villainess and I hissed her and shot imaginary bullets at her, but she fascinated me so much that my dreams were never free of her until the movie serial was ended and the characters forgotten.

I wanted to know something about Elizabeth, her background, where she came from, where she was going, who she was. I made her talk about herself, hoping with every paragraph, every word, that she would tell me something that would make me respect her.

She told me about her childhood. It hadn't been too happy. Her father and mother had quarreled a lot. Her father had been a jockey, a flyweight, a vaudevillian, a newspaper reporter, and finally a circulation manager of a small county paper.

Her mother was from what she called a pretty good family, well-educated but pampered and spoiled and not too "trustworthy." Elizabeth said she disliked her mother but she didn't mind the old man. They'd given her a good education. She'd started with private schools but was finally kicked out because she gave all-night parties in her room. Then she went to high school. Her diploma was withheld because a girl said she'd stolen some things from a department store. It was true. She'd swiped a compact and a pair of gloves but her old man settled for them. Then her mother paid plenty to get her into a small college someplace in Missouri. One night she was found nude in the men's dorm and kicked out. She giggled when she told me that. "And you know, Walter, it was so silly," she said. "I hadn't done anything. As a matter of fact, I was still a virgin. That's more than most of the girls could say. We were just playing strip poker, that's all. I always was a bad card player."

She finally ended up in a business school and got a job as a secretary. Beyond that she refused to tell me, so I asked her what happened to her folks.

She shrugged. "Dad started to drink a lot and was killed in some kind of a street brawl. And Mother, I don't know. She died, I guess. In a rest home. I don't know."

I tried to find a note of sympathy in her voice, a line of sadness in her face. There were none. "I don't understand you, Elizabeth," I said. "I loved my mother. She died when I was little but I loved her. Even my old man, who used to beat me, I didn't mind him. When I heard he had a stroke it made me sad. A little. Like it would make you sad if you heard someone else's dog got run over. Even if he was cross."

She pulled her lips tight across her teeth, tight as an elastic band, then she spoke through her tight lips. "Just because a couple of people are your mother and father, why do you have to respect them? Or like them? Their names were Jim and Eloise. They were people. People I didn't like. Who didn't like me. Especially."

I didn't say any more but for a moment I felt sorry for her. I didn't feel respect but I felt sorrow. I think in a way I know what she meant. I had a pretty good picture of her mother and father. After she fell silent I went over the picture in my mind, scraped together from the bits and pieces she told me. Her mother had been a beautiful pampered woman. She went to the sulky races one day and saw a good-looking sexy guy driving a handsome mare. Through her connections she wangled an introduction to him. She wangled him. They were married. He was the horseman of the hour and her old man had some dough so it was even Steven. After the newness of sex wore off they stayed together for various reasons. First it was the year 1904 and people didn't get divorces so quickly, and second they wanted to stay in the old man's graces. Pretty soon they had the baby, Elizabeth. Then the World War came along and he went off to war like a hero and came back like a hero. He'd won some amateur boxing contests in the army and decided to train for the flyweight championship. Elizabeth was left in care of a nurse while Ma and Pa toured the boxing circuits. He won a few titles and was offered a vaudeville tour. Elizabeth's mother wanted some more glamour so she went on the Keith Orpheum Circuit with him. Elizabeth was still left behind, with governesses now who didn't understand her.

When her mother and father came back the grandfather died and left them some dough and they started out again, this time for Europe. Elizabeth was dumped into a boarding school. And by the time they decided to reclaim their baggage she'd grown up into a stranger. Finally three strangers attempted to pick up the threads of a domestic existence that never did or never could exist. Eventually the money left and the quarrels came. And the stagnation.

And that was the atmosphere Elizabeth Frazer blew out of, and despite it she achieved a semblance of an education. So is education the answer to delinquency? To crime? Not really. Not school education. Some of the worst crimes are being committed by so-called intellectuals. It starts farther back than schools, the right kind of training. It starts in the minds of the parents. Maybe Elizabeth was right. They weren't Father and Mother. Their names were Jim and Eloise and they were strangers to her. What can be done with parents like that? It still doesn't seem right to drown them.

I felt sorry for her.

But it still didn't explain my fascination. It's like when you're little and keep passing that house that's haunted. You know you shouldn't go in. It's dark and cobwebby and dank and gruesome. The steps are busted and they creak when you put your big toe on them. Tramps have left paper bags, old bourbon bottles, and pieces of dirty, undignified paper all over the porch. A dead cat's carcass careens precariously on the broken shingled roof above. There's an odor of damp wood, termites, and broken plumbing about the place. And way deep inside, way in the interior, there might be found anything from the headless horseman to the body of a stillborn child. But you've got to go in the house and see for yourself. You can't just keep passing it day after day, you've just got to go in. You're driven to it. You're driven to defy your parents and your schoolteacher and your principal and your own better judgment and enter that defiled domicile with its rumored ghosts. The fascination has got you, and while it's upon you nothing else matters, home, school, or the coming picnic. And that's the way you feel about some people. When you grow up and get hair on your chest and chin, and iron in your jaw and head; when you bounce hopes instead of toys on solid cement, that's the way you feel about some people. And that's the way I felt about her. And if you were just looking at the outside of her you might feel that way, too. Because there were very few women who were any more beautiful. Sometimes God wraps the devil in velvet.

The devil and I rode side by side, safe as in the inside of the crater of an active volcano, and we arrived, eventually, in California.

Chapter 3

When we got to that little dump of a town in California it was like a breath of fresh air in the midst of a blast furnace. California's always good to get to and then good to get away from. It's good to get to because when you get to the desert that air lifts you up and you float over, especially at night. Most tourists rave about the heat of the desert in the daytime. It isn't the heat of the desert. It's the heat from their own stupid tempers because they make a mistake in going through it in the daytime. But to me it's good both in the daytime and in the nighttime.

There's a freedom about the air and the air isn't always free. The air in a cell isn't free. Every cubic foot of it has been paid for again and again.

As we drove to that desert town and I saw it rise up out of nowhere like a neon rabbit rising out of a magician's hat, I forgot she was with me. I forgot that her bleached head was resting on my shoulder in that childlike sleep and I remembered my first trip to California. Later I remembered why I remembered it—because this town that stuck up out of the desert before us was the same town that I'd spent my first night in when I was alone once. Alone and sad but with only the sadness of aloneness, which can be peaceful.

I opened the windows of the little hotel I was in and I took a deep breath that lasted all night long. I didn't move from those windows all night long. I couldn't believe the air. I couldn't believe the trees. I couldn't believe the smell of real live orange blossoms that weren't left over from an Italian wedding. I say Italian because I'd only been to two weddings in my life. One was a shotgun wedding where I guarded the guy with the shotgun, and the other was Italian with mock orange blossoms and a groom who'd just hacked his way through six iron bars to get to the wedding so he'd be married before the police put him back in again. I'd known him for years. I went to school with him. He'd quit in the seventh grade before I quit in the eighth grade. That made us very close the rest of our lives.

And so I sat in that car with her and remembered all those things. I guess she felt my thoughts because she woke up, batted those big eyes, yawned, stretched, looked out at the town and the horizon, the neon mirage, and said, "Oh, my God! I hope there's a beauty parlor in that town. I just broke my last nail."

I could have told her what she broke it on but I was trying to be a gentleman. I was too damn tired to be anything else.

She wouldn't tell me whether she had any money left. After the sixth time I stopped asking her. But after seeing that town and remembering a few pleasant hours in my past, I got my second wind again, which gave me renewed courage, so I asked her again and this time I was going to be damned mean because if she hadn't answered the way she did, I was going to beat the hell out of her.

Of course she answered me the way she did, which was the unpredictable way again. She took a cigarette out of a jeweled cigarette case. I guess that was the only thing she filched out of the drawer besides the money. Then she carefully lit the cigarette, looked at me, smiled slowly, and said, "Of course I have some money left. I have fifty dollars." Then she giggled that horrible giggle and said, "Don't spend it all in one place."

I ought to have hit her anyway for that crack. God knows I'm not too bright, but I can't stand old vaudeville gags at eleven o'clock at night in the middle of the desert when you're so tired that even a murder is difficult to remember.

We didn't say any more until we got to the middle of the town, but I made sure we weren't going to drive to the same hotel that I'd once been in. I couldn't have taken that. Anything but that. And I knew the hotel because it had two great big palm trees in front of it. So I found a hotel that didn't have two great big palm trees in front of it and we went in.

We registered as man and wife, using a phony name I thought up over a cup of coffee in a Chinese restaurant. The name sounded like a horse you wouldn't bet on but it was good enough for us for a couple of years.

Yeah, we went into that room to stay one night. We went into that town to stay twenty-four hours. We went into that state of California to stay a couple of days and we stayed three years.

A guy said a minute could be an eternity. Another guy said an eternity could last a minute. But where in the hell is the guy who forgot to say that three years with evil is less than a second and more than a lifetime? Don't look now but he's sitting right next to you, only he doesn't know it. He doesn't know the awful end of evil—the awful long, long days that come when you discover that evil's been sitting with you at your board and sleeping beside you in your bed and that it'll never go away until you write your name on that big fat check —write it with a pen dipped in that blood that's too damn yellow to be recognized as a signature.

I stopped signing checks long ago because I never had any bank account.

We didn't stay in the hotel long. Just a couple of nights. Long enough for her to buy a few things she needed, like a housecoat and a sweater and skirt. No matter how much taste that kind of woman has, when they insist on wearing a sweater and skirt, the kind of sweater they wear is always two sizes too small and the skirt's slit up the side almost to the hipbone. At least it looks like it's going to split a little more when they sit down.

So we took the housecoat and the sweater and skirt and the memory of a brief past and went to a little motel that I found on the edge of the town. Twenty dollars a month, two rooms, a kitchen, and a garage. The bath was quite a walk from our cottage. At first I was unhappy about that. I should be unhappy about baths! I'd never been bath-conscious before, but since I had a beautiful, clever murderess to live with I thought I should be clean physically even though I never could be mentally. So that long walk, walk, walk, walk! Right foot in front of the left foot. Left foot in front of the right foot. Right foot in front of the left foot. That walk to the bath was a pleasant one because I got away from her a while. I suppose it was the only pleasant walk I'd ever known. Thank God that obsession, that right foot in front of the left foot, has gone from me now. When it left I knew I was free again.

The motel wasn't so bad. And when she got on that little flowered housecoat and stood over the stove cooking bacon and eggs and talking a mile a minute, like she usually talked in the morning when you didn't want her to but when it sounded good because your thoughts had driven you crazy all night long, I had a feeling for her, a feeling that she kind of belonged over that stove, even over a stove that I might buy her—someday.

She was a damned good actress. And the food didn't lie in your stomach in a lump like I expected it to. But I had long since made up my mind that what I expected to get from her, I never would get.

The garage was at the side of the motel, one of those things where you drive under a shed. The first night I drove the car under the shed and I kept it there for two months. I destroyed the license plates we had stolen and I bought me a can of automobile paint and a spray, and in the daytime when she was in the house reading borrowed magazines or writing letters that never would be sent because I wouldn't let her send them, I painted the car so it wouldn't be recognized.

I've learned in my life that you can do too many things to keep away from detection. The less you do, the more chance you have of not being found. It's a mental thing really. I didn't have any fear of being found. I didn't give a damn! And she didn't think about it because she didn't think about anything but herself and the present moment. And if she didn't think about it she couldn't be frightened. It was the only right thing about her—the only right thing. She lived for the present moment so she lived without fear. But her present moments were all evil, so what the hell?

In a sense she'd get there, to that awful reckoning point, sooner than the guy who was afraid of his evil. Because when you're afraid, sometimes you do little things that deter you, make your path deviate from the wrong one, and it takes you a little longer to get to that bloody hell that's waiting for you. It all adds up to one thing—that life and everything in it is a paradox—a touch of hate and a touch of love—a touch of heaven and a touch of hell. And it was hell to paint that car to make it look like it hadn't been painted by an amateur.

When I got it painted I let it set in the garage. And while she was making friends with the few people in the court I went out and looked for a job. That was always a hard thing for me to do because I never wanted to find one but I knew I had to find one then. So the first place

I went to, I found one. People who can't find a job can't find one because they pass by places where they could find one and don't go in and then keep telling you over and over again that they wish they had one.

I got a job as a mechanic in the Carleton Motor Company. I should have got a job as a locksmith, I'd picked enough locks in my life. But I made more money as a mechanic, at least enough to keep her in new housecoats and permanents. Because even with my left hand I'm a hell of a mechanic. The serial numbers that I've burned off of motor engines, if laid end to end, would make the devil's social security number. So besides the dough I had another good reason to get a job as a mechanic. I wanted to burn off the serial numbers on our—her car. And I wanted to steal me a blank bill of sale in case I decided to sell the car. I knew all the angles and intended to work them, but this time I really didn't care whether they worked or not. This time I really didn't care because I knew the end.

Chapter 4

After the first day in the garage I went home feeling tired, not exactly happy, but tired. And on the way home I thought of myself in the light of a married guy for the first time. I thought of her standing over that stove with the little wisps of blonde hair falling over her face that should have been greasy but never was. And I thought of the slippers that she might put by the chair as she did once before. She didn't this time because we didn't have any. And I thought of the *Carleton Evening News* laid out on a table made by me out of an old packing crate. And I thought of the nice newly painted car in the garage, the car that I didn't own and couldn't drive yet. And I thought of the five dollars that we had in our coffee-tin bank. And I thought of the dishes washed and the paper put away and the money counted and the slippers put under the bed. I thought of a night in the arms of a beautiful woman who loved me very much because I'd just saved her life and because I was damned good in bed. And then I added up all those thoughts and scraped the blood off of them and swept away the hate and the bitterness, and by the time I got to the house I was whistling a tune that sounded like Mendelssohn's "Wedding March" after you've forgotten how the rest of it goes.

I walked into the house like a guy who had just been made happy by a dame who'd said yes and a preacher who'd said, "May you live in peace." But as I opened the door, I realized she wasn't standing over the stove with or without a knife in her hand. She was talking a mile a minute and there was someone in the room she was talking to because she didn't act for nothing or no one.

I heard her say, "Oh, I won't be here long. Walter and I—I mean my husband and I were just on our way to Los Angeles. We just stopped off for a little while—you know, the desert and all that. I haven't been—I mean he hasn't been too well and the desert is good for him, or so they say. Of course, he may not be able to leave, I mean he may not want to, but I'll go anyway. I have lots of friends in Los Angeles—I mean, well, at least one, and I'll be able to stay with her. She's an old friend from Minnesota or, well, one of those Western states. I never ask where people come from, you know. I never believe it's any of my business."

She didn't hear me come in. She had her back to me, but the woman she was talking to saw me and I don't think she heard much of the conversation because she was looking at me with that curiosity, that unexplained curiosity, and I knew why. She wondered why I just stood there and didn't say anything.

But I waited until Elizabeth finished and then I said, "Hello, Elizabeth. Entertaining this evening?"

But she didn't bat one of those big eyes. She didn't open that sensuous mouth and hold it in a pose that said, "Oh, my God—you!" She didn't even catch her measured breath. She scarcely turned. If she did turn, it was—what do they call it?—imperceptible.

But she answered me. Oh, yes, she answered me. She said, "No, Walter, Mrs. Hargraves and I— You've seen Mrs. Hargraves. She lives across the court. She and I were just talking about—well, you know what women usually talk about. But don't you fret. I already have dinner on the stove."

Mrs. Hargraves got up. When she got up she was a fat dumpy woman. When I first looked at her, she looked tall, but then she had a surprised look, her mouth had dropped open, and her face was longer that way, her whole body seemed longer. Thought can do that. But in reality she was a small, dumpy woman with a small, dumpy, evil mind. I found all that out later, much later. In fact, too late.

I put my hand out to Mrs. Hargraves. "How are you, Mrs. Hargraves? Glad to know you. Glad to know neighbors. You never know when you might need them." I smiled and waited. And Mrs. Hargraves said the expected thing.

She giggled and said, "You're so right. You just never know when you might need neighbors. You can be sitting on your front porch and you can be perfectly safe and then all of a sudden just anything might happen and well, then you really need a friend, don't you?"

"Like the chair breaking, Mrs. Hargraves?" I asked. "If you're ever sitting on your front porch and the chair does break, call me. I can fix it. I can fix lots of things."

I looked at Elizabeth. She got my thought. I turned to Mrs. Hargraves. "I can fix lots of things," I repeated. Then I turned to Elizabeth again. "I got a job today as a mechanic. So you see, Mrs. Hargraves is right, you never know."

Mrs. Hargraves was on her way to the door by that time and she was in a pretty good mood. I'd made her laugh and I'd made her forget what Elizabeth had just been saying about Los Angeles, but I hadn't forgotten.

Mrs. Hargraves said her polite farewells and went on across the court. And after she left, I threw my hat in the ring. Elizabeth was waiting to catch it.

"So a guy's waiting in Los Angeles for you, is he? Well, let the son-of-a-bitch wait! Let him wait until I get good and ready to send you to Los Angeles—until I can go with you. I knew you hadn't killed that fat ugly face for nothing. So you killed him for another guy—another guy who has more money? But you didn't expect one more guy to come along, a guy who had more brains than you and more brains than the other one. But I pity the other one anyway. I pity him because he has to wait for you. I pity anyone who has to wait for you because he waits for hell! I wish I could speak to this other guy. I wish you'd give me his address so I could write him and tell him not to wait. Because if he waits he waits for the Four Horsemen and you'll be riding the last horse—the one called Death! And when he comes riding along with you on his back there won't be room for another guy. But you'll make room for him and he'll have an unpleasant and uncompromising ride to hell!"

She wanted to speak, but she knew if she said one word, this time I'd really hit her. "Look, Elizabeth," I said, "I want you to get this straight once and for all. You're going to stay here with me as long as I feel it's necessary to stay, and you're going to keep your mouth shut! I don't care how many Mrs. Hargraves you have here in the house. Have lots of them. Invite them in for tea. Have a big party. Get drunk! But if ever again I catch you telling them about you or the millions of guys waiting for you, I'll put you right beside that ugly face in Middletown, Minnesota! Because this time I'm saving myself and if it means saving you, too, I'm gonna be damn sure you play it my way!"

She knew she couldn't answer me, so she got up calmly and started for the kitchen.

"Wait a minute," I called to her. "I'm not through yet." She walked back into the room. Not too far but far enough.

"And why the hell do you think I'm saving you? Whether you think so or not, I could've got out of that apartment house and left you there. It was your murder, not mine. I saved you for one reason only and I've told you that many times—for myself! You're pretty dumb to stage that phony murder and think you were gonna get away with it, but I don't believe you're so dumb that you don't know why I saved you. I know you haven't forgotten that kiss and I don't intend to let you forget it. I know I'm not the most unattractive man you ever met and I bet I wouldn't be too damn wrong in saying I'm one of the most attractive you've met except my pockets aren't full of dough, but they *can* be." I stopped and waited and she did just what I hoped she'd do. She walked a little farther into the room. So I repeated the last line. "But they can be, Elizabeth," I said.

I saw the moneybag look in her eyes. She was already in the money house counting out the gold. She walked a little closer to me. "And they *might* be, Elizabeth," I said again quietly. The words were just enough. They made just time enough for her to get right up to me and I saw that smile starting, that flicker of a smile, and I finished it for her in my arms.

And that was the beginning of my biggest lie. It was the beginning of those nights in bed that I knew could be there. And I guess after all, at that time, that's all I wanted. I knew damn well I'd never make any more than any garage mechanic unless I started the little tricks again—the racing forms, the phony dollar bills, the hot furs, the shakedowns, but I wasn't going to start any of those rackets for her. I was just going to keep her with me as long as I wanted her, as long as I wanted her in bed. I wasn't going to think about the next day. I was going to be like her. I was going to live for the moment and lie for the moment. I was going to mix honesty and dishonesty and hate and love and hot and cold. I was simply going to live like other people do. Except other people don't always live with a murderess, a woman who has actually murdered. But even that I was going to force out of my mind.

So after that first night in bed, I woke to a new day. Not the kind of new day that people awaken to when they decide to live that life of truth and beauty, but a new day as far as my routine was concerned. I was going to begin step by step to build that wall around her and me so that no one could get in—no one like Mrs. Hargraves and no one with a blue coat and brass buttons and a gun on his hip. And then when I built it up as securely as possible, then I was going to sit back and wait. But years later when I finally asked myself what I was waiting for, I didn't have the faintest idea.

When I think back on those years, I wonder how the hell they went so fast. Once I saw a guy sit at a big desk in a big office of a big insurance company, and that guy sitting there made me realize how unexplainable time is, how undependable. To some people time means it's too long, to some it's too short, and to some lucky ones it doesn't exist at all. I had to go in the office to see about an insurance policy a friend of mine had. I was to be a sort of witness for my friend. He had fire insurance and he burned his house down and I'd been there the night before he did it.

I knew he was going to do it. And even though you know they're going to do it, after they do it you can hardly believe it. I don't know why he wanted to do it. I guess he did it because he had such a nice face and such a lousy house. Later, in a book I found, I read about people with complacent faces. They're the ones that have a lot of little termites hiding in their square heads just waiting to pop out. And that guy had a lot. I nicknamed him the firebug after that. But I guess I had a lot of termites too, because I was at the house the night before and I acted as a witness for him so he could collect the insurance. I told them how it happened. I told them I saw my friend, the complacent one, drop a match into a wastepaper basket and that we were sure the match was out when we left the house but we found out later that the house had burned down and that the wastepaper basket was made of some inflammable material and shouldn't have been sold for a wastepaper basket.

It was a damned lie because the guy never had a wastepaper basket. His house was so full of crap that you couldn't walk through it. He didn't have anything worth keeping. And if you don't have anything worth keeping, you don't have anything worth throwing away. But anyhow, he didn't get the dough. They proved he didn't have a wastepaper basket, and even if he had had one he shouldn't have thrown matches in it. He took a rap for the attempted fraud, but it didn't hurt me because I proved that I was drunk at the time.

But that isn't what I was getting at. When I went into that insurance office, I saw this insurance guy turn the calendar on his desk, and he flipped away a year in three seconds by turning those pages real fast. I flipped away three years without turning the pages of a paper calendar ... without even turning one page.

We came to be very good citizens of that little town in California. I even went so far as to join the American Legion. We went to dances in an old ex-beer hall. Mr. and Mrs. Walter Blodgett, we finally called ourselves. Mrs. Hargraves became, not our friend, but her closest friend. It was a funny combination, Mattie Hargraves and Elizabeth Frazer. I don't know what Frazer taught Hargraves or Hargraves taught Frazer, but it wouldn't be worth writing down on a piece of toilet paper.

But Elizabeth Frazer tried to teach me a hell of a lot. I thought she had taught me, but the years that came later convinced me she hadn't. She hadn't taught me enough that I couldn't forget, because I've made a hell of a stab at forgetting it. And I have forgotten it way down deep inside of me. It's only the surface that remembers. The surface greets the day, but the way-deep-down inside greets the night, and the night's when you live with your own soul; when you take out that dirty broom that's all ugly bristles and you try to sweep away the remnants of that ugly face, of all the ugly faces you've ever known. And if you've got a strong arm, even though the broom's dirty and has no bristles, someday you get it all swept away. God does it for you.

Chapter 5

When you bum around as long as I have, you're bound to meet a lot of crummy people. During the depression I lived in a ratty apartment house in Hollywood, and most of the time all I had to eat were oranges swiped off of trees in someone's backyard, sample packages of cornflakes that were left at the door, or homemade gin that I aged myself and sold to the neighbors. I knew a bootlegger who later became a movie star. He was a pretty good guy. Tough, up the hard way, no education, but an old lady that made wonderful Italian spaghetti and an old man who played the races when he wasn't trying to eke out a living selling old clothes from door to door. I know the kid's setup wasn't the best in the world, but he became a movie star just the same.

I knew plenty of dames who'd been kept and those who were keeping. The gal that lived next door and shared her rations with me had been well kept once. Before the crash. She used to say to me, "Walter, the worst tramps in the world aren't walking the streets. When I was young and healthy I had so many clothes I couldn't get 'em all into the apartment. I used to give 'em away. I kept my family and a half dozen bums and now none of 'em will even speak to me. They're in church thankin' God they're not like I am."

She'd cry on my shoulder and ask me to try to help her. She wanted me to buy her cocaine so she could forget. She was a "cokie" and died in the apartment along with a chow dog, her only friend. They didn't find her body for three days and the dog had gone mad. I took up a collection to bury her body, cover it over with a hunk of steel so that her family and friends wouldn't have to look at her if they ever ran across her in some cemetery.

I lived in a cheap hotel in New York and my best friends were an alcoholic actress who'd had one big hit, then tried to drown her following failures in alcohol, and a racketeer who ran the pinball setup in Jersey. He raised blue-ribbon Boston bulls and painted godawful murals on restaurant walls, bright blue scenes with Italian gondolas sailing along unnatural-looking water. He thought he was a second Rembrandt. I knew he was a killer but it never entered my mind to either censure him or try to reform him.

I didn't delve into brains then. I didn't even think once of wanting to find out what made all the screwballs tick. But the years I lived with Elizabeth in Carleton, California, I met so-called normal everyday people, and when I say in some cases they're a hell of a lot worse than honest-to-God bums and grifters, I can prove it. I had a lot of time to study them, and the little termites rattling around in their heads make just as large a noise.

When you're not too deeply interested in something, and leave it alone or toss it off, you're pretty safe. But when you start to get interested in something, want to figure it out, particularly if it's a person, you've got to beware. It begins to be suspicious of you. In other words, in order to get along in the world you have to give the world up. In order to keep people out of your hair you got to keep them away from your hair. You got to keep out of sight of people.

While Mattie Hargraves and Elizabeth spent a lot of time together I never interfered. They went shopping, had tea, lemonade, coffee, shared their daily gossip. Occasionally both families would eat together. Sometimes at the Hargraves'. Sometimes at our place. Charley Hargraves and I never had anything in common. He was a quiet taciturn little man who worked in a shoe store all day and read history books at night. I didn't know what he thought about anyone or anything and he didn't often give me the chance to know. But I had nothing against him.

Mrs. Hargraves I didn't like at all. She was too much like Elizabeth might have been if she'd been born like Mrs. Hargraves was.

One day I came home from the garage a little earlier than usual. I brought Spike, a colored kid, home with me to help clean the house and do some odd jobs around the motel. Spike was O.K. He wasn't very bright but he was honest and had a sense of humor.

Elizabeth was at the grocery with Mrs. Hargraves and before we were through cleaning they came back. Neither Spike nor I saw them coming up the walk to the cottage. He'd pulled the moth-eaten rug off the floor and was going to wash it for me. Without looking he stepped out the door to shake the dirt out of it. I heard a scream and ran to the door. Mrs. Hargraves and Elizabeth were just coming up onto the porch and Spike hadn't seen them. He'd dusted the dirty rug in Mrs. Hargraves' face. She screamed and choked, coughing and spitting dirt and dog hairs. Elizabeth, who was trailing her, bumped into her, lost her footing, and took a spill on the steps. Milk, eggs, onions, potatoes, the whole works went flying. It was good slapstick stuff but I didn't have time to laugh.

Mrs. Hargraves blew up like an angry rhinoceros. She picked up a paper off the porch and whacked poor Spike across the face. I ran out the door, grabbed the paper away from her, and shoved her into a chair. Spike hadn't moved. He'd turned white, then back to brown again, but he hadn't moved.

Old Lady Hargraves' face was dirty and streaked and she was shaking up and down and from side to side like a tub of old bacon grease. "You dirty nigger," she yelled, "you get out of this court!"

"Shut up, Mrs. Hargraves!" I said. "Shut up or I'll throw you off the porch. The kid didn't mean it. He didn't even see you coming."

"Get him out of here! I hate him. I hate the lazy critters!"

She started to cry like she was going to develop a swell case of hysterics. I pulled my arm back to slap her and Elizabeth jumped me. "Don't, Walter," she screamed, "you're liable to hurt her!"

"I'd like to slap her well into the African jungles. The stupid ass! Can't she see Spike didn't mean it?" I turned toward Spike, but the doorway was empty. I looked across the side lot next to the motel, and there was the poor guy running like a bat out of hell.

I turned back to Mrs. Hargraves. "What kind of a human being do you call yourself, anyway? Would you have acted like that if it'd been your husband who'd done it instead of that poor kid?"

She settled herself into the chair. Now that Spike was gone she felt calmer. "I hate niggers," she said. "They're dirty and you can't trust 'em. He did that on purpose. They're risin' up against us, I tell you!"

Elizabeth was picking up the groceries. She started into the house for a broom to sweep up the broken eggs. "I don't think he saw you, Mattie," she said.

"He saw me all right, Elizabeth!"

"You're a goddamned liar," I said. "You know it was an accident. You and your puny Midwestern morality. Your kind don't belong in the open spaces. Why don't you go back to Circleville, Ohio, or wherever the hell you came from? No, I know. Go to Georgia! Go south! There you could hate with company. There you'd have company. There you and your gossipy old friends could build your puny hates into that monster that'll destroy you someday. That's destroying you today!"

I turned away and walked quickly toward the door but her words followed me. They were calm and spoken with the kind of venom I knew her tepid exterior hid. "You just be careful what you say to me, Mr. Blodgett. You just be careful, that's all. I ain't a spiteful woman but if I wanted to I could say a few things you might not like. So be careful!"

Even though the veiled threat shook me clear to my boots, I went on inside the house and let her pick up her things and get home the best way she could.

I tried not to dwell on what she said, but that night after dinner I told it to Elizabeth. "What did she mean, Elizabeth?" I said. "What did that old bat mean? Have you been shooting your mouth off?"

Elizabeth was ironing a shirt for me. She set the iron down on the board, tested it with her finger, then gave me one of her bland stares. "It's nothing, Walter. Except a few weeks after we were here she caught me reading the paper about ..."

She stopped and walked over to the sink to wet a towel. I followed her, took hold of her shoulders, and swung her around facing me. "About what, Elizabeth? About what?"

She tried to pull away from me, "Ouch, Walter. Don't!"

I let go of her and waited. She walked back to the ironing board. "Oh, you know," she said, and her tone was more casual. "About the ... well, the murder in Minnesota."

"I thought I told you not to think about Minnesota or the murder or anything you've ever known before this."

"Well, but people are human. They got to think and talk. The papers were full of it. As a matter of fact, this was her paper I'd stolen off the porch, a Los Angeles Sunday paper. I don't think she saw the article. I tore the page out and put the paper back on the porch. I know she didn't see it. Anyway, that's been a whole year now. Over a year. She didn't mean that."

"Well," I said, "if she didn't mean that, why did you bring it up? What do you think she meant, Elizabeth?"

She shrugged. "I told her you and I've been quarreling lately and that I might leave you. I think that's what she meant." She said it carelessly enough but she averted her gaze. She'd just picked up the iron again to finish my shirt. I grabbed the iron from her. She screamed and backed away from me. I slammed the iron on the board and followed her into the bedroom. I know she thought I was going to kill her.

I shut the bedroom door and let her have it. "Listen to me, you bitch. If you've got any more ideas about leaving here you better get them out of your head! Because the minute I know you've beaten it I'm going to call the cops. Do you get that? I'm going to call the cops and tell them who you are!"

When she saw I wasn't going to throttle her she got her courage back. She sat down on the bed and dropped her hands in her lap dramatically. "But Walter!" Her abnormally high voice rose two octaves. She studied her hands a moment, then looked up at me pathetically. She was dying to cry, but it would take more than a Bermuda onion to open those little-used ducts. "But Walter," she whined, "how long do you think I can go on like this? Ironing and cooking and sewing? Things that are foreign to me, things I never intended to do. You can't expect to hold me here forever, locked away from the world, the world I love. It's been two years already. We just can't keep on living this way. Look at this place. A joint. A miserable packing case. Walls cracked and peeling. The furniture something that I wouldn't have in a maid's room. And the neighbors! Oh, my God. Walter, I can't listen to that Hargraves woman any longer. Please!"

I waited until she finished the act. It was damned well done, like an appeal from a lady. I stood and looked at her until the effect of her histrionics wore off of herself, and then I said very calmly, "And why not, Elizabeth? What's to prevent us from living like this year after year, century after century?"

She clenched her fist and pounded weakly on the hard bed. "But 'Walter! My God, Walter, it isn't decent! It isn't even existing. I planned it differently. I planned it differently a long time ago. And even you, you said it wouldn't always be like this. But I don't believe it now! You'll never be anything more than what you are, a bum! A mechanic. A mechanical bum!" She began to laugh. I walked over to her. Close. She saw the menace in my eyes. She stopped laughing suddenly and put her hand to her mouth to suppress that horrible screeching.

"And you're a lot better than a bum? Is that it, Elizabeth? When we first came here I told you that I'd make a lot of dough someday. Maybe I will and maybe I won't, but I'm gonna take a few years and find out. And you're gonna hang around until I do find out! And I'm thinking you'd better hang around too. This has been a good hiding place. Figure it out for a minute. Use that great brain of yours. You've been living here, openly, for two years. You know the sheriff. You say hello to him. You know the policemen, the firemen, the mayor. They nod to you on the streets, give your gams a second look. You're safe. Damned safe. That's been proven. Stay that way, Elizabeth. For a little while longer. There's no way to make money in jail."

She took her hand down from her mouth. Her lipstick was smeared all over her face. She looked like a wax doll that had been left in the sun and was beginning to melt. I saw the speech had made a little impression. She batted her big eyes and said, "But you can't make money in that garage, Walter. Here we are living like pigs and I'm used to good things. That's what I was born for and I'm going to have them!"

I figured there was no use. I sat down on the edge of the bed and took one of her restless hands in mine. I couldn't force her with anger. I couldn't faze her with realism. You have to give it to children the sugarcoated way. She saw my changed attitude and her hand relaxed and her smile was almost soft. "Elizabeth," I said, "let's don't quarrel any longer."

She shook her head no, tossed her hair out of her eyes, and looked at me so innocently that for a moment I forgot everything about her except her beauty. Her eyes were like rich blue velvet that had never been worn. I would have liked to say that to her, but I knew it wouldn't come out like poetry and wouldn't be appreciated like poetry.

She took hold of one of my fingers and twisted it around hers. Like all children, she was well aware of the mood. "I do love you, Walter," she said. "You're awfully good-looking and you make love like no one else...."

"And I'm smart and entertaining and trickier even than you are."

She laughed. "Yes, but you're not doing like you promised. You're not making any money so that we can have a beautiful house and a new car and pretty clothes. I want you to look well dressed, too. Oh, I saw the most beautiful suit in an ad in a magazine. It was Harris tweed and it had big shoulders and high plaits in the trousers and oh, you'd look so handsome in it."

It was a screwy thing. Most of the women I'd known were nicer people, but not one of them was ever interested in what I should wear. I held her hand. Tight. "All right, Elizabeth," I said, "we'll have those things, but you've got to give me a little more time. I'm working on a big deal and it's going to take a little more time."

She caught her breath and looked up at me, from under the arches of her brows. "Are you telling me the truth this time, Walter? Honest Injun?"

"Honest Injun," I lied.

She put her head on my shoulder, her arm went slowly around my neck, and she shoved me gently onto the bed. The whisper in my ear I didn't quite get, but I knew what she meant.

That night, after we'd gone to bed, I woke up suddenly. The air had got cold like it does in the middle of the night in California, but it hadn't got that cold. I was wet ice. My feet were like rocks of wet ice and my palms were as damp as if I'd dipped them in cold water or the blood of a friend a long time dead. I listened but there was no sound. I looked over at Elizabeth. She was sleeping quietly, peacefully, as she always slept. I took a deep breath and it cut into me, sharp knife points into my chest. Then I knew! It was my conscience again. This cold air and wet clamminess, these sharp pains were a conscience that I only knew I had when it hurt this way. Two years of this sickness. How many more, dear God? How many more before I could either get her what she wanted or rid myself of what she had that I still wanted?

Yeah, you can know a lot of people when you're free and unencumbered with the last evil, and they're just people to you. They don't make you wake up in the middle of the night with ice water coursing through your veins. But living like I'd been the last two years when there was plenty of time to study me and the other fellow is when you get a chance to see why the grave awaits all men and some sooner than others.

Chapter 6

Things have happened in my life in threes. I was born the third month on the third day. It was three o'clock in the morning that awful night when I lay awake on that operating table. It was exactly three o'clock when the doctor raised the knife and brought it down on my arm. It was the third of April, the rainy third of April, when I walked into an apartment house, a well-lighted, comfortable apartment house in a town in Minnesota. And it was three years, two months, and three days that I lived with her. Three days to the very minute on the third day of the week at three o'clock in the morning that I walked into the house and found her gone. And it was only three steps from the back door—three of my steps—well measured, to that small funeral pyre she left behind.

What can you make out of the figure three? You can turn it around on its side and it makes a W—that's my first name, W—W for Walter. Then you can turn it around the right way again, and it makes a B almost, if you add another line. And *if* you add another line and make it a B, it could mean burn, bitch, burn! And if you turn it upside down again, facing the W, it makes an M —M for murder!

I know I haven't got a great mind. Most of the times in my life I wondered if I even had a mind. But although the slate has been wiped clean since those horrible hours I spent before I was convicted of murder on circumstantial evidence, I still don't understand how they could have convicted me. I don't understand why I couldn't have talked myself out of it. I don't understand why I couldn't find where the cards were stacked. If I could've found out where they were stacked, I could've kicked them over and they would have made sense. They would have made a poker hand—a full house for me. I say I don't understand, but there are so many things that none of us understand. And yet I'm beginning to understand. I'm beginning to stack the cards myself, my way. I guess I'm just learning to deal myself a hand from the top of the deck. But the fact remains, I was convicted of murdering Elizabeth

Frazer!

When I saw that little pile of junk and crap out in the backyard of our motel it didn't mean anything to me at the time. I thought, It's funny Elizabeth isn't here, and what in the hell's she been burning? I knew something had been burned. Not recently, not in the last few minutes, because there were no embers, and there were very few ashes. And I knew that morning there hadn't been any ashes because I notice everything, particularly out-of-the-ordinary things, even though they're just ashes. I've had to sweep away enough refuse in my life, mine and other people's, so I kind of sensed there was something wrong. I saw the evidence that there was something wrong, that all wasn't quite right with the Blodgett household.

Of course, the first thing I did was stand and think, think of where she could have gone and why the hell she didn't leave me a note or something. I'd run out the door quickly, looking for her, but I walked back into the house and my steps were a little more thoughtful, methodical.

I went to the closet, first, to see if maybe she'd run away from me and gone to Los Angeles, to that guy I knew she had waiting for her. But her clothes were all in order. They were too much in order. They looked as though they'd been carefully hung up, too carefully. She wasn't a messy person, but she had a little habit of sticking a hanger in a dress so that one sleeve of the dress usually hung off the hanger. But each one of her dresses, and there weren't many, was hung too carefully. The sleeves were where they should have been and the tips of the toes of her shoes were in a straight line. So what's missing? I said to myself. What dress was she wearing? What shoes?

I stood another moment. Her sweater and skirt weren't there. I ran to the dresser. I opened it like a thief opens a dresser drawer when he hasn't much time, when he hears that key being turned in the lock. I opened the second drawer and the third. She was wearing her sweater and skirt all right. Now I said to myself, What does she have on her feet? She couldn't have gone very far in house slippers, and yet I knew she had gone a hell of a long way because her house slippers weren't around. They weren't in the closet. They weren't under the bed. They weren't thrown carelessly on the floor near the armchair.

I sat down and lit a cigarette. What's the hurry? I kept saying to myself. Why are you thinking ahead? And what are you thinking about? She's just next door talking Mrs. Hargraves' fool head off. But wait a minute! Mrs. Hargraves goes to bed at a reasonable hour. A reasonable hour? I looked at my watch. It was three-thirty in the morning. Mrs. Hargraves wouldn't stay up for anybody or anything, not even a choice bit of gossip Elizabeth Frazer might want to tell her. So where the hell could she go at three-thirty in the morning? There was only one restaurant in town and she wouldn't be caught dead there. Dead! Dead, I said to myself. Dead. Dead! *Dead!*

I jumped up quickly. I had to see Mrs. Hargraves. I had to see someone!

Did you ever sit peacefully in a room, nothing had happened to you during the day except something peaceful and nothing had happened to you during the night except something peaceful, and your thoughts were on little trivial things that didn't matter, that weren't important? And you reached in your pocket for a pipe or a cigarette and you lit the cigarette and watched the flame flickering and you smiled that soft peaceful smile, not wondering if everything were right with the people in the world, but knowing it was right with you so it couldn't be anything but right with any of the people you knew in the world, if there were any people? So after the cigarette you sat back, and still with that soft slowness, that meditative stillness that they tell you exists once in a while, you sat back and sighed and wondered just what your next move would be? Whether you would read the paper, a book, or just think a little more? And then all of a sudden, like a scream arising from the bottomless, stagnant pit that was always empty, you heard an ambulance siren cutting the darkness of your peaceful night! You'd heard it many times before and hadn't thought much about it, but this night you heard it and it penetrated not into your brain but into your heart, and you knew that that siren meant death and destruction, not to some unrelated person but to someone you knew, and you knew it so vividly that you had to do something about it. And when you did something about it, when you got up and forgot your slowness and hurried into your coat and hat and started on a run to follow that scream of the siren; when like all little boys you began to chase that ambulance but not like all little boys for no reason, but for a reason that you knew in your heart, and when you arrived at the scene of destruction you knew there'd be no surprise, because there on the pavement lay that person that you'd thought about, that you knew would be there—a person whose name you knew! No surprise. And that's the way it was with me that night. I knew. And I knew the person's name too well. And I knew when I found out what I knew, there'd be no surprise.

I woke Mrs. Hargraves up. I woke her husband up in the next bed.

Mrs. Hargraves put on a ratty-looking kimono. Her face was all wrinkles and concern as she followed me back to the cottage. Her face was all wrinkles and concern but her voice sounded like a machine gun without any bullets in it. She shot off her words but they didn't get anywhere.

"She was here at twelve o'clock, I tell you, Mr. Blodgett. I saw her lights on. I was sitting here on the porch and I saw her put the lights on and off. I think it was twelve or perhaps twelve-ten. No, maybe twelve-fifteen. Yes, because I got up then. It got cooler and I got up."

We were in the house by that time. I'd already explained to Mattie that wherever she was, she was wearing her sweater and skirt and house slippers. And wherever she was, she looked damn foolish in just her sweater, skirt, and house slippers.

"But I just don't understand. There's no place in the world she could go to now. Even if she was dressed up. Have you called the police? Have you called the hospital? I know she wouldn't go down to the restaurant now. She had plenty in the house. She had plenty in the house she told me herself because she was expecting you to come in later."

"She's not anyplace in the house," I said, "and she's not in any of those other places!" I was on the back porch by this time and I practically slammed the door in her face, but she opened it all right. She opened all the doors, even when you didn't want her to. But this time I wanted her to. I guess I even liked the fact that she was rattling on and saying nothing, nothing I hadn't thought of before.

She followed me to the backyard and that small pile of rubbish. I wanted her to do that, too, because I knew I was going to find something in that rubbish. I didn't know quite what, but I knew it wasn't going to be a surprise. I didn't want Mrs. Hargraves there because I wanted to weep on her broad shoulder, because I wanted her motherly instincts around me; I just wanted a person around when I found it.

She watched me digging in the rubbish. "What in the world are you looking for here? It seems like a silly thing to do, especially at three-thirty in the morning. Why, it's almost four. Shouldn't you start looking for her? Shouldn't you take out the car? Mr. Hargraves will get up and help you. He said he would."

I gritted my teeth. I wanted to say, "Shut up, you silly fool. Shut up, you goddam ass!" But I didn't want her to shut up. I didn't want her to go away. Yet I didn't want her to see what I had found. I dropped the stick I'd been poking with and I turned to her, and it was a damn good thing there was no light on my face because she would have seen its blankness, its cold, pale blankness in the moonlight. But there was no moonlight so she just heard me say, "All right, Mrs. Hargraves, I'll get out the car and I'll start looking for her. You don't need to bother Mr. Hargraves. She might have been worried tonight, or moody. You know how women are? I guess husbands worry too. I'll just get out the car and start looking for her. I'm sorry I bothered you, but you know how husbands are sometimes."

My voice was so calm, my apologetic voice was so calm, that what could

Mrs. Hargraves do but smile? And it seemed to me like a broad smile, a warm one it seemed to me, and I accepted it. She turned away and started back toward her cottage, and it seemed to me that as she started back there was a casual shrug of her shoulder. It seemed to me that my whole world at that moment was just seeming. It was a world of unreality, and unreality is just seeming. So I accepted the fact that she seemed to be casual and understanding. As she walked on over to her back door she threw another seeming thought over her shoulder at me. She said, "Let me know, Mr. Blodgett, when you find her. I'm sure it'll be all right, but let me know. Good night."

I nodded. "Good night," I said. "Thank you, Mrs. Hargraves. I'll let you know."

And I started back into my house too. But as I came near that pile of rubbish I skirted it. I walked around it as though it had a sign on it that read "Scarlet fever." I remember when I was a little kid my mother made me go around the block, two blocks if necessary, to avoid passing a house with those signs, those horrible signs on them—scarlet fever, measles, smallpox.

I walked back into the house and sat down. I wondered how long I would have to sit, because I knew she wasn't coming back. And I knew if I took the car out it would be a senseless, aimless ride to nowhere. Yet I had told Mrs. Hargraves I was going to take the car out. But I knew if I took that car out and started down that road, started down any road leading to anyplace, I would never come back. And if I never came back I would never be sure that what I found was really what I found. And if I was never sure then, if somebody else found what I thought I'd found, they'd be certain as hell to come looking for me.

Curiosity. Deader than a cat they say curiosity kills you. So you die a million times before you do die.

How long I sat, I'll never know. But when it looked like it was going to spell bright dawn any minute, I got up and walked on back outside to the object that was causing me to act like a drugged man. And when I got out there, I wasn't alone. I wasn't alone with death and I wasn't alone with life because Mr. and Mrs. Hargraves were out there poking around and finding what I thought I'd found; Mattie and Charley Hargraves, fully dressed and fully aware of a situation that I hadn't even begun to become aware of.

And even to this day, I'm not quite aware of it. I'm on the outside looking in, an outsider. To be outside of things looking in or looking on is so much better, really. If they don't become too much a part of you, or a part of you at all, you can get rid of them. That way you can, someday, get rid of evil. It just goes away because it sees you're not too interested.

And you're not too interested because you don't quite understand, you're not fully aware.

Mrs. Hargraves didn't speak to me. She didn't speak to me but she looked at me. She looked at me and this time her expression didn't seem to be warm, didn't seem to be concerned, at least not about me. Her face was blank, that same blankness that I've seen so many times in my life. But she didn't need to say anything because what she had in her hand said it for her. She was holding a long stick. It looked like a broom handle, and hanging on the end of it was the goddamnedest thing she could have possibly discovered at that moment. Hanging on the end of that stick was a partially burned girdle, Elizabeth Frazer's girdle, one she'd been wearing that day because it was the only one she had to wear.

Tragedy, real tragedy, is always underlined with a morbid humor. At least my tragedies have been. And I guess everybody's is if he has time to think about the humor of the situation, if he allows himself time to recognize the underlying humor.

I've been in a hell of a lot of fires in my life, mental and actual. I've been in a burning building, in the middle of a city of many buildings. I've been on a burning boat in the middle of an ocean of no boats. I've been in a forest fire, up on the top of a mountain looking down on it. And I've been in the middle of a fire in the Michigan woods, miles from a fire engine and too close to a lake to want to jump in. I saw a lodge burning and twelve cottages around it. There was a high wind blowing the wrong way for safety. I had to get down on my hands and knees and dig trenches, backstops. Sure I was scared. Everybody was scared. But in the midst of these physical and mental conflagrations the damnedest thing happened. The owner of the lodge ran into her hut that was burning. She ran in to save her worldly possessions and she came out holding a kerosene lamp in one hand and in the other a comb with some dirty hairs sticking to it.

I started to laugh but it got no farther than my thoughts because when she saw me she handed me the kerosene lamp, and falling all around us were burning embers the size of a large umbrella. So I stood there like a dope holding a kerosene lamp, wanting to laugh like hell and knowing that maybe the next minute my arm would be blown off, or I might even have to jump into one of the deepest, coldest lakes in the world in order to save my skin. And that night when Mrs. Hargraves poked that burned girdle in my face I wished to hell I had a lake to jump into, and yet I wanted to laugh all over again.

But Mr. Hargraves opened his mouth first. It was one of the few times I'd ever heard him speak without being spoken to first. And I wish now I'd never heard him. Because sometimes even yet I can hear those words, although they don't make my blood curdle or my skin creep up on the back of my neck. In a voice that was cold steel he said, "You needn't take the car out, Mr. Blodgett, and go looking for your wife." Then he opened his hand, and in his sweaty, sooty palm, black from poking around in the ashes, there was a small gold-plated wedding ring.

I paid ten bucks for that ring and ten years of my life because he found it that night in those ashes. But that's not all he found and he was ready to tell me about it right then, in that same tone, in that same deathlike tone. "That's not all I found," he said, and he reached into his pocket and brought out a broken piece of bridgework. And that's the second time I wanted to laugh, because I didn't know Elizabeth Frazer wore a bridgework. I knew about all the other false things, but I didn't know about the teeth. And when you come right down to it, they were what really and finally convicted me.

The scene at the funeral pyre of Elizabeth Frazer Blodgett in the early dawn of a beautiful August day in sunny California was very well played by the three characters known as Mr. and Mrs. Hargraves and Walter Blodgett. It wasn't a hammy scene. Nobody would have thrown any orchids, either, but it was damn well done, nevertheless. Our voices were held low. They were calm, stagy voices. Our actions were casual. That made the meaning of the scene more important. Mrs. Hargraves didn't rattle on for nothing like she usually did. She was still the same character, but she didn't make it corny. She said what she had to say, which was enough, and her old man added the periods. I didn't add very much because nothing added up for me.

They didn't need to tell me how long they'd been searching in that pile of junk, because they had their wares laid out on the ground like a rummage sale. And I guess I was supposed to buy back the articles. There was a piece of Elizabeth's house slipper. There was a sleeve of her burned sweater. The skirt was missing entirely. Leave it to Elizabeth, stripped for action. Anything to show her legs, even in death. And there was a lock, a very small lock of her burned, blonde tresses. I found this. I told the court later about how carefully that little bunch of hair was lying on the ground just on the edge of the burned space. But Mrs. Hargraves trumped my ace. When I found the hair all bunched up like that as though it had been placed there by a hand that had gone, that was supposed to be burned up, Mrs. Hargraves accidentally knocked it out of my hand. So after I told it in court it didn't mean very much because when it was picked up later it was found scattered all over the ground. Anyway, the court didn't choose to believe anything I said.

And even that night when I said to Mrs. Hargraves, when I spoke my very first words, which I repeated later on the witness stand, even Mrs.

Hargraves' blankness turned to disbelief. For my first words were "I don't understand it. I know what you've found and I know what it means, what it seems to mean, to all of us. But you've found just things. Even though they're here, even though they've been burned, even though it seems to be evidence of murder, they're just things. Where's the burned flesh? Where're the bones? Where are the little pieces of ashes? Dust unto dust. Even I can see, here in the dawn, even without a bright light, that they're not around; that there's not a part of her here … not a real part … just manufactured things. Even that hair that's her own except for the peroxide, what does it mean? It's not attached to her, not to any real part of her."

I stopped and took one of those deep breaths, but they weren't ready for me to stop. They didn't believe me but they wanted to hear me to the end. And when I saw them staring like that, waiting like little kids wait when they're waiting for their mothers to tell them they can go out and play again, then is when I actually laughed. But the laugh didn't come out all round and warm and happy. It was bitter and it hurt. It was a laugh that hurt. I really never knew before that a laugh could hurt that way. But I was laughing because I remembered another phony murder set, staged by the same master hand. And even though Elizabeth wasn't really around, she was there more than if she had been there. It was like I was expecting her any minute. And yet I knew that back door wouldn't slam unless the wind slammed it, or the ghost of an evil mind that surely must still be living someplace.

I know Mr. Hargraves thought I was nuts. I know that he was the one that suggested a psychiatrist. And though I hated him at that moment because he was married to Mrs. Hargraves, I was grateful later that he remembered the laugh and told the court he thought I was nuts. I'd never met a psychiatrist before and it was fun trying to outsmart him. It was fun and it wasn't difficult, but it didn't mean a damn thing.

When Mr. Hargraves got over the shock of my laugh he said, "Mrs. Hargraves has already called the police. She called them right after she left you. She didn't tell you because we wanted to make sure first that what she saw, when she walked out here with you, was really true."

"She wanted to make sure that what she saw was really true so she called the police first. Is that it, Hargraves? They're a hell of a long time in coming, don't you think? But then, there are only a couple of them in Carleton. But tell me something. Why didn't Mattie call me first when she discovered what she thought she did? I'm the one that's interested. I'm the guy that's lookin' for her."

I moved closer to Mr. Hargraves. He began to look frightened. "Oh, don't worry," I said, "I won't get violent. I won't fight the law. I won't even cut your throat, although I'd like to. As a matter of fact, I won't even act too concerned, because it seems to me that you and Mrs. Hargraves aren't too concerned about how I might feel. She was my wife, you know. And though I don't act like a shocked man, I don't have much feeling left. Because I know something, Mr. Hargraves, I know there's something mighty phony about this!"

Mrs. Hargraves started to interrupt me. I think she even got a kind of sympathetic but pained expression on her face. Maybe she was going to try to offer sympathy, or maybe she thought I suspected her, or maybe she was just having one of those second thoughts. But I didn't even care if she had a fifth. I wouldn't have cared if she'd screamed and beaten her chest and started a little wailing wall all of her own, because I knew she didn't give a damn whether Elizabeth Frazer was dead or not. She wanted to play murder and I told her that.

"You want to play at murder, Mattie, don't you? You want your name in the paper. You want to be a witness and convict a man. Not just any man, not a stranger or a casual friend. You'd love to convict me! You've hated me ever since I told you off about Spike. Over a year ago. All right, that's O.K. by me. I'll play along with you.

"I want you to look down on the ground at my feet. You see that small space that's been swept or maybe shoveled away? I think that's done on purpose. You know what the police will do? I'll make you a bet. They'll go through that pile of ashes with a fine-toothed comb, but they won't find any physical part of Elizabeth Blodgett, half-burned or completely burned. They won't find it because it isn't there! But like you and like myself, they'll see that that place has been swept and shoveled away. And they'll say that I or someone like me buried all the little bits and pieces left of a human body. And they'll dig up your backyard, and our backyard, and the whole world's backyard, trying to find it!"

This time I moved up closer to Mrs. Hargraves, within an inch of her hawklike nose, and I screamed the remaining part of my momentary defense. "But they won't find it, Mrs. Hargraves!" I shouted. "And they'll wonder why in the hell the guy who must have burned her, and must have buried her remains, didn't bury the stinking rummage sale of used articles he left behind!"

Mrs. Hargraves moved back a pace, away from my venom; then she turned to her husband. "Charley," she said, "the police are here."

The police had arrived and were running through my house, were already on the back step, had slammed that door I'd waited to hear, but I wasn't even aware that they'd driven up.

Chapter 7

Christmas! I had to wait from the first part of August to the week before Christmas until my trial started. Then the court took a recess for Christmas.

There used to be a lot of snow in the world. I often wonder whatever happened to it. It doesn't snow as much as it used to. Oh, maybe some winters are colder sometimes, but it's not like when I was a kid.

I sat in that cell on Christmas Eve, and even though it was hot and dirty and the guard wasn't singing any Christmas carols, I couldn't help but remember Christmases that I've known; that I'll never know again unless I become like a child again, like they tell you you have to do to enter the Kingdom of Heaven. The Bible's a great book. Even a Gideon Bible left in a crappy hotel room; even that kind of Bible the bums use as a coaster for cracked highball glasses is a great book. But so few people know how to read. My mother had a little Bible. It must have been pretty ancient because the leather had almost all peeled off. She kept old, yellowed snapshots in it and a faded, crumbly rose left over from some romantic or tragic escapade.

I never knew my mother as well as I would have liked to. She died a long time ago when I was very little and it was around Christmas too and all I could think of was, Gosh, now I'll bet we won't have any tree. We didn't have any. Mothers of people like me always seem to die when people like me are little. Maybe that's why we turn out to be people like me.

Near where I lived in a small town in the Middle West we had a long high hill, called McKinley Hill, and during the school holidays just before Christmas when the sky began to get darker, quicker, and the holiday snow fell just as it should have fallen, in large chunks that made it easier to pack down tight to the streets, we got out our sleds, our red racers and flying bobs, and we belly-busted down that long hill from early morning until far into the night. Far into the night on that bobsled I coasted down McKinley Hill, just missing two-cylinder cars and rickety one-horse wagons crossing the intersection, going home to their well-stocked cellars and well-lighted hearths. Many times I scooted under the wheels of a wagon without thought of danger.

Danger! It lurked in the gray cement of the cell walls just waiting till I turned my head so it could stare out at me. And no matter which way I turned my head, it stared out at me. It hid under the dirty covers of the gray bed, and every time I moved the blanket an inch, it made a noise like a death rattle. It kicked at my heavy, laceless shoes until my toes ached. And that hissing sound, like a busted steam pipe, like a Dr. Jekyll brewing his evil, like a snake just ready to strike, it came from the bars across my window. And funny, through it all, louder and even more penetrating, I could hear the hurried shouts of unsuspecting kids in a world of hard-packed snow that hadn't yet turned to slush.

It's better to be in a crummy Forty-sixth Street bar up to your memories in sawdust and cigarette butts, buying a round of beers for the B girls, barflies, and bums, listening to the scared, squeaky-voiced waiters and whisky-soaked contraltos; it's better to hear your Christmas carols sung through a comb covered with tissue paper than to spend Christmas Eve hung to a warden's bedstead with the shadow of a bloody cross spilled all over your face. I hate martyrs! The guy that says it doesn't hurt to pound a nail through your hand is a bloody liar!

The trial was like a long road that you walk sometimes when you're dreaming. The farther you walk, the closer you get to nothing. And then your feet begin to sag like they were filled with lead. Only you realize that they're not heavy with lead, they're heavy with mire. You keep sinking down into mire and then you know you'll never find an end to the road because pretty soon the quicksand comes, and you can't even walk anymore. And then pretty soon the end comes and you can't even talk anymore. But with dreams you wake up.

Living to most people is a row of loose ends that can't get together long enough to be tied up. If they could be tied up they'd make a circle. To live in peace is to live in a tight circle where everything adds up inside of you and inside of your circle. When someone starts to tie up the loose ends of anything, he has to have a lot of patience and a lot of guts. And he has to reach way back into the past. I watched those loose ends of my life, and of Elizabeth Frazer's life, pile up so high that there was hardly any room left in the court for the jury or the spectators.

Elizabeth Frazer's first crime happened on the day she opened her mouth and yelled to be born. She didn't yell, she screamed. And only I know how she screamed, what it sounded like even at that early age, because she never improved upon that scream. But it was kind of fun listening to the lawyer tell about all of her other crimes.

I guess the only wedding band she ever wore was the one I bought her. She never stopped long enough to get married. They were trying to convict me of murder. But they convicted her of even greater crimes—selfishness and lust!

Through the court I finally found out about her recent past. She only worked twice in her life, that is worked and got a pay check for it. She was fired from both jobs. The reasons stated were normal enough, lack of ability and lack of enthusiasm. But her first boss said there was some petty cash missing. And her second boss didn't say anything about the forged signatures on his charge account until after he stopped sleeping with her, which was evidently a few months after he fired her. Then he started to prosecute. I'm sure it wasn't because of the charge accounts, but because she stopped sleeping with him. But she came back with a countersuit of breach of promise, settled out of court. It was all in the record.

So her first major crime was the murder of the ugly face in Middletown, Minnesota. But nobody believed that was her major crime. The judge didn't believe it. The jury didn't believe it. And the prosecuting attorney didn't believe it. He hammered at me like a bad carpenter driving nails and he wasn't going to stop driving the nails until they hit home, no matter how many it took or how bent they became. And he said the same things over and over again, asked the same questions and answered them before I could even swallow.

"Why did you run away that night of April the third in Middletown, Minnesota? If it weren't your murder and you didn't know the woman, why didn't you stay and prove to the state that you hadn't taken a man's life? Or did you take it? We have only your word for it. We can't ask her. We have only your word for it. And these people here."

He stopped his slobbering and pointed to those same sad-eyed, wet-shawled faces that I'd herded out of the door that night. Of course, they looked a little older and sadder, droopier. Over three years had passed. Even three years can change a man. I often wonder if they found them in the same position I left them that night ... standing in a brightly lighted hall, pounding on a door that would never be opened. No, I'm sure they found them doing simple everyday chores. And they walked into their so-called comfortable homes and dragged them out into the bitterness of a courtroom that smelled of old murder.

Mrs. Garrity, with the mole on her nose, was probably standing over a hot stove cooking her old man's dinner when the police walked in. Her old man was at a union meeting and they had to wait for him. Mrs. Garrity was so anxious to tell him the gore that she almost grew another mole while waiting for him.

The thin man with the red string tie was asleep under a week-old newspaper when the law called on him. He lived alone, so the abrupt awakening was kind of a shock. But he got over the shock quick enough. The police were right. They were law, the law he paid for out of his own tight pockets.

Mr. and Mrs. Samuelson were just sitting down to dinner. Mr. Samuelson was asking the blessing, repeating words he didn't know the meaning of, when suddenly the rap came on the door. And the baked potatoes and the red cabbage and the Lord's blessing had to wait for murder.

And the young woman with the pudgy hands and nails, home manicured, too red; the young woman of the ten-cent-store glass-covered hands was on the phone making a date with the divorced gentleman across the court when the police interrupted her conversation and her night in the hay.

But in exchange for their hard, uncomfortable seats in a courtroom smelling of old murder, they got excitement, and they got it free—excitement and real live entertainment that they'd wanted for three long years. Many times they'd dreamed of this big show, wondering if it would ever happen and if they'd be a part of it. And now suddenly they were a part of it and they didn't even have to pay amusement tax. Lucky people.

I smiled over at them, my best witness smile, then I turned to the lawyer. "Ask them what I said when I saw the body that night. They'll tell you because it was a damn good speech and they'll remember every word of it, especially about my right hand, my phony right hand."

The lawyer picked up his hammer and nails again and this time he pounded them into my right hand. "How do we know the man was stabbed by a right-handed person? Only your fingerprints were found on the knife."

"They must have been funny fingerprints," I said, "because I didn't touch that knife with my good hand." I looked over at the row of stony-faced experts. "They told you," I said. "They told you he was evidently stabbed by a right-handed person. I only guessed that night, but they're experts. They don't guess."

The prosecuting attorney took off his glasses and wiped them carefully on his sleeve, stalling for time. But he needn't have stalled. He needn't have taken any time out to think. He was going to have all those answers anyhow, no matter what I said. The final one would come from his lips. "The evidence that the experts have offered in which they have stated that he was *probably* stabbed by a right-handed person is not conclusive. It is merely problematical. It's been over three years since the night his body was discovered."

He paused for breath and it was the pause I needed. "Then why don't you bring him in here?" I said. "I'll bet he looks pretty now. All flaky guts, long hair, and maggots!"

The spectators stood up to look at my bitterness. The jury leaned forward until they were hanging out of the box at almost a right angle. The judge pounded with his gavel, short, angry raps.

"Sorry," I said, and turned to the pink-eyed prosecutor. "But stick to the point! You're not trying me for the murder of John Isaacs in Middletown, Minnesota, but of Elizabeth Frazer in Carleton, California. And if you're not careful I'll demand a retrial!"

Had I had a lawyer he would have stood up too. He would have sniffed with his great legal majesty and repeated my very words. But I didn't have a lawyer. I didn't even have a public defender. I didn't want anyone to defend me. I could defend myself much better, because as far as I was concerned I was defending myself against nothing. And you don't have to have anyone help you defend yourself against nothing. For you see, I didn't believe Elizabeth Frazer was dead!

But they did. They had their evidence. Their gory exhibits were laid out on a table like a traveling salesman places his wares. Only they were traveling salesmen for Death, Incorporated.

They had Elizabeth's not-too-pretty-to-look-at bridgework, which was made by a dentist in Atlantic City. The dentist had died, but his assistant dug out the files. They were her teeth all right, three of them, pearly white, in a crooked row hooked onto a hunk of tin. Pearly white, but with a not quite masticated crumb stuck in the middle of one of them. That determined what she'd eaten for dinner the night she was murdered. It wasn't caviar and no woman would have ordered it unless she was awfully hungry.

Exhibit B—hair. A hank three inches long of bleached hair. The hair had been burned, but it had also been cut as if by a knife or a pair of manicure scissors. My row of sourpuss experts was called in again. Yes, the hair had been definitely cut, they said, so their decision on that point was in my favor.

When my time came to talk about that little bunch of hair I looked the jury square in its bloodshot eyes and said, "People don't cut their hair while they're burning to death in a pile of rubbish in the backyard of a two-room motel. But people might cut their hair off like that while they're standing in front of a mirror. Then they could, if they wanted, burn it a little so it might look like it had been burned a lot more. And they would, too, if they intended planting a murder on someone else."

Exhibit C was a wedding band that hadn't melted because it was made of gold wash on stainless steel. So it didn't melt because she hadn't been burned in a blast furnace.

And then there were the pieces of girdle and sweater and house slipper.

But no ashes. No ashes and no bones of Elizabeth Frazer. So where were they? At this point you tell me.

How the judge wished he knew! How the brilliant lawyers for the state wished they knew! How the jury longed for their discovery! How the spectators waved their curiosity from side to side! And how I sat and smiled my three-cornered smile, which didn't last very long!

For days they questioned me. They fought with me. They threatened me. (With what? Death?) They cajoled. They wheedled and needled and bargained. (My life for theirs?) They tried to make me admit that I'd swept or shoveled those bits and pieces into a little pile and then buried them. Just as I'd told the Hargraves they would.

They even tried to make me say I'd put those little pieces of ash and bone in an envelope and then hid the envelope. "Where?" I asked the lawyer. "Where did I hide the envelope? Perhaps I mailed it, air mail. Watch for your postman."

When I got Mrs. Hargraves on the witness stand, when it was my turn to question the witnesses, I leaned over and hissed into Mrs. Hargraves' bland witness-for-the-state's face, "What did I tell you, Mrs. Hargraves, the night we found this pile of rubbish?" I pointed to the exhibits. "Didn't I bet you they'd dig up the world?"

Mrs. Hargraves nodded. In the nod there was the same fear of me she had had that night.

I continued, "You owe me some money, don't you, Mrs. Hargraves?" Mrs. Hargraves started to deny it, but I'd learned my trade from the prosecuting attorney. I didn't give her a chance. "Because you don't think, Mrs. Hargraves, that even if they dig up all of Carleton, California, that they'll find any trace of Elizabeth Frazer, do you? You don't believe she's dead. You didn't hear her scream for help or watch me drag her mutilated body out into the backyard. You didn't see me light a match and burn up a human being that you and I knew as Elizabeth Frazer, did you? *Did you, Mrs. Hargraves?*"

Mrs. Hargraves spluttered, "I didn't say I did. I didn't say I did."

"No, you didn't, Mrs. Hargraves," I said. "So you know that if they dig until doomsday they won't find anything but dirt." I paused a moment, and turned in the direction of the jury; then before Mrs. Hargraves had a chance to answer again I turned back to her. "Because you don't believe she's dead, do you? *Do you, Mrs. Hargraves?!*"

Mrs. Hargraves' eyes popped open and rolled around like they were on hidden pivots. "I didn't say I did," she repeated. "I didn't say I did."

I was finished with her. I smiled. It was one of the few times I'd smiled since the trial started. "That's right," I said. "You didn't. So I'll stand my ground. Under me they cannot dig. Witness dismissed."

My closing speech to the jury in defense of the accused, the masterpiece I'd worked on for two nights, almost all night long, wasn't the greatest speech ever heard, but it carried weight. I saw the jury take the weight of it and hide it in their weary brains.

"Circumstantial evidence," I began, "should be eliminated in the murder trial, but because some of us are so strong in our weakness that we won't admit our guilt, we must be hung on what they call circumstantial evidence. Our lives must be taken because of things. Things such as a burned girdle, a piece of neatly cut hair, a broken tooth, a house slipper that can't be worn again. But circumstantial evidence is not enough to convict a man of murder—particularly when there is no corpus delicti! No corpus delicti! Yet in a book I read once, an encyclopedia, it said, 'If a person is charged with murder the prosecution must prove the death as by the finding and identification of the corpse or by evidence of criminal violence adequate to produce death and to account for the disappearance of the body. In other words the corpus delicti in such a case consists in the death of the person *alleged* to have been murdered and the criminal agency of the *alleged* murderer in producing death!' End quote.

"What is the evidence of criminal violence that my antagonist, the attorney for the state, has dug up? Has he proven that I was at the house when she was supposed to have been killed? No. Just because the state can't account for a few hours of my valuable time doesn't mean I was where they hope I was. And has it been proven yet whether she was burned alive or killed first? Has it? No, it has not! And furthermore, the brilliant attorney for the state hasn't the vaguest idea of the weapon that might have been used. As a matter of fact, he can't even prove that she's actually dead. Except for things. Things that were carefully left behind as if done on purpose.

"And what could be that purpose? The only thing that has been proven during this trial is the fact that Elizabeth Frazer, now missing, was a criminal. She was a criminal in more ways than one. I don't think there's anybody in this court that in his heart doesn't believe she killed a man in Middletown, Minnesota. I know that there isn't a person in this court that doesn't realize what a hateful person she was even in daily living. I wasn't the only man she had in her life. You saw the men in her past dragged through this court, and strung up and taken apart for every one of us to see. But I believe there's one man that none of us has seen yet. Not another guy who might have murdered her, although that's possible, except I was the one chosen from the beginning. The cards were purposely stacked that way. *And* except I don't believe she was murdered. But a guy that I'm sure she had waiting for her someplace. A guy that I wouldn't let her get to. So she planned her own murder, a murder that she knew would convict me and free her.

"If her friend Mrs. Hargraves had told the truth, or perhaps I should say, if she had gone back into her memory and pulled out a day three years ago, she would have remembered something that Elizabeth Frazer said that would make everybody here realize what I realize; that Elizabeth Frazer had another guy with more money that she was waiting to get to, that she'd been waiting to get to for three long years. But our kind neighbor Mrs. Hargraves hasn't a very good memory. You see, all of her life she's wanted her name in the papers, so, like the state, she's built up a case against me for her sake. Oh, not that she hadn't heard Elizabeth Frazer and me argue. Who doesn't argue when he's that close to a woman? When he knows a woman so well that a murder she's committed ceases to be a crime and becomes just an ordinary fault? But when Mrs. Hargraves was asked to repeat those arguments here, she couldn't repeat one word of them and make them spell sense. But she tried. She tried pretty successfully. For you see, Mrs. Hargraves is a respectable married lady who dotes on horror, reads every paper-backed murder mystery ever written, yet gets by because she stinks of lavender and old lace. And I'm a bum who doesn't like to read even a newspaper, who hates the smell of violence in every form, yet couldn't make anyone believe me if I was wearing a monk's robe and carrying an honest-to-God recipe for eternal life.

"If I had a lot of money or a big name that spelled Rockefeller backward I wouldn't have been dragged into a court of law. But if by mistake or someone's bitterness I had been, my raft of bright-eyed yes men interpreting the law would have seen that I wouldn't have had to stand trial—because, I repeat, there is no corpus delicti!

"Do you know what that means? If no corpus delicti has been established, there has been no murder! So what are we doing in this court, ladies and gentlemen? Why am I here? I'll tell you why. Because I'm just a little guy, a bum, a wanderer, a tramp that rides freight cars and walks along crooked railroad ties, that calls the gutter his home. I'm just a little guy that was caught a couple of times for little rackets. If I wore a white collar and sat behind a shiny mahogany desk and juggled accounts—made black columns where red should be or vice versa—I'd have a better chance. Not a better chance in life, you make your own chances in life, but a better chance in death—to escape it! To escape the penalty for sin.

"All right! I'm the scared victim of my own stupidity. And all the loose ends of that stupidity have been tied here today—tied together like a string of putrefying sausages. I don't like to look at that string any better than you do. But I can stand here in front of my row of scarlet sins and not see murder lying with them.

"O.K.! I'm not asking the great white-haired judge or the kind-eyed jury or the hissing lawyers or the eagle-eyed experts or the enthusiastic witnesses to free me from this charge—this charge of murder on circumstantial evidence without any corpus delicti. I'm just asking for leniency. Leniency for me and the little guy, all the little guys all over creation who can't pay for leniency, but have to stand up in front of a jury, a judge, and God and plead for leniency. Plead for it and die for it before they really have to die!"

When I sat down I even saw a look in the prosecuting attorney's face that wasn't there before. It wasn't a look of sympathy and it wasn't a look of amazement. It was just a quick look that you couldn't put your finger on. A quick look that passed too soon.

The jury was out only a few hours. God was pretty good to me as far as time was concerned, because even the closing speech for the state wasn't too long, but it was right to the point. Maybe it was wrong to the point, but the answer was there just the same. And I knew that answer long before the foreman of the jury stood up, long before any of them went into that room to cast their ballots. The answer was "Guilty!" *But with a recommendation for leniency!*

The state closed every link in the chain. They tied every loose end without fanfare, without persuasion, without too much high-toned legal language. As a matter of fact, the attorney's speech didn't even sound like a closing argument. It was just plain facts and quick—to the point. (1) Motive. (a) Mrs. Hargraves said we'd been quarreling the last year. Mr. Hargraves heard us, too, time and time again. Elizabeth told Mrs. Hargraves that I'd threatened her day after day and that she was trying to get away from me. (Elizabeth provided my motive.) (b) I might have killed to cover up my part as an accomplice in the murder of John Isaacs. (But that was scratched off the record. They weren't trying Elizabeth Frazer for the murder of the ugly face and they weren't trying me as an accomplice.) (2) Evidence—circumstantial. (a) The absolute disappearance of Elizabeth Frazer. (b) The funeral pyre and its contents. (3) Character of defendant—anything but good. (a) One year in the Ohio State Penitentiary for forgery. (b) One year in Joliet for blackmail. (c) Six months in Lincoln Heights Jail, Los Angeles, for illegal betting.

Not a habitual criminal, but an enemy of society all of his life, ever since leaving home. Held down only two known jobs; one at a race track in Caliente, Mexico, at the two-dollar window, the other as a Carleton automobile mechanic—job ending in murder.

But the one sin that I thought I'd committed more than any other they didn't dwell on. They didn't dig up the women in my past like they dug up the men in Elizabeth's. But then, I'd always played honest. That's the one thing and the only thing in my life that I've really been put-it-on-the-line honest about—sex! The recommendation wouldn't get me into Heaven.

So they didn't make much fuss about Elizabeth's and my common-law marriage. Maybe the judge was sleeping with his secretary. Maybe that's why he was so tolerant with me. The jury recommended leniency, so he gave me twenty years. Twenty years for murder in the second degree.

Minimum, twenty years! Maximum—life!

Leniency!

I must write that judge someday. He might need a letter of thanks about now.

I won't send Mrs. Hargraves a bill for one life. She'd never pay it. She died a year after the trial ended; fell out of her porch swing, rolled over the edge of the porch to the walk, and landed in such a way that her neck was twisted under her. Broke! Like the chain of the swing broke over her, tired of carrying her bulk. A clean break. I could have fixed that swing for her.

I heard that they kept up a two-year search for Frazer's remains, her guts that should have been strung up to light a Christmas tree for the "hot seaters," the guys that didn't do away with their corpus delicti.

Chapter 8

After I was convicted in California I was suddenly shipped back to Minnesota. It looked like I was to stand trial there for the murder of John Isaacs. One life sentence wasn't enough. They were going to make sure my future was taken care of. I was thrown on the train with a couple of guards and told to keep my mouth shut.

When we arrived in Minnesota I was taken to Middletown, to a dingy wooden courthouse, and there in an office I met my first surprise. I met my defense attorney, hired to represent me. That was a novelty. I could sit back and listen to him this trip. He came up to me and shook my hand as though I were a visiting celebrity. "Carver's the name," he said, "J. Alden Carver, and we're going to see that you're exonerated."

He was a little bald-headed runt of a guy with nose glasses that kept falling off every time he tried to emphasize a point. He sat down next to me and I thought for a moment that he was going to take hold of my hand and squeeze it, there was such an intimate air about the whole thing. "I'm representing the legal firm of Carver and Lamartina. Do you know Minneapolis?" I shook my head no. "Well," he sucked in air through a hole in his uppers, adjusted his glasses, and continued, "my firm has been hired by William Walker of the Walker Manufacturing Company of Minneapolis. They make electrical equipment. Mr. Walker read about your plight in the newspapers and he wants to help you."

"Wait a minute," I said. "That's enough. Let's get this straight first. I can't take many more shocks. I'm down here to stand trial for the killing of John Isaacs, a guy I never met in my life. And instead of being slapped into jail, I'm brought here and told that I got a good chance of being exonerated on account of a Mr. William Walker, another guy I never met. Have I got that much straight? O.K., Carver, you make the rest of it just as clear. I haven't got much time. Only fifty or maybe sixty years if I'm unlucky and live that long."

He laughed self-consciously, then patted my hand as though I were a prodigal son. "It's like this," he said. "Mr. Walker was—how shall I say it?—a ... a friend of the so-called Elizabeth Frazer, lately deceased."

He glanced up at me and I don't know whether he blinked or there was a twinkle in his eyes. Anyway, he was waiting for me to deny the death part of it. I looked at him blankly, so he cleared his throat and went on, "Mr. Walker feels that knowing Miss Frazer as he did, well, you aren't guilty. Do I make myself clear now?"

"Perfectly," I said. "In plain words, Mr. Carver, he's one of the guys she took for a ride and he wants to help out another guy that went on the same ride. Only a little farther."

He nodded. "And so we have called the district attorney, and Mr. Walker's going to testify at the hearing, and—" He stopped and opened a briefcase, dragging out some legal-looking papers. "We have two witnesses who can testify as to your whereabouts on and before the night of April the third when the murder was supposed to have taken place. And we have a third witness, too."

I shook my head. I was just coming out of a dream. This man before me was a character I should have left behind in my dreams. I shut my eyes for a few minutes, then opened them, expecting Carver to be gone. But he was still there because I could see him and hear him. "I have here," he said, "the stationmaster of the Middletown Station. He said he saw you jump off the freight train and stand out in front of the station in the rain for a few minutes. Then he saw Elizabeth Frazer wave to you from her window in the apartment house. You crossed over to the house. He says he watched you go in. Do you remember seeing him at all?"

I smiled. "Listen, Mr. Carver," I said, "I don't remember anything but the fact that I got into that apartment the front way and went out the back."

Carver went on talking as though I hadn't spoken, and I began to remember what my thoughts were as I stood in the rain under the eaves in front of that station the night I met Elizabeth. I was sure that I was alone in a lonely, lonesome world. I saw no one watching me. I watched no one. There was no one to watch until Elizabeth appeared in that window. As Carver went on to explain the rest of the deal, I was fascinated by the thought of the train master seeing every move I made when I didn't see him, didn't know he was within spitting distance of me. More than two people in this world have eyes in the back of their heads.

I brought myself back to the present and listened to Carver. "Isaacs had been dead for two days and you were only in the apartment for half an hour. I also have the testimony of a man who lived next door to Frazer and Isaacs. He was out of the country when your trial started in California. When we finally located him he testified that a couple of nights before you arrived in Middletown he heard Isaacs and Frazer quarreling. He heard her threaten him, then there was a rumpus, a loud scream, the sound of a body, or something that resembled the sound of a heavy body, falling to the floor, then silence. He said he didn't have time to go investigate, and anyhow, he figured it was none of his business. He says he didn't think any more about it until he read about the finding of the body, and by then he said he didn't see any sense in reporting what he knew. Frazer had disappeared and he figured the case had been dropped."

"So he didn't have time," I said. "Well, that's understandable. Some people don't have time to stop for trains at crossings either."

Carver smiled at this. "Well, it doesn't matter now," he said. "He's going to testify for us."

"Go on." I was getting amused. "What other little guys are going to come to the rescue of another little guy?"

He looked me over so carefully I began to think he was taking my measurement for a new suit. "I don't think you remember the third witness."

"I don't remember any of them," I said.

"He was on the same freight with you from Canton, Ohio, through to Illinois, Johnson Junction, I believe. There you both got off. You took another freight to Minnesota and he went on east. That was about the time Isaacs was killed, according to our medical authorities. The county coroner disagrees. Nevertheless," he shrugged and continued, "your friend remembers the date. He said it was his birthday. We had a difficult time finding this man, but I put an ad in the *Hobo News*, adding the words 'large remuneration,'" Carver winked at me, "and the man showed up."

I laughed. "Took a fast freight, I suppose. Yeah, Mr. Carver, now you've hit home. You've met one of my friends. I remember the guy. It was his birthday and all he wanted as a present was a handcar. He kept telling me that someday he was going to have a lot of money and own his own handcar. Maybe he was right."

Mr. Carver put the papers back in his briefcase and zipped it shut. "That's about all, Johnson. Except I'm sure you don't have a thing to worry about. They'll lock you up here in jail tonight, but we're going to be in the judge's chambers tomorrow with our witnesses and you'll be exonerated. Free! That's the way justice works when you have enough money to pay for it."

I let that crack pass. I was interested in the word free. "Free," I said, "means that you can walk out and go home if you have a home to go to. Remember I got twenty years or more to spend in the sunshine state."

Carver looked embarrassed. "I'm sorry, but I mean free as far as Minnesota is concerned."

"Well, that's good. I don't like the cold winters here."

He stood up and took my hand. "Mr. Walker is anxious to meet you," he said.

"Yeah, and I want to meet him, too." I thanked him and walked to the door with him. "Yes," I repeated, "I want to meet him, too, Carver. I want to meet a guy with all this influence."

As soon as Carver left they took me to the Middletown jail, where it would have been a cinch to get out, to escape, but I was too curious about all these people who were helping me. I had to stay until the next day. And anyway, escape? What does it mean, really? Does it mean getting out of a place that's barred and guarded and electrically wired? Does it mean being a Houdini tied up in a strait jacket? Does it mean running out of a house, leaving your wife and kids to shift the best way they can, and going to the South Seas to become a beachcomber or draw crazy pictures in the sand? Does it mean quitting school in the eighth grade and running away from home to roam the world until you're convicted of the murder of someone who isn't actually dead yet? Does it mean to sail the seven seas in a dinghy that belongs only to you, or to race to the top of a mountain and pitch a tent, sleep on a bed of twigs that nobody would want to claim? Or to live in a forest primeval with the four-footed friends that will never rip out your guts, stick a knife in your back, steal your money or your house or your wife—or your country?

No! There's no escape by running, by sailing, by soaring, by flying, by crawling, by dying. The sooner the world finds it out, the better. The escape is within you. The escape route lies within you. To seek the hidden resources within, the strength that so few of us are aware of, the strength that lies within us, the sufficiency, the power that we possess to deny all the unpleasantness, to refuse to accept it, to make it disappear. That is possible. I learned that that is possible.

The next day we met in the judge's chambers, the guy across the court, the stationmaster, the bum from Johnson Junction, and Mr. Walker and I. Walker was a handsome guy. Big and well-built for his forty-five years, and dressed like he stepped out of Brooks Brothers' front window, the Brooks Brothers in New York with the expensive clothes. I bet Elizabeth didn't have to tell him to dress up. He had a star sapphire on his little finger and his gold cuff links were set with smaller sapphires. He took my hand hard, like a real guy. "I'm glad to know you, Johnson," he said. "Glad to help you out if I can."

Brother, I thought, helping me out is right. And how many other guys are benefiting by it? The Middletown Courthouse will probably be able to put up a new façade and the judge will take a long vacation. "Johnson Junction" will get his handcar and the guy across the court can put some money in the bank. The Middletown stationmaster will ride in luxury in his private car. Carver was right. It cost dough to do what Walker was doing for me.

I sat down with him until Carver arrived and we talked about Frazer. I told him the deal. I think he believed with me that she wasn't dead.

Then he told me about how he knew her. "I introduced Isaacs to her," he said. "Isaacs worked for me. I fired him after he and Elizabeth started going around together. He got another job with a concern in Minneapolis. He was a pretty bright man.

"Yes, I was really in love with Elizabeth. If I'd have been free I might have married her. I escaped that horror, I guess. But she fixed me up anyway. She left her mark. She met my wife one day by appointment. I didn't know anything about it. She told Helen about us, asked her to give me a divorce. Helen wasn't well at the time and the doctors felt the shock of what Elizabeth did quickened her death. I loved Helen very much, had always been devoted to her, but the fascination that I felt for Elizabeth had been hard to throw off. After Helen passed away it was a terrible burden to bear, knowing that I had something to do with her death. I began to hate Elizabeth. I finally threw her out and Isaacs was waiting to pick her up.

"That's about it, Johnson. And I've been waiting all these years to pay her back some of the misery I suffered. I'm glad it happened this way, I mean as far as I'm concerned. I can now feel that I've not only paid her back, but helped someone in the bargain."

He stopped and smiled at me.

"That's the part I like about you," I said. "The rest, about Elizabeth, is the same story. Mine and Isaacs' and God knows how many more." He knew what I meant.

The inquiry went as Carver planned it. The man across the court did his testifying, and then the stationmaster and my freight-hopping friend. He probably bought his new handcar with the dough I know Walker gave him. I hope it makes him happy. But one day I expect to see the car abandoned by the tracks ... someplace.

There wouldn't be so much fighting in the world, for love, for money, for prestige, for territory, for handcars, if people remembered how easily they tired of new things.

I didn't have to go to trial in Minnesota. They shipped me back to California to start my original sentence. I never forgot Walker's kindness. That's when I began to believe there might be a God.

Chapter 9

How can you tell people you want to be left alone? How can you make people understand you want to be a tramp, a bum, a wanderer; that all your life you've studied to be one, that you like it? How can you force the world, even a small part of it, that small part that surrounds you, to keep away from you, to keep away from you and let you think what you want to think, do what you want to do, at the time you want to do it? How can you walk in a crowd and be invisible?

You can't crawl in a hole, because somebody will be bound to dig you out. Somebody will come along and see your foot sticking out of that hole, and they'll be so excited that they found you, any you, that right away they'll take hold of your foot and pull you out of that hole.

You can't go up on top of a mountain that nobody's ever climbed, because somebody will climb it someday. Somebody will get a screwy idea in his head and want to climb the only mountain that's never been climbed, and he'll find you there.

You can't live in the city, because the noises of the city can even penetrate through six feet of cement. The subway runs under you with a roar, the skies are filled with a roar over you, the bells ring inside of you, and the static whirls around you and through you, and so you become a sounding board for the city.

You can't shut yourself up in the country in a space separated by water or flat land or hills, because there isn't enough room for everyone in the city, and before long a city settler will stake a claim and run up a fence next to your space. Then sooner or later the settler will hang over his fence to look inside your space and you.

But there's got to be an out to the inside of everyone.

And there was an out for me, but it had to work through a murder. I had to find that aloneness, that space that nobody could look over, into, by being shut up in a cell for ten years. In ten years I was paroled. I had to serve only ten years of my sentence.

Ten years! That seems like a hell of a long time. But it took those years and a few more to discover how to live inside me, any place, so that eventually the outside, every place, wouldn't touch one part of me any longer.

It took me ten years to learn how to think in a straight line because a cell with a square floor and a square ceiling and four square walls is a square, straight line. All square lines that are straight end inside of you. So that at the end of those ten square-straight-line years I walked out into the bigger space, into the noises of the city, and it was like a release after the healing of a malignant disease.

And had I been stronger than I thought I was, the two recuperating years that followed would not have been called a relapse. But even ten years are not quite enough sometimes to build a defense that will stand against the hate and the revenge that the world holds up in front of the not-yet-healed invalid. Well, that's all right, too, because the relapse is natural for some people. The two years constituting my relapse were part of the plan. The two years of afterbirth sickness were necessary to clean up the bloody remains, the bits and pieces of the operation that were still clinging to me. Then one day the way was clear. The recovery was complete.

It's better to be completely well at forty than to be well at thirty and die at forty. It's better for me. For you it's better to work it out your way. But work it out before the loose ends are tied around your neck and swung over a scaffold and you hang until dead. It's better to die in bed—natural.

There're an awful lot of hates around. I don't mean the big hates like races and countries hating each other, envying, coveting. I don't mean big personal hates like Hitler's was or Mussolini's. Take it further back than that, like Pompey's and Caesar's and Napoleon's. I mean the little guy's hates. No wonder we're in such a hell of a mess. Big hates only reflect the little ones that are within us, within you and me.

And there sure are a lot of little hates in prisons. That's what builds them and keeps them occupied, I guess. When those big iron gates opened to me I wanted to go through them different than the other guys do. I wanted to take a little love in with me, or maybe it was superiority. I didn't want anyone to think I was like those other haters. I've always wanted to be different. Maybe that's why I've got attention from big shots like Walker was and the warden. The warden was a big shot to me. For the time being. He was my boss for a few years, so he was a big shot. I got attention from him. I got sympathy, even. I got freedom. Eventually. At first I thought he was being considerate because I was handicapped with a bum hand. Or that he warmed up to me because people have always warmed up to me as though I'd done something important in the world, for it, to leave with it after I was gone. Yes, the warden treated me pretty swell and not because I went in with a different thought than the other guys, but because I went in—innocent. I finally found out that the warden didn't believe I was guilty.

When I first arrived he called me into his office to talk to me. I sat down in a big easy chair opposite French windows that opened out onto a beautiful garden. He had snapdragons and stocks and delphinium and beds and beds of pansies and the biggest damned sweet peas I ever saw. I sat and looked out that window that opened onto beauty and freedom and I don't think I heard much of the first part of the warden's talk. I was convinced that one way to cure inveterate haters would be to throw them into a garden like that and tell them they had to till the soil for the rest of their lives. Never let them out. I wonder what they'd do. Pull the sweet peas up by the roots or learn to love them like I eventually did? We've come a long ways from the Garden of Eden.

He must have noticed the dreamy look in my eyes because he stopped whatever lecture he was giving me and said, "It's a pretty picture out there, isn't it, Walter?"

I nodded and smiled and focused my eyes on him for a while. He wore thick spectacles, bifocals, and even at that it was pretty hard for him to read. His eyes were washed-out blue as though he'd been looking at the sins of others for so long they had all but blinded him. He had another handicap. He was short and walked with a limp. He threw the left side of him out front first, then the right seemed to follow a few minutes later. And instead of a booming voice full of self-righteous authority, his voice was low as if he'd spoken a lot in his life and with evident authority, but still he didn't want to force you to listen. You had to be quiet to listen, and his words were well-rounded, meditative words. He chose them for their gentleness and power. After I got adjusted to his voice I liked to listen to him.

He spread his hands out on the desk like he was embracing it. I looked at his hands. They were long and thin. Artistic. His hands talked even more than his voice. "I may sound silly, Walter," he said, "when I tell you I want you to be happy here. But I do. If possible, I want you to find yourself. Some of the men have. One even wrote a book and became famous later on. I have a symphony orchestra here. Some of the men are doing beautifully and they never played musical instruments before, never had the desire to. If you're interested in music ..."

I shook my head. "Don't know a thing about it. Never listened to it much. Only swing stuff."

"That's a pity," he said. "There are a million different avenues of escape into contemplation through music. Well, there are other things to do. Sports. I have an excellent library, too. Maybe you'd like to work on the paper. We're even setting up our own radio station. I notice you never got a high school diploma. We have a broad program of academic training. We teach subjects ranging from basic reading courses to work on a college level. You could earn a grammar or high school education, Walter. Day or night classes. How about it?"

I nodded no to everything and my eyes drifted back out into that garden. I saw a red-breasted bird light on a pepper tree near the sweet peas. He started to sing.

I gestured toward the window. "That's music," I said.

He looked out and we both listened to the bird.

He turned back toward me. "How'd you like to work in the garden?" he asked.

I guess my face must have lit up. He went on, "What I'm going to say to you, Walter, is a little off the record. I guess you think it's pretty odd that I've called you in here so soon and talked to you like this, but I've been studying your file very carefully. I find out a lot about my men that even the law courts don't know. I think you love people like I do. Maybe you're not so aware of it yet, but you will be. People, women in particular, seem to have been the cause of most of your troubles. You've been a sucker, Walter."

I laughed. "Women are the cause of mine and men are the cause of women's. It's a screwy world, isn't it?"

He laughed with me. Soft. Musical. Lilting. I'll never forget his laugh. It sent chills up my spine like symphonies did to other people. "I'm a bachelor, Walter," he said, "for that very reason, women. I taught philosophy once at a major university. I got mixed up with a woman. It didn't turn out so well. And the more education I got, the more confused I became. It wasn't until I took this job that I found happiness. In helping others, I guess. Yes, in helping others." He got up and walked to the window and stood with his back to me. "I think you like nature, too. In a few months I'm going to give you a job, there in my garden. We'll see ... we'll see." He turned back to me and I sensed that the interview was at an end. I got up and shook hands with him and they took me back to my cell.

That was the beginning of my friendship with Warden Masters.

I went to work in his garden. I discovered my green hand. I discovered that my good left hand was a green hand. Masters said his flowers grew larger and his vegetables better to eat because my green hand fostered them. He had a sense of humor, too.

He used to ask me to come into his house and smoke a cigarette with him and listen to him philosophize. He picked out a bunch of books that I was to read. And that's how I learned to concentrate. Really concentrate, for the first time in my life. I found that books made me forget. As long as I was interested in a book and it had a lot of pages until the end I could even forget why I was where I was. But as soon as I finished one book and before I started another I would think of her, Elizabeth, and wonder where she was or what she was doing. It wasn't until I'd been in the can about eight years that one day I suddenly forgot to remember her.

After Masters got me to reading and I read everything he loaned me—some of the books on philosophy and some of the classics were damned hard to get into but I made it—then he taught me a little about music. From Schopenhauer and Spinoza and Nietzsche and Shakespeare and Dickens and James and Wordsworth and Longfellow and Poe to Beethoven and Brahms and Wagner and Tchaikovsky and Grieg and Strauss and César Franck. Then when he saw I was absorbing all of it he suggested the night course again for a high school degree. "You need it, Walter," he urged me. "No matter what happens to you on the inside or outside, you'll profit by it."

I finally gave in, and four years later I was a full-fledged high school graduate. A little too big for short pants and a little too dumb for a professorship, but I got an education, an education that it would take most people a lifetime to acquire, because the basis of it came from Masters.

He and I would sit in the twilight of his room and listen to Chopin waltzes and he'd tell me a little about the guy and his love for George Sand. Then we'd play Tchaikovsky and he'd tell me about him. It was a peculiar thing, when Masters talked about musicians like Tchaikovsky or poets like Oscar Wilde, he seemed more interested in them than the others who led what you might call more mundane existences. I often wondered if his loneliness could have been a little like that of those men. Perhaps that's what made him friendlier with me. But that didn't matter. I didn't care what his hidden desires or frustrations had been as long as he treated me O.K. Some of the guys in the can told me that Masters could really be tough. Brutal. I never saw any of it. As far as I was concerned, he was the finest human being I'd ever met, and I needed damned badly to meet him when I did. I'd seen enough of the other kind.

If anyone had told me that being locked up for ten years would teach me the love of literature and music, the acquisition of a bona fide diploma, the value of friendship, I'd have called him a damned liar. It shows you that you never know what's going to happen from minute to minute. So only live for the minute. What happened yesterday can't be recalled, and tomorrow you don't know a bloody thing about. So today is important, and if you don't fight today and accept it, it holds a lot of surprises. It did for me, and my second surprise was my parole. After ten years of contemplation and study I was paroled into the bigger space called freedom.

I know Masters hated to see me go, that is leave him, but we never really leave the good we've found in others. And as I discovered later, unless we're awfully strong, we never really leave the bad. Or maybe I should say until we're awfully strong we never really leave the bad.

I was sitting in Masters' office. We were talking about things that had nothing to do with me or my life in prison when he suddenly swung his chair around toward me. "Walter," he said, "you've served over half of your sentence, counting the time off for good behavior, and I think it's time we made out an application for your parole."

I jumped out of my chair as though I'd been shot from that well-known cannon. "Repeat that, Warden," I said.

He smiled. "I've already spoken to one of the officers of the state parole board. A good friend of mine. I have the parole application here." He pointed to his desk. "I want you to make it out right away."

"You did this," I said. "You've arranged this!"

"I haven't done anything yet, but I do have a great deal of influence with the parole board in this state. Your case will be reviewed very carefully."

I walked over to him. If there weren't any tears in my eyes, they were in my heart. He knew that. He stood up and took my hand. "You see, Walter," he said, "I never believed you were guilty. Of murder. Now, after knowing you like I do, I'm certain of it."

I held onto his hand. Tight. Like a little boy might hold onto his father's hand after they'd gone through great danger together. I tried to thank him but I couldn't talk, and I knew if I could have talked the words wouldn't have made sense.

He went on, "It may seem unusual, Walter, that I have so much faith in you. But your case has been unusual. Right along. You're an unusual person and unusual things happen to unusual people. I think perhaps someday you might prove what I believe you're capable of—that is, prove a life that's worthwhile."

I let go of his hand and walked toward the French doors to his garden.

His words followed me. "I don't mean, Walter, that I want to hold you down to a promise that you'll be a great success, a material success. When I say worthwhile I mean that you'll learn how to live a simple, unencumbered life, unencumbered with the many mistakes that most of us make, the mistakes that you've made that I hope are behind you."

I looked out into the garden, the garden I'd been taking care of for ten years, and I nodded my head. "I'll try," I said.

"I know you will. I'll make it as easy for you as possible. If the parole board agrees with me—and I'm inclined to think your record here and my, shall we say, influence will convince them—I'll see that you get an even break. You must keep in touch with me."

I turned toward him. "If I don't," I said, "I wouldn't be very grateful, would I?"

"I just want you to work hard. That's all." He walked over to me and put his arm around me. "Now don't think about this. Forget it. Lose it. Let it go. Then it'll work out all right. It'll be O.K., I know."

He walked over to the desk, picked up the application blank, and handed it to me. I glanced at it briefly, then looked up at him. He gestured toward the application blank. "There are some things on there that I'm sure you'll want to talk over with me. The question of a job. I don't believe you have one you can go to, have you?"

I nodded no.

"Well, I'll fix that up. You take the form back with you and don't worry about any of the points there. As for the judge's signature, I've already contacted him. When you get the application made out we'll send it to him to sign."

He walked over to the door with me. "Now forget it, Walter," he said. "Just answer all the questions truthfully and leave the rest to me. You see, this is just another proof that regardless of any obstacle or obstacles, truth will out. Inevitably."

And he was right. It wasn't long afterward that my parole was granted and I was on my way to a job Masters had arranged for me.

The truth will out. Trite or not, I remembered those words. For a long time. I had a damned good reason to.

I'd been given my printed instructions, the rules governing prisoners on parole. The day I left I was with Masters looking them over. On the first day of each month I was to forward by mail to the state parole officer a report of myself in accordance with a blank form to be furnished me by the state parole officer.

I noticed a rule about operating an automobile. It was strictly forbidden. Masters had got me a job in a parking garage in San Francisco. "What about this Rule Three here, Warden?" I said. "The one about the civil rights? I'm strictly forbidden to drive any kind of motor vehicle. I'm a mechanic, you know."

"You'll be in the office of the garage," he said. "It's the best thing I could get for you at present, but," he picked up a piece of paper from his desk, "I have a friend in New York, Arthur Henaston. Lives on Long Island. If you ever decide to go to New York, I want you to look him up, Walter. He has a lot of money, a big home, big factory. If there's an opening he'll hire you as a gardener on his estate. Or perhaps in some other capacity. He and I are very old friends. Just tell him I sent you. I'd like to see you continue your gardening. You're good at it."

I took the paper he handed me and put it in my pocket. "But what about New York? Will the parole board let me go to New York?"

Masters grinned. "Rules governing prisoners, Number Two. Quote. 'Should you desire to change your employment or your residence or should you desire to leave the county in which you are employed you must first obtain the written consent of the parole officer.' Unquote."

I smiled. "I can read," I said. "But do you think they'll give me permission?"

"If they don't, write me when you get ready to go. The thing is you get to work and live like a normal member of society, and you'll get the right kind of leniency."

Leniency! There was that word again. Well, at least I'd found one guy who knew the meaning of it ... Masters.

When I said good-by to him and my last ten years I felt like it was a final good-by to a war buddy, a guy that had made it possible for me to live a little longer, a guy who'd deflected, with his own body, that bullet that was meant for me. And I went outside those big gates, unencumbered, save for a few bucks the state awarded me, a temporary job, and a new suit of badly fitting clothes in the pocket of which was a slip of paper, a slip of paper with a man's name on it who might hire me as a gardener on his estate regardless of my ten years in a cell, regardless of the crime that most people would say still hung over my head. I didn't feel anything hanging over my head. Unless freedom carries a weight with it. But my freedom didn't carry any weight. My first few months of freedom were so without earth weights that all I wanted to do was just walk the streets of the city and look into the faces of people, every person who hadn't been where I'd been, who hadn't yet experienced a rebirth or who didn't want to experience one.

I walked the streets of the city to look in the faces of just people. And I forgot about the man in New York who would give me a job as gardener because I wasn't ready yet to enter into a career with any degree of permanence. Pretty soon I knew my recuperation would be over and I'd be ready. Then one night it happened. Not the end of my recuperation. That wouldn't have made my pulse quicken or that so-called blood run cold as they tell you it does when something cyclonic takes place in your life. No, the recuperation, or rather the end of it, would have been simple and right and natural, but this thing that happened, this cyclonic event, was not like that.

I'd been working in Frisco in this garage where Masters had sent me. It was only a part-time job, but I'd been there for over a year, minding my own business. I didn't have many friends, the guy who ran the garage, a couple of waitresses at the restaurant where I usually ate, my landlady, and two fellows who roomed at the house where I lived. I didn't want any close friends. I didn't need them. I'd had plenty of people in my life. Now I just wanted quiet. I was happy just being quiet, keeping my thoughts to myself, for myself. The less people knew about me, the easier it would be for me to travel when I decided to go, if I ever did.

One night I was sitting in a little dive on Market Street, sitting alone, quiet, having a bottle of beer, minding no one, no one minding me, when it happened! When she came in! It never would have happened, I never would have seen her, had I not broken one of the parole rules. The sacred book said we weren't to drink, "under no circumstances enter into a place where liquor is sold or given away." I was probably the only guy in the world trying to abide by that. But then, I had Masters to think of. And the night I didn't think of him was the night I slipped into that bar and she came in. The minute I saw her legs I knew. I didn't need to look any farther but I did. She was wearing a sweater and skirt. A sweater too tight for her and a skirt split up the side so that you could see more of her leg when she sat down, if she ever did. She did, but not next to me. She sat in a far corner of the bar, and the first thing she did was take out a compact, a big purple tortoise-shell affair, too big for her small face, and she powdered her nose, like I'd seen Elizabeth Frazer do a million times. Then she batted her big blue-green eyes that were so much like the sea when it's blue, and so much like the sea when it's green. Then she wet her finger and ran it over her lashes, the lashes that made long shadows on her too-white face. Then she took a comb and ran it through her bleached blonde hair, and as she did she leaned over or back or someway so that her V-neck sweater fell away from her neck and I saw that shoulder in a pose I'd seen a million times before. Even when it had the crust of someone else's blood on it, it still shrugged that careless, too-casual shrug that said to everything and everybody, "Later. Much later."

I sat staring like a madman. Like an idiot I drooled surprise and disbelief and hate and revenge. The hot smoky room I was sitting in, staring at a ghost, a ghost to me, got cold. An icy blast blew in through the door that opened out onto a hot night and I pulled my coat collar up around my neck. I even put my head down inside my coat like a drunk, like a dope searching for a new dream, but when I raised my head to look again she was still there. And she was more alive than before, because she was talking to a guy at the next table and I heard her voice. I wanted to slap my hands over my ears, but even if I did I knew I'd hear it just the same. I knew that voice would carry into a room I was sitting in thousands and thousands of miles away from the point where the voice began. It was hers all right. It was high and squeaky like a rusty hinge that nobody would ever oil, because nobody lived in the house. The voice didn't come out all throaty and warm like I'd hoped it would.

I got up so quickly that my groin hit the table and I lost my balance, catching myself before I fell over onto the floor and the manager threw me out for drunkenness. I turned toward her and made my way through the tables separating us. The people at the tables followed my progress like people do when they watch a speeding car dart through traffic dangerously and without regard. I got up to her just as she finished one sentence and was about to start another. She looked up at me startled, the unformed words still on her open lips.

I clenched my hands until the nails were cutting into my palms. I clenched my teeth. I shut my eyes tight and swallowed dry hard swallows, then I spoke and the words came out like sound blown through the wrong end of a funnel. "Elizabeth," I said. "Elizabeth."

The guy she'd been talking to jumped up and started over toward me.

"Wait a minute," the girl said. "Don't, Jerry. The guy's nuts or drunk or somethin'. Don't smack him." I opened my eyes just in time to see Jerry unclench his fists and mouth.

I nodded my head. "Yeah," I said, "the guy's nuts or drunk or something." I turned away. "Sorry," I muttered. "Sorry. Sorry. Sorry." I started for the door. Her words followed me.

"Yeah, Jerry, poor old guy. He's nuts or sick or somethin'. Elizabeth. That's a pretty name, Jerry. I hate mine. Do I look like a Maude?"

I didn't hear what Jerry said, but he must have said something funny or dirty because she laughed. But the laugh wasn't all scratchy and jagged and horrible. Her voice was better in a laugh.

As I went to put my hand on the door I saw a mirror above one of those gum machines. I stopped and looked in it. The first thing I saw was the girl in the background talking to Jerry again. I noticed then that she couldn't have been over eighteen. I stepped closer to the mirror. I saw my own face. I couldn't have been under forty, although I might have passed for thirty-five. I was tall, thin, still fairly well built. My face was thin too, but there were lines in it, and not lines that spelled youth. And my hair was gray, almost all over gray. Poor old guy. Not because forty was old or I looked even older or even younger, but because I had forgotten to remember that ten years change a man and a woman. Elizabeth would be the same age, around forty. Her sweater wouldn't be quite so tight or the shrug of her shoulder so casual. Elizabeth! A nice name, the girl had said. And a name that I thought I'd forgotten, but evidently remembered more surely than if I'd never spent those ten years trying to forget. Elizabeth, who left me a phony funeral pyre and ten years of too much time, was still alive to me.

The moment I walked out of the door of that dive on Market Street I knew that my old sickness had not returned, but a new one had taken its place. A new sickness of old hate, instead of an old sickness of new love. The relapse was upon me. For before I could realize the full meaning of the recovery of freedom, I was on my way to find Elizabeth Frazer if I had to search streets of cities the rest of my life. I was on my way to revenge, for I was certain that Elizabeth Frazer, or the ghost of what she once was, was still around someplace.

Chapter 10

I met a guy once who said he'd lived in Tibet. We were riding a freight together. It's a cinch he didn't belong on that freight. He would have looked better in a loincloth riding a magic carpet. But he was broke and had to get somewhere fast. A lot of us throw away our loincloths for just that reason. This guy said he could study people better when he traveled steerage. The real subjects he wanted to help lived in houses by the side of train tracks. He said they needed the spiritual and he was the guy to take it to them. He was like a Baptist missionary wrapped in an Oriental rug.

I didn't believe everything he told me, but he had a philosophy he said he learned in the Orient. I don't know whether he could walk through fire or jump on broken bottles like I once saw an old African do and come out unharmed, but I've got to admit he had a sense of calm that I've never seen before or since. He interested me a lot, but I didn't go for his placid face too much. It made me nervous to look at those smooth planes of his cheeks, the limpid quiet of his eyes. When he talked of great emotional upheavals, told me of the disasters that had driven him to seek this peace, his expression never changed. He looked like an oil painting when it's young before it begins to crack and fall apart and cost a thousand dollars.

He said, "Walter, it takes years and years of contemplation to find this quietude of soul, where nothing material matters. Where it doesn't matter what you've got on, what you eat, or where you go. Where all is calm. Even. It takes years. You think you've got it, then puff, it goes away like a smoke ring and you have to keep seeking, studying, sorting your thoughts, throwing away the bad, the personal, the selfish, the evil, and keeping the good, the unselfish, the all-enveloping. Then the peace comes again and stays with you maybe for years. Until something else comes into your life to upset you and you begin all over again. The struggle is glorious. And then one day the peace comes to you for good. A great blanket of softness, of calm, covers you and beds you down, and nothing touches you any longer."

"I don't like it, yogi," I said. "No color. Where's the color? I like to explode and hate and love and explode again."

He smiled, but even then his expression didn't change. The smile vanished quickly like the smoke and his eyes remained the same, clear and penetrating and still. "Fire burns you up," he said. "It cleanses. It tears your insides out and cleanses you, refines the gold from the dross. You'll welcome it someday, but don't think it'll come easily."

The fire that burned in me, forcing me to seek Elizabeth after those ten years I didn't like. It burned the inside of me all right, but the peace that's supposed to come afterward didn't come. Ten years I'd spent in the quietness of a cell, in the presence of a man who had that stillness, Warden Masters, and yet as that phony Hindu said, the stillness wasn't mine to keep. Yet. I had another fire to walk through, more empty and broken beer bottles to jump on, until nothing hurt any longer.

I sorted out my thoughts, but I didn't throw away the bad and keep the good. I sorted my thoughts as if I were sorting money. The pennies I put there. The nickels here. The dollars over there.

Where would I look first? There was no sense in going to Los Angeles, trying to find a mythical Elizabeth Frazer that might or might not have been there ten years before. I would go to the original scene of my so-called crime. I'd go to Carleton, California, and find the Hargraves, Charley and Mrs. Hargraves. Mattie Hargraves might know where Elizabeth might have gone. Elizabeth might have told her once in their stupid exchange of stupid confidences. Had I known Old Lady Hargraves was dead this whole story might have been different. Might. Might have been. The sorrows of the world are soaked in the thoughts of what might have been.

I reported to my parole officer and was given permission to leave the county. As soon as I found work in Los Angeles a parole officer would be sent to check up on me, but my monthly report was to be mailed to San Francisco. I thanked the guy. "Don't thank me," he said. "You're doin' O.K. No bums or grifters hangin' around you. No gettin' into trouble. You're doin' O.K., Johnson. Keep it up."

Trouble, Mr. Parole Officer? I haven't even begun to learn how to spell the word right.

I told him to give my regards to his friend and mine, Warden Masters, and my legal and personal obligations to the state were completed until the next month.

I gave my radio and what junk I had in my room to my landlady, paid all my debts, bought a new suit and hat, and had just enough dough left to take me to Carleton, California.

It was a blistering hot day when I arrived, regular desert weather. The guy who'd picked me up at the depot took me into town and dropped me off near a gas station. I went inside the restroom, brushed off my clothes, and washed my face. I leaned over the washbowl and I got such a cramp in my stomach I could hardly straighten up. I was scared, I guess. Or nervous. Maybe I thought I might find Elizabeth still alive and sitting in our little two-room motel, just as I'd once left her, waiting for me to come home from the garage, rocking back and forth chatting gaily, and what I thought was unsuspectingly, to Old Lady Hargraves. Or maybe I was nervous and scared because I was afraid I wouldn't find Hargraves at all. People not only change in ten years. They move. They move away and sometimes don't even leave a memory you can follow.

My cramp went away, but when I came out of the washroom I was so weak I could hardly stand up. Hungry. That was it. I was hungry. Before I could face any of them I had to have a cup of coffee. I had around forty cents left. I tossed a coin to see which I'd do first, go look up Old Man Hargraves in the shoe store or eat. My stomach won. I walked across the main drag to a diner that used to have pretty good food. It was two o'clock and I was glad the place wasn't crowded. Someone might recognize me, and I had had enough of that kind of curiosity. I looked around for a familiar face. I didn't see any, so I slid onto a stool at the counter. A pimply-faced high school brat was cleaning up the dishes, stacking the dirty ones on top of the clean ones while he lit a cigarette and rested for a minute. He'd probably been resting all day.

I didn't see anybody willing to wait on me. A squatty-looking little guy with a big white apron on was standing at the grill flapping a hamburger. He had his back to me.

I grabbed the menu off the counter and looked it over. The prices had gone up since the last time I visited the joint ten years ago. Twenty-five cents for a hamburger and coffee. Ten cents for a couple of doughnuts.

Well, that'd have to be it.

The bus boy was still resting, taking deep puffs of his cigarette and watching the smoke come out of his greasy nostrils. After I had watched him, it didn't look so appetizing, but I wanted to smoke too. I reached in my pocket for a cigarette. The pack was empty. Damn! I couldn't have a doughnut and smoke too. But I could borrow a cigarette. I nodded to the boy. "Lend me a cigarette, fellow," I said. "I haven't got any change right now for that machine. And I don't know how soon I will have any."

The kid looked surprised but didn't refuse me. He reached in his shirt pocket for the pack and tossed it down the counter. "Don't take any more'n one." He grinned. "They cost seventeen cents in here."

I ignored him and took two, shoving the pack back. I started to light up, and that's when I saw the little man watching me. He'd turned from his griddle the minute I'd started talking, and he was staring at me like he'd seen a ghost. He still had the cake turner in his hand. I could smell the hamburger on the griddle. If his hand remained that way suspended in space, that hamburger would be a goner.

After I caught him watching me I turned full face and showed my teeth in what was supposed to be a smile. "Good afternoon, Charley Hargraves," I said politely. "Your hamburger is burning."

His mouth came open but he swallowed the gasp before it made any noise, then he turned back to the griddle and slid off the hamburger. His hand shook as he tossed it on the roll. He fixed the sandwich but I knew he wasn't thinking about daubing the bread with oleo, or slapping some chili sauce and mustard onto a hunk of lettuce. He was thinking about me, sitting there as though I'd just come in to lunch, sitting like a solid and respected citizen waiting for his meager repast so he could get back to his job. And that's the way I looked, too. But he knew damned well it wasn't true. Inside him he knew I was sitting there at that counter for the first time in ten years, that I was in this town for the first time in ten years, and that I had a damned good reason for being there, that I wanted something pretty bad or I wouldn't be there. I wanted something more important than a hamburger sandwich.

He turned and avoided looking at me as he slid the sandwich down to a guy at the end of the counter. He walked to the coffee urn, and as he poured out the guy's coffee I said, "Make that two, Charley."

The bus boy had finally taken the dishes back to the kitchen and I felt that Charley and I were all alone. He felt the same, I'm sure. He poured the two cups of coffee hesitantly, as though he were waiting for some interruption that would take his attention away from me or vice versa.

"One sugar, no cream, Charley." I spoke through his hesitation. He jerked and the hot coffee ran over and burned his hand. He set one cup down and picked the other up, put some sugar and cream in it, and set it down in front of the guy. Then he picked mine up and started toward me.

"You forgot the sugar, Charley," I said and smiled. He gave me a sheepish glance and went back for the sugar. When he started up to me again his movements seemed more sure. Maybe my smile had something to do with it.

He set the coffee down. "How's your wife, Mattie?" I asked.

He looked straight at me, into my eyes for the first time, and a thin film shaded his myopic ones. I could see it even through the thick lenses of his glasses. "Mattie's been dead for many years," he said, and turned away from me.

I took a big gulp of the hot coffee to cover my surprise and the beginning of my disappointment. Before I could speak he made a quick turn back toward me. "She died a year later," he said. "Accident. The swing. Fell out. Her neck was broken."

I had to bite my lip to keep from laughing. "I could have fixed that swing for her," I said.

He didn't pay any attention to my last remark. He put his hands on the counter and leaned toward me, staring into my eyes. "What are you doing around here, Walter?" he said. "Why did you come back?"

I laughed this time. "Well, believe it or not, I came in here just to get a hamburger. Honest Injun."

I stopped abruptly. Honest Injun. That was what Elizabeth always used to say. I shut my eyes and prayed hate. When I opened them Hargraves was still there, apparently waiting for me to continue. "I just came in to eat, Charley," I repeated. "Will you fix me a sandwich? I've been traveling all night and all morning without anything to eat."

He didn't move. Just stood with his hands on the counter for support, waiting for me to say what he thought I should say.

I got a little mad. "Fix me that sandwich, Charley," I snapped at him, "and some fried potatoes and a piece of pie and make it on the house! As soon as I've finished eating I'll tell you why I'm here."

A firecracker going off in his pants couldn't have turned him any quicker. He shot to the grill and began fixing my sandwich. It was a good thing the rat poison wasn't handy. I watched his short fat hands fly over that sandwich board. I never thought of Hargraves as a fast worker before. I wondered what made him give up the shoe clerking business.

He got my sandwich ready, fried the potatoes, cut the pie, and set out a couple of doughnuts. Some mechanics came in and diverted him while I ate my food. I listened to him talk to the other customers. It didn't make sense what he was saying, but I knew, for his sake, it covered up his fear.

He was scared crazy of me, had been ever since that morning we found what he and Mattie and the court thought was Elizabeth Frazer's body. To him I was a bona fide murderer.

The mechanics finished eating before I did, slid off the stools and up to the cash register where the toothpicks stood in a dirty glass holder. Hargraves had to walk past me to get to the register to ring up the sales.

"Got a cigarette, Charley?" I spoke low. He didn't stop or even acknowledge that he'd heard me. But after he rang up the checks he took twenty cents out of the register and walked around the counter to the cigarette machine.

I turned around and watched him. "If those are for me," I said, "I smoke Camels."

He got the cigarettes out of the machine and walked back behind the counter, stopping in front of me. "That'll be seventy-seven cents you owe me, Walter."

I took the package, tore it open, and threw him the three pennies that were inside the cellophane package. "Seventy-four and try and get it."

He didn't answer at first, but he looked like he was going to cry. He bit his lip as though to stop it from quivering, but I found it wasn't crying he was about to do. He was mad.

"Lookie here, Walter Blodgett," he exploded, "you and I never was very friendly and this ain't no time to start bein'. Why even when you lived next door and Mattie and—and Eliza—" He hesitated.

"Go on. Elizabeth. Say it, Charley."

"Even when Mattie and your wife was seein' each other, you didn't know me well enough to call me Charley. Even then."

"That's right, Charley," I smiled.

"And now after all these years you come back here and get friendly. Even borrow money. I don't want to see you. I ain't got nothin' that you want. Mattie's gone and I been workin' here in this diner for the last two years, mindin' my own business, livin' in a room in a house with nice people. Tryin' to make my life over."

I took a puff of my cigarette and blew the smoke out slowly. I wanted him to calm down. He was shaking all over.

"What happened to the shoe store job you had for so many years?" I said.

He settled back with his thoughts, sighed, picked up a greasy rag that was lying near him, and started cleaning the food spots off of the counter. It seemed like a reflex action. "They fired me," he said. His words were slow now and tinged with pathos. He was nicer. His attitude was nicer. He was talking about himself now, and that made his voice more tolerant.

"After the trouble and the trial, so many people came into the shoe store to see me that Mr. Levy said I was causin' trouble. No one was buying any shoes. They was just looking at me like I was some kind of novelty. They didn't even give me a bonus when I left, and I'd been there eighteen years. That's people for you."

"I didn't get a bonus either," I said, "and I spent ten years on a job I didn't ask for, that I wasn't paid for. That I hated."

The rag stopped moving across the counter. He looked up at me and his rabbit eyes got big and scared again.

"Yeah, that's right. I'm not an escapee. I'm a parolee. I'm a good friend of the warden's. The state likes me. They let me go. And I'm here for a reason. I don't want to mess up your life like Elizabeth and Mattie and you messed up mine. I just want some information. Then I'll get out of your hair and you'll never see me again."

"Information?"

"Yeah. What time do you finish here?"

"Four o'clock."

"O.K. I'll be back and pick you up. We'll talk in your room." I slid off the stool.

"Wait a minute, Walter. You ain't aimin' on makin' any trouble? A scene?"

I shook my head. "Nope. I just want you to try to remember something for me, that's all."

He relaxed considerably, picked up the rag, and tossed it to the bus boy, who was coming through the kitchen door.

I walked to the door and turned. "But don't run away, Charley," I called to him. "Then I really might get sore."

He didn't answer me verbally, but I saw him nod and I walked on out into the desert sunshine with a prayer on my lips that what I wanted to know wouldn't be too hard to find out.

Chapter 11

It was just getting dusk. The red-bronze shadows of the desert came through the windows and fell across Charley's wrinkled face. As he rocked back and forth in an old wooden rocker the shadows moved with him.

We were sitting in his rented room and he was telling me how much he missed Mattie. "It was awful, Walter," he said. "The first few weeks it was awful. I just went around in a daze. I didn't eat or sleep. I didn't know how to do them things alone. I didn't know how to eat alone or sleep alone. Or even get up and get dressed alone. I went around town half dressed."

"Maybe that's why the shoe store fired you," I said.

"Oh, no." He looked over at me and there was no hint of humor in his eyes.

I was sitting on his unmade bed. I'd taken off my shoes because my feet hurt and I had one knee propped up in front of me. We were relaxed for a moment, Charley and I.

"Oh, no," he repeated. "They fired me right after the trial. Mattie didn't die until a year later. She had to live to see me humiliated, to see me lose my job."

"That's the trouble with people, Charley," I said, "they get to depending on each other too much. They have no inner life, no sufficiency. So when they lose the only person they depended on, they have nothing left."

"I know," he shook his head, "but try and change. It's easier to just go on living with memories that are unhappy than to try and change."

"To change takes courage," I said, "and you bet damned well I've had to have plenty of guts. I've lost everything. All my life. I'm always losing things. When I was little, I lost marbles and penknives. Then when I grew up it was jobs and people and time. But I've had to change, to go on changing."

He stopped rocking and looked over at me. "What do you want to see me about?" he asked sharply.

I took my feet off the bed and reached for my shoes. "I want to find out something about Elizabeth. Where she might be now."

He jumped like he'd been shot out of a rocket. If it hadn't been so dark in the room I could've seen his pop-eyes rolling around in his white face. But the shadows were deepening.

"She isn't dead, Charley," I said.

He started to say something, then he got up suddenly and went to the window, pulled back the dirty lace curtains, and slammed the window shut. Then he turned back to me. "Switch the light on by the wall, there." His voice had fear in it.

I smiled. "Why? Let's talk in the dark."

He brushed quickly past me to the wall by the door and snapped on the light. The disheveled room loomed into view real and solid. It made him feel safer.

"O.K., Charley, ghosts don't walk in the light and Elizabeth won't walk through here unless she happens to be in the vicinity. Because, you see, she isn't a ghost."

He sat down again in the rocker, on the edge of it this time. He would be ready to leap quickly in case a ghost paid us a call.

"But—but you killed her, didn't you? Didn't you, Walter?" His voice rose almost to a shout. "You killed her and burned her body in the backyard. We saw the ashes. We saw them. Mattie and I. Didn't you, Walter? Didn't you kill her?" The hysteria he was suddenly exhibiting frightened even himself. He glanced toward the door to see if he were heard by the people downstairs.

I walked to the hall door and made sure it was closed. "Elizabeth isn't dead, Charley," I repeated. "I didn't kill her. You didn't. Mattie didn't. Nobody killed her. She's alive. I'm sure of it. I know it! I know she's around someplace. Maybe not in Carleton. Maybe not in Los Angeles or Frisco or San Diego or Fresno. But she's around. In this country. In this world somewhere. Now, she and Mattie were pretty close. You heard how close they were. At the trial Mattie said Elizabeth confided in her all the time. She even said Elizabeth told her that I was going to do away with her someday. That helped convict me. If you remember."

Charley dropped his head on his chest and I knew what he was thinking. Not about me and my misfortune, or of Elizabeth and hers, but of Mattie.

I went on, "Now, if Mattie and Elizabeth were so close, Elizabeth must have told her at some time or other about the guy she had waiting for her in L.A. She may have even told her where he was waiting. What the address was where he lived."

He shook his head. "I don't think so, Walter. Mattie never told me."

"Women don't tell men everything. They tell other women. They even make up things to tell to other women, but they don't tell men everything."

He sighed. "I don't think so, Walter," he reiterated.

"Well then, if you don't think so and we can't recall the dead to find out, did Mattie leave any effects that you didn't destroy? Any letters or scraps of paper or anything we could dig out that just might have something on them that would lead us to Elizabeth?"

He sat and thought for a moment. "Well, Mattie did leave a lot of junk. The only thing I kept was," he got up and ambled to the closet door, opened it, and leaned over, "this here box." He pulled a cardboard box from the closet. "I piled some old letters of ours in here. Mattie saved those and some papers and clippings. Little things that meant a lot to her." He began rummaging through the box. "You know, little keepsakes."

I got up, walked over to him, and leaned over. "Didn't you ever go through the box before?"

"Oh, sure." He began laying things out on the floor. A moth-eaten New

Testament, a pressed gardenia, some of their old love letters, a nail file, a couple of yellowed Urichsville, Ohio, *Chronicles*. "I been through this a dozen times but I never paid a lot of attention to some of the letters. They was just old letters from her relatives in Urichsville, Ohio. Outside of them, I know everything that's in here."

"Well, drag them out," I said. "Find them. Maybe there's a letter in there from a relative in Urichsville that mentions Elizabeth. Maybe Mattie told them something about Elizabeth. Something even I don't know."

He dug down in the bottom of the box and scraped up some letters. I grabbed them out of his hand. "Wait a minute, Walter. Be careful of them. Don't tear them. I want everything in this here box left intact."

"I'm not gonna tear them. I'm just gonna read them. If I tear them I can't read them. Right?"

I walked over to the bed and sat down. My hands were trembling as I opened the letters. They were from relatives all right. "Dear Cousin Mattie, Did the earthquake last night do much damage? We worry about you out there...." "Dear Aunt Mattie, Ain't it funny? It's cold here and you're dying with the heat out there...." Etc., etc.

Charley sat down and helped me read them. We had gone through about eight apiece and hadn't found a mention of Elizabeth or me, and the letters were written at the time we were living next to the Hargraves. "You'd think," I said to Charley, "that Mattie would have mentioned Elizabeth or me."

I reached down on my lap to pick up one of the last letters and I couldn't believe what I saw. I tried to reach for the letter but my fingers grew stiff as though they'd been paralyzed. I read the address again to be sure. "Elizabeth Blodgett, Melvan Motel, Carleton, California." And up in the left-hand corner the return address. "Hollyjoy Apartments, Hollywood, California." And even if the man's name wasn't tacked onto the return address, I knew a guy had addressed the letter. I looked at the date. Stamped two days before I found what was supposed to be Elizabeth Frazer's burned body lying in a junk heap out in back of our cottage in the Melvan Motel.

When I was finally able to grab hold of the envelope I turned it over quickly to open it. The seal had already been torn. I looked inside the envelope. Nothing. Not even a scrap of paper. "The letter's gone," I shouted. "Someone took the letter!"

I searched frantically through Mattie's other letters, then I looked over at Charley. He'd stopped reading and was watching me curiously. "The letter!" I shouted again, and my voice was hoarse with excitement. "A letter addressed to Elizabeth but no letter there." I held up the envelope.

He took it from me and looked it over carefully.

"Oh, this," he said. "I remember. This came to the motel afterward, a couple of days after you all were gone. It had been misdirected."

"Well, where's the letter?" I said. "Where's the letter?"

Charley thumbed through the letters on his lap. "I don't know. Mattie must have opened it, and that's not like her. I remember her saying something about the letter and should she hold it or send it to the dead-letter office or give it to you or what. But they'd taken you off to jail and Elizabeth was gone, so I told her to destroy it. I supposed she did."

He got up and walked back over to the box. I followed him. We went through the box again with a fine-toothed comb. Nothing else. Just the envelope. Mattie must have taken the letter with her to hell.

Oh, well, it was all right. I calmed down. At least I had an address of a guy Elizabeth must have been corresponding with while she was living with me, the address of a guy Elizabeth might have got to, an address that was ten years old but that didn't matter. There were hotel and apartment registers and files and people living around who remembered. Sometimes.

I put the envelope in my pocket and thanked Charley. I even offered to help him put the things back in the box, but he didn't want any help.

Then I made a speedy exit. No curtain speech now. I'd found what I wanted.

As I walked down the steps of the frame house where Charley had the lousy room with the nice people, I could see him as I left him, sitting on the floor in front of the cardboard box gently putting back the rifled keepsakes, stroking them softly as if they were living memories. He didn't care about me or my passions. He didn't care about Elizabeth. Dead or alive. It was Mattie that occupied his thoughts. That asked and answered his questions. I was happy that that picture of Charley was the last of the Hargraves.

It was seven o'clock by the time I got out on the highway, and the only picture I carried with me then was of Elizabeth, Elizabeth Frazer Isaacs Blodgett, the wandering corpus delicti.

Bumming the road is a fascinating racket. Maybe that's why I was a bum most of my life. It's a peaceful racket, too. Especially now. Some people, you and all the rest of the hard-working moles, call it a lazy man's existence, an ignorant man's job, a no-good guy's life.

I met a helluva lot of good guys on the road. Most of the time a lot better than I met inside houses. They like nature. They like the trees and the mountains and the cold mountain streams, and the smooth, silky highways, and the black-as-tar moonlit highways, and the rough masculine rock-pitted roads, and the warm, lush dust of the country roads and the smell of clover and hay and barley and cherry and peach and apple blossoms. They stand in awe before the orange trees with their aroma, sweeter than a new bride's breath. They love to sit in the shade of an oak tree and listen to the sounds the country day makes. They like the slow-moving streams, the sluggish water. They thrill before the singing brooks, the fast, daring rivers. They'll sit for hours watching the salmon run and jump and leap in the cold productive northern rivers.

They like other people. They like to talk to the "bo's" they meet on the road, share a bit of gossip, a sandwich, a "tailor-made" cig, a pack of Bull Durham, a quarter, a dime, a penny for some Dentyne at the next cowshed station.

They like to meet in the woods or old dried river beds, or fields where nobody goes, abandoned mines, or houses or stone quarries. They got the best damned grapevine in the world. It's better than telephone, radio, cable, or air mail. They grapevine their fellow bo's and tell them where the next jungle is, where they can stop and bed down for the night, where a few of 'em, sometimes five or six, ten or twenty, forty or fifty even, can get together and build fires and share food and smokes and talk about that other world, that dreamworld where everyone is fighting over torn maps and nonexistent boundaries.

Don't censure those guys. Don't tell the world it's those guys that stop at faraway houses, rape little girls, murder housewives, steal precious possessions, or kill livestock, sucking the blood from a pet chicken's neck. Oh, sure, that kind of guy joins the bo's once in a while. But he's an alien. He's as much a foreigner as the workingman would be or a white-collar joe who met the bo's in an obscure jungle, or a guy from Washington bedding down in the woods, his head on a pile of old war debts.

The bo's have got the alien spotted, all right. He's the real transient. He looks for cities mostly where he can ply his trade of pickpocketing, thieving, murder, and rape. He meets up with the road gang when he has to. But they don't want him, and when he's with them they change the hiding place of their meager pennies, stick their "tailor-mades" in a secret pocket in their pants, roll up their valuables in their overcoats, and sleep on the coats.

The real bo's of the road don't like the cities and the drawn faces in the cities and the white faces on the highways and the evil ones in the alleyways. They took to the road to get rid of those very faces, to blot them out with the newer, fresher images of the country. And if once in a while they lift a few cents or swipe somebody's lunch or pilfer the chicken house, it's from necessity, not greed.

It's a peaceful life now with the other world as it is, the man-made world in such confusion and chaos. It's a peaceful life, this hitting the road, and if I hadn't the newer picture of Elizabeth Frazer, framed in bright red revenge, in the world's type of revenge, in my mind, I would have stayed on the road forever and probably been a lot happier because of it.

When I left Carleton I had two hundred miles to hike to L.A. One guy picked me up but dumped me out after fifty miles, so I hit the road, and it's a damned good thing I did. I met a bo who shared a couple of cheese sandwiches with me, some coffee out of a battered thermos, and a hunk of gum. I gave him two tailor-mades. We caught a ride on a cement truck that dumped us part way to L.A. and we bedded down for the night. It got cold and I had no overcoat. This bo built us both a couple of fires on some old bricks and stones he found. Then he waited till the fires burned out and only the hot bricks remained, wrapped me up in his overcoat backward, buttons down the rear, and told me to lie down on top of those warm bricks. I did and slept like I was in a pre-heated, satin-sheeted Waldorf bed. It was a warm sleep. Good. Forgetting.

When we parted on the outskirts of L.A., near Alhambra, we shook hands, this bo and I, and he slipped me a quarter.

Yeah, hitting the road isn't the worst profession in the world. In most respects it's the best. It's a lot better than wearing a spiked crown or brass medals of hate.

Chapter 12

When I think about how hard I tried to find Elizabeth it seems weird now. That's because I can analyze it. I couldn't then. I tried to. All the way from Carleton to Los Angeles I tried to analyze why, after those ten quiet years, a mere coincidence would set me off again, onto that merry-go-round, into that mad fun house, down those perforated slides, and through those winding dingy stairways, in front of those warped mirrors that contorted your very thoughts. I know now what drove me on. Not hate or any of its outgrowths like revenge or envy or jealousy or hurt. But desire, pure desire. Not love. Desire. Sex. I still had a tremendous physical urge for Elizabeth, an unadmitted urge, a latent, buried urge, an urge that I wasn't aware of then. An urge that I called, humanly enough, hate. I hadn't got Elizabeth Frazer out of my system. She was a liar, a thief, a murderess, a high-class whore. She'd planned my futile destiny and forced me to seek the contemplative life before I was ready to seek it. She caused me to be shut up behind cold steel bars. She had broken off my lazy career in the middle of it. I had lost ten years of my life, and yet with all of it I still remembered those nights, those rare minutes during the day, when her beauty, her feline charm, when her evil fascination blotted out the more lurid evil of her soul, the grimy part of what she actually was. And even though it would seem difficult for a normal, everyday, practical mind to understand my submersion, other men and some women who'd lived more physical lives would see my point. Walker had been and still was an influential man, a bright man. She'd broken up his home. She'd murdered Isaacs. She'd left a wake of dissolute human beings in her path, and I felt that she was still traveling her well-plotted ground. There must have been others after me.

Anyway, our story started a long time ago, with a forbidden tree in a lush, well-watered garden.

Brother, what a dump the Hollyjoy Apartments were! Maybe they were nice when Elizabeth lived there, if she ever did, or when her friend lived there ten years before, but they were a dump when I arrived.

They were in the middle of what had once been a pretty good district in Hollywood, but the transients and hangers-on had taken it over and it was tough. That was O.K. I knew a lot about cheapness. Toughness. I could deal better with tough people. The manager of the Hollyjoy was that kind of people. She opened the door of her apartment and let me see just enough of her to know that she was wrapped in a dirty flannel kimono and her yellow-gray hair was up in leather curlers. She had a pudgy face, turned hard. Little furrows of distrust and greed ran down her nose, ran up from the flat part under her chin, to the corners of her mouth. The furrows were deeper in the bridge of the nose and pulled her eyes closer together and made her look like the cover of a cheap mystery novel.

She gave me a drawn-lipped stare and her eyes narrowed. "What do you want?" Her voice was a flat Kansas monotone.

I stuck my foot in the door and swung it open. I don't know why I did it. It was a cheap theatrical gesture derived from pure orneriness, but it worked. She suddenly stepped backward, catching herself before she fell over a moth-eaten red plush chair. The gesture unnerved her for a moment, made her aware, announced me as a guy to listen to. I saw right then that she was used to grifters. I shut the apartment door and smiled.

"How are you, Mrs. Maloney? I got your name from the box downstairs. I want to talk to you a moment."

She backed up a little farther into the middle of the room. "Who are you?" Her flat tones took on a little color.

I smiled again. "I'm not a bill collector," I said. "I haven't got a bloody thing to sell and I'm not on the lam from anything or anybody. I just knew if I didn't shove my way in you wouldn't listen to my story. Sit down."

She walked over to me, her eyes mean as sin. She was braver now. Maybe I wasn't lying. "You got a hell of a nerve," she said. She stood looking me over, her evil eye cataloguing. "Got a cigarette?" she asked.

The sudden flip to her words startled me. I shook my head. "No, I was just going to ask you the same."

She smiled for the first time and showed me decayed brown teeth. "Tell me what you want, and if you ain't after my money or my old man I'll get you a smoke."

She must have liked my looks, added me up pretty right, otherwise her smile, as senile as it was, wouldn't have been so trusting.

I sat down in the red plush whorehouse chair. "Were you the manager of this apartment house ten years ago?"

She shook her head. "Christ, no," she said. "I jist came in from Arkansas 'bout two years ago. Been here in this dump for six months."

"I see. Are there any books around? I mean registers or files I could look over?"

She squinted her pig eyes. "Shamus?" she asked.

"No, Maloney, I'm just a guy lookin' for a dame that lived here ten years ago. I don't want her for any particular reason except—well," I looked over at her and winked, "the usual thing. I been out of the country since I saw her last and I'd like to get reacquainted. That's all."

Her look told me she knew where I'd been. "Well, how come you shoved your way in on me like you did if that's all you want?"

She was asking me the leading questions. I was right about her when I first lamped her. Her profession wasn't just managing an apartment house. There were other things. What I didn't know, but they weren't within the law.

"Get me that cigarette, Maloney," I said, "and I'll tell you my ugly story."

She got up and shuffled to a dinette, opened the cupboard between the dinette and the kitchen, took out a pack of Camels and a bottle of bourbon. That was fine, if she poured me a drink, too. I was hungry as the devil but I could use a drink as a substitute.

She poured us both a slug and set the bottle back in the cupboard. "O.K.," she said. "What's the score?"

She walked back into the room. I got up and took the slug of bourbon from her, set it down, then lit our cigarettes.

"I'm looking for a dame named Elizabeth Frazer. Or she might be using the name of Johnson or Blodgett or Isaacs. Or more than likely it's none of those. Just keep the Elizabeth and pick a last name."

Maloney laughed and swallowed her bourbon without finishing her laugh. The drink and the laugh ended in a loud gulp. Some of the whisky slid down from her mouth onto her lower lip. She wiped it away with the edge of her kimono.

"Some dame, huh?" She set the glass down on the end table near her and shot the next question at me with all the force of a bulldozer and the timing of a professional. "What were you in for, buddy?" she said.

It was her strike this time. I looked at her for a moment, then I figured it was the best thing to tell this kind of dame the truth. I took a drink of my whisky, more politely without dripping any on my vest, looked up at her, and said, "Murder! I took the rap for a dame."

She grinned. "For Elizabeth Frazer or whatever the hell she's callin' herself."

"Right."

She got up quickly, walked over to me, took my glass, and started back toward the cupboard. She was all energy now. She moved quickly, lithely, almost gracefully. She liked my reason for looking for someone. She understood it. She sympathized with it. She condoned it. She knew what stir meant.

She poured us both another shot, and while she talked and drank she took her hair out of the curlers. I looked at it and realized it was a futile hope. Her hair was beyond the easy curling stage. It came out like a pig's tail, kinky in the middle and straight on the ends. In her youth she must have had it dyed every color in the rainbow. Now that it was getting gray and she was getting gray she was trying to reclaim an unknown softness.

She told me there weren't any files or registers around, but there was one woman in the apartment who'd been there a long time, ten or twelve years. The dame was a gossipy old rabbit hutch but would probably remember Elizabeth if she ever lived there.

"And even if she just visited here," she added, "because this dame knows everyone that comes in and goes out. She's got a front apartment and all she does all day long is look out the window and watch the tenants. Gets on your nerves. I'd tell her to move but I ain't got any real good excuse. She don't break nothin' or git rowdy. Just sits and looks."

I had to wait until she got her hair combed out and a house dress on. She dressed right in front of me, that is she stood in the dressing room doorway and I could watch her if I wanted to. I only looked once. Not out of curiosity. It was just natural to look at her while I was talking. She leaned over to pick up her house slippers and I saw that she'd been shot in the back. There was a scar just above her last vertebra. The bullet must have come too close for any comfort.

When she was dressed she grabbed the keys off the bureau, and we walked to the door.

"If she ain't home," she said, "I'm goin' into her apartment anyway to see if she got her cat a box like I told her to. I'll leave her a note, then you can come back later. Her name's Goldie Lewis."

After Maloney's stuffy apartment the air in the hall hit me like a tornado. Those two slugs of bourbon had just about floored me. One more and Maloney and I would have tangoed off together. I hadn't been drinking and on an empty stomach it wasn't so good.

We walked up the stairs to the second floor and down the hall to the front apartment, Goldie Lewis's apartment. I knew if Goldie had lived in the apartment house ten years ago and she was the kind of dame Maloney said she was, she'd remember Elizabeth, that is if Elizabeth had ever been there. Not Goldie or anyone else in this kind of a joint would ever forget Elizabeth, because the minute they saw her, even if she were wearing a Hoover apron, they'd know that she didn't belong in poverty row.

When Maloney and I walked into Goldie's cluttered apartment and saw her sitting there in the middle of a heap of darning, dirty dishes, unmade beds, and cat hairs, talking to her girlfriend "Countess Evelyn," I thought I was meeting my stepmother, reincarnated; I ran away from home just because of the kind of dame Goldie Lewis was. My stepmother was the same kind. The Countess and Goldie were tearing apart a neighbor they both knew. They'd finished with the hors d'oeuvres and were just starting to rip open her backbone for the main meal.

For about a year after my own mother died my old man sat around the house emptying gin bottles, then one day he got up and dressed in his Sunday best, the shiny blue serge and brown suede shoes his boss had handed down to him, slicked back his hair with some white Vaseline, drank a cup of coffee, and left the house stone sober. Later that evening he came back with my stepmother. They'd been married that afternoon. He met her about three weeks before in some roadhouse gin mill where she worked as hat checker. My old man was pretty good-looking and she probably checked his hat for nothing.

I had a little sister a couple of years younger than I who died in a diphtheria epidemic a few years later. Sis and I were home when the newlyweds came back that evening. We didn't like this new stepmother. We didn't like her the minute she walked inside the house. We didn't like her even before she walked in. We saw her from the window getting out of Dad's old bus. She got out of it like she was stepping over mud, and when she saw the dilapidated, unpainted frame we were existing in she gave it a stare that would have turned hot water into ice cubes in less than a minute.

My own mother, who died when I was ten, was a wonderful woman. She'd been a practical nurse. She was soft and gentle and gracious even when there wasn't anyone sick around. And when there was, she was more gentle. Everybody that Mom touched seemed to get well. She was the only one who didn't. She loved my old man too much, but that was all right. The ten or twelve years he lived with her were the finest he ever knew.

Mom had a pretty good education and wanted us kids to have one too. The old man and she used to fight over it. He didn't believe in his kids going to a school run by narrow-minded teachers, biased school boards, and crooked politicians. He had something there, but they were only ideas, because when he married my stepmother he married a narrow-minded, biased, deceitful dame. Sex will excuse anything. Even murder.

I stood my stepmother for three years, then I ran away. She'd never owned anything in her life until she hog-tied Dad, then she made his life hell. She did the house over, filled it full of ugly bric-a-brac and whatnots and chairs nobody could sit on, and she ran the poor guy into so much debt that I couldn't get enough dough for decent shoes to wear to school.

When she got the house done and a bunch of new clothes that would have looked better on a performing seal, she dragged all the "cats" in the neighborhood in to see herself and the house. They used to have teas and cocktail parties and sometimes an old-fashioned sewing bee that usually ended in a drunken brawl. The reputation of any dame who wasn't invited to my old lady's parties wasn't worth the time it took to tear her to pieces. They did it quickly.

I had a pal whose old lady was a Polack and a swell mother. The day I heard my stepmother lay her out and in an early grave was the day I quit school and took to the road to get away from what the bright guys who eulogize people in books call Americana.

Most of the people are the same all over the world. Bitchery has nothing to do with boundaries. Narrowness has nothing to do with nationalities. The end of the world will come pretty damned quick. Only this time we won't have our backs turned.

Goldie Lewis was ten shades worse than Maloney ever could be. She looked and tried to act respectable, but every time her eyes changed moods, the mask lifted. A person could know where he stood with Maloney. She was probably mother to a half-dozen con guys and she wasn't so pure herself, but she was steady with her character. Goldie shifted with the wind. If the wind blew crooked, Goldie blew with it. If it blew pink, if it blew red as revenge or black as hate, Goldie was with it. Goldie would have looked natural holding a flaming torch and trying to keep up with Danton.

When we first went into her apartment she was pretty annoyed, then she took a second look at me. I smiled my best movie-hero smile and she softened a bit. Old Lady Maloney introduced us and told Goldie what I wanted.

Goldie put her finger to the red smear that was her mouth and started the gray matter churning. "Let me think. Ten years ago. That's a hell of a long time, ain't it? Yeah, but I remember her all right. Her name was Elizabeth." She leaned toward her friend Countess Evelyn, the phony countess who was really a movie extra. "Remember that dame, Ev," she said, "that moved in here with that fat guy you was always tryin' to make?"

Evelyn tried a blush but it didn't work. She frowned over at Goldie. "Why, you louse," she said, "that guy didn't interest me. It was him always tryin' to pick me up. Wanted to drive me to work and all that. Yeah, I remember her. She had bleached hair and when she came here she didn't have no clothes with her. Just what she was wearin'."

My heart began to pound. "That's Elizabeth!" I said. I tried to keep my voice normal. "How long did she live here? Do you remember, Goldie?"

"I like him." Goldie smiled over at Evelyn, indicating me. "I like the way he said Goldie. Sounded real intimate."

Maloney sneered. "Come on, Lewis," she said, "the guy ain't lookin' for you. You're here. Easy to find. He's lookin' for a dame named Elizabeth."

Goldie huffed up a bit. "Well, I'm tryin' to remember, ain't I?" She turned to me and her manner was less brazen. "I didn't like her at all," she said. "She was snooty, had airs. I used to watch her come and go. I was sick then. Had to stay in a lot. He bought her a whole raft of clothes. Expensive. Fur coats and things, and it was hotter than hell that fall. He wasn't a bad-lookin' guy. I don't know why he was livin' here. It wasn't so much a dump as it is now," she pointed this at Maloney, "but it wasn't the Bel Air neither. Yeah, I hated her guts and I didn't even know her. Ain't that a lulu? She wouldn't speak to none of us. They was here I should say about two or three months after she arrived, then they up and left." Goldie took a deep breath and was going to start again, but I couldn't wait for any more historical references.

"O.K., O.K., I think you got the right dame, but what was the guy's name? Did you ever meet him?"

Goldie laughed and showed the other gold she was hoarding in her mouth. "How the hell am I supposed to remember their last names this long? I wouldn't have remembered her first name except you said Elizabeth and it sounded right. Besides, I ain't a jukebox that you can keep droppin' nickels in. My record's broke now."

She picked up the darning she'd dropped behind the chair when we came in. Countess Evelyn got up and started to the bedroom. It was the exit music all right.

Maloney threw a dagger stare at Goldie. "Listen, you silly blonde jerk," she said, "this guy's a pal of mine. Don't be startin' any of your Christamighty stuff. Information in this country is still free. Tell him what he wants to know and cut the wisecracks or I'll throw you out of here someday."

Goldie laughed. "Look who's talkin'," she said. "Who's gonna help you throw me out? The President? You can't put me out unless I'm causin' a rumpus. Your kind ain't runnin' this country no more, Maloney. Keep your belt buckled. The people's got a chance to put in their two cents now."

Maloney snorted. "You're a fatheaded fat ass, Lewis. You're too dumb to be runnin' around with ideas in your head!"

I saw that it was going to develop into a female cat fight or maybe even a political argument that would have been hilarious, but I thought I better stop it. I motioned for Maloney to shut up. "Look, Goldie," I said, "I won't bother you anymore, but thanks a lot." I stood up to go. "At least I know Elizabeth was here. Anyway, your description sounds pretty accurate. Thanks a million."

Goldie was pouting on account of Maloney. "She's a helluva dame to be lookin' for, that Elizabeth," she said, "but you might try Laguna. Laguna Beach. That's where they went when they left here. I found it out from the garage boy." She hated to tell me this, but she didn't want Maloney to think she didn't know everything.

Maloney winked her granulated eyelid at me. I had a grin on my face as big as the San Francisco Bay Bridge. Laguna Beach. Ten years ago. Ten years ago Elizabeth Frazer left the Hollyjoy Apartments and went to Laguna Beach. My grin faded suddenly. So what? How the hell could I trace her when I didn't know either the guy's name or her alias? Laguna Beach might be small, but not that small.

Maloney helped me out on this. "Would she be usin' the same name, Johnson?" she asked me. "The name you knew when she ran out on you?"

I shook my head. "No," I said blandly, "because, you see, she's been dead ten years."

I heard the slamming of a door and Countess Evelyn's surprised mug leer into the room. Goldie had dropped her darning and was staring at me as though I'd just performed a miracle, like cutting Maloney in half with a penknife. I liked this tenseness. This was sport now. I had an audience, composed of three decadent dames who never got anything for free. Well, I'd give them some drama for free. Even though the state had buried her, I still believed Elizabeth was living. I would convince them, too.

I waited until my audience got its breath, then I told them the whole story, from the beginning, from Middletown, Minnesota. It would make good drinking conversation for them later that evening. In a few years they could regale their rickety grandchildren with the tale of the man with one hand.

When I finished telling them, Goldie blew through the hole in her front teeth. "Hot damn," she said, "what a dame!"

Countess Evelyn lit her eighth cigarette. As soon as I'd started telling my story she'd come into the room and sat down. I'm sure it was the quietest any of them had ever been.

Maloney was fascinated. She forgot her old man and the cops that were after him. She walked over to me and gave my phony hand the once-over. "Son-of-a-bitch," she said, "if that don't look real. It's a good job."

The Countess began to perk. "Goldie," she said, "we gotta help him out. Don't you think if you tried usin' that dopey brain for once that you could remember the guy's name this broad, Elizabeth, was staying with?"

"I don't know, Evelyn," she said, "I just don't know. Wait a minute!" she snapped her fingers. "Go down in the hall and call Norma. She met the dame one night while she lived here. I think her and Russ played poker with 'em. Maybe she can remember their names."

The Countess made a quick exit. While she was gone Maloney and Goldie and I celebrated with a Tom Collins Goldie fixed. By the time Evelyn got in touch with Norma and started Norma thinking, the three of us were pretty plastered.

Evelyn came back and her nervous face was working overtime with excitement. "I got it," she yelled. "Norma said she thinks the dame's name was Elizabeth Denton, and you're right, she and the guy moved to Laguna. And about three years later when Norma and Russ were in Laguna they ran into them in a bar. They live on a high hill right off the beach highway, and she says they're probably still around because they got married and bought some kind of business down there."

I threw my hat into the air. "Countess Evelyn," I said, "if I weren't so drunk and had another dame on my mind you and I would hook up right now."

The three of them laughed, we all had another drink, I said good-by, thanking Maloney in particular, and left for Laguna.

When I left them their latent female animosities for the time being were drowned in the bottom of a highball glass. It had been an interesting morning for me, too. I had proof now, almost positive proof, that Elizabeth Frazer Denton was still alive and very near. Very!

Chapter 13

I hopped a ride down to Long Beach, and stopped off in the Star Café on Peach Street. There was an old pal of mine working in the Star. I met the guy in Frisco and he told me his old lady owned the café and if I was ever in Long Beach, etc. I made it a point to be in Long Beach, to happen along Peach Street, to suddenly come upon the Star Café. I had to. I was hungry.

Everything blots out of your mind when you're really hungry. If you were homesick before, you're not any longer. If you were tired you forget about being tired. The success that you've been praying for for so long is shoved way in the background, is even forfeited for a hamburger sandwich. And every joint you see looks like the Ritz dining room. The cheapest hot dog, the most poisonous potato salad, tastes like roast pheasant. Keep a mob hungry enough, then feed them at the opportune moment, and you can rule the world. So hide your freedom in your spring vegetable garden.

My pal at the Star Café was nice to me and packed me a lunch, and his old lady put a quarter in a little church collection envelope she took out of her purse. I found the envelope tucked in the wax paper in one of the sandwiches. That quarter is what I entered Laguna Beach with. The guy that picked me up let me out on the other side of town and I had to walk back about a mile. It was nice to walk along the highway gazing out at the blue Pacific, but it was no way to look for Elizabeth Frazer. I had to have some kind of job, and jobs weren't as plentiful as they had been before I was thrown in the can. At least they weren't in Laguna. The tourist season wasn't so hot.

I made the rounds and had my choice of only two jobs, dishwasher in Ferguson's Waterfront Café or car washer at Jim's Combination Gas Station–Garage. Jim said he couldn't use a mechanic, he was one himself, but if I'd lower my standing in the union and take the wash and polish jobs for a while he'd throw some extra car work my way now and then.

Jim owned the garage himself. He was a boy about twenty-five, had a couple of kids and a mother-in-law to keep, and he wasn't a very good mechanic. He knew it, but he was scared to take a chance with me. He'd lamped my phony hand and thought that since he wasn't so hot with two hands, how the hell could I be good with only one?

But he looked like a pretty nice joe, so before I accepted the job I told him that, as my employer, he'd have to sign a report for the parole board every month.

He stared at me a long time. "You don't look like you'd been in the can," he said.

"Thanks, but that's no answer."

He shrugged his shoulders and grunted. "What the hell," he said, "somebody's got to hire you."

I got the car wash job and in two days worked my way up to assistant mechanic. Jim got all gummed up trying to do a valve job on a Caddie so I took over.

One day a big Oldsmobile sedan came into the garage to have a spark plug and battery checkup. A guy brought it in in the morning before I opened up. Jim had got me a room in a little shack on the beach, near the garage, so I opened up every day.

When I got there and found the Oldsmobile, there was a note on it saying the keys were under the front seat. I drove the car into the garage to wait for Jim before I did any work on it.

When I got out of the car I took a good look at it. It was covered with mud and sand and the inside was dusty enough to be good topsoil for a vegetable garden. I figured if the guy was a regular customer he wouldn't be averse to having his car cleaned up, so I washed the tub. When Jim arrived he laughed at my presumptuousness but said the guy was O.K. and would probably be happy I gave it a wash job.

After I finished I had a couple of minor repairs to do on a Ford and it wasn't until later that evening that I thought about the Oldsmobile at all. I took a call that came into the station. It was from a dame by the name of Hanley, Mrs. Hanley. She mentioned the Oldsmobile and wanted to know when it'd be done. I told her it was finished and she said she'd pick it up right away.

I hung up the phone and went out and told Jim. He laughed. "That screwball," he said, "she always does that. She wants to use the car tonight so she beats her husband to the garage, picks up the car, and he don't see her until after dinner." He shook his head. "She's a smart one."

I shrugged. "What the hell," I said, "dames are always smart ones and what can you do about them? I'll back the car out."

Jim hadn't finished the conversation. "Do about 'em?" he said. "What I do about my wife. I tell her when to come and go and that's that. She ain't puttin' nothin' over on me."

"Come and go," I mumbled. "Yeah, that might be easy to tell them. But it depends on where they want to come and go. If they decide they want to come and go someplace else, they'll figure out a way to do it. Sometimes it isn't so pleasant."

Jim rolled out from under the car he was greasing. "I thought a dame caused your trouble," he grinned.

I was in Mrs. Hanley's car by then and had the motor going. He couldn't hear me above the roar of the motor but I heard him all right. I answered him. "And when I find the dame," I said, "she won't cause anybody else any trouble. Not for a long time."

I backed the car out, parked it in front of the station, and was just getting out when I glanced down at the registration slip fastened on the steering wheel. It was made out to Elizabeth Denton Hanley! Elizabeth Denton! The Elizabeth Denton I had come to get. Elizabeth Frazer Denton, the cat with nine lives.

Coincidence is a screwy thing. Some people don't pay much attention to it. They simply call it coincidence and go on about their and someone else's business. To me coincidence is reason, a reason. In other words, there was a reason for me to pick out this particular garage to work in. There was a reason for the guy to hire me, to be nice to me and find me a room. There was a definite reason for me to back that Oldsmobile out of the garage. Some religious folk would call it divine reason. Some infidels would say evil reason. I just say reason. Because that something beyond us that some of us recognize as God, when we call on It or if we call on It, It usually directs us. I was directed to that garage for a reason.

And when the reason walked into that garage to collect her car I was waiting for her. I got her keys out and had them in my hand, and when she walked up to me, smiling, I knew the reason for my being there. It was an omen. It was a sign telling me to quit searching. It was a sign not from God, but from the devil, who was having a hell of a time with me providing clues and coincidences and reasons for me to be someplace so he could laugh at me and say, "Look, you silly jerk, stop searching for a woman that belongs only to me. Pick yourself another dame. Frazer belongs to the devil."

Because the fat, bleached, unsexy, voluminous-bosomed dame with the face that looked like an ad for Serutan who walked up to me and asked for her keys couldn't have been my Elizabeth if I'd seen her in a nightmare, inside out and upside down. And to cinch it, Elizabeth Denton Hanley's voice was a low rumble, like a thunderstorm on a sleepy day, a pleasant low rumble that suggested a warmth Elizabeth Frazer's scratchy soprano would never have, that Elizabeth Frazer would never have if she lived to be a hundred. Her warmth was all reserved for bed.

I'd failed again, but I knew it didn't matter so much in the final summing up. It wouldn't make me stop searching. Failure couldn't do a thing to me permanently. Failure and I were old companions and you don't fear an old buddy. You have no self-consciousness before lifelong pals. You don't listen to old friends. Although I felt a sharp disappointment for a moment, I made up my mind to pay little heed to this failure.

When my disappointment died down, my curiosity flared. I wanted to know if this dame, Elizabeth Denton, or Mrs. Hanley, was the one Goldie Lewis told me about. So when she thanked me for washing her car and was about to leave I called to her to wait a minute. She'd just opened her car door to get in. She swung around and eyed me skeptically.

I ran over to her. "I'm sorry, Mrs. Hanley," I said, "but all of a sudden it just came to me where I saw you before."

She looked at me closely and her eyes narrowed, but it wasn't a mean emotion I saw. On the contrary, it was curiosity, the same emotion I had. She didn't say anything, so I had to follow my opening attempt.

"The Hollyjoy Apartments. In Hollywood."

She blushed, and as with a lot of fat people, the blush started way down on her breastbone and moved up to her forehead as if a pink spot had been thrown on her from a low angle and moved upward.

I knew I'd hit a homer but she wasn't going to acknowledge it so quickly. "About ten years ago," I added. "I met you through Norma and Russ. I forget their last names."

The blush left her skin whiter than was natural. She shook her head slowly. "I never heard of them," she said.

"But the Hollyjoy," I repeated. "I lived there. I'm sure it was you."

She turned from me abruptly and got in her car. "Ten years ago is a long time to remember anything," she said, and started the car.

I knew she didn't want to remember for obvious reasons, at least obvious as far as what Goldie had told me was concerned. She and her present husband, Hanley, hadn't been married then, and no doubt they'd both had other obligations.

I was afraid Jim might lose her for a customer so I tried to apologize. "I'm sorry," I said, "but I was so sure. I'm sorry, Mrs. Hanley, but people make mistakes."

She turned in the seat and looked at me for a moment, then she smiled softly. "Yes," she said, "people do make mistakes." She shoved the car into gear. "And some," she added, "are better forgotten."

I got to thinking about it after she drove away. I was sorry I'd opened the wound. She was probably happy now, and as she said, some mistakes are better forgotten. I could have taken a lesson from Mrs. Hanley.

That night I took a walk on the beach. I found a lonely rock overlooking the beautiful Pacific. I sat on top of the rock and pretended it was the world I was sitting on and that I had command of not only the entire universe but myself as well. That didn't last long.

When you get down to it, I actually didn't know what the hell to do. I didn't know where the hell to go or why. I didn't know what to think about. I didn't know how to think straight like I had done the last few years in prison.

Quiet is a wonderful thing. A world without people is a kind of static heaven. When you're someplace where you can't buy newspapers, or hear people yelling, or the terrifying sound of death-dealing automobiles, you can acquire a little peace. You can think a little clearer. The pilgrims must have found that out. But though I was sitting on top of a rock on the edge of an ocean, I was far from a pilgrim. Only a few yards away from me were people on the sand around a fire and they were shouting and screaming aimlessly. The smell of roasted weiners drifted toward me. The man-made odors and sounds mingled with the smell of grease and oil and the roar of traffic up on the beach road above. And far out at sea I saw a boat blinking its lights at me. If they were signals I didn't recognize them. I couldn't read symbols in things.

I slapped the palm of my hand on the rock so hard it stung for two or three minutes. "Damn it," I said aloud, "damn it! I know Elizabeth is alive. She just has to be alive! But where? Where can I look now?"

The dead ends had been struck. There was only one other guy who might be able to provide some kind of lead. If I contacted William Walker, the man who'd helped me in Minnesota, he might be able to do the same again. If I told him I was certain she was in Los Angeles ten years ago, he might be able to remember someone she knew there, someone she'd told him about. It was a cinch to find Walker, if he was still alive and in Minneapolis, and I saw no reason why he shouldn't be. His electrical equipment company was still in Minneapolis. I'd seen advertisements in magazines.

It was my last stab, and as weak as it was, it made me feel sure that there was still hope.

That night I composed a letter to Walker and sent it off. In a couple of weeks I had my answer. His secretary wrote and told me Walker was in Los Angeles on business. He would be staying at the Biltmore for a couple of weeks.

I was excited when I got the answer. Here, I thought, was another potent sign that Elizabeth was around me someplace. All roads seemed to point to L.A. and its environs. The territory around Los Angeles was getting hotter and hotter. Even Walker was there on business.

I asked Jim to give me the day off, took a bus to Los Angeles, stopped at the Biltmore, and called Walker. I made a date to see him that evening for dinner.

He was overly cordial to me, like he'd been the first time I'd met him in Middletown. He congratulated me on getting paroled, and told me I looked a lot better than when I went in. When I told him my mission he said he'd do everything within his power to help me find Elizabeth. For a moment I thought he seemed a little too eager. I don't know.

"What do you mean within your power?" I asked him.

We were having cocktails in the Biltmore bar and there was a kind of cozy, intimate atmosphere about our meeting. I felt that I could be frank with him and he'd be the same with me. At least I convinced myself that was the way I felt. He was a millionaire and I was a poor misguided mechanic with a bum hand, but I wasn't such a bad foil for him. He knew a lot of things I didn't know and I knew a lot of things he never would know. You can have good conversations with that setup.

"Well, Walter," he smiled at me warmly, "you believe that Elizabeth isn't dead. You have a reason for that belief. You have proof, personal proof. I don't know anything but what I read in the papers and the reverse of that, which is what you've told me. Now I could give you some money and a lot of contacts that would be open sesame to you. I could give you the help of the police, the FBI maybe, and perhaps you'd be able to find her, if she's around. But, Walter, I don't feel that that's what you need, that kind of help."

He stopped talking for a moment, took a sip of his whisky sour, then before I had a chance to answer him he swung around toward me and looked at me hard. It seemed like a good, straight, honest look. "I think you need a job, Walter," he said. "Something you like, a job that you feel would eventually give you an advancement. Your mind should be occupied, your mind and body, so that there would be no time to nurture this obsession. And it has become an obsession with you. You're not aware of it, but it has. Before long it'll cause a psycho-neurotic state. Then you won't be good for anything. Then you won't even be able to find yourself."

I looked down at the table and clenched my fist, hard, tight, against my knee. I wanted to pound on the table, or better still, I wanted to pound my fist in Walker's face. But I couldn't. I knew he was right. Whatever his motive, I knew he was right. But I also knew that whatever he said to me wouldn't matter, that I'd continue to look until the desire pooped out or they eventually picked me up and threw me in the psycho ward.

Walker was aware of my attitude. He beckoned the waiter. I sat there like a stupid drunk while he paid the check. When we got up to go I felt better. The sickness of indecision suddenly left me and I was hungry. We went into the dining room, and on the way there I thanked Walker for his kindness.

He didn't say anything more about Elizabeth until we finished dinner, then he sprang a surprise suggestion. "You might go to my branch office here on Alameda Street, Walter, and look over the employment records. Elizabeth worked for me once, you know, and perhaps if she were badly in need of a job and happened to be in this vicinity she might try my plant. It's a nebulous idea, I know, but anything's worth trying." He smiled. "I mean for you anything's worth trying."

I got his point and smiled, too. He went on, "I'll arrange for the employment records to be at your complete disposal. You can also interview any of the employees who were at the plant ten years ago. There will probably be quite a number. My employees are pretty loyal. The stenographic department isn't large, and I'm sure there would be someone there who would remember Elizabeth Frazer ..."

"If she was ever there," I finished it for him, and laughed. I had a good reason to laugh. I had a lead again. My purpose in living had been strengthened.

The next morning I telephoned Jim and told him I wouldn't be back until the following day, then I spent eight hours in Walker's plant. I had the joint in an uproar because I was a friend of the big boss. Everyone was swell and tried to be helpful, but I didn't find anyone who had ever known Elizabeth Frazer. It looked like it was going to turn out to be a bum lead until I met an accountant, a Mr. Pritchard, who told me there'd been a girl by the name of Elizabeth Neindorf that had worked in the plant ten years ago. She'd left suddenly to go to Chicago and everyone thought it was strange. She'd seemed so happy there. She was a good worker. When she left she told no one, not even her boss, that she had been contemplating this move.

We looked up her records and found that she'd gone to work there just about the time Elizabeth Frazer hit Los Angeles, after the Carleton affair. I was pretty excited again about this lead. Then my bubble burst. Pritchard told me Neindorf had a mother who lived with her.

"How well did you know her?" I asked.

"Pretty well, Mr. Johnson. She was a quiet girl. Shy. Pleasant. I liked her."

"No, Mr. Pritchard." I shook my head. "That couldn't be my wife. I'm so sorry, but that couldn't be Elizabeth. In the first place, there wasn't any mother. Anywhere. And in the second place, the word shy wasn't in Elizabeth's dictionary. She was blonde and brazen and beautiful. If you'd ever met her you'd never forget the day."

Pritchard's watery blue eyes took on a reminiscent and somewhat covetous expression. "I've never forgotten the day I met Elizabeth Neindorf," he said.

Then I got it. I knew why Pritchard had remembered Neindorf. "Are you married?" I asked him.

The glint left his eyes and they returned to their routine blankness. He nodded. "Yes," he said, "twenty years. And if my wife were missing, like yours, I don't think I'd start looking for her."

This surprised me. I didn't think the guy had that much guts. Clerks that sit on high stools, year after year, adding columns up and down and backward and forward and right and wrong, never seem to have many guts. But they must have a hell of a lot more than most people. Than me, for instance. Because they're able to sit on that stool, year in, year out, sit in that cluttered cottage with the high mortgage, listen to that same female voice rant and rave and cry and moan and wave its troubles about, to sleep in that same cold bed and dream those dreams of freedom. Yeah, they must have more guts than anyone realizes.

I patted the guy on the back in what I hoped was an understanding gesture. "No, Pritchard," I said, "I don't think your Elizabeth is the one I'm looking for. But I'll take her name and address anyway. If I'm ever in Chicago I'll look her up. Tell her you said hello."

This time his eyes sparked with a different emotion and I knew he was going to spill his dreams all over the front of me. I didn't have the time or the patience to listen to him, but what could I do? The guy seldom had anyone to talk to, anyone he wasn't afraid to confide in. I was a stranger. I would probably never be back by there again. I'd been through a lot. I'd been hurt and unhappy. I would understand.

He told me he got off at five-thirty. Would I wait for him and we could have a drink and some dinner?

"O.K." I said. "My mother was Irish. I've never been known to refuse a party."

We went to a Chinese joint downtown, across from the Plaza, and there Mr. Horace Pritchard told me his life, his one brief interlude that was his whole life. He told me about his affair with Elizabeth Neindorf.

"We met a few months after she came to the plant," he said. "I was thirty-two. She was around twenty-seven or -eight. I wasn't bald then. Not even a little bit. My hair was thick and wavy." He ran his hand over what was left of his thick and wavy hair. The last ten years had been pretty rough on Horace. "The minute I passed her desk and looked into her eyes we both knew."

He stopped and stared lovingly into his chop suey. Then his eyes took in the whole joint, from the colored paper lanterns hanging down from the ceiling to the bottle of soy sauce dripping onto the spotted tablecloth. This Chinese chop suey parlor had been their meeting place. Now it was his temple.

Their romance was the regular run-of-the-mill clandestine affair. They go on every minute. Every minute in every office, store, factory, or mill in the country. In the world. Elizabeth Neindorfs abound like rats in the back of a Greasy Spoon restaurant. Washed-out blondes with skinny legs and flat chests. Nice girls. Not too bright. Not too pretty. Not too dull. Not too homely. Average. Average girls with average educations from average homes, leading average lives.

He told me the more lurid details of their great love, and in my mind I added the obvious. Elizabeth Neindorf had never got married because she had an old mother to keep. By the time she was twenty-seven all the fellows she knew had bypassed her, were married, had homes and families. The younger ones coming up weren't interested in her and the old ones with money wanted the young ones with beauty. So, what's left? The Mr. Pritchards. The average married men with average incomes and average homes and average wives. The Pritchards who've come to the conclusion that romance is dead, but that doesn't keep them from looking in the graveyard. The Pritchards meet the Neindorfs and the consequence is usually a couple of broken hearts. Maybe a broken life or two. Only two things can result from the affair. It eventually has to break up to preserve the home and children. Or the home has to break up. If the Pritchards and Neindorfs marry, it just takes a few more years for Miss Neindorf to turn into Mrs. Pritchard and Mr. Pritchard to fall back into his old routine. It's the less monotonous to have the affair break up. That way the memory is always alive. That way the memory still smells of sachet. The love letters are still legible, bright with a purple bow.

I promised Horace that if I ever got to Chicago I'd look up Elizabeth Neindorf.

I don't think he had the slightest hope that I would. But there he was dead wrong. I had every intention in the world of seeing Neindorf, and as soon as possible. Although I was positive Elizabeth Frazer would sooner lift her skirts to a tomcat than Horace Pritchard, it was my last lead and I was going to run it down. There was no place else I could look, so I figured I might as well go to Chicago.

I didn't want to stop and figure out how far wrong I was, that is wrong from outward appearances. Frazer didn't have any mother. She said her mother died a long time ago, if you could believe anything she said. And if Frazer, for some one of her ulterior motives, had let a namby-pamby like Horace Pritchard make love to her, she wouldn't leave him and go to Austin, Illinois, to live quietly in a middle-class suburb of Chicago. Elizabeth was after pay dirt, and so far she'd done everything, murdered and arranged a murder, to further her gory career. She wasn't due yet to end up in an ancient yellow frame house, working and caring for an incapacitated mother. Mother's Day, to Elizabeth Frazer, was better known as Sunday, a day most people didn't work.

I stayed at the gas station in Laguna for a couple more weeks. I had to wait for permission to leave the state. I got in touch with Masters. He arranged it for me. I was to report to the parole board in Chicago the minute I landed there. Masters and I had a good conversation over the phone. It was swell hearing his voice again. No matter what your problem is, hearing a calm voice with strength in it telling you everything's going to be all right seems to make everything all right. Even evil seems all right.

I didn't tell Masters what I was going to Chicago for. All I wanted him to know was that I'd been working. I told him I hoped someday to surprise him, pay him a visit, that is if I ever achieved that worthwhile something he thought I could achieve. He laughed and said, "That's all right, Walter. I don't expect you to conquer the world in a few months, in a few years. Just keep going, straight, like you have been. And when you see trouble coming, walk the other way. That'll make me happy, Walter."

Walk the other way? Not toward it, Masters? Not over it or through it or with it? You have to get close to trouble to destroy it. To kick it out. For good. At least I thought so. But I thought a lot of things were right that were subsequently proven wrong. Wisdom doesn't always come with age. My aunt was old and she died an idiot.

When I left Laguna, Jim had a kid come in to take my place washing cars. He told me if I ever came back I could have my job again. Jim liked me, the part he could understand. The part he couldn't understand is what took me to Chicago.

With all the odds against me! A tinhorn gambler will do that. You and I do it every day. We know we can't win. We know we only have a few more dollars. We know there are a thousand chances to one of that lucky three not turning up, of that point not being made, of that marble not getting into the right slot. But invariably we'll play our last dime. When we know we haven't a chance of winning we'll still stay until the game's over, with the score sixty-three to nothing in favor of the other side, hoping against a dead hope that our team just might come through.

And we never win anything either. Guys like Walker win. Do they gamble, I wonder? Or do they play it straight? Somehow they hit the sure things. I began to wonder if Walker had anything to do with this gamble of mine. I mean, did he fit in someplace that I'd overlooked?

Maybe I was just getting suspicious. Maybe I was forgetting to be grateful.

Chapter 14

Elizabeth Neindorf's house was on a quiet, elm-lined street in Austin, Illinois, a small town a few miles from the Chicago Loop. The lady next door told me they'd been living there for ten years, and old Mrs. Neindorf hadn't been to Chicago in that long.

The house was a musty faded yellow frame that looked smaller than it was. I stopped in front of the unpainted picket fence and debated whether to go in the front way like a visitor, or take the back door like the bum I resembled. My only suit of clothes was dirty and unkempt, my shirt was ragged, and my hat was battered into a misshapen hunk of felt that looked more like a wad of dirty dough pulled down over my head. When I'd started from Los Angeles I was clean, at least. But the trip took me longer than I expected. People don't give you rides so readily now.

I went around to the back door and knocked. I could hear the old lady clumping down the stairs. She opened the door a small crack and her withered face stuck out at me.

I tipped my bashed-in Homburg. "Is Elizabeth at home?"

She squinted at me and shoved the door almost shut. Only one eye was distinguishable through the crack.

"No, she ain't," she said, "she ain't to home. What do you want her fer?"

I hoped she could see my smile. "I'm a friend of hers," I said. "Worked with her in Los Angeles. Horace Pritchard wanted me to look her up."

The door slammed in my face and I could hear the lock being turned. The old lady obviously didn't like Pritchard.

Well, there was nothing I could do to make her like him. I walked down the driveway to the front of the house. I could feel the old lady watching me. I could feel that evil eye upon me. I glanced toward the second-story window and I saw the closed blind move ever so slightly.

I stood out in front of the house. A clock somewhere near me chimed four o'clock. If Mrs. Neindorf's daughter, Elizabeth, worked, she wouldn't be home until after six. What the hell could I do till then? And the second question was why? I was sure I was barking up the wrong Elizabeth this time. This was the only time I was positive that I was wrong. The appearances were all against it. This town, this house, this strange old woman peering suspiciously out of the second-story window, Horace Pritchard and the job, the steadiness of working, the stability. None of this belonged to Elizabeth Frazer. But I stayed on. I had hope with the others and no hope with this, but I stayed on. At least I could give her Horace's love.

I started to walk down the street to the corner drugstore, and as I passed the house next door I heard a woman's voice, "Mister—mister, wait a minute, will you?"

I stopped quickly and turned in the direction of the house. A dame was leaning out the window waving to me. She had on an old-fashioned dust cap and a gingham house dress and was a woman about forty-five years old.

I opened the gate to her house, walked into the yard, and up onto the porch before the front door popped open and her dust cap appeared. She had a pleasant face underneath the cap. As a matter of fact, it was a trusting face, otherwise she wouldn't have asked me to sit down on her porch and wait for Elizabeth.

"I seen you at the Neindorfs'," she said. "I was out in the back. I didn't mean to listen, but I heard what you said and saw Old Lady Neindorf slam the door in your face. She can't see so well and she is kinda peculiar to boot, so I thought I oughter call you so's you'd know about her and maybe you'd like to wait for Elizabeth here? She don't get home till about six-thirty and I'm sure she'd like to talk to you. I'm very sure since you said you was a friend of Horace's, if you know what I mean."

She said it all in one breath, and after she finished I took a deep one too as though it had been I who'd done the talking.

"Do you know Horace?" I said.

She smiled. "Elizabeth and I are good friends," she said.

I nodded. "It's cool here on the porch." I took off my hat and wiped my forehead with the back of my sleeve. It was November but Chicago was still sweltering. Pretty soon the wind would start to blow across the lake and the cold weather would be upon the city with the snows and ice and sleet and slush and it wouldn't leave again before the following April. I was beginning to miss California.

The good neighbor's name was Davis and she asked me if I wouldn't like a spot of lemonade. I hadn't drunk lemonade since I was a little kid. I thanked her kindly and drank two glasses of it. She brought the Austin paper and I read this until I dozed off. Mrs. Davis went back to her ironing and about six o'clock she awakened me and asked me if I wouldn't like to go around on her back porch and wash up a bit.

I washed my face and hands and combed my hair, and by that time she informed me that Elizabeth Neindorf was coming down the street.

I wanted to act like I knew her. I hurried around the front and stared toward the corner. I saw Mrs. Davis watching me. The normal thing would have been to run down the street toward Elizabeth Neindorf. That's what Mrs. Davis expected me to do. But I knew that would be worse than just waiting for her. I better approach her calmly at first.

I couldn't see her face from where I was, but she was just about the height of my Elizabeth. She was wearing a suit, a hat, a shoulder bag was thrown over her shoulder, and she was carrying a big sack of groceries. I couldn't imagine Elizabeth Frazer lugging groceries home after she'd put in a hard day's work in an office. Not at this late stage in her life, anyway. Elizabeth Frazer surely wouldn't cook a meal for an ailing and very peculiar mother. An ailing "daddy" maybe, a poor rich son-of-a bitch that she was praying would die soon and leave her some dough. Yeah, for that kind of guy she'd cook dinner all right. She'd cook an eight-course dinner three times a day every day in the week if she thought he'd get indigestion and die from it.

Elizabeth Neindorf was taking a hell of a long time getting to me. I was showing nerves. The palms of my hands were wet. What the hell? That's silly, I thought, this tall drink of water coming toward me could never be my Elizabeth. Or could she?

But again I was right! Miss Neindorf was all of three inches taller than Elizabeth Frazer. She had yellow, gray, light brown, half-red hair worn in a bucket bob. She was nearsighted and her rimless glasses were octagon-shaped. They didn't make her look any different than anyone else looks with glasses.

Her skin was nondescript and as indescribably muddy as her hair. There were red blotches around her nose and chin where she'd been picking at the blackheads.

She was flat-chested and skinny-assed, and if so much of her hadn't been turned under for feet she'd have been taller than she was. She had on a tweed suit that hung on her like grandfather's suit on the family scarecrow. Her white collar was mussed and wilted and I could see that she was mad at herself for wearing a heavy outfit on such a hot day.

I waited till she got fairly close to me, then I stepped out to greet her. She strained her eyes at me. I didn't want her to toss the groceries in my face for being fresh, so I smiled briefly and began my story. All I needed to do was mention Horace's name. Her plain face lighted up like a floodlight at a Hollywood premiere. I took the groceries from her and on the way to the house I explained about her mother not letting me in.

She laughed lightly. "I'll fix that up," she said. "Mamma probably thought you were Horace. She never liked him, you see."

I nodded. "I know. I found that out."

If Horace had arrived in the flesh she couldn't have been any happier. I waited outside until she explained to her mother that I was a friend of Horace's and not Horace, then she invited me in to dinner.

It seemed like an awful letdown to be invited to dinner at the Neindorfs', but there was not much else I could do, no place I could go at the moment. I had to have a little time in which to think the rest of this thing out. After this disappointment, even though I expected it, I was kind of numb, lost all feeling for the time being. That's when folks like the Neindorfs are useful. You don't have to think, to be bright or clever or sharp or intellectual, with the Neindorfs. They take you for just what you are at the moment.

During dinner the old lady didn't speak to me, but Elizabeth chatted as gaily as a monkey at four-o'clock tea. After dinner I helped her with the dishes and then we sat out on the porch and had a cigarette. It was peaceful and quiet on the porch, sitting there looking out onto that old street that was so indicative of this great solid, stolid Middle West, that I wished I didn't have anything else to do ever again. I wished I could just sit there night after night in the cool of twilight and remember only the pleasant things of the past, forget the imminent present, and refuse to dwell on the dubious future.

We sat on the porch until after twelve. Elizabeth got chilly and went in to get a wrap. When she came back she brought some hot coffee and cheese sandwiches.

She talked about Horace. Incessantly. Told me the same things Horace had told me, but I tried to be a good listener. I liked this Elizabeth. She was homely, frustrated, full of small talk, but there was an honesty and stability about her. She was nervous, unhappy, and terribly lonely, but she had an innate kindness, a great patience. Anyone who year after year keeps pleasantly waiting for something big to happen in his life has to have great patience.

They had an extra room and Elizabeth invited me to stay. I could have stayed forever if I'd wanted to. Elizabeth liked me too. I wasn't a young Adonis, maybe, but I still had my good points. I was tall and healthy and had sympathy for anyone who'd been in love as deeply as she had been. I had deep-set brown eyes and wavy gray hair and I had a quiet tolerance, a true sophistication that would attract her. I could have lived in that home forever. I could have married Elizabeth Neindorf if I'd been able to, and if I never wanted to work again it would have been all right with her. There was a peasant quality about her, too. She would have worked for the man she loved.

But I couldn't stay. Even though it would have been an easy life, except for the old lady, I didn't love Elizabeth Neindorf. And someday I would've walked out of her house and left her in a much worse state than Horace left her. I couldn't do that to another human being. To Elizabeth Frazer, maybe. But not to Elizabeth Neindorf.

As it was, I hung around for a couple of weeks. I was pretty tired and it provided a good rest. Elizabeth wanted to find me a job, but I put the nix on that. I told her I'd stay around, fix up the yard, do some odd carpenter jobs that were needed, fix the fence, the back steps, and do some plastering inside. That would pay for my room and board. But after I was through I'd have to move on. I had to move on. Where it didn't matter, but I had to go someplace, look for that something, that someone that kept getting more and more illusive. Elizabeth thought I was searching for an ex-wife and that I felt about her like she did about Horace. For that reason she understood my restlessness. I'm sure if she hadn't had the old lady she'd have packed a knapsack and gone with me.

The day I left she gave me a secondhand suit of clothes she bought in Chicago for me, packed a lunch, and handed me a couple of bucks. I didn't want to take it but she began to cry and the tears made her greasy face look so much worse that I grabbed the dough to keep her from bawling. I told her as soon as I landed someplace I'd get a job and send the dough back with interest.

"You don't have to ever return that money, Walter," she sniffed. "And if you ever need any more you just write to me. You got a home here too, Walter. You got a good home to come back to."

"Thanks, Elizabeth," I said, "I really appreciate it."

Even Old Lady Neindorf got friendly that last day, shook my hand, and thanked me for plastering the cracks in her drafty bedroom. I guess she was happy to see me go. She wouldn't have to share her daughter any longer. She was a possessive old hag and Elizabeth would have been better off if she'd croaked. That wasn't a very nice thought, but I'd have liked to see Elizabeth happy. It took so little to do the job.

When she walked out to the gate with me she reached for my hand and the tears began to come again. I knew my exit would have to be quick or I'd be flooded out. I leaned over and kissed her on the cheek. "Oh, Walter," she sobbed.

I turned and started quickly down the street. As I passed Mrs. Davis's house next door I saw her in the window waving to me. When I got to the corner the excitement in the lives of the occupants of 202 and 204 Elm Street in Austin, Illinois, had left as quickly as it had come.

I stopped at the corner and looked back. Elizabeth was still standing at the gate, her hand to her cheek, the cheek that I'd kissed, and I was glad that I couldn't see the tears.

I felt pretty good in my secondhand suit and clean shirt she'd washed and ironed for me, and as I rode down to the Loop there was a certain freedom about the way I felt. But when I got downtown and realized I didn't know where I was going, a sense of depression hit me and I wanted to die.

I went to the Greyhound Bus Station, got a travel folder, and sat down to study it. Las Vegas, Reno, Santa Fe, the last strongholds of the wild West. I'd been west and hadn't been too happy. Detroit, Ann Arbor, Charlevoix, Lake Michigan. The great woods of northern Michigan. I was in the woods already. St. Louis, Kansas City, Arkansas, the plains of the fertile and unfertile Middle West. Elizabeth Frazer wouldn't like those open spaces. The vastness of the Kansas flatlands would frighten her. When we'd crossed the desert on our famous trip to California she'd shuddered at the loneliness of space she couldn't see across. She had to see things close to her, to be able to reach out and touch them, hold them, destroy them.

The South. New Orleans. Now, that might be a place where she'd go. The Vieux Carré. Behind Spanish grillwork, through a brick patio, back in an eaved studio room. Dark in the room. Voices hushed, almost indistinguishable. Faces indistinguishable. Color? Black. White. Yellow. The blue smoke of sensuousness enveloping the room. No! Not Elizabeth. No French Quarters or Left Banks or Greenwich Villages. Not for Elizabeth. Greenwich Village! New York! Sure. New York! That would be her beat. Park Avenue. Beekman Place. The Drive. Connecticut, maybe. I threw the travel folder on the floor of the bus station.

If you haven't got any brains, a hunch is a good substitute.

I went to the phone and called the parole board in Chicago. I talked to the guy who knew my case, asked him about the chances of seeing him as soon as possible. He gave me an appointment that day.

When I went to see him I explained my problem. "I can't get any decent work here in Chicago," I said, "and I want to go to New York. Warden Masters has given me the name of a man in New York who'll probably give me a job. He said my records could be transferred there, if I plan on staying permanently."

The parole officer, a man by the name of Ed Hammond, was studying my files. He acted as though he hadn't heard me, but he finally looked up and said, "I don't know. This'll probably take a few days."

I began to get nervous. I didn't want to go back to Elizabeth Neindorf's and I didn't have enough money to go to a hotel for any length of time. "I haven't got much money," I said, "not enough to hang around here that long. How about a phone call or wire? If you get in touch with Masters—"

Hammond squinted at me to get a better look. His eyes were small anyway, and when he squinted they seemed to disappear right into his head. It was like looking into a face without any eyes. I turned away to hide my nervousness. He tapped his pencil on the desk, glanced over my file, then looked up at me again. His thoughts must have tied up, because the next time I looked at him his eyes were where they should be.

"What kind of job do you plan on gettin' in New York?" he said. "Since you been out you've had two different kinds of work, in a garage in Frisco and a mechanic's job in Laguna, California. You haven't done a damned thing since you been here. Just what is your profession, Johnson? Just what do you want to settle down to?"

I detected a distinct note of sarcasm. "Gardening," I said. "I can work for this man in New York, this friend of Masters'."

"You learned that the last ten years, huh?"

I nodded. "I like it," I said.

"Well, I'll tell you, Johnson, I can teletype. I'll contact the parole board in San Francisco."

"But Masters," I repeated. "He'll arrange it."

"Procedure. I've got to get in touch with them first. If you really plan on staying in New York permanently and have a job to go to, I don't see why your records can't be switched there. But get located someplace. It seems to me you've had it pretty fair all along the line."

"Masters," I echoed.

Hammond finally changed his expression. He grinned at me. The grin didn't exactly resemble a ray of sunshine lighting my dark day, but it was a help. "You're a great publicity agent for prisons," he said, "and probably the first guy I ever met who fell in love with a warden."

I laughed. "He's a great guy," I said.

"So I've heard. O.K., Johnson, come back about four o'clock this afternoon. We'll see then what fate has in store for you."

I thanked him and left and thought about fate for a while. Fate, that little word that can excuse a lifetime of lousy mistakes.

I went to a drugstore, bought a cup of coffee and a magazine, and I tried to read. But it didn't do any good. I was as nervous as the day Masters told me there might be a hope for a parole. What the hell would I do if I had to go back to L.A.? Wait for fate?

I stopped trying to figure it out and decided a walk would do me good. I walked around Chicago until my feet were sore. I passed a couple of cheap bars and contemplated whether I should go in for two or three quick ones. Then I remembered parole officers don't like you to get in the habit of drinking in the daytime, or any time, for that matter, so I went back to the same drugstore and had a coke and before insanity set in. I looked at the clock and saw that it was ten minutes to four.

When I went into see Hammond he was grinning again. I said, "Either fate was good to me or you take things perversely."

"O.K. It's O.K. As soon as you get to New York you report there. Here." He handed me a letter. "That's your written permission, and this," he handed me a slip of paper, "is the address and phone number in New York City. You see this man Steve Elliot. His extension number's there. An officer will be assigned to your case, and if you stay your transfer will be arranged."

I took the letter and paper and put them in my wallet. "That," I said, "is the shortest red tape in the history of the United States government. Thanks a lot, Mr. Hammond."

Hammond nodded, but as I turned to leave he threw me a parting remark. "With your kind of influential friends," he said, "you should go far." The remark sounded a bit facetious.

I smiled back at him. "Just as far as New York," I said. I don't think he got it and I didn't stop to find out.

When I left Chicago and started bumming to New York I figured it'd take me no time at all. I was dressed fairly well, my mind was exceptionally clear, and I had a few bucks and some cigs in my pocket. But I figured wrong. Way wrong. The first night on the road I took sick. A bo found me lying at the side of the road, took me to an old barn, and sat up with me most of the night. I had the flu, I guess. All I know is I was damned sick.

The next morning this bo left an old coat that he'd thrown over me and a couple of aspirin he laid beside me. I was asleep when he left. When I woke up I discovered the switch. In exchange for his coat and aspirin he'd taken most of my dough and every damned one of my cigarettes. At that, he probably saved my life.

I lay in that barn all the rest of the day praying that no one would find me. When you get sick, if you're not too sick, you have a greater desire to live. You lie awake thinking up excuses as to why you should live a little longer.

By night I felt better. I managed to get up on my feet and drag myself to the highway. A truck driver picked me up. He saw that I was pretty sick, got me some soup and coffee, and let me sleep in the back of his truck. The next morning when he let me out I felt well enough to continue. I'd made my excuses to God as to why I should live a little longer.

Chapter 15

I hit New York in the middle of its first snowstorm. God! New York in the winter, white with snow and the frost from some poor bum's belly. New York with its lights blazing, but so far out of reach that the warmth from them can't penetrate when you're way down in that gutter on Broadway. New York with its vermin and ermine all mixed up in a crazy quilt that your grandma would never dream of patching. New York with its first nights and old nights and nights misspent, ending up in a rock-pitted bed with the inky waters of the East River washing your hairy face of all its impurities, and adding a final sin to your soul.

I've known New York in all of its moods, with all of its faces. And even when it can't find a face to meet the day. When it hides under the gray covers of an army cot in a bedbug-infested hotel room, with a floor covered by dirt, cigarette stubs, two psychopathic mice, and a buffalo nickel.

I've known it from the rosy-hued angle when the lights spell out champagne, satin sheets, penthouses, and stolen rides on the Weehawken ferryboat.

I've known it on a crisp November morning when Fifth Avenue never seems long enough although it runs alongside the most beautiful park in the world with a lake in the middle and a white swan on it that you swear will have to turn into a princess any moment.

And I've known it on Second Avenue and Third and Tenth and Ninth when the rabble of voices speaking languages you'll never understand makes the merchant-laden streets of Arabia seem as quiet as the rifled tomb of an Egyptian mummy.

There are a million worlds, a million countries, in New York, like there are a million faces and people and buildings and dogs and cats and merchandise and traffic and bars. Let's not forget the bars.

But the last day I landed there I saw it like I'd never seen it before. I saw it through a magic lantern with all of the magic gone and the lantern blown out and turned inside out. I saw it like a dead man looking through eyelids drawn tightly together by a thin layer of dirty wool. I just didn't see it or feel it, and it didn't see me.

I was still sick and the people jostled my poor fever-ridden bones this way and that. The horns honked at me like a flock of geese blocking a toad's way. I couldn't get away from it and I couldn't get through it or by it or even with it.

I was barren and sick of an old longing and of plain downright pain and hunger. The only fire that was left within me was fed by a feeble spark of revenge. Even that had almost died.

When I landed at Forty-second and Broadway I had the much-written-about dime in my pocket, and I found that down an iron grating as I walked along Forty-second Street. A dime in my pants pocket and two pieces of paper in my coat pocket. On one piece of paper, dirty and torn from a couple of years' travel, was a man's name, Arthur August Henaston, Woodmere, Long Island, the man Warden Masters had said might want a gardener. I could picture his garden now, covered with slush and dirty snow. On the other piece of paper was the address Hammond had given me. I would contact the state. Later on.

When I got to Broadway I decided to flip the coin. Heads, I'd call Mr. Henaston right away and send him belated regards from the Warden. Tails, I'd wait till the next week, or the next week, or the next. Or maybe I'd never call him. Maybe I'd tear the piece of paper into bits too small to be put together again. To be discouraged is one thing. But to be sick besides or because of it is no condition to be in, especially when you're broke. I flipped. Heads! I'd call Henaston and ask him for a job. I'd have to appeal to someone for help before they called for me and laid me away in a roseless grave. Don't let anyone kid you, the "little foxes" are a heavy load. Even if you string them together they wouldn't make a cape large enough to hide the hump of hate on your back.

I walked up Broadway toward Forty-fifth. I turned down Forty-fifth to Eighth Avenue. I saw a restaurant in the middle of the block and headed for it. I went into the restaurant to use the telephone, and like a man who had courage I walked up to the bartender. "Where's the phone, fella?" I asked the marble-eyed joe.

He leaned out over the bar to point toward the rear, and as he did a drunk standing next to me swung around to take a look at me and his hand with the glass of beer in it hit the bartender's arm and the beer did a triple wing and landed down the front of me. I looked like a stray dog right out of the reservoir. Maybe it was a good thing the drunk spilled the beer on me. It made me look more disheveled than I was, but rightfully so. And maybe that certain fate I'd been hearing about wasn't haunting my footsteps either. The second time I'd been inside a bar since my parole, and the only time I should have been in one. The long arm of coincidence was reaching out for me again.

The drunk with the spilled beer turned out to be a nice drunk, the kind you don't mind, the kind you like a little, especially after he offers to buy you the beer he spilled on you.

He giggled and pounded the bar. "A beer for the gentleman with the wet hops on his vest."

The bartender gave the guy a sour grin, handed me a bar rag to mop up the "wet hops," then poured me out a glass of two-bit foam. I never saw anything look better. It looked better than clean sheets after forty days and forty nights crossing the Red Sea.

I drank two or three beers and forgot all about the phone call, forgot about wardens with souls and gardens with weeds, even forgot the fact that it was almost zero and I had no overcoat or any place to hang it. I'd found a warm spot and a friend, the kind I could understand. That made two warm spots.

With every drink the drunk took I had to take one. We finally ended up at a table with two slugs of whisky and our voices raised in raucous song.

My first night in New York wasn't going so bad after all. By eight o'clock I had everything anyone else had. I had a warm roof over my head, a glow in my stomach, and a hot friendly breath in my face.

Even though it didn't make any sense, I had a conversation to pursue with a pal and a promise of a bed with the same pal. He was carrying a torch for an octoroon in Harlem and I was a good listener. I kept lighting the torch for him, so that by nine-thirty that night we were good enough buddies that he'd allowed me to order black coffee for him and a dinner for me.

What else is there in life? *What* else? A woman that you either hate or love. He had one that he loved and I had one that I'd forgotten to hate for a moment. And it's during those moments that prayers are answered. They're never answered when you're waiting for them to be answered. You can't wait around for prayers and things to be answered. You have to stop waiting, and then the thing you're waiting for either comes to you or it goes away.

It would have been much better, maybe, if mine had gone away.

The restaurant we were in was near the show district. Right around the corner there were two or three theaters, and up the street several blocks there were two or three more. My drunken pal, whose name was Brigadier Jones, informed me that the best show he'd ever seen outside of Minsky's was right around the corner and that shows were good things to make one forget sorrow.

I looked at him through my half-shut eyes. "I thought I was making you forget," I said.

He squinted at me and the slits in his face looked as though they were about to cry, then he fumbled in his pocket and instead of a handkerchief he brought out two tickets to the show. He was going to take his girl to see it that night, and now he didn't have any girl.

I reached across the table for the tickets. Two $4.40 tickets to a play called *You Asked for It*.

I laughed and threw the tickets on the table. "You asked for it," I said, "and it's too late. Too late for you and too late for me and an hour and a half too late for the show."

"Oh," Brigadier said. "Oh, thass too bad. Too late, huh? Well, les' get the check and go home then. You stay with me on account of I'm lonely and—"

"I haven't any other place to stay," I finished it for him, and motioned to the waiter.

Brigadier handed me his wallet and told me to take out enough for the bill. When I saw all of the money in the thing, for a moment I was almost tempted to take a few bucks for the morrow. Then I remembered Arthur Henaston and my job. Maybe. And I also remembered that taking things wasn't very nice and got you in real bad.

As I started to count out the money to pay the bill, the restaurant, which had been pretty quiet, with the exception of Brig and me, got very noisy. Suddenly a lot of chattering females and guffawing men marched up to the bar like a bunch of fascists taking over a Munich beer hall. Brig had put his exhausted head in his arms and laid it to rest on top of the table, but when he heard the sound of happy voices he raised his head a few inches, ogled the bar, mumbled, "Intermission," then went right back to his table-bed.

I handed the dirty-aproned waiter a bill and was just about to put Brig's wallet back in his pocket when I heard it!

You see, I'd got up and walked around the table so I wouldn't upset Brig's rest until the waiter came with his change, but the sound of what I heard froze me in my tracks, my walleted hand in mid-air. It was a laugh, the goddamnedest most horrible laugh I ever heard. And I'd heard it a lot of times, too. I'd heard it when I was awake. And when I was asleep it had haunted me. I'd heard it in the middle of the desert and on the top of a mountain. I'd heard it in Texas, Arizona, Nevada, California. And once I thought I heard it in a dive in San Francisco. But this time I *did* hear it in a restaurant on Eighth Avenue off Forty-fifth Street in New York City of a cold winter's night.

When I got over my shock I turned around and faced the bar. There sitting on the bar stools were six or seven diamond-studded people. They were all in evening clothes and loaded with rocks and not the kind you find at a marble quarry. There were three men and four women. And none of them too young. None of them under forty.

At the far end of the bar was the one that I was pretty sure had done the laughing, because there was still a smile on her face, but it didn't blot out the evil in her eyes. Maybe no one else would have noticed it, but I did. Her eyes were blue and there was no twinkle in the blue. They were cold eyes. I couldn't see their exact emotion, but I knew it was calculating.

As soon as I could take my stare away from her eyes I looked at the rest of her. She was what you might call a well-dressed matron. She had on a black lace evening dress. At any rate it was long and covered her legs, and her black gloves covered her arms. And there were two diamond service stripes on the outside of her gloves. And thrown over her shoulders was a silver-fox cape, silver, the color of her hair. She was well dressed all right, well dressed and well massaged and well creamed, but none of it hid her forty furious years, or her one hundred and sixty-five pounds, or her soulless face topped by that phony sheaf of silver. It was a good disguise for someone who didn't know her as well as I did, and someone who wasn't looking for her as hard as I was, and maybe if she hadn't laughed I wouldn't have known her. But there's nothing hidden that won't someday be revealed. At least that's what a right guy said once. A guy who lived too many thousand years ago to be of much influence now.

Well, I'd found it. At last! The night I stopped searching I walked right into Elizabeth Frazer Isaacs Blodgett with the names and none of them hers. And what did I do? I stood there like a half-baked moron and the only thing I could think of was How can I say anything to her when I don't know what she calls herself now? What fools we mortals be! Another guy said that, but he didn't live quite so long ago.

If I'd been a bright guy I would have picked up a chair and slung it at her or I would have run out looking for a cop. Or maybe that wouldn't have been so bright. Cops never believed me anyhow. Maybe what I did, just stand there, was the smartest thing I could have done, except before I could make my feet move or my mouth move, they'd swallowed their drinks and were getting ready to go back to the theater.

When I saw her being helped off of the bar stool, then's when I began my dazed walk toward her. But just as I put one foot out Brig woke up and yelled at me. "Hey," he said. "Come back here. Where you goin'? You got my wallet!"

I turned around for just a second, just one little second, just long enough to toss the wallet to him and say, "I'll see you later. The waiter's bringing your change." And when I turned my head back toward the door again they were gone.

As I started to run out after them the son-of-a-bitch waiter got in my way with the change. "Take it to the drunk at the table," I bellowed, and beat it out the door.

I ran to Forty-fifth Street, pushing the crowds away from my face so

I could see her. But I must have been on the wrong street or in the wrong town or the wrong world because she wasn't around anyplace. How the hell, I said to myself, could they've got away that quick?

I went on up the street and stopped in front of the theater Brig had the tickets to. The intermission crowd was just going in. I shoved my way through them and round them and passed them, but I might as well have gone to the aquarium to look for a herd of buffaloes.

I couldn't go in the theater unless I went back and got Brig's tickets, and if I went back and got them he'd insist on going along, and then we'd both get thrown out.

Elizabeth, if it was Elizabeth (after the first shock passed I was beginning to doubt my own eyes), didn't see me and I didn't want her to ... yet.

So I stood out in front until the show was over, and by the time the crowd came charging out I was so cold and stiff I probably wouldn't have recognized myself if I'd run into a full-length mirror.

The object of my frantic search was within my grasp and I couldn't reach out.

Chapter 16

What is there in human nature that makes anticipation, whether it's anticipation of a love or revenge, so much sweeter than the realization, even so much calmer, almost deadlike? Don't answer that. It wouldn't be right for anyone but you. I'd be sure as hell to believe something different.

That night I slept in a charity flophouse in the Bowery. Yes, I slept. For the first time since I left my four walls I slept the innocent sleep of a bright new baby or a well-heeled murderess.

I guess it was because the search was over and the revenge hadn't yet begun.

The next day I began to play the game differently. Instead of combing the highways and byways and getting nowhere except where I started from, I looked in the telephone book and found Arthur Henaston's business phone number. He had an office on Lexington Avenue and a factory in Brooklyn. The Henaston Washing Machine Company. His product, as I discovered later, was called the Henaston Handy Washer and there were three or four factories scattered about the country. It was a very successful concern. Henaston was the president and its biggest stockholder.

I tried for two hours to borrow a nickel from one of the bums around me, but could only scare up two cents and a St. Theresa medal, so I decided to put an extra hunk of newspaper in my shoes and hike to Lexington.

If Henaston would hire me for a while I could get on my own two feet instead of a couple of Hearst newspapers, buy some clothes, put a few gold coins in my pocket, and start to haunt the places where Elizabeth might go, like theaters, swanky bars, East Side restaurants, Fifth Avenue shops, Park Avenue walks. I figured it might take years and every cent I could earn but Dr. Frankenstein never gave up. He had a monster to make and I had one to tear to pieces.

I walked from the Bowery to Henaston's office and I smiled most of the way. I couldn't get a certain picture out of my mind. I couldn't stop imagining how Elizabeth would look in a sweater now. Lines in your face can make you unhappy, but a fat ass in a split skirt can't very well sit down.

You know it sounds silly now to tell it, but I had a dream once, an ambition. I only had it for a little while and I think all in all it came to me about three times in my life.

I felt it first when I was eleven years old. One night I'd been particularly bad at dinner and my father made me go upstairs, but I didn't go clear up the stairs. I sat in the hall where we had the pictures painted in oil, badly painted and unnatural. I've mentioned them before. One of the pictures had a boat in it, a boat sailing on a sea too blue to be real. And I looked at the picture so long that I was on the boat sailing over that glassy blue sea. I was on the deck and it was so peaceful and right. And from the deck I could see the shore line and little white fishermen's shacks dotting the shore. And way over near the foot of a small slope was my house. I knew it was mine because it was the only one that had smoke pouring out of the chimney. I thought that that was the sign of well-being, because the real house I lived in didn't have a fireplace or a furnace. It had a coal stove that only heated the room it was in.

Then I dreamed a little bit longer and I went inside my house with the fireplace and there were painters' easels all round. It was a beautiful studio and I was a painter. I painted the soul of things. And people came to see my paintings and shuddered a little because I painted the soul of things.... Would that dream be sort of an undefined ambition? Or would it be an omen?

Then again I had a similar experience. Before I quit school in the eighth grade I had to read a story aloud to the class. It was a pretty powerful thing and it must have been good because my teacher said it won a prize. As I read I could feel the class with me. I could feel the teacher with me. And before I finished the story I was playing the game again. I was a great actor and these people around me were my audience. And as I talked their bodies swayed with the rhythm of my words, and their eyes filled with tears at the sound of my musical voice, and their spirits soared with the import of the potent meanings.

When I sat down again, at my desk, I almost forgot where I was for the moment.

And I had the feeling again when I walked into Arthur August Henaston's important office. I couldn't say anything for a few minutes. The secretary looked at me as though I were in the wrong place. She was just about ready to say, "Down the hall and to the left," but she didn't because she must have sensed there was something wrong.

My knees began to shake, sweat poured down my face, and I had to sit down. Maybe I was hungry. Maybe it was a hangover. But I don't think so. I think it was that thing again, that dream, that thwarted ambition. Big offices with big, well-upholstered furniture and long windows and an easy air of activity always fascinated me. And that day, when I walked into the richest office I'd ever been in, I knew suddenly why they'd always fascinated me. I wanted to be somebody. I wanted to do something important that would make people catch their breaths when my name was mentioned, or when they looked at one of my pictures, or heard one of my poems read, or when they just came into my office and sat down.

I wanted to be somebody! Well, I was somebody all right. An ex-convict, forty years old, with not one possession in the world ... except revenge. A bright career.

Mr. Henaston saw me immediately. The Warden's name was like magic. They must have been very good friends. Of course, when he took a look at my unshaven face and the slept-in clothes he did a take, but as soon as I started talking the air eased up a bit.

First he wanted to know how his friend the Warden was, and then he wanted to know how long it'd been since I'd had a good meal, and if I needed clothes. That was obvious. And if I'd be willing to go to work immediately, live in a room in the butler's quarters over the garage until he could get the caretaker's rooms refinished. Then of course he finally asked me what I'd been in for.

"Murder." I looked at him squarely in the eye. "Circumstantial evidence. Twenty years. Ten of which I served."

Peculiar guy, Henaston. He'd winced when he looked at my tough appearance, but when I said murder he didn't bat an eye. I thought for a moment he was going to say, "Good. Sign here." It was one of those looks, but instead he said, "Too bad. But we all make mistakes. Your salary will be one hundred a month, room and board. And I'd like to buy you your first suit of clothes and a shave." He smiled. "And you can get your dinner. Here." He shoved a hundred-dollar bill at me. "Your first month's salary and charge the clothes to me. I've an account at Saks. I'll call them."

I mumbled my grateful thanks and started to get up. "By the way," he leaned over the desk, "I didn't get your name. Johnson?"

"Walter Johnson," I answered quickly, "but I'd prefer to use another name, my mother's maiden name, Lukens. Johnson Lukens. I don't want a convict's name all my life."

Mr. Henaston leaned back. He was a big man. I hadn't seen him stand up yet, but I imagined he was tall, too. His hair was fairly thin on top but heavy at the sides. He wore rimless glasses and I couldn't see his eyes very well, but I figured they must be kind. He had on a dark blue double-breasted suit and his vest was piped in white. He looked like a drawing of a high-powered executive and that's what he was.

"I can understand that name business," he said. "People are so prone to censure. Lukens, eh? Dutch?"

"I guess so," I said. "Van Lukens a long time ago."

He began to write something on a pad of paper. "Johnson Lukens. All right, Mr. Lukens."

"And about the forms I have to fill out—you know, for the parole board. I have to have my employer's signature."

"Just send them here. My secretary will take care of them."

I thanked him and as I turned to go I said, "Oh, I forgot. How big is your garden? And is there anything special I should know about it? Any rare trees that I should read up on, or flowers or vines?"

Mr. Henaston smiled. His teeth were too white and too even to be his own, but they were an expensive job. That reminded me to get a few of mine fixed. It would cost me this time. The state supplied the dentist before.

"You don't have to do anything but water the lawn today. I'll take you through the gardens when I get home. Mrs. Henaston will be happy to get some intelligent help. You see, the last gardener we had left only a few days ago. This is our lucky day. I mean yours and mine."

"Thanks," I said. "I'll see you later."

When I left his office I had what they call mixed emotions. Coincidences piling up on top of coincidences. People too nice. Drunks and rich people. New York was being kind. Why? Why? I kept asking myself, because way down inside the farthest layer, I felt I didn't deserve it. I was still on the wrong track, but for some strange reason the train wasn't coming.

But when it did come the switches were O.K. No sidings. And I was on the main track ... all right.

Chapter 17

I once thought that you could probably learn a lot from the birds and the bees. And that people who'd been unhappy and mixed up in the outside world could enter the world of the little creatures and green things and learn how to live all over again. I guess I got that from a children's book, because working with and close to the earth didn't give me an awful lot of wisdom. Maybe I only worked with my hands.

When I first took a gander at Henaston's estate I wanted to sling my carpetbag over my shoulder and hop the first freight out. The place was enormous, thirty-four rooms, eight baths, three patios, a swimming pool, tennis courts, aviary, and stables. The grounds around the house spread over so much territory that if you decided to take a walk you practically had to take a hatchet along to mark the trees so you could find your way back.

My two rooms and bath in the gardener's cottage looked like a suite in the Waldorf, at least to the footsore character I was when I arrived.

The housekeeper told me not to let the size of the gardens throw me because I was just the resident gardener and would have two or three people to help me. In other words, for the first time in my life I was a boss.

I wanted to ask the housekeeper why the other guy left the job but I didn't have to ask her. "You only got one worry," she told me, "that's to make the missus like you. She don't like many people."

I nodded and continued to lap up the lunch she'd had the cook prepare for me. "I'll try," I said.

"She don't monkey around much, but when she takes it in her head to check up on you ... look out!"

"Any kids around?" I asked. "I noticed they got three horses and a pony."

"Nobody rides Bessie anymore. The kids are grown up. One's at boarding school. Alys, the young one. The other's at Yale. They're his kids."

"I see. And what about Mrs. Henaston? What's she like? I mean, what do you think about her, Mrs. Strapp?"

Mrs. Strapp looked at me over her bifocals. "I'm paid to keep the house going as right as possible. Nobody gives me any extra for my opinion." She glared at me, although it wasn't an unkind look, then she left me alone. That was the beginning of my first day in the Henaston household.

I spent the end of the day with Henaston while he showed me through the gardens. I didn't learn a lot from him, except what my duties would be, but it didn't matter much. I really wasn't too curious about any of the Henastons. I just wanted to work alone and live alone and plot alone. I had a mission, insured by the devil.

And then one day my mission was completed.

I'd been working for about four months and everything was going along fine. I'd seen Henaston two or three times and he seemed pleased with my work. The grounds didn't look any better than they had when I arrived and they didn't look any worse. There were a couple of Cécile Brunners that Henaston seemed quite fond of and they hadn't been doing very well, so I applied my little knowledge of roses, plus my green hand, and the bushes seemed to be perking up. He liked that.

During my third meeting with him I found out he liked boats, too. And we talked about sailing for a few minutes. He had a yacht that he managed to get away on whenever he managed to get away, and he said he'd take me on a trip someday. I felt that Mr. Henaston liked me, too. I didn't know why. I was sure it wasn't because I could trim Cécile Brunners and make them take on new life, or because I liked the sea. Somehow I felt it was because I'd been where I'd been. And it wasn't because he felt sorry I'd spent the best years of my life behind bars, but because he understood some of the things I'd been through. He was a peculiar guy. He was taciturn in a way, but not thoughtfully so. He was well mannered, but I don't know, it seemed sometimes the manners were thought out carefully a long time ago. And that maybe a long time ago he was a different kind of guy. In other words, the family crest was there but maybe it wasn't his. And yet I knew he was a pretty powerful figure in the business world. That didn't spell either, because I knew a Brooklyn thug once who had eleven top hats and a wife from the social register. But it didn't do anything to the inside of him. He was the same. A face-lifting lifts only the face.

I hadn't met Mrs. Henaston yet. I guess it wasn't her time to inspect the outside. But I'd heard several things about her from the cook and chauffeur. To the chauffeur she was beautiful; to the cook ugly. I don't know what the upstairs maid thought of her. The cook said she was smart and the chauffeur said she was "kind of a dumb dame." I didn't hear the housekeeper mention her mental powers. The chauffeur said she dressed like a million and the cook said she had terrible taste. The groom said she never came out to the stables any. She didn't like to get herself "dirtied up."

So my picture of Mrs. Henaston was pretty vague. But as I said, it didn't matter much just as long as she left me alone.

My day off was Wednesday. And on this particular Wednesday I'd gone into New York early in the morning to make my accustomed rounds looking for Elizabeth Frazer.

It was March and a pretty cold day. I didn't feel very well, so instead of staying the night like I usually did on Wednesday, I decided to go on back to Woodmere.

I think I was beginning to like my life, to like it so well that I wasn't quite so eager to pursue my revenge. The thrill of it was dying away.

When I got on that train for Long Island and knew that inside me that warmth of wanting to get home was beginning to take possession of me, I realized I'd changed a helluva lot; that I'd found another path in life, a patterned path that the small people take, the small people who make up the world of patterned paths and horny hearths. And I liked it. I was proud of me.

I smiled at the conductor. I smiled at the faces peering over their evening papers. I edged up closer to the tweed-covered commuter next to me. I could feel the warmth of his routined soul and I liked that warmth. He was going home like he did three hundred and sixty-five times a year. But the important thing was, he was going home. I felt one with him. I could ride with these people. I had a home, too, with smoke coming out of the chimney. I could talk to these people about trees and gardens and patterned paths. I could tell them about my rosebushes and the hydrangea and the hyacinths and the many different kinds of ivy. And the horses. I could tell them about the horses that belonged to me, at least for a little while. They belonged to me when I was with them. If you watch anything long enough it belongs to you. It belongs to you while you're watching it.

I could talk about kids, too. The cook had one and so did the chauffeur. I'd got to know them pretty well. They came to my cottage to visit me. And they were mine, too, while they were there.

Someday in this world no one will own anything. There'll be no personal possessions. We'll only own what's with us at the moment. And if things keep on going the way they have been, even the space around us will only be ours for the minute that we're allowed to stand on it. And time? If we have any, it won't be ours for long, either. Things are rushing by awful fast. Reach out your hand and grab onto something before it all goes away.

A murderer's mind works in different ways depending on the type of guy he is. One type of mind becomes one type of criminal and then commits one type of crime.

There's what they call the archfiend, whose art is cunning. He commits the horrible murders, almost in defiance of laws of every kind. He defies you to solve his bloody riddle. He's a "riddle me this." Maybe if he wasn't so busy committing crimes he'd be poring over a crossword puzzle or reading a detective story or listening to a radio quiz.

There are lots of armchair horror fiends that never leave their armchairs, which is a good thing for the world. Playing games is always a lot of fun to people, all kinds of people, most everybody. The murder game is no exception. As a matter of fact, to some people it's the most interesting riddle. Particularly to the best thinkers.

Then there's the stupid criminal who commits stupid crimes like small holdups, housebreaking, purse-snatching. When he kills he kills because of stupid fears, because he's afraid of being caught, or being hurt or being killed.

It wouldn't be hard for him to become the cold-blooded killer type, the gangster, that is if his ego gets bigger. And if his ego gets bigger his crime gets bigger, his fear becomes bravado, and then he kills anything that stands in his way.

The emotional murderer is the one that's hardest to detect, because he's liable to be your best friend, or your wife's sister, or your own brother, or the young widow that lives next door; the "I could kill that guy" type who someday gets an inflamed emotion and doesn't know what he's doing. Maybe his wife lies to him about another guy, or someone steals from him or cheats him in a poker game. If it's the other way around, maybe he lies to his wife. If he's a doctor, maybe he's got a nurse or secretary he's carrying on with, and when his wife finds it out she gets one of those inflamed emotions and bingo, they're all gone, wiped out with a bread knife or anything that happens to be handy. Many just ordinary fights between ordinary people end in murder. The animal instinct, or what they call the animal instinct, screams protect yourself ... kill him before he kills you, and so another murderer is born. The desire for sex, money—yes, and freedom—provide motives.

But where did I come in? Except too late.

I didn't feel I belonged in any of those categories. I wasn't an archfiend. I've always hated quiz games, violent sports like that.

I wasn't a bank robber running from the cops. I'd been in some petty rackets, but I never thought of running when I realized I was going to be caught.

My emotions had never urged me to a pitch of "seeing red." And God knows I'd spent ten years waiting for freedom, so I didn't need to look for it anymore.

So? I just wanted to add up the figures again, make them spell. The court convicted me of murder, so I was going to second their motion. I was going to add it up for them, double check, to prove that, after all, they were right. I was going to give that twenty-year sentence a reason and at the same time get rid of a human vulture.

And I couldn't have been more wrong had I decided to run naked through a busy city street hacking pedestrians' heads off with a dull meat cleaver.

The day I turned my head and saw her close to me again, for the first time in over twelve years, I didn't exactly think of murder. No ... just revenge ... all kinds of revenge, which started first with the little kinds.

When I came home that Wednesday I went out in the yard to do a few things I'd neglected, like dig away some weeds over by the stables, inspect the fruit trees (we'd had some pretty cold days), and see that the guy who tended the greenhouses had done everything I'd told him.

I didn't usually work on my day off, but it's when we break up that old routine that things happen.

I was on my knees digging out weeds by a cement path when I felt someone standing over me. I thought it was one of the grooms watching me, so I didn't pay much attention until I heard a voice. A voice that sounded like the last squeak of the trumpet on Judgment Day. I stopped what I was doing so quickly I almost dug the spade in my hand.

"Do you usually work on your day off?" the voice asked.

The voice! The voice I'd waited so long to hear, that I'd searched for for so long, had finally come to me. It just didn't seem right. I felt like a guy who'd cheated death too often.

I took two or three deep breaths, then stood up, straight, and stared at her, before I spoke. And when I did speak, the words I said were "No, Elizabeth, I don't. But as usual Fate got in my way again. It's had a habit of doing that."

I don't think she heard anything I said but the one word "Elizabeth." I saw her go white, then rock back and forth on her heels, like a toy Humpty Dumpty. I thought for a moment that she was going to fall my way. I couldn't have stopped her. I wouldn't have stood in her way. I would've moved aside and let her fall. I could stand and watch her crumple unto death and not lift a finger of my wooden hand to help, unless it helped her die faster.

But she got control of herself all right. She got back to herself. In fact, she pulled down the blinds that covered her eyes, blotting out any knowledge or connection with the past, but this time she was a bit too late.

"Don't pull any fast ones, Elizabeth," I said. "I know all the answers now. Just go on being the great lady and I'll go on being the gardener.

We're too old, you and I, for much else." I paused and added up my thoughts, then I went on, "Only don't be getting in my way, Mrs. Henaston, because I got a little house over there now," I pointed to my cottage, "and inside my little house are all kinds of implements of torture. You know, like knives and things like that."

She drew her lips together, tight across, as if a rubber band had suddenly snapped across her mouth, then she turned and started slowly down her patterned path to the big house.

But I saw her eyes. I saw her eyes open and close quickly, mirroring the past and adding a new picture to the future.

As I watched her now comfortable figure start down that path I called after her, "I didn't plan this on purpose, Mrs. Henaston. I didn't know until now what was in the big house on the hill."

I saw her hesitate, but ever so slightly, then she moved on until she disappeared among the heavy trees and foliage that sheltered the path and I went back to my cottage. And instead of dwelling on the amazing thing that had just happened, instead of shaking with the joy of reaching my goal, I pushed it all out of my thought. I pigeonholed it in my mind, to take out later when I'd had my dinner, fixed the fire, put on the slippers she wouldn't have placed by my chair; when I could sit down comfortably, pack my pipe, which wasn't peaceful any longer, sort through the evening papers, then drop them quickly as I brought out of the closet of my mind this amazing thing that had just happened.

People never believe the real things in life. They read made-up stories and believe the stories, but when they read real things in books they say, "But that never happens in life." My life would make more than one story that nobody would believe.

I sat in my chair by the fire and imagined I could hear Elizabeth cursing the long arm of coincidence until her exotic bedroom was blue with hate.

After all of the changes in the world everything was exactly the same again. Mrs. Elizabeth Frazer Isaacs Blodgett Henaston was going to have to get up and find me around someplace. One murder wasn't enough. But her mistake wasn't murder. It was the mistake of only one murder. She should have laid *me* beside Ugly Face. And yet if she had, there would have been something or someone else. You can't get away from the me's that reflect the real you.

Get away?

I sat up straight in my chair. Get away? Of course she'd figure she could get away again. She could get *me* away. She'd bungled the job, but it wasn't too late, not for a woman like her. All she needed to do was to find me alone some night, any night, every night. Tonight! I got up quickly and ran to the door and locked it. I locked the windows down and turned all of the lights out but one.

There were plenty of places right around the estate where she could bury my body. What'd she have to lose now? Everything as far as her life was concerned and nothing as far as I was concerned.

Yet, I said once that ten years can change a man or a woman. They had changed her considerably, on the outside. But the expression in her eyes and the ice in her voice were the same.

But what was the inside of her like now? Now that she had everything she'd always wanted—all those things she'd lied and cheated and stolen and murdered for? Was she still willing to gamble with another murder? Or could she keep from gambling and still keep what she had? Particularly her peace of mind. Peace of mind. Did that still make no difference to her? Did she still live for the present only? And what a present! Mrs. Arthur August Henaston III, wife of A. A., millionaire president of the Henaston Washing Machine Company. Poor rich guy.

Wait a minute. Whoa! Maybe he knew about her all the time. Maybe that's why he hired me. He surely must have recognized my name. But she didn't know about me before today. The look on her face said as much.

I got up and started to pace the floor. I know I must have talked out loud. But I just talked questions. I had no answers.

And how was I to find the answers? Not by planning to find out. That I knew. When the time was ripe I'd find out. I'd find out all right.

Circumstantial evidence!

When the time was ripe.

Chapter 18

I didn't see Elizabeth again for a couple of weeks but I wasn't ready to see her anyway. I had some sleuthing to do. First I wanted to find out something about Arthur August Henaston.

I found a biographical sketch in the public library. He was said to be worth in the neighborhood of three million and had made it all in the last twenty-five years. That would mean that he didn't start piling up the dough until he was about thirty.

The biography was very sketchy concerning his years from one to thirty. It told where he was born, Montreal, Canada, and that he'd gone to school at McGill University, but never graduated; that he was the son of poor but honest Montreal farmers. He came to the United States when he was twenty and went into some kind of insurance business.

When he was thirty he began to dabble around in the stock market and made enough to buy a patent on a washing machine that he now manufactured.

He was married to an Elaine Hammermill who graced him with two children and then died. A few years later, when he really began to amass his fortune, he married a certain unknown woman from California, an Elizabeth Winfield. Winfield. Where in the hell did she dig that name up? Or was it her own? I doubted it.

But the thing that interested me most was the fact that little was known about Mr. Henaston in his early twenties, and the more obvious fact that Mr. Henaston married Elizabeth the very year almost to the day that I began my sentence for the murder of Elizabeth Frazer Winfield.

If I'd been a newspaperman or had enough influence to get into the files of some big paper I could have dug into the morgue and probably found out what I wanted to find out sooner. But I found it out anyway, and I didn't find it out by searching for it.

I had become pretty well acquainted with my parole officer, and the day I went into New York to the library I went to the parole board to drop off my monthly report. I had Henaston on my mind, trying to figure out how I was going to find the information I wanted.

The parole officer, Steve Elliot, was checking my report and asking me routine questions about my job. I was answering him in that automatic way a person answers familiar questions when he's thinking of something else when I suddenly woke up to the fact Elliot was talking about Henaston.

"He's a nice fellow, Henaston," he was saying. "I'll never forget the day I first met him."

I came back to the conversation with a startled expression on my face. "Henaston? Yeah, he's swell. Great guy. Been wonderful to me."

I looked at Elliot and my mind began to function again. He must know Henaston pretty well. This was the second or third time he'd mentioned him to me. Nothing concrete until now, except in connection with my job, but why should Elliot know Henaston? How could their paths have crossed? These two unrelated personalities? I studied Elliot a moment. He was a man about sixty-five. Henaston was perhaps eight or ten years younger. Elliot looked as though he'd been working for the government for a long time. At least, he had that imperturbable, robot-like patience that seems to be attached to clerks and those who've had to interview the public all their lives. He was the direct opposite of Henaston. There was always a bustly air of activity about Henaston that made you feel he'd never known anything but big business, quick decisions, impulsive hunches that paid off. Elliot gave you the feeling he'd never known anything but details, important, cumulative statistics revealing the strength and weaknesses of humanity. But there is something here, I said to myself. And I had to find out what it was. What it was that I was supposed to find out, because I knew as soon as Elliot mentioned Henaston that it was a lead. Thoughts like rubber balls. Bouncing back. My thoughts about Henaston, intense as they were, had bounced right back to me.

I made a move to go. It was a definite move, but my remark was casual. "I'll tell Henaston you sent your regards," I said.

"Oh, no," he answered quickly, "that's not necessary. It's been so long. He probably wouldn't remember. Wouldn't care about remembering. He's come a long ways since then." He smiled at me. "Let that be an inspiration to you, Johnson."

"Yeah," I said, "it is. How long's it been since ..." I hesitated with my deduction but not too long, "since he used to come up here?" I finished the sentence in a hurry hoping to God I hadn't been too presumptuous.

"Oh, 'bout twenty or twenty-five years. I was a young fellow then, too. Him and I used to gas about a lot of things. He was pretty bright."

"He still is," I said.

"That's what got him in trouble with that insurance company in the first place. I don't know how guilty he was. But grand larceny—" He shrugged. "Ten years. He only served, let's see, about three years and four months. That was the minimum, I think, less the time he received for good behavior. Of course, he had to make out his report every month for seven years."

"Yes, I know," I said.

He grinned. "Yep, I been around for quite a while and I've seen Henaston really shoot up. The last day he had to report up here was his happiest day, I bet. Now look at him, a multimillionaire, ain't he? And they say America's not full of opportunities. If that was some countries he'd still be in the pen."

"Then a guy can live things down, huh, Elliot?"

"Sure. Who knows about Henaston around here? He came from California, too. Made new friends. A new life. Hell, it's good. I don't think I told more'n three people about him. And they don't matter. I wouldn't have talked to you but I knew you was in the know, workin' for him and all that."

He got up to leave his desk. There were a million questions I'd have liked to ask him but I didn't dare, and anyway, I really didn't need to know any more than I did. I knew just enough about Arthur August Henaston to play "heavy, heavy" when I was ready to.

On the way back to Woodmere I sat on the train and began to piece it all together. When Henaston got out he went to New York. Approximately seven years later he married Elaine Hammermill. He lived with her for five or six years. During those years he played the stock market and bought the washing-machine patent. Then when he was going good the first Mrs. Henaston died, leaving him two kids. Then he met Elizabeth Frazer someplace, evidently in Minnesota because one of his plants for the manufacture of the washing machines was in Minneapolis. Old Bloat Neck Isaacs had evidently worked for him after Walker fired him. When Henaston met Frazer it developed into a great thing, and even though she did get away from Isaacs, she couldn't get away from me for quite a spell. But when she did she got to Henaston O.K., and she'd been with him ever since.

Well, well, well. So Arthur August was a brother con and from the same can. That accounted for his knowing my friend the Warden. So he had some things he was trying to forget, too. I didn't know whether Elizabeth's evil deeds were added to the things he wanted to forget, but if so he was still in for a bit of repentance. His beads would still be pretty black. And I was eventually going to make them blacker.

It didn't take me long to figure out the method of my revenge. It didn't take me long for two reasons. First, when you finally arrive at the point where you can begin wreaking your revenge, especially after ten or twelve years, you're impatient. You want to do it all at once. It's like when you dream about wanting something or someone for a long time, when you get to the very point, just before you get it, you're in such a hurry that you almost bungle the job. In other words, when you want someone real bad you sometimes cease being subtle and become frenzied or corny or just downright simple, and you end up by losing the very person you could've had. That's the way with revenge. That was the way with my revenge. I found her and I wanted to get started right away. So I did. And number two, the second reason it didn't take me long, I wasn't very bright building my hate up into something big, not like she was, at any rate, so I chose a very simple method. The old drop-of-water gag. It was good a thousand years ago when it wore the stone in two, so why the hell shouldn't it still be good? I'd drive her nuts with the little things, the details that pile up, one on top of the other, until the mountain is so big you can't see over it any longer and you finally have to destroy it. And that's what she finally had to do.

I started weaving the net by sending her a rose every day. Every day I picked a red, red rose, picked it from her own greenhouse. And when I went up to the house with the flowers Mrs. Strapp ordered for the day I saw to it that the one rose was placed in Elizabeth's crystal bud vase and put in her room.

At first it didn't mean anything to her. But repetition is a screwy thing. One day she woke up and stared at that rose and wondered. Then she remembered that she'd been waking up and staring at it for quite a few mornings but she wasn't cognizant until this particular morning that, until I arrived, the rose hadn't been there before. So sure, she asked Mrs. Strapp, and she told her it was my idea for "the missus." Later when Mrs. Strapp was telling me about it I asked her casually how the missus took the information. "She didn't say one blamed word," Mrs. Strapp said, "not a word. She just made one of those cold stares that goes through you like a Chicago wind in winter, turned on her elegant heel, and walked away."

I laughed. "O.K., Mrs. Strapp," I said. "If my thoughtfulness isn't appreciated we'll just forget about it. She can wake up from now on and stare at herself in the mirror. That'll start her day off lousy."

Mrs. Strapp loved me for that. I can hear that belly laugh now, like a fat pack burro heehawing on the rim of disaster. Mrs. Strapp was scared of Elizabeth. She needed her job badly and it wasn't often she got a chance to hear someone else say the things she'd been thinking for five or six years.

For the following week or so I tried the letters. I sent her a letter every day mailed from a different spot. Sometimes it was Woodmere, sometimes Port Chester, Westchester, Manhattan, Brooklyn, the Bronx. One day I rode the ferry way over to Staten Island just to post her a letter from there. It's maddening how revenge can control every part of you. Even your humor doesn't escape. It becomes tinged with the evil too.

I never saw her receive one of the letters, of course. But I got a good mental picture of the first couple of them. She knew my handwriting, so she probably opened them furtively behind one of her many closed doors. Maybe she expected a love note in the first one. Or a threat in the second. Or a "touch." But when she opened the first and the second and the third and maybe the fourth, because I don't think she opened any more of them, she never found what she expected. She never found anything. Because there was nothing to find. No long letter, no note, no line, no word. Just an empty piece of paper. Empty like her head. Blank like her eyes. Cold and sterile and unproductive like her soul.

Finally the flowers and letters were not enough. So the telephone calls. I began calling her in the mornings and awaking her from her beauty sleep. "Hello, Elizabeth," I would say, then wait. At first she didn't recognize my voice. She was merely angry because someone had awakened her. So, sensing her anger, before she could say anything but hello, I'd hang up. Then one morning she caught on. She banged the receiver, and even though I wasn't near her window, had I been I'm sure I would have seen her bite her sensuous lip to keep from screaming, throw her fat but still sexy body from the bed, and pace the room like a gutted tigress with all her entrails trailing.

I waited a few days, then I rang her up at night. At eight o'clock, at ten and twelve and two and three and once at dawn, "the dawn, Elizabeth, that you and I shared as one." The only time I ever thought I understood her was at dawn when she lay in my arms, her blue eyes batting out the hurried seconds before the latent desire was made unlatent and a moment of ecstasy melted into what I thought might be understanding someday but was only a suspended state of blankness, her own particular brand that took on different shapes depending upon the situation.

And then one day the game of telephone calls got dull, that is for me, because we never stop playing unless the game gets dull for us. We don't change our colors for others to see, to soften the glare for them. We pick out the new masks or change the old make-up for our own sakes, because we're tired of us, because what we wanted and thought we might get isn't any nearer to us and the game's not progressing. So, when the game's not progressing, change it! Forty-love can go on a hell of a long time. If you're nearsighted you can get pretty dizzy watching the same balls go over the same net.

I decided to send Mrs. Henaston a wire, a wire with words in it, words she wouldn't like but words I knew she'd read and pay attention to, for I was going to ask her to meet me. But I didn't have the chance. Even as my hand reached for the telephone to call in the wire I heard the knock on the door of my little cottage and I had my first important visitor.

It'll be a long time before I forget that face. When it comes back to me now it doesn't come back in all its tragic meaning, but it comes back all right. Like a photograph, white on black, that you can't see through to the inside or behind the eyes. Or like a painting by someone who can't paint insides, only faces. And what a face it would have been to paint if you were the type of painter who painted the inside on the outside! I wish I could do it. It would hang in the gallery called posterity.

It had hate in it and hope. And hopelessness and pain. And painlessness and the pallor of tragedy after the tragedy has worn thin, worn into numbness.

The minute I opened the door and saw Elizabeth Frazer standing there I knew that she'd changed a hell of a lot, changed before the new change had brought more tragedy, her kind of tragedy. I knew she had changed enough in the last ten years so that just knowing I was near her like an evil conscience had at last given her a warped semblance of a conscience.

I opened the door wide. She walked past me into the room and sat down before either of us spoke. As I watched her walk by me fearfully like someone hurrying by death I saw another change, physical. Mrs. Henaston hadn't eaten much in three weeks. The toll was being taken in pounds of flesh, too.

When she got seated and I'd closed the door she looked up at me and straight into my eyes, and I saw the picture of the nights without sleep, the sleeping tablets and cigarettes and quick shots of whisky. Her eyes were not the blue of the sea any longer, but of the ocean during a prolonged storm. Her face was thin and white and the long shadows on her cheeks looked like smudges made by a piece of charcoal held in a hand that wasn't too steady.

"Walter," she began, "I can't stand this any longer. What do you want? What do you want of me? Why don't you go away and leave me alone?" She fumbled at a purse she held in her hand. I watched her open it and take out a roll of bills. "Here." She thrust the money at me. "This is all I could get, but there's over two thousand dollars." I looked at her a long time, until she had to take her eyes away from me. Then I said, "Put it away, Elizabeth. It wouldn't pay for one night of the ten years."

Then I saw her do something I never saw her do before, not even during the years I lived with her. I saw her start to cry, cry like any other woman, any other human being, might do when the net had closed around him so tight that there was no way out anymore.

I watched her for a few minutes, watched her without sympathy, without feeling of any kind, and then I said, "It won't help, Elizabeth. The water all ran under the bridge a long time ago. Let's just start with today. Now. Two thousand dollars seems like a lot of money to me, but it isn't to you, because if we're going to play with money I want more than that. I want as much as you can get and as often as you can get it. Beg, borrow, steal. You wouldn't be against stealing, would you? Not from your own husband, anyway. I want enough money so that I can use it to cover up all those hours I spent trying to cover up for you while you slept in the countinghouse." I saw her blink her eyes and then stop crying like someone had suddenly shut off a water tap. She wanted to talk but she didn't know quite what to say yet, so I went on.

"I'm going to hang around here until I get the money, too. I know what you've been through the last few weeks. But I have no sympathy for you and I'll never have any. But it's funny, right now I have respect for you. For the first time since I've known you I have a funny kind of respect for you. That's because I've seen you suffer a little bit, because I know that you're finally capable of some kind of suffering. For a long time now you've been living in a new world that you made for yourself out of your rotten one. You like it. Sure you like it. Who the hell wouldn't? You're supposed to be a respectable woman, charming, wealthy, hanging on the edge of a blue book.

"And now in a second, in the second it took to convict me or kill John Isaacs, everything that you've got, that you planned for in your bloody way, could be snatched from you, and it might be, too! But the worst part's that you can be snatched from it and hung high on that scaffold you built for others. Hung high by the neck until dead!

"No, of course you don't like the picture. But the tears or anything else you might think would help don't mean a goddamned thing now, because I'm in the driver's seat driving like a bat out of hell and you aren't my only passenger! Mr. Henaston won't like the ride either."

As soon as she heard me mention his name, and I wonder now if that isn't the only thing she heard, she stood up so quickly she had to grasp onto the sides of the chair to keep from falling.

"Don't!" she screamed. "Don't do anything to him. Please don't! You've worried him enough already with those horrible notes and phone calls. Please, Walter!"

"Oh." I walked over close to her, so close, in fact, that she had to move back from me. "So he knows about them, huh? That's why you're putting on this act? He's discovered one of the ghosts in your attic. He's known all along, hasn't he, Elizabeth? He's known who I was ever since I arrived. What's he gonna do about it? About me?"

Her expression was incredulous, the tone of her voice. "He doesn't know. No, he doesn't know, Walter." This wasn't an act now, I was sure. I knew when she was lying. "What makes you think that, Walter?"

"Because he knows my name, my real name. He's known it ever since I came to work here."

"It wouldn't matter," she said. She was calm now. She wanted to prove her point. She spoke clearly, out of her sudden stillness. "He never knew about you. Who you were."

"I don't believe that!" I shouted.

"But it's true! We weren't here when your—when your trial was going on. I never told him about you. We were in South America. We left right away." Her voice began to rise again. "We stayed there two years. He opened a branch office down there. I got him to stay. I didn't want him to know about you. I don't want him to know now. But he's beginning to wonder what this is all about. And I won't have it, Walter! I won't! I won't! *I can't afford to!*" That horrible voice that she used for screaming, that chalk-on-the-blackboard screech. I clenched my fists to keep my nails from curling backward. Her face had blown up red like a circus balloon about ready to pop. It was time I moved away from her. I wasn't ready yet for that slap in the face. I couldn't take so cheap an insult this late in the game.

When I saw her deflate and turn white again I picked it up from my new position and though my tone was lower it didn't lose any of its meaning. It grew in intensity because my words grew in importance. At least to me. To her, nothing grew any longer. I knew that. Everything stood still. Stagnant. Or died, because she wanted it that way.

"So, Elizabeth, you really found someone you love? Or is it love for a man? I don't believe it. I think it's the love for a man with money. Because if I went to him and told him everything I know, he'd sure as hell kick you out, wouldn't he? Wouldn't he, Elizabeth? He couldn't afford all of your scandals added to his. Yeah! I know a few things about the guy you love, too. So don't worry. All you need to do is to get me as much money as you can and as often as I ask you. That's all. It's very simple."

She started to step toward me. I moved back so she could pass me, because I knew that she was going to begin one of those silent walks to the door. When she got to it I was there ahead of her and opened it for her.

"Oh, yes, and about the two thousand. I can use that as the first payment."

She turned toward me and held out her hand that was still clutching the roll of bills. As I reached for them she opened her hand and they fell to the floor. I laughed and kicked them over to one side.

"Thanks, Elizabeth," I said, "and come to see me often. Knock, because the door will be locked from the inside."

She turned her face back to the door, walked on outside and straight down the path to the house on the hill, and not once did she turn back or stop to call good-by over her shoulder.

The interview was at an end. Abrupt. Swift. Unsatisfying. Like it began. Unsatisfying. Like everything that began with her. Like everything that ended.

What would she do now? What would her husband do? Was it true that he didn't know about me? I could hardly believe it, yet I didn't think Elizabeth was lying. And what about Isaacs? Did he know about John Isaacs in Middletown? About Elizabeth Frazer's life before John Isaacs? If she hadn't told him, would she tell him now? About me? About Isaacs? About herself? Would it matter if she did? Or if she didn't? Or if ... ? To hell with it! Mathematics never interested me because I couldn't add up so well when the figures got too big. Two and two? Sure, that made four. But what comes after four? The guy with the greater calculations, the guy up there, above me, above you, from now on He would have to do the calculating.

I shut the door and locked it and then stooped down to pick up the two thousand. I looked at it lying in my hands, and all of a sudden I wondered what the hell it could buy.

Chapter 19

In the Bible there's a quotation from St. Paul that goes like this: "The new birth is ... waiting for the adoption, to wit, the redemption of our body."

Now, whether you've ever read the Bible or not, or whether you have read it in some off moment and still don't believe it or understand it, St. Paul said what I just quoted. And when one of your lives seems to be over and another may be beginning any moment, regardless of what you have or haven't believed, you often turn to the Bible.

You turn to it for help, and that's what I did. I didn't turn to it for help because I was burning to death in the hold of a ship or because my plane was dropping or because I didn't have a job or any money or any place to sleep, or was sick and helpless or discouraged and lonely. I turned to it because I was in doubt, and the kind of doubt that had a sense of finality tacked to it. I felt that the end of things was really coming. That at last I was going to die ... someway ... somehow.

And yet obviously I was still perfectly whole and comparatively safe, and had a bank account of ten thousand dollars.

Elizabeth had sent me ten thousand dollars in cash over a period of a few months.

But one day I woke up with this doubt. First, I knew damned well there wasn't going to be any more money. Second, I knew that the cat-and-mouse game was definitely at an end and that it was going to have to be either Elizabeth or me.

Now, I could have run away. I had the dough and the opportunity. But the money didn't mean anything to me any longer, and the opportunity only meant another trip to find what was once Walter Johnson. And I could have sat in the same chair and rediscovered Walter Johnson if I'd known how ... if I'd been ready to find out how.

So instead I sat in the chair and tried to read the Bible, tried to make it mean sense, make it apply to me. And I thought of my mother, could hear her soft voice speaking aloud a verse from Psalms like she used to do when I was too little to understand anything but the warmth of her voice. And I thought of Masters and his gentleness, of the yogi who'd been to Tibet, of the quietness of some people. Of calm and quiet ... and ...

That was where I was sitting and what I was thinking when she came to visit me for the second time.

It was the spring of the year. We'd had several spring thunderstorms in the last few days. And as I sat there trying to figure out the meanings in the Good Book and how they might apply to me in case I was going to take one of my last breaths, I noticed that it was raining again. It had rained in the morning but had stopped at noon.

I got up to shut the window. As I started to walk away from one of the side windows that opened out onto a small clearing surrounded by a clump of trees through which you could see the stables, I looked down on the floor and noticed some mud right under the window. I stooped down closer to the floor. Mud! Mud made by footprints ... and not my footprints. I looked out the window and noticed that right underneath it there were other footprints in the soft ground. Footprints made by a person with feet much smaller than mine and wearing high-heeled shoes.

I turned quickly toward the center of the room. There was no mud anyplace but under the window. I stood for a moment, then my eyes took in the entire room and the door leading to my bedroom. I could see through it into the room and the closet in the bedroom. The closet door was standing open. I stared at the door so long that it seemed to move. But after a few minutes I realized that it was one of those optical illusions. The door hadn't moved an inch. But if anyone was hiding in the closet, that person could certainly sense my fear.

I had quickly to give her a reason to think I wasn't afraid. That was my first step.

I went around to all of the lamps, numbering three, and I turned them out, leaving the bedroom lamp on, giving me enough light to see by. Then I started slowly toward the bedroom, trying to fake a yawn that could be heard in any part of the small house.

As I passed the closet door in the living room my eyes were attracted by the doorknob, because the light from the bedroom reflected into the living room and fell on the door of the living room closet. I saw the knob turn very slowly, then click back again. If I hadn't heard the almost imperceptible click I'd have sworn that it was another illusion. But I'd heard the click.

Good! Whoever was in my house was in the living room closet. That was a break for me.

I went in the bedroom and undressed, standing in full view of the living room closet door. If the person in the closet was looking through the keyhole she got a pretty good show for her stolen ticket, because I stripped down, then walked to the bed, pulled down the covers, got in bed, and switched off the lamp. And with hardly a second's hesitation I rolled out of bed onto the other side, stuck the pillow under the covers, and darted into the bedroom closet, pulling the door almost shut, leaving just space enough for me to watch the show. I had a reserved ticket, too.

I had to wait, I guess, about ten minutes, then I heard the click of the doorknob again, and I saw her step into the bedroom doorway. At least I saw the shadow of her as she raised her arm and pumped three bullets into a feather pillow under the covers of my bed.

I knew she'd have to stop to unlock the front door, or open the window if she was going to leave the same way she came, which gave me time enough to put on my robe and grab the only weapon handy, a flashlight I kept on the night table for just such an emergency ... an unexpected visit by a lady.

She'd got to the window before she heard me coming. When I got inside the door of the living room she must have thought she'd seen a ghost, because as she turned quickly around toward me and raised her arm and the hand still holding the automatic, her hand hesitated in mid-air, her whole body poised briefly, suspended like her hand as though a shock had run through her entire system and caused numbness for a moment. And in that moment I raised my arm, which was steady, and flung the heavy flashlight at her, hitting her squarely between the eyes. She fell back against the window, dropping the gun on the floor. I made a dive for it just as she crumpled up underneath the window.

I switched on a lamp and walked back to the window and the heap of flesh under the window. She had a cut on her head between the eyes and the blood was trickling down onto her dove-gray negligee. She was breathing heavily and her eyelids were fluttering as if she might come to any minute.

I stood over her like an executioner with an ax in his hand waiting for a head to roll off, a head that hadn't been cut clean. As I watched her trying to come back to consciousness, making that eternal struggle, I wasn't actually thinking about what had just happened, or what was going to happen. I was thinking about something that had happened a long time ago and yet was clearer to me at that moment than it had been even a long time ago.

Because the same scene was being played over again, and repetition makes things clearer. A rainy night, a small comfortable room, a man wearing a robe with two pockets in it. In one pocket a wooden hand and in the other pocket a gun, not a knife this time, but a gun.

The audience couldn't see in the pocket, so whether it was a knife or gun made no difference. The end was the same.

In the comfortable room there was also another figure. A figure in a soft gray negligee, a negligee with blood on it. Not on the hem of it this time, but on the top of it, around the neck. And the figure in the negligee was older and fatter and the white shoulder twisting out of the mass of gray material wasn't quite so alluring.

The man in the room was older, too, and thinner. And the robe he wore was longer, covering his once virile frame. But the scene was the same. The details that were different wouldn't have been so noticeable from a distance or they might not have been remembered over such a long space of time.

The lines of the circle had met. Like they always do.

She came to in a few minutes. I dragged her onto her feet and sat her down in the chair I'd been sitting in before she left her hiding place. And at the point of her gun I forced her to write on the flyleaf of the Bible I'd been reading and which was still lying on the table by the chair. And this is what she wrote; the content was my idea, the style hers: "I, Elizabeth Frazer, alias Winfield, Blodgett, and Henaston, killed John Isaacs in Middletown, Minnesota, sixteen years ago. Three years later in Carleton, California, I faked my own murder, thereby causing Walter Johnson (Blodgett) to be convicted of that murder. Tonight I tried to kill Walter Johnson, alias Johnson Lukens, because," and I let her add the rest and this was it, "I think I've repented enough. I have everything to live for and he has nothing."

She stopped and glared hate at me. I smiled. "Sign it, Elizabeth," I said.

Signed, "Elizabeth Frazer Henaston, April 3."

April 3! I laughed and pointed to the date. "Look, Elizabeth," I said, "the date. It's the same. Or did you know that? Is that why you added it? It's the same date that we met. Sixteen years ago, April the third. Three. My unlucky number. Lucky now."

Without waiting for her reaction, without even looking at her, I raised my arm, my good left arm, and the steady hand with the gun in it, and I heard a gasp and saw her bloody face turn frigid, as if a sack of dry ice had been dropped over her head and frozen her face into immobility. She was scared. She was scared stiff. She was a poor, silly, stupid, scared human being. Skip the human and let's face it. For the first time in her life she'd found something more terrifying than herself. Her death! She didn't want to die.

"I don't want to die, Walter," she said, "I don't want to die." Her voice sounded far away. The echo came back and hit her in the face. "I'll do anything if … if I don't have to die!"

"Anything, Elizabeth? If I told you to go and kill Arthur Henaston and I'd let you live, would you kill the only person you've ever loved, the only person you say you've ever loved? Would you do that, Elizabeth?"

She looked at me and her expression never changed. Again it was as though she heard only what she wanted to hear. "I'll do anything if I don't have to die," she repeated.

I couldn't help laughing. I couldn't have helped it if my life had depended upon it instead of hers. "Well, the truth will finally out." I shook my head. "Don't worry. I'm not going to kill you, Elizabeth. No, I won't kill you. You see, you only kill people you love a lot or hate a lot. I feel nothing for you. A great glob of nothing. And you know when I discovered it? Right now. A second ago. A minute. A day. A week. A year. A lifetime. Yeah, I've learned too much to toss it all away with a piece of lead. I know that now. I've learned too much." I hesitated a moment, waiting for some sign of understanding or even recognition that she at least followed my words. I looked in those cold blue eyes and realized they were colder now because fear had been removed, the fear of death, the only fear she knew. Her brain was beginning to tick again. Beat upon beat. The pulse was slowing. Steady, Elizabeth. Escape is not that near. I smiled. "But I could kill you, Elizabeth," I continued. "I could blow your brains out and no one would care. Not even the law. Because, you see, you've been dead for years."

I started to laugh again, but the three shots that rang out, one on top of the other … One on top of the other. Three. The three shots were like sudden periods in the middle of an incomplete sentence. They stopped all words, all thoughts, all noise but their own, all life but mine.

I looked at Elizabeth and her head rolled over onto her chest and the Bible dropped from her hand and the voice behind me said, "It wasn't like shooting at a pillow, was it, Johnson?"

I turned my head and saw Arthur Henaston standing in the doorway holding a .38 in his hand.

Chapter 20

I can see Henaston yet. In that doorway standing as still as death, still as Elizabeth's body in death. I can see him as he walked slowly into the room, into my cottage, as though he were entering it for the first time. I can see him as he sat down beside her, quietly, as if even the scraping of the chair on the floor might awaken her from her final sleep, and I felt sorry for him. I guess he loved her in spite of her evil. If he loved her because of it, then what happened later was inevitable.

He knew about John Isaacs. He carried the weight of that around with him all the time he was married to her. She'd met Henaston after she'd hooked up with Isaacs. She'd tried to get away from Isaacs legitimately in order to get to Arthur. But Isaacs caught on and she finally had to murder him. Then she stumbled over me. I was her nemesis. Her mistake. She should have run out of the apartment and left Ugly Face there to rot alone, but she had too big a flair for the dramatic. She thought she saw a way to involve me. She saw me, a bum, standing in the rain by the train tracks, and she said, "There. There is a worthless son-of-a-bitch, I'll give this dead body to him. I'll will him my corpse." But she played it all wrong. She overplayed the drama in it and we made our exits together.

And all this time Henaston, the poor sap, was waiting for her. He saw the papers about Isaacs' murder. Sure. He knew Elizabeth well enough to figure that it was her murder, not mine. Not the nameless bum's she made her exit with. The minute he read the papers he knew Elizabeth had arranged it, but he waited just the same. He waited for three years until she finally broke away from me. He was fascinated with evil, too.

She could have got away from me sooner than she did, but I believe Henaston felt that she should let the murder die down. He didn't admit that, but I'm sure it was his suggestion that she lay low for a while. He wasn't all light and sunshine, either. There was evil there.

She'd been corresponding with him while she lived with me. Even Old Lady Hargraves knew that. She'd arranged for Elizabeth to telephone Henaston the day before she left my bed and board. Elizabeth made the call in Mattie Hargraves' front parlor. Mattie was a bigger skunk than I thought. But she carried her secret, Elizabeth's secret, to the grave with her. I think she really felt I'd found out about Henaston and murdered Elizabeth. That I'll concede her.

Henaston said he knew Elizabeth was staying with someone in Carleton and he waited until she could make a clean getaway. He flew out from New York and met her in Los Angeles. Their rendezvous was at the Hollyjoy Apartments, but I don't think they were ever joined by Goldie Lewis or Countess Evelyn or the Countess's friends Norma and Russ.

There in my cottage, over Elizabeth's dead body, Henaston swore that they went to South America and that he never knew a thing about me or the "murder" in Carleton until this night, until he followed her to my cottage. It's pretty hard to believe, especially when everybody reads newspapers. They can be bought in South America. They're even printed in Braille, too.

He said he followed Elizabeth to my cottage because he'd seen the letters and heard the telephone calls. But he didn't know who or what the object of his jealousy was going to turn out to be until he saw her come out of that closet in my living room, stand in the bedroom doorway, and pump three bullets into the pillow she thought was me.

He was hiding in the bushes outside my front window. It wasn't a very comfortable stall there in the rain, but he stayed for the whole show. He wanted to hear the score. It added up for him all right. But then, he was better at mathematics than I was.

He told me he'd come to kill the guy she'd gone to meet. But he stayed to kill her instead. Maybe I shouldn't have felt sorry for him.

Before I left I saw him sit staring at her lifeless body, blubbering like a spoiled brat who'd just wrung the neck of his pet cat because the cat had scratched him once too often. Henaston bumped Elizabeth off because of that mountain of things I mentioned before. Those little things had grown into a mountain he couldn't see over any longer.

At last he said, "I could stand anything but the fact that she didn't really love me."

Sure, Arthur, I thought, we all feel that way. It's the best motive in the world—for murder.

"Sure, Henaston," I said, "I understand."

He looked at me like a man fresh out of a bad dream. "Get some clothes on, Johnson," he said. "For the police."

I looked down at my robe. I'd been standing there listening to him talk, so interested in his sorrow-ridden explanation, his regret and reason for murder, that I'd forgotten I was in no condition to meet the police with or without a dead body in the room.

"Get some clothes on," he repeated, "and call the police."

I went into the bedroom and got into some pants, shoes, and a shirt, and grabbed my coat out of the closet. Then I remembered Elizabeth's gun. I reached into the pocket of my robe and took the gun out. I walked back into the living room. "Elizabeth's gun," I said.

He held out his hand. "Give it to me."

I handed it to him. He took out his handkerchief and wiped it off carefully. "No use your being involved in this again."

He took the gun in his own hand and slipped it into his pocket. I waited for a moment, then started toward the phone. His words stopped me. "Go get Ronnie," he said. "Go get my chauffeur, Johnson. Tell him to come down here right away. You can phone from the house."

I stopped at the front door as though waiting for some final instructions. There were none. He didn't turn toward me again. When I left, I left him sitting like Salome brooding over her pet prophet's head.

I went outside. It was still raining. A thin, cold rain. I put my coat collar up around my neck and started running toward the garage. As I ran I remembered another night and another rain and a path along the railroad ties and the whistle of a distant freight and a woman in a window, waving....

I ran upstairs to the chauffeur's apartment over the garages. He was still up.

"There's been some trouble," I said. "At my cottage. Mr. Henaston wants you to go down there right away."

He looked puzzled but dropped the book he was reading, switched off the radio, and reached for his coat.

"I'm going up to the house to telephone," I said.

"What's the matter? Is the old man sick?"

"No," I said, "not that way. Mrs. Henaston is dead."

His eyes narrowed and I'm sure I saw a smile cross his face, though I wouldn't swear to it.

"Use my phone. Do you know the number?"

"I don't need one," I said. "I'll just ask the operator to connect me with the police."

He was at the door by that time. He swung around and stared at me. I nodded. I don't know whether he knew exactly what the hell my nod meant, but he didn't stop to find out. He shot out of the door and down the steps before I could pick up the receiver. And it's a damned good thing he did, too, because he got to the cottage just in time to see Henaston kill himself.

The note Henaston left completely exonerated me. One of the bodies he left completely released me. Forever.

I'm three thousand miles away from there now. I'm farther away than that. In spirit. I'm working with the earth again, growing things. Out of tough soil this time. Dry. Hard. Desert. It's different. I love the desert. It's good for you. It's big and roomy and free. I'm a hell of a gardener now. See? They're growing!

I don't know what people are doing.

THE END

Diamonds Don't Burn

GERTRUDE WALKER

1

She wished John hadn't driven her to the station. It made her feel guilty. There he stood, his kind, gentle face watching her as she got on the train. His kind, gentle face staring at her, but his quiet, thoughtful mind on something else. On his school, for he took his principalship of the high school as importantly as a man would take the presidency of Harvard; on the meeting with the school board to select a new vice-principal since the decease of Miss Simpson; figuring out what to do about the needs for a new gym, a better-staffed commissary. There he stood thinking of millions of things far from her, but saying, "Buy yourself a new hat, Clara. It'll make you think you've got a beau." And then laughing at his pleasantry, his attempt at a witticism.

If he hadn't have said that. How could she leave him like this? But she had to. How could she do this to him? But she was going to. For eighteen years a fine virtuous husband. And for eighteen years a virtuous wife. Lonely. And now thinking of being no longer lonely, of being no longer virtuous.

She heard the warning whistle of the train. In a minute she would be off and she would try and erase this picture of John from her mind. And in the three hours it took to get from Westfield, this small upstate town, to New York City she would make herself forget everything but why she was going to New York. Not to shop for new curtains for their house. Not to buy a new hat, as John had so jokingly suggested, but to keep a rendezvous with love.

The train gave a lurch and as it did so her bracelet with the gold St. Christopher caught on the rail guard of the platform. The spring ring which held it snapped open and the St. Christopher flew into space.

"I'll get it, Clara," John called.

But even as he ran the train began to move away, slowly at first and then it gathered speed until John was merely a lonely figure down the tracks searching valiantly for a St. Christopher, a good-luck piece. John had given her the medal and she was a bit superstitious about it. It had protected her. At least she thought it had protected her, in some instances that might have proved fatal. There was that time on the boat on the Hudson River. They were visiting friends and had taken an excursion boat. It was actually the day John had given her the medal. After they had reached their destination, up the river, they stood on the shore watching the boat depart and before they could turn away smoke began to rise from the lower deck and it was just a matter of minutes before the river boat was an inferno of flames. Two hundred people perished and yet John and she were safe. From that time on, the St. Christopher had meant protection to her, yet she was neither a Catholic nor Irish enough to be genuinely superstitious. Now the St. Christopher was gone. She wouldn't be wearing it for the first time in ten years, and for the first time in eighteen years since her and John's ideal marriage she was going to meet another man at his hotel and she was going to stay with him there because she could no longer help herself.

Desire. What is it really? Is it a face, a body, a moment, a mood, an atmosphere? If anything, it is an atmosphere. As nebulous as that seems, it is an atmosphere of thought. We can so let our frustrations go that we can become immersed in an atmosphere of desire. And then if we are enmeshed enough to have to find an outlet it can be anyone. The grocer boy, the iceman, the man next door. Or one's own husband if he is interested. But because he is no longer interested is why we find ourselves in this predicament.

This was the excuse Clara gave herself. And it was probably right. But where was that needed strength that was so necessary, that was imperative to deny this new desire? Where was the strength she had had before? Or was this new desire more tremendous in its intensity— or had the years of frustration piled up too high?

It was John himself who had brought Roger home to dinner. Roger was a bank teller in the Westfield, New York bank where John banked. Clara had never seen Roger before, but she knew the moment she saw him she could never again say, "I have never seen that man before."

The dinner that she'd worked over so carefully to make it nice for John and his friend Roger was of no import after she met John's friend Roger. It was good that the two men ate the dinner and seemed to relish it, that they seemed to have a good conversation over their coffee and brandy; but, for her, eating was out of the question. She was not a drinking woman, but even John agreed that she drank a little too much that night.

She couldn't take her eyes off Roger. He was not handsome by youth's standards. Nor by youth's measurements would he be unattractive. He was a bit overweight, but for a man nearing forty it didn't seem unattractive. His face was round but not too round, not chubby. It was a ruddy face, but mostly from wind and sun. There was nothing pudgy about his face. His eyes were blue. It was his eyes. They were a deep blue and as you watched his expressions change his eyes would change also, from a deep blue to a light blue to a sea-green. It was incredible. And when he laughed his eyes crinkled, curling up at the corners and almost disappearing, and then you saw his long black lashes, so long they looked as though they were pasted on.

After three martinis the "Song of Solomon" kept coming to her; the beauty, the sensuousness of those verses swam in her head ...

> *"By night on my bed I sought him whom my soul loveth;*
> *I sought him but I found him not....*
> *Who is this that cometh out of the wilderness like pillars of smoke,*
> *Perfumed with myrrh and frankincense? ...*
> *Thou art beautiful, oh my love,*
> *Terrible as an army with banners....*
> *Turn away thine eyes from me, for they have overcome me...."*

But he didn't turn his eyes away, and as fate would have it John excused himself to go upstairs to do some work on the book of philosophy he was compiling and writing, leaving her and Roger to talk together. They couldn't talk and so they decided to play gin rummy.

She would never forget that game. As she sat in the train to New York trying to blot out the newer picture of John searching frantically for her St. Christopher she remembered the game of gin rummy and her and Roger's first meeting.

"I don't play very well," she heard herself saying, which was far from what she was thinking. She was looking at Roger's hands as he shuffled the cards. They were long, thin hands, not stubby, short and efficient as she imagined a bank clerk's hands should be; they were artistic hands and on his ring finger he was wearing an immense intaglio ring. Not the natural black or brown onyx or cornelian but an emerald green with a dragon intaglioed in the stone. He saw her looking at the ring and quickly slipped it off his finger, passing it over to her.

"Emerald onyx. Chinese carving. May be old. May not be. But definitely a collector's piece. I picked it up in San Francisco many years ago."

She studied the ring. She tried it on. It was massive, much too large for her. She laughed and when the laugh came out it sounded self-conscious. Now why did she laugh? It wasn't apropos. Where were her poise, her sophistication, that subtlety that went with low-cut gowns?

"They said the ring was bad luck. But it's brought me only good luck."

As she handed him back the ring their hands touched briefly. She caught her breath, looking up at him under her newly arched brows. They held the look, their eyes meeting that way for that too-long moment.

She turned away. She felt like Salome dropping her seventh veil:

"Come to me, Jokanaan …" Your head is at stake.

He dealt the cards as though he'd been used to playing often. She tried to form her rummy hand but every jack and every king had his face.

He had his hand fixed before she knew what cards she had. He looked over at her. "You live too much within yourself," he said suddenly. "It shows all over you. John said you stay alone here day after day, that even at night he has to leave you often to work on his book. It isn't good for a person. Especially one as attractive as you. You must have contact with people, flattery occasionally. An unfed ego can be dangerous."

"I have no hobbies."

"That's bad."

"I tried hooking rugs, but it wasn't for me. I used to paint. Sunday painter."

"Tell me about your painting."

She laughed. "I had no encouragement."

"Didn't John encourage you?"

"He said they were dreadful. And they were. They were great blobs of paint. Not even cubistic."

"Impressionistic, they call it."

She laughed again. "They were impressionistic, all right. Impressions of—" She hesitated.

"Of what?"

"Frustrations, I guess." She answered it herself, truthfully. She saw by the look on his face that that's what he surmised.

"I'd like to see your paintings," he said.

"Oh, you'd see nothing particularly Freudian about them. They'd puzzle even a psychiatrist."

"Where are they? Could I see them?"

"I tore them up. Burned them."

"Oh. I think that's too bad. I'm sure if I ever had, well, the guts to sit down and try to paint, try anything artistic, I think I'd keep the stuff. Show my friends my talent."

"If I'd shown my paintings to anyone, John would have died. They were really ridiculous."

"How about sports? Did you ever play tennis? I play every morning before I go to work."

"I was quite good when I was in college."

"Why don't you play some morning? With me." She stared at him. He smiled. "That's right. With me."

She didn't answer him for a few minutes. She was trying to remember where her tennis racket was. In the attic? No, it was in the basement in an old trunk. Her golf clubs were there, too. She and John used to play some golf. But it had tired him too much when he had such important work to do at night on his book. If they'd only kept up the golf. Maybe being together, relaxed and having fun, would have brought them close again.

"Well?" Roger was waiting.

"Well, I ... maybe I can. Some morning, if I can find my racket."

"Tomorrow morning."

"What?"

"Tomorrow morning."

"But ... I ..."

"I'll pick you up at a quarter to nine. I have to be at work at ten."

"But John ..."

"He leaves at eight, doesn't he?"

"Seven-thirty."

"Tell him you and I are going to play some tennis. Get you out of the house for a while. Why should he mind?"

"I don't think I'd better."

He put his cards down carefully, with slow deliberation. Then, without warning, he reached across the table, taking her hands in his. "Clara."

His voice was husky. She watched his nostrils quivering ever so slightly, with that inner pulsation that she was feeling all over her body.

"You can't escape it. You might as well say yes now, because I'll haunt you."

She didn't have to ask him what he meant. She tried to pull her hands away but he was on his feet and pulling her towards him. She fought it but it was no use. His arms were around her, her head was back, her lips parted.

They clung together as long as they dared. When she pulled away she was shaking with not only desire but guilt. She listened. There was no sound upstairs, no footsteps on the stairs. She hurried over to a wall mirror to straighten her lipstick, her hair, to calm down her flushed face. In the mirror she could see Roger behind her wiping the lipstick from his mouth. Then he crossed to the card table, picked up the cards and put them back in the box.

She turned around. She was still shaking. But she had a speech to say. "I can't go with you tomorrow. And I think you'd better leave now. I'll go upstairs and tell John you're going."

He didn't say anything. He merely smiled, self-assured, confident. He knew just about how long her decision would remain permanent. Until the next morning, when he would stop for her for tennis and she would be ready.

And she *was* ready. After he left, without realizing it, she was making preparations. She went down in the basement and found her racket. She found her tennis shoes and a shirt and some white shorts.

The next morning, while preparing John's breakfast, she told him she was going to play tennis again. She hesitated briefly when he asked her with whom. But she needn't have hesitated in telling him because it didn't seem to cause a ripple in his calm. Rather, he seemed to be extremely happy that she had found a partner since he didn't play too well and had no time, and she needed the relaxation.

She and Roger played every day for three weeks with the exception of Sunday, when she was home all day with John, when Sunday became a prolonged nightmare of boredom until she could see Roger the following morning.

They both knew that tennis couldn't go on forever, that they couldn't keep out of each other's arms forever. Twice during the three weeks she had had breakfast with Roger and there had been a brief respite. They had kissed, but she was careful not to allow it to go on. There were always people watching. Walls of eyes. While they were on their way to the courts, they had run into several people they both knew and they had to be very careful not to look ecstatic in each other's company.

The next time John suggested that Roger came to dinner she vetoed it very quickly. She didn't want John to see them together, for it was difficult to hide what she felt when she looked at Roger. She had told John that she saw enough of Roger in their daily rounds of tennis, she couldn't stand having him to dinner. John had seemed to accept this as a bona fide and plausible excuse.

But the game of forty-love couldn't go on indefinitely. It had either to culminate or one of them had to win. It was Roger who won his point. He got her to promise she'd meet him for a weekend in New York City.

It would be so simple, he said. She could go away for a shopping trip. She used to go to New York without John—why would he question it now?

She told him she'd sleep on it, but she, like himself, knew the answer without having to ponder, to weigh the guilt against the desire. It was inevitable.

When she thought about the consequences, when she allowed herself the agony of thinking about them, she was admittedly afraid. Confused. Unhappy. She tried to analyze why this thing between her and Roger had happened. Her analysis was correct. She didn't need a psychologist or a psychiatrist. She had been lonely and frustrated for many years. John loved her deeply, but was no longer interested in romance. He accepted. She never accepted. She challenged. And their love was no longer challengeable. It was latent, if anything, laid away like a whatnot in a glass case. Inanimate. She wanted animate love. If John had realized this he might have been able to do something to prevent what was happening. But his self-absorption was blinding.

It had been for a long time now. As far back as five, six years. She remembered when her emotions began to become so pent up. It was when John started his book. The book required a great deal of research. Night after night he stayed in the public library until closing time. When he came home, although he would stay up long enough to have hot chocolate with her, he would be uncommunicative. And when he went to bed, whether it was a week night or Saturday or Sunday, he went to his own room and slept alone. After a while her pride got the better of her and she stopped asking him to sleep with her. His excuse was that he was exhausted. She knew it was true, that he didn't love her any the less. She knew it in the daytime, that is. At night she only knew she was miserable and that he whom she loved was a million light-miles away.

She tried desperately to understand. But it was difficult. One who has never written a book, or rather, one who has no talent for the arts, who does not have a career or hobby he loves deeply—it's difficult for him to understand the kind of self-absorption of those who write or compose or paint, especially those who are fanatically in love with their work.

Knowing she was not and probably never would be capable of true understanding, she had offered her services to him anyway. She offered to learn to type again, to help him save money on typing. She enrolled in a stenographic night course at the Westfield High School where he was principal. She'd once taken a stenographic course before she went to college, but since then had never utilized the knowledge.

While she went to school he worked either at home or at the public library. When he worked at home she took the car to night school.

In her class was a Finnish boy, a Displaced Person, Doiva Moininen. Several times during class he'd asked her to help him. One night she saw him waiting for the bus and offered him a lift to his rooming house. That's how it had started. He was younger than she, by five years or more, a blond behemoth, all muscles and wistful smiles, with an accent as intriguing to her provincial self at that moment as an accent is always intriguing to the glamor-starved.

At first she tried to say it was that old mother instinct of the childless woman approaching her forties, but this psychology had a hollow sound. She finally forced herself to come face to face with her desire and in so doing she was able to know it for what it was. Revolting as it seemed to her at that time when she uncovered it, still it could not be denied, a physical desire for an attractive man by a sex-starved woman.

In admitting it she was able to fight it, to conquer it, albeit she had to quit night school in order to shut the door more forcibly. For to face the object of the desire, after the decision to fight it to its death has been made, is the mistake that most people make and then they have the effrontery to call the affair inevitable.

It was her typing that suffered the most and John good-naturedly fired her as his secretary. Next, she had tried to do some research for him, but her mind was not the index kind. She couldn't, however hard she concentrated, arrange facts in their chronological order, nor could she seem to pick out the most indicative facts John needed. So she lost that job, too, but they both had a good laugh about it.

For a year or so she had managed to force herself to find things to do—knitting, which she loathed. Hooking rugs, only one of which she was ever able to finish, and it wouldn't lie straight on the floor. She finally bought herself the canvases, oils, brushes and a book on Grandma Moses. But, as she'd told Roger, what came out of her brush was far from a great primitive. Her paintings antedated the acknowledged primitive. They belonged on the walls of prehistoric caves. Perhaps if John *had* encouraged her ... encouragement might have given her the impetus to continue, but she knew that encouragement alone could never have created in her a talent she obviously did not have.

She eventually resorted to the familiar female pattern followed by frustrated wives of busy men. She decided to redecorate the house. This particular day she'd gone to town to buy some new curtain material. On the street in front of the Boston Store, Westfield's best department store, she met an old college chum, Glen Field, a former Ohio State football great whose fame and glamor had once punctured her girlish reserve.

Meeting her like this so many years later, even though the rigors of war had left him bald, and the battle with the world highly nervous, he still retained a certain glamor for her. They recalled all the fun, the gay, heedless, always improbable forays they'd been a part of, and most often the avid ringleaders. It was like opening the college year book, years later, at a time when you're particularly happy, for then you can recall the gay moments.

Glen had been married and divorced and was now selling a line of ladies' shoes on the road. She didn't question him too much about his job, although she did make one *faux pas* by jokingly asking him if he'd seen or read "Death of a Salesman." When she saw the strange hurt, or—what was it?—a desperate denying of the play's truth in his eyes, she turned to the past, a happier subject for him.

He loved to hear her rehash his football exploits almost as much as he loved to brag about them to anyone who would listen. A perennial collegian wearing his ribbons on his now fat chest, walking as though he were wearing padded football pants, his feet encased in cleat-soled shoes. Even when he talked, using his beef-like hands for explaining, illustrating, one could clearly visualize those hands wrapped round the old pigskin again.

The day she rediscovered him they went into a coffee shop to have lunch and she watched him pick up the French roll. He picked it up as he would a football he was about to pass to an end. She ducked slightly as though he were going to toss it over her head at the oncoming waitress. But, unaware of her analysis as well as his gestures, he calmly sliced the roll down the middle and slapped the butter on it, and she got the giggles. He laughed with her, thinking it was merely an outward expression of her happiness at having found him again.

After that they met two or three times. Every time he came to town that year he called her.

When she felt herself succumbing to desire again, desire for this man, who under normal circumstances, and particularly as he appeared then, would never attract her, she tried not to see him. She had the right thought. She had the inner strength. And then one day it happened. Not the consummation of desire, but the end.

They had gone to his rooms in the Starker Hotel to have a quick drink before she went home. He was leaving town that night and she had made up her mind never to see him again.

He had brought her a pair of sample shoes from New York, the first present, and after he mixed her a drink he gave her the shoes to try on.

He was stooping down, helping her on with the shoes. He took hold of her foot in his big hand. "Size four and a half." He held the foot aloft as though he were a sculptor of feet and hers were posing for an immortal statue.

She laughed. "You look like a sculptor," she said. "Remember, it's really a foot of clay."

"I always loved your feet," he said. "They're still beautiful. In school, I can remember your walking along the Long Walk toward the Psych building. You had a nine o'clock. I used to come along about then. Remember?"

She nodded, eagerly remembering.

"On my way to my nine o'clock at University Hall, I used to watch your feet clear down the walk until you turned off to the Psych building. I guess I was always late for my nine o'clock. It was your feet."

She laughed again. "It was your nine o'clock, English. And you were awful in English."

He had the new shoes on her feet, pressing here, pulling there, like a shoe salesman in a store. Then he suddenly looked up at her, his eyes bright as an eagle's, the glow in them on fire. She could actually see the red circles of fire rimming his pupils. His big, beefy hands were flailing out towards her. He was lunging at her.

She pushed on his big chest until he let go of her and then she kicked one of her shiny new shoes right in his face. The four-and-a-half-inch heel caught him in the eye. She began to laugh wildly.

"Now you'll have something to explain," she said. "Hit in the eye with a heel. Or should I say by a heel?"

His eye began to puff up. She'd kicked him with the power of a mule kick. His fat, pudgy face looked as though it were going to fold into a good cry. He got up off the bed and walked over to the dresser to look at himself in the mirror, to punch around his sore eye as he punched around ladies' feet.

It was all over. Anything she had felt for him was now smothered in a laugh. It had been a bear hug with psychotic undertones.

She took off the new shoes and put them back in the box and put her own shoes on. He was still looking at himself in the mirror when she stood up. He turned and walked into the bathroom to wash out the eye. He didn't seem to care now whether she stayed or left. He acted as though she had never really arrived.

She stuck her head through the open bathroom door. He was standing at the washbasin pouring some boric acid into an eyecup. "I can see now," she said, "why you became a *shoe* salesman."

She'd meant to say it with a laugh but it didn't come out that way. It sounded exactly as she felt—derisive and disgusted. She didn't care about hearing his rebuttal, if any, but as she went to leave she had a parting glance of him in the medicine cabinet mirror. He'd lowered a hot towel from his fat face and she knew she had hit a bull's eye, figuratively *and* literally. He was a fatuous sensualist with an abhorrent fetish which he had no intention of stifling. His look told her he knew that she knew.

She crossed the hotel room, picked up the new shoes, tossing them on the dresser as she crossed to the hall door. "Give the four and a half's," she raised her voice so that he could hear, "to someone else. With prettier feet. Some women will do anything for an ankle strap."

She slammed the hall door so hard that she shook the entire hotel in its ancient frame.

When she got home that night she was so nauseated that she couldn't eat her dinner. Where was her mind? Where was her reason? Her dignity? Her self-respect? Where were her frustrations leading her? Down perilous paths. In byways and alleyways. Guttersnipe sex. She didn't want that. For that she was not brought into the world, raised, bred, trained, taught, educated, smoothed, polished and stamped with the diploma of dignity.

All she wanted was what others wanted, too. All she wanted in the world was closeness and warmth, and she wasn't getting them from the right source, *John*. So she had been seeking them in an ersatz substitute. She wanted closeness and warmth and someone not only to love her physically but gently, someone who would be interested in her mundane activities, dull as they were. To listen when she talked. To smile when she smiled at them. To remember her with flowers and notes and promises that were kept.

And then suddenly Roger was there, brought by her own husband, incognizant John. Roger, epitomizing everything she'd been desiring. He was interested in her activities, uninspiring or not. He listened when she talked. He smiled when she was happy and was unhappy when she was sad. He had brought her a flower every morning they played tennis. And he loved her gently as well as physically. He knew just the right words to say, the right gestures to make, and when she was with him, blinded as she was by this, his human illusion, she firmly believed he was the man for her. When she was away from him she wasn't quite as sure. But then, paradoxically or humanly, and she knew that moral man is paradoxical, she couldn't stand being away from him.

And what was she going to do about it? Just what she was doing or trying to do. Forget about where it was going to end. Move along with the fast-moving stream. Head up. Out of the water. If the falls came, if the stream divided into a roaring ocean, then would be time enough to think about a life-saver, to figure a way out.

She'd always thought of herself as a person of integrity, forthrightness, that is, before the physical became such an issue in her life. She hadn't told John about the Finnish boy or Glen Field because she hadn't actually succumbed. She had fought those desires and had overcome them. But with Roger it was different. Her thoughts were so concentrated upon him that sensible, honest reactions were out of the question. He hadn't asked her to get a divorce, to leave John, to live with him—to marry him. And she didn't know, on her part, whether she actually wanted her freedom. It was much too early in their romance to ascertain this.

Roger never mentioned the triangle they were jammed in. On the contrary, his was an acceptance. If she'd stopped to analyze his attitude or him, if she could have been objective about him, which of course at this point she couldn't, she would have realized his was an acceptance all too casual. He, like the daredevil, prepared the pool, measured the distance, then leapt without looking. But, unlike the daredevil, he was cautious that his leaps were not too high and his water the right depth. He never took unnecessary chances. When it looked as though it might be developing into danger he turned in his key. And danger to him meant one thing, the usurpation of his freedom.

Of this Clara was, as yet, not aware.

She had planned on registering at the Welling, a midtown hotel where she and John had often stayed in the last ten years. She was to meet Roger later on at his hotel. If John had to get in touch with her it would be less unusual, less suspicious if she were at the Welling rather than a strange hotel.

Suspicious! She shuddered. What a horrible word. A word used by and for and concerning a criminal. If she played at this game long, wouldn't she, too, be a criminal? (Wasn't one of the Ten Commandments "Thou shalt not commit adultery"?) The stories were full of the results of these affairs. Suicides. Murders. Scandals. Broken homes. Ignominy.

What would happen to John's reputation if her and Roger's affair were found out in Westfield? He would have sympathy. She would be the villain. More importantly, what would happen to John inside? Oh why, oh why was she having these upsetting thoughts?

She suddenly realized she'd gone far back in her thinking, reliving a past that really had no meaning for the present, envisioning a precarious future that had not yet and might never arrive. Was it because of the long train ride to New York? Only three hours but it seemed like three years. She loved to ride in the train. She thought this day would be wonderful, a new May day, the beauty of the country in the spring. Spring seen through a train window, through eyes of desire. Her thoughts should be filled with the anticipation of this weekend.

Roger had gone on ahead and was no doubt already at the Alton Hotel, where their rendezvous was to be. Rendezvous! Clandestine! Words she'd seen over and over again in the scandal sheets ... "Their clandestine love has been uncovered, their rendezvous was a tiny love-nest" ...

It was the St. Christopher! She shouldn't have lost the St. Christopher. Everything would have been all right if she hadn't lost her good-luck charm. Luck! There was no such thing. One made his own luck. How could everything be all right when, according to society, it was all wrong? Society? What society? Whose society? Society as it is today? Rotten to the core!

Even her seat on the coach was unpleasant. There was a fat man next to her who smelled horribly of bay rum and the musty clothes smell of a suit that had been pressed too many times without cleaning. He went to sleep with his feet spread out on the seat opposite. His snores cut the humid air in the coach like a foghorn through a misty night.

The paper he had been reading was on the floor near her feet. She leaned over and picked it up. The headlines screamed at her, invisible fingers laying open her guilt: HUSBAND MURDERS WIFE'S LOVER!

Shuddering, she dropped the dreadful sentinel. She stood up, moving toward the center of the aisle. She walked to the front of the coach and got a drink of water. That wasn't what she wanted. She wasn't thirsty. She crumpled up the cup and dropped it in the refuse container. She took out her cigarettes, fumbling around in her bag for her lighter. She couldn't find it. She must have packed it with her things in her overnight case. She found a packet of matches in her purse and started for the observation platform. She had to have a cigarette and some fresh air. Or some fresh air and a cigarette. She *had* to clear her thoughts from this depressive thinking. She had to *stop* thinking. Thinking ruins everything.

As she arrived at the observation platform there was the sudden squealing of the train's brakes, the sickening crunch of the impact as the big locomotive came in contact with a vehicle. She fell against the glass door leading to the platform, which opened and deposited her outside on the platform in time to see a man's headless body dragged down the tracks after the train hit his truck at a crossing.

She became so ill that she scarcely had time to reach the ladies' room before the nausea struck in full force. She stayed in the restroom long after the train started again, after the tracks were cleared of bodies and debris.

They were over an hour late, but time made no difference to her now. It was as though she were crossing the turbulent English Channel, which she had done in her college days. The pit of her stomach came up to hit her under the chin and the lights in front of her eyes flickered like a spent neon sign and she wanted to die. When it was all over she had one of those frightful migraine headaches.

When she arrived at the Pennsylvania Station all of the joy she was to have felt at being in the world's most exciting city on the most exciting adventure was dissipated because of the grinding, blinding headache. She could scarcely see to hail a taxi. When she got one, she forgot for the moment where she was going. Oh, yes, the Welling. She gave the driver the name of the hotel and settled back in the seat and then the rain began. A thin rain at first that suddenly burst into a spring thunderstorm.

Instead of the rain depressing her more, it began to clear her head, to blot out the agony of that dirty, unhappy train ride, made unhappier by her anguished mental probings. Even her headache ceased. She opened the window of the cab, letting the rain slash against her hot face, cooling the fever within, and she remembered a poem from her youth:

> *"I walked in the rain last night*
> *It beat full down in my face....*
> *And a sense of oddness crept o'er me*
> *That I was one of an unknown race,*
> *That I was a child of the new-born rain*
> *And reared by the restless wind.*
> *As I walked I dwelt on this theory*
> *And have doubted my kith and kin...."*

Before they arrived at the Welling on East Fifty-fourth she was beginning to come alive again, to get tuned with the present, with New York, to pulsate with the excited, semi-hysterical beat of the city. Up Broadway to Forty-second. Yes, the people were still there queueing up in front of the theatres as though TV didn't exist. She looked down Forty-second. The burlesque houses, God bless them, still shouting their wares or lack of wares. Forty-third. Forty-fourth. Forty-fifth. Up that street toward Sixth, next to an Automat was the Hotel St. August where she and John had stayed on their first visit to New York together after their marriage, their first anniversary. They had stayed there because it was named St. August and the month was August and they were in love. A silly reason, but you do silly things when you're happy. The hotel was theatrical now and probably in the same state of self-respecting decay as it was then.

She and John had been too absorbed in each other to care about the cracks in the ceiling, the peeling paint, the worn steps, the elevator they lovingly christened the "lateavator." They had seen the ballet, gone to the Roxy, seen some Cornell play and one in which Helen Hayes was starred. She couldn't remember the names of either of the plays. They'd had late breakfast at the Automat, sighing over its wonderful coffee.

Why, oh *why* was she thinking of John again? Roger was whom she was supposed to be thinking about. Roger and the ecstasy that came when she was near him.

John must be thinking about her. That was it. Perhaps there was a bad storm upstate and he was worried about her.

Had she loved John a lot when she married him? Was that thrill the same as it was now with Roger? Less? More intense? She remembered she hadn't wanted to meet John. He was a blind date. On that first date she hadn't given him much thought; in fact, was slightly bored with his seriousness. But for some inexplicable reason she made two other dates with him. On the third date she realized that she loved him. She wasn't in love with him, as she told him, but she loved being with him more than anyone she'd met in years. After two or three more dates she realized she was in love with him and it had lasted eighteen years. And even now she couldn't say she didn't love him. She adored him. She couldn't contemplate what life would be without him. But life with him was not what she wanted either.

Why *had* this happened? Why had John shut himself away from her? Built a seemingly unscalable wall between them? She could have been happy the rest of her life with John if he'd only continued to want her physical closeness. "He had neglected to nourish the flowers of their love." That was a line she'd heard on a TV show the night before she met Roger. It was corny, but she remembered it because it was true.

Now that she was thinking about it, maybe John wasn't just tired physically, mentally. Maybe he was tired of her. Maybe he just hadn't forgotten to nourish their love, the little amenities that were important to him once not just neglected, not even thought about, because he was no longer in love with her. This was an angle she hadn't contemplated. But now that she thought about it in the light of John's character, if he did no longer love her, he would never admit it to her. He would go along quietly until something or other forced him to admit it. Because he could go along without love, probably for many years.

When had he begun to forget the thoughtful little things he used to do? It was their thirteenth wedding anniversary. He had forgotten it completely. When she reminded him of it he had seemed, not embarrassed, but annoyed. Annoyed with himself? Or with her? At that time she hadn't stopped to analyze which it was. She remembered he had sent out for some flowers. The anniversary before that he had picked out a present for her himself, the overnight case she was now carrying to New York.

After that anniversary his secretary remembered the date.

Yes, she knew he was busy on the book then, thinking about it constantly. But that year he continually refused to go out with her, either to dinner or to friends' homes. And yet there was the time when he refused to go that she'd come home and found he'd gone out to a school board meeting and dinner afterwards at his vice-principal's. And he'd never mentioned the affair to her.

Was she a fool? Did he have someone else he was seeing? No, she would have found out. It wasn't anyone else, she was sure of that. It was the book. She knew he spent most nights at the library. It was simply the fact that he didn't love her any longer. Surely that was it. Whenever they heard their piece playing "Easy to Love," she still got the same thrill as she had the night they met, when they first heard it played. But he didn't feel the same. She'd caught him on that. He didn't even remember the name of the song, and he would have if he still cared.

Were these really excuses she was inventing—these indications, so-called, of his lack of interest—excuses to cover her infidelity now? Oh, God help me, she prayed, to understand, to work this thing out the right way for all of us—for John, for Roger. For myself.

The taxi driver was waiting for her to get out of the cab, staring back at her through the open door. She paid him and moved, as in a trance, into the lobby of the Welling.

The desk clerk handed her a key and a message. The message read, "Eight o'clock, Room 515." It was from Roger. She looked at her watch. It was five o'clock. She would shower, then lie down for a few moments, collect her weary self before she met him.

She had felt that they shouldn't appear together in a public place since they all had friends in New York, so they were going to have dinner in his room at the Alton.

She could go to the room without causing any appreciable notice and in the morning she would leave and go back to her own hotel. But the morning would take care of itself. Tonight was the night.

Tonight *was* the night. Maybe she should use the old Coué System, repeat, repeat, repeat it until it became an actuality, until the thrill came back. Tonight is the night, Roger.

Anticipation? A tremor of fear? How would it work out? She hoped she would seem suave, sophisticated about the whole thing. She hadn't been with a man for a long time. But desire, she knew, has a beautiful habit of taking care of all of the details that might otherwise appear gauche.

2

There was still rain in the air and a slight breeze when she awakened at seven o'clock. Not meaning to sleep over an hour she had slept even after the desk clerk had called her. She had to hurry.

She caught a cab at exactly a quarter to eight. By the time she arrived at the Alton her heart was beating out of her body with excitement.

She didn't want a bellhop at the hotel to grab her overnight case, assuming she was a new guest, so she used a side entrance to the hotel and, without once glancing toward the desk, she searched for the stairs. She hurried up the stairs, shielding the overnight case as though it were a diplomatic briefcase full of stolen state secrets.

As she reached the fourth-floor staircase she passed a man standing in the shadows. She quickened her pace but he seemed as anxious to avoid her as she him. As she passed him he snapped the brim of his hat down, shading his face, but she got a fairly good look at him. Although she noticed him mainly because of his furtive attitude, once she looked into his face she was quite intrigued. Not in the way she was with Roger but because this man was so handsome. One of the handsomest men she ever saw. Then she smiled to herself, thinking, "Isn't it odd, when we see beauty in one man, when we are in love with beauty, we seem to see it in everything, or rather, we notice it in everyone else?"

She hurried on up to the fifth floor, stopping in front of the door marked 515, hesitating a moment before she knocked. "The time has come, the Walrus said ..."

But she didn't have to open the door. Roger had heard her and opened the door before she could reach out her hand. He pulled her forcibly into the room, because of the seeming reluctance on her part.

He took her in his arms. She laughed. "Don't knock my hat off," she said. Now wasn't that a stupid thing to say before the King? Her mind was full of nonsensical rhymes and fragmentary quotes from old books.

He released her and she took off her hat. She was looking at a wall mirror, fixing her hair, when she saw him slip her overnight case in the bedroom.

He came back into the living room smiling. "I've ordered a wonderful dinner," he said. "Squab. Wild rice. Champagne. Crêpe suzettes."

She sighed with pleasure and walked to the long windows. He had chosen an expensive suite overlooking the park. That was so indicative of him. Everything planned with finesse, with thought toward the beauty of the surroundings, the atmosphere. Central Park in the spring. Could anything be more beautiful seen now through the eyes of love?

The evenings were getting longer and, even though the darkened shadows fell across the trees, the lights were not all on yet. She could remember during the war, during the blackouts, how strange New York seemed. Gay cities without lights were like dead things, or blind men, strong still but groping in the dark unable to understand why they were crippled.

He came to the window, standing directly behind her. "'And now the red light fades swiftly ... and there are voices in the air, and somewhere music, and we are lying here, blind atoms in our cellar depths ... and while we lie here at evening and the river flows and dark time is feeding like a vulture on our entrails and we know that we are lost and cannot stir ...!"

She turned, shuddering perceptibly. "How morbid. What is that?"

He smiled. "Thomas Wolfe. I was trying to remember something he said about New York. Something beautiful. But instead those lines came to me from *Death to Morning.*"

"Don't," she said. "Think of something light. Poetry. Do you know any poetry? How about Elinor Wylie? 'Angels and Earthly Creatures'? Or does anyone read poetry nowadays?"

He grinned. "Elinor Wylie?"

> *"The whole of him except his heart*
> *Was lying straight and still,*
> *And that was pulling his ribs apart*
> *To climb the top of a hill.*
> *"Get up, get up, the sheets are clean;*
> *The pillow is smooth and even;*
> *Climb the hill for we have not seen*
> *One half our fill of heaven."*

She laughed, delighted. "Oh, you do know Elinor Wylie. That was 'Robin Hood's Heart.' I haven't remembered it since I was—well, quite eighteen. A freshman in college. 'Robin Hood's Heart,'" she sighed, remembering.

He took her in his arms. "Your heart. Mine."

He held her close to him. She was frightened again and wanted to pull away, but when he started to kiss her the fear left and she gave herself to the kiss, the caress. Suddenly he was unfastening the neck of her dress. She tried to protest but the look in his eyes warned her. It was a different Roger she was seeing now. Passion was reddening his face, causing his eyes to be mere slits fastening on her like the eyes of a vulture watching its prey. She pulled away, backing into the bedroom.

"Don't, Roger. Please! Not now."

He followed her. Pulling down the blinds in the bedroom he turned to her again. He pulled her to him and began kissing her face, her eyes, her neck, her breasts. In John's most abandoned moments he had done nothing like this. Then came mounting tension until the crisis of their desire.

The exhaustion of it caused her to sleep and when she awoke later on Roger was gone, but he had thrown the blanket over her.

She got up quickly. It was very dark in the room. How long had she slept? Where were her clothes? In the closet neatly hung up. She called, "Roger …"

His voice answered her from the next room. "Here, darling. Get dressed. Dinner will be up in a second."

"What time is it?"

"Almost ten o'clock."

She had slept longer than she realized. She went into the bathroom to shower. In a few minutes she came out to him again. She was dressed but he was in a pair of slacks and a smoking jacket. Maybe she should have just worn her robe. She hadn't even opened her overnight case. Still it was really better for her to be dressed when the waiter arrived with the dinner.

He was smiling at her. "Will you forgive me?" he said. "But I've been waiting a long time."

"It was better that way," she said. "It gave me less time to think."

He laughed and handed her a lighted cigarette. "We have the entire weekend. And it still won't be long enough."

They sat for a few minutes watching the lights of the city. They sat side by side near the window, but he didn't take her hand, didn't touch her. He was polite and charming, gentle, romantic, but his forcefulness was gone. It was as though friend and friend sat side by side in the gathering twilight ... "The friendliest of lovers and the loveliest of friends ..."

Roger was no new hand at this game. Had she known what he was thinking, had she been able to fathom the psychology of this moment as far as he was concerned she would have realized, and perhaps shockingly, that this was all part of the plan, that it didn't just happen, that this was the way he had it worked out. He knew women, or thought he did. One did not strain his masculinity to extremes with some women. Clara was not the ordinary type of woman who goes to men's rooms. He knew it had been a long time since she had had anything to do with the physical and in eighteen years she had never known or would not, at this late stage, know the kind of physical love he was capable of giving. Had he waited she might have allowed her fear to mount and turn into a sudden revulsion. So this was his psychology and he knew it would work.

Although she fascinated him, although his mind had never really been free of her since the night he met her, his pattern of love-making remained the same as it had always been with the many women before her. He had never married because of the self-knowledge of his restlessness, variability. But it had never made him cease to search for the woman who might be his partner in life, even now, now when he was past forty. At this point he didn't know whether Clara was the one, didn't particularly care, hadn't given it much thought because, if it were to be, later events would drop into their proper places.

There was a knock on the door. It was the waiter with their dinner. Roger opened the door and the waiter wheeled in the cart. Clara stood in the doorway looking out into the hall. A man was entering the room next door. He was a heavily set man around fifty, rather flashily dressed, an expensive diamond glittering on his little finger. He stopped to wipe the perspiration from his flushed forehead and that's when he saw her in the doorway. He smiled at her. She didn't return the smile, shutting the door quickly. Afterwards she wondered why she hadn't smiled in return. Wasn't that stupid? Rather, it was selfish. The poor man must think her very rude. But, attractive as was the man she'd seen previously on the stairs, this fat man was ugly. She didn't want to think about ugliness, now.

Had she analyzed her thoughts more closely, had she had time to analyze her thoughts by taking a moment more away from her concentration upon Roger, she would have realized that when one is in love she does not necessarily see beauty in everything or everyone. She merely notices beauty in the *beautiful* which she had not consciously noted before. When one is happy, walking with head up, eyes wide open, smile ready, the horizon is larger and the beauty of detail more vivid.

Roger was helping the waiter set up the table. It was all there, from the one rose in the bud vase, the caviar hors d'oeuvre, through to the champagne and Grand Armagnac brandy afterwards.

A dinner she would surely never forget. It was a passing thought, but had she actually known how this night would be imprinted in her brain, how it would color her future, she wouldn't have waited for the squab and wild rice to be served. She wouldn't have even waited to pick up her overnight bag. She would have run out of the hotel. She would have rushed home into the arms of security, safety, with the speed and swiftness of a winged Mercury.

There is and always will be more to consider than just ourselves, regardless of how well guarded our secret moments seem to be. Though Roger and Clara could not be fully cognizant of the outside world, it was there and, before they could stop it, it would soon envelop them both in its tentacles of destruction. No one is safe. Locked doors, barred, mountains so high few can climb, the waste spaces of the desert—there is no place where one can hide today. From the outside world. Isolationism is an idea only. From the past.

They had finished their dinner and were having their brandies. It was around eleven o'clock. They had talked about everything they seemed to have in common and then for want of conversation she began telling him about the man she had seen in the hall.

"He tried to avoid me, I'm sure. Pulled his hat down around his face so that I couldn't see him. Aren't people odd?"

He smiled. "Now, of course, I wonder why he did that, too. We'll probably never know."

"It's like looking at people on crowded trains or in buses. They have little furtive movements. They do odd out-of-the-way things. You wonder what makes them tick and why their reactions are as they are. One day I was riding in a bus down Fifth Avenue and there was a young boy sitting next to me carrying a squarish sort of box. Like a box from a toyshop. There was something ticking in the box. At first I thought it was a clock. Then I thought maybe it was a bomb. Several people began to hear it and watch the young man. He knew it and every so often passed shy, secret smiles to a girl up the aisle from him. She would nod at him, as though only they shared the secret. After suspicion had been completely aroused, they got off and went on their, I suppose, merry way. And no one ever found out what it was about."

He laughed. "And it was best for you not to try to find out. If you had said anything they would have held you for a witness. That is, if it had been an explosive or something like that the boy was carrying. Or you might have been bumped off for identifying the chap. Like the guy who turned in that crook, Willie Sutton, 'The Actor'. He was murdered for his trouble."

"It's best," she said, "to live completely within your small circle, because when you step out even to give aid, you're in quicksand, aren't you?"

"That's why," he said, "I never hang around the scene of an accident or any kind of confusion. You know, like you see all the time. There's always someone wanting to give his name. I run. And I would in extreme cases. Even if I knew. Even if I had seen something. It's none of my business. My motto is 'leave well enough alone.' I'm well enough when I'm alone." He got up to pour her some more coffee. "Well, we're safe now, my love, from the outside world. For the moment. And the moment is all that counts. Yesterday's gone. Tomorrow never happens. So we have today. This moment's all we've got. And nothing can take that away from us."

But his philosophy lost its proper effect. It was punctured very quickly. For he'd no sooner said this than they were startled by the crash of glass, followed by the sound of a window slamming shut. It was like a sudden shot, the sound of the window. Clara jumped up, fear on her face.

He shook his head, smiling. "It—it was nothing, Clara. Only a window in the next room. It's quite windy tonight."

Then they heard the shots. Two of them. One on top of the other.

"*Those* were shots, Roger!" This time she grabbed at her throat as though the next ones would be aimed at her.

Roger, alarmed now, had risen and was starting for the door.

"Don't open it!" she shouted.

But he'd already opened it. A man was running past the door, a snap-brim hat pulled down around his face. Roger ran out into the hall, staring after the man. He noted briefly that the man was carrying a black overnight case. He turned toward the room next to his. The door was open. He stepped into the room.

On the bed lay the fat man who'd smiled at Clara, his pajama top open, showing an enormous expanse of hairy chest, like some waste desert. Streams of blood flowed from two holes, one in the man's chest and one in his abdomen. That the man was dead Roger had little doubt. He turned and ran back into his own room. He shut and locked the door.

Clara was still standing where he'd left her, as though she were unable to move, as though rigor mortis had finally set in, in her body, too.

"Get your overnight case!" He barked the order to her. "In the bedroom!" A general on the field of action. "You've got to get out of here. Quick!"

They heard the sound of doors now, opening up and down the hall, of feet running toward the room next door.

"Someone was shot, Roger? Tell me!"

He nodded, hurrying past her into the bedroom to get her suitcase, since she didn't seem to have the power to do it herself. He came back like a runner in a tag race, passing the suitcase to her. She dropped it on the floor at her feet. He turned her round as though she were a marionette and began helping her on with her coat, which he'd brought from the bedroom closet.

"You mustn't stay here, Clara. You've got to get out! If it's murder, if you're here, if *we're* here, we'll be questioned. And I'd really be in Dutch. I used a phony name when I registered."

She stared at him, wide-eyed.

"To protect you, both of us," he explained.

"Oh, my God!" She began to come to. "I knew it'd end like this. I just knew. I had a premonition after I lost my St. Christopher this morning."

"Premonitions be damned! Things like this happen sometimes. Who can help it? A stupid, ignorant superstition didn't cause it. It—it just happened. Who the hell knows why?" Roger's nerves were showing, too. "Go on. Get going! It'll save us a lot of trouble if you're not found here. They'd slap our names over all the front pages. We'd make a hell of a story, too."

"What are *you* going to do?" She seemed to be a silent figure in a sea of flames. There didn't really seem to be an exit.

He pushed her toward the door. "Never mind about me. I'll get out, too."

The phone started to ring. "Don't answer it," he shouted.

She certainly had no intention of answering it. He opened the door to the hall.

"Oh, Roger!" She was on the verge of hysteria. "*Why* did it have to end this way?"

"Go on, Clara. Don't look back! Remember Lot's wife. She looked back and was turned into a pillar of salt."

She nodded but she was in no mood to comprehend parables. She stepped gingerly into the hall. There were ten or twelve people already congregated at the victim's door. She could hear the word "murder" running through the murmur of the crowd. Her terrified face showed such confusion she didn't seem to know which way to go. God! She'd never get out!

What had happened? *What* had happened? And why, *why, why? Why?*

"Go back to your own hotel." Roger lowered his voice. "Don't stop for anything."

She nodded again, pushing her way through the gathering crowd, easing herself towards an empty space near the elevators.

Roger shut the door to the room and lit a cigarette, trying to get control of himself. If he hung around he'd naturally be questioned. So close to the murder they'd want to know what he saw, what he heard. He'd have to get out before they caught him, too. With the alias, with not being able to explain Clara, it would be hell to pay. They'd make a front-page story out of him and Clara.

The excitement was now sweeping along the halls, more of the curious arriving, pushing their eager way to death's door, desiring a surreptitious peep at death, but not their death, of course, someone else's.

The elevator had arrived and was emitting a cage full of official-looking men, excitement marking their faces also. Clara tried to push her way through the men, into the elevator, but the men staring at her rudeness frightened her.

She turned from the elevator and ran swiftly down a corridor where she thought the stairs should be. But she had run into a darkened corridor, a dead end with a fire escape ahead. The only light was from the fire escape sign.

She turned to run back the other way and as she did so she bumped into a man. The impact of their bodies was so forceful that she dropped her overnight case. She reached around on the darkened floor, found the case, then straightened up. The man was staring at her, his cruel face confronting her frightened one. She gasped. It was the good-looking man she had previously seen on the stairway. Only now he wasn't so handsome. His face was full of hate and fear. An evil face, his mouth curling sadistically at the corners, his eyes mere slits of anger. He took hold of her arm roughly, his grasp paining her. He shoved her against the wall.

"Get out!" His words were a low snarl.

She began to back down the hall. She watched him stoop down and pick up his overnight case, then run toward the window with the lighted fire escape sign above. As he stepped out on to the fire escape he turned back, giving her a brief parting glance. Viciousness had crowded all beauty from his face. His look said that if he had time he'd see to it this woman who bumped into him would never bump into another person. But there was no time. For either of them. Footsteps. Shouts. Closer. Coming closer.

The man turned and ran down the fire escape. And Clara, not fully cognizant, turned again in search of the stairway.

As soon as she reached the safety of the street in front of the hotel she looked at her watch. It wasn't too late to get the last train to Westfield. But what would she tell John? She had seen no shows, bought nothing. Not even a memento for him.

She hesitated a moment, glancing back towards the hotel. The lobby was filling with policemen. They were pouring out of cars parked at the curb. People were running, following the murmur. She turned to hail a taxi. As she turned she bumped into a man. This was getting tedious. Bumping into people. She was losing her sense of direction, of equilibrium. The man tipped his hat apologetically, peering into her frightened face. She must get away from the Alton before someone grew suspicious.

She began to run toward Fifth Avenue. This time she really lost her equilibrium and hit the side of a building, knocking the wind out of her. She stopped to get her bearings. A taxi driver saw her and pulled up to the curb. She climbed gratefully into the cab. Once inside she relaxed a little. In relaxing she began to go over what had just happened, to envision the ensuing possibilities if Roger were questioned. She was sure he wouldn't mention her name, but what if they held him as a witness or something? If they thought you'd seen anything and didn't want to talk, they had ways of making you talk. They could make a tongue-tied man talk.

But Roger was clever. He'd get out of the hotel before he was caught. She knew that. She *had* to know that. She mustn't think about what had happened, what might happen. She must not *think!* She must not even ask why. That was thinking. Blank out your mind, Clara. Shut the door. Pull down the steel blinds covering the iniquity, the resultant fear.

You've done it before. You can do it again.

What did she really want now? She wanted *security*. She had had a narrow escape. The handwriting on the wall was all too apparent. Security was all that she wanted. Who has time for sex when his life is in danger? There's only one thing more important than love: self-preservation, which includes the desire for permanent safety.

As she entered the Welling lobby she stopped by the cigar stand. She would buy John a new pipe as a present. She picked out one she thought he'd like, a meerschaum, German made, with a large bowl. He didn't have one like that.

She paid for the pipe and walked to the desk. She stopped to ask the clerk about trains to Westfield. The clerk looked at her anxiously.

"What's the matter, Mrs. Harris? Are you ill?"

"Ill?" Yes! Yes, that was it. She was ill. She would be ill. It was an excellent excuse. She stepped to one side, peering at herself in a wall mirror. Her face was drawn and white. She didn't look ill. She looked dead.

"Yes," she said in her still frightened voice. "I *am* ill. Would you put a call through to my husband in Westfield? I'll take it in my room."

"I could call the house doctor."

"No. No, thank you. I'll be all right. But I don't think I'll be able to complete my vacation. I must go home."

The clerk nodded understandingly, sad with other people's sorrows. Thirty-five years a hotel clerk, listening to everything from senility's whine to youth's wail. His own sorrows, regrets and joys so mixed up with the guests that he no longer knew what it was he was sad or happy about.

She hurried to her room. When she entered, the phone was already ringing. John's voice sounded as anxious as the clerk's face looked. Should he drive in after her? No, the papers said there might be storm. She would take the last train. He could meet her at the station.

She hung up and took her first steady breath. Then she called the desk clerk. He said she could just make it to the station if she left at once. She grabbed her coat and overnight case and ran to the door.

She got to Pennsylvania Station just three minutes before the last train for Westfield pulled out. Her escape seemed to be completed. But what about Roger?

She didn't have time to buy an extra, but she didn't suppose the story had broken yet.

Besides Roger's problem *she* had a serious one to consider. She'd seen the man at the fire escape, perhaps the murderer. No doubt he was the murderer. She'd seen him making his getaway down the fire escape. She figured she was probably the only person who had seen him who could clearly identify him. This was a problem for her conscience alone.

The man had perhaps killed someone. He should be apprehended. If the someone he had killed had been her husband or brother or lover she would want to see him apprehended, would feel strongly about it, would feel that people should help if they had the ability or knowledge. But how could she, in this instance, be an informer? Unless her name were kept out of it. There was no possible way for her to go to the police, for she felt sure the police would not keep her name out of it. And it would involve everyone, John, Roger, herself. If they never caught the murderer, three reputations would have been ruined. All for nothing. Yet, with her description of the man, they might stand a chance of catching him or knowing who he was.

She knew that John, in her place, regardless of the circumstances, would go to the police. Roger, in her place, would keep quiet. He had told her so. He had said, "I leave well enough alone."

But Clara? What was she going to do? She was going to wait. Like Scarlett, she was going to think about it in the morning. She had made enough decisions for one night. "Pull down the blind again, Clara. Pull it down."

3

No one would have figured Mike Grant for a gunman or a petty crook or—a murderer, and yet he'd just murdered a man in room 518 in the Alton Hotel.

Mike's B.A. was Columbia, School of Journalism. He hadn't been a very good pupil, or an imaginative writer, although his Short Story Prof was quite pleased with his talent until the national magazine to which he sold a short story discovered that it was a steal, almost verbatim, from one they'd published twenty years before, written by a top writer, since deceased. Mike swore he'd never seen the aforementioned magazine, was much too young at the time to be able to read. But the magazine took him to court. The case was settled by his returning the money to the magazine and the magazine's writing an apology to its readers and in defense of the dead writer. Mike was thrown out of school but later reinstated. He graduated without honors. No *cum laude* he. And what few friends he had were irreconcilable.

None of this tended to make him particularly bitter. He had so many assets, he felt. He had a profile that would put a Greek god to shame. He had a degree in his pocket that would never make him a millionaire, but he had youth, intelligence and inventiveness on his side. And he had a strange and wonderful imagination, even though he couldn't write. It wasn't that he couldn't write. He didn't really want to write. He'd discovered that it was hard work, unglamorous. What fun could a guy have in life with the seat of his pants constantly glued to the seat of a chair? And yet he'd taken up journalism because it interested him. The interest, sadly enough, hadn't remained at a fever pitch.

Whatever he chose to do after college he knew wouldn't hurt his family, because his family consisted of one father, a father who very seldom saw him and when he did his greeting was a cocktail and his au revoir a small check. Mike's mother had passed on when he was two and the grandmother who raised him only lived to see him enroll in Junior High. From that time on, around the age of twelve, Mike was on his spectacular own.

When the thought of his childhood assailed him at all, a dark brown taste, as nasty as the paregoric he used to have to take, welled up in his throat and he felt as if he might have to vomit.

He never liked his grandmother. She was old and cross and no longer understood the ingenious or rebellious, and he was both. She had not, he realized when he grew older, been a very happy woman. Her husband had left her years before and she never even found out where he'd gone. But, as Mike selfishly rationalized, she wasn't very bright. Nor did she ever attempt to improve her mind. He figured that was why her husband had left her, so she deserved her martyrdom.

He was glad that she died, releasing him. But the funeral had come on a most unfortunate day, the day of a school picnic. There were to be egg races, and foot races and sack races, many opportunities for him to glorify himself with his prowess, to impress the teachers and pupils who were not usually impressed with him. He hated the funeral proceedings with such intensity that he vowed he would never, as long as he lived, in any manner whatsoever outwardly or inwardly, pay tribute to the dead again.

His father had come to Woodmere, Long Island, where he and his grandmother lived, bringing with him his second wife, who acted like Mike felt, as though death had been very thoughtless to interrupt her usual routine, whatever that was. And Mike never found out, because, shortly after he went to live with his father in New York City, his father and stepmother (if she could even be deified with that description) were divorced. And again Mike was glad of the release from what would have obviously been another tyrannical domination.

His father? Mike had no grouse concerning his old man. When he thought about him at all he thought of him as an inanimate object, useful as money is useful, but easily dismissed.

His father was home so seldom that Mike, from the age of puberty, practically lived alone. Because of his innate ingenuity he was quite capable of living alone and plotting his daily life alone. He could even cook his own meals. He kept the house as neat as though he were a young girl with a natural mother instinct.

Mike's father in his selfish way was proud of Mike and, when he brought any of his business associates home for a cocktail and dinner that their part-time maid stayed to cook, Mr. Grant pointed out Mike's cleverness. "A good boy," he used to say. "Best ever born. Never causes me a minute of trouble." He had apparently never heard of the adage, "Still waters run deep."

When his father would compliment him, Mike would smile boyishly, his handsome face lighting up, diffusing its glow, spilling over on to the fatuous guests its fatal charm. The women, in particular, were fascinated with the boy.

Seeing that his father quickly turned to other subjects, Mike would excuse himself and go to his room.

But who studies little boys' eyes for that flicker of derisive humor? Who has time to pick at their brains, lay open the devious, devilish subterfuges?

Mike cooked because he was inventive and liked to make up things; making up new dishes was a part of it. And, more importantly, he cooked because he got hungry when the maid wasn't there, when his father was having dinner out, which was most of the time. Having few friends, and trying to believe he didn't need them, he was very seldom invited to other children's homes for dinner. This, outwardly, didn't seem to bother him, but there were times, in his bed, alone in the apartment, when he cried himself to sleep from hurt that he was not understood. The hurt left, but the pride remained, a fierce pride bottled up so tightly that it was taken to be arrogance. And it was a form of arrogance, for he felt that others should understand his great genius, whatever it was, without his having to give of himself to others.

He kept things neat, particularly his own room, because he gave attention to the details that interested him, and because he was a natural planner. Plans must be kept clear of extraneous details. Plans must add up, neatly, if they are ever to work.

And Mike was good, if one may call it that, because he was a thinker. Whatever he did that was bad he was able to cover up with his outward charm and his quietude of person. There were many things he did wrong, but even in school he had the faculty of getting out of things, being able to toss the blame elsewhere.

To say that at an early age he developed a wonderful self-sufficiency but no sense of morals is not quite right. Rather, it went farther back than that. He was a hybrid. He was born where devils mated at the crossroads and no one ever came along to chart him another path. His warmth, if it were there, if it were ever to be there, whatever it was reserved for, had not as yet appeared in his life.

When he graduated from college, having no past to dwell lovingly upon, a present as empty as the look he sometimes got in his steel-blue eyes, he settled down immediately to work out his future.

Women could be had when desired or when necessary. A wife would get in his way and children were something he didn't understand, having never been a child, so the cozy love nest, the wedding cottage, were as dull as eating at a cafeteria every day.

His father magnanimously and without malice aforethought gave him one year to get on a paying basis. In that year he had to plan his future and that future must consist of money enough to travel first-class the rest of his life.

The year seemed scarcely long enough to plan a lifetime career as carefully as he usually planned the pleasurable things, but if he buckled down he could manage it.

He was sure that, when his father died, the extravagant way he lived, he would leave only debts, so Mike knew that to live the rest of his life in the manner in which he wished he would have to make his own money in a more or less illegitimate way. He might have chosen a legitimate way but it would have taken him too long.

He didn't have enough of a stake to gamble and he was really a poor gambler in the accepted sense, that is, when it came to games of chance and so forth. He could probably get away with a bank holdup but there was too much danger in that. There was the risk of having to kill, which as yet he didn't wish to contemplate. There was the more dangerous risk that the receipts from one holdup would not be enough and he'd have to stage a couple more. Con games, gigoloing, society stickups were out because he didn't want to mix with the public. He didn't make friends as easily as one should for that type of racketeering.

He knew there was a good market for stolen gems in South America and this appealed to him. He wanted to travel, and one of the places he wanted to go to was South America. A jewel robbery or diamond robbery in the trade would be the answer.

If he were to execute a diamond robbery in the trade he would have to know his stones well, his markets, his merchants in New York.

A diamond robbery fascinated him. Anybody could hold up some loaded dowager and lift her jewels, individual as they were and easily traced.

But cut, unset diamonds. That was different. They would be easy to sell in South America. But what steps should he take first?

He went to the public library and crammed on gemology and the art of the lapidary. He studied stones in the raw. He memorized the types of cuts, how they were cut. He studied the particular diamonds that were rare. He learned where the finest gems were found, how they were mined, where the markets were, how sold and how priced.

Armed with this knowledge, he toured the finest New York jewelry shops looking for a job as salesman. A store on Madison Avenue, Buckingham Ltd., hired him because of his knowledge of gems.

Buckingham's created their own jewelry in their workshops, and this was a break for Mike because in that way he could get to know the diamond sellers from the downtown market.

Diamond merchants walk the street loosely carrying fortunes in diamonds. Sometimes in packets, sometimes in cases, more than likely in their coat pockets rattling around like marbles in a little boy's hip pocket.

After a few months working at Buckingham's, Mike discovered that a man by the name of Max Burnsides from Baltimore was one of the best diamond men in the trade, sold to the biggest houses and no doubt carried with him a great amount of unset diamonds. He began to watch for him and each time he came into the store he made it a point to talk to him, ask him questions relevant to the trade, showing his interest in the profession.

One day the two men were able to have lunch. Mr. Buckingham, owner of the store, was not able to keep a luncheon appointment with Burnsides. Mike, knowing this, asked Burnsides to lunch with him. It took a little nerve for a salesman to ask one of their buyers to lunch, but lack of nerve had never stopped Mike before.

Burnsides, affable and pleased with Mike's friendship, insisted upon taking Mike to lunch. They went to a crowded restaurant off Thirty-fourth Street. Mike, hating crowds, was annoyed with the man for dragging him clear to Thirty-fourth from Fifty-first and Madison, but Burnsides had been adamant.

"In this restaurant," he said, "they have the best corned beef in town. I want you to have the privilege of eating the best corned beef in town."

Mike hated corned beef; but this day his charm had to be turned on full force if he were going to be able to find out from Burnsides what was uppermost on his, Mike's, mind.

"I love corned beef," he told Max and tried to mean it.

They had to wait for a table and, when they found one, it was in a small corner of the restaurant near the kitchen door. The heat from the greasy kitchen and the noise of the garrulous voices of the ego-ridden merchandising men, commonly known in the trade as salesmen, were doubly irritating to Mike. It seemed as though things had not started out well at all. He wanted to ask Burnsides a lot of important questions concerning the diamond trade, leading to the opening he desired, and a Thirty-fourth Street hash house wasn't exactly conducive to an exchange of confidences.

But, as soon as they had ordered, Mike realized he needn't bewail the atmosphere. Burnsides, himself, was garrulous and loud and loved to talk, apparently oblivious of everyone around him. Good fodder for the pitchfork with which the wily Mike was going to prod him.

He waited until they'd eaten their corned beef special and Burnsides was slopping up his custard dessert to begin his third degreeing.

"You—you sell to all the biggest shops, don't you, Mr. Burnsides?"

"Ummh?" Burnsides looked up from his custard. As he did so his tie trailed in what remained in the dish.

Mike quickly grabbed a napkin and tried to help him take the custard off the tie.

Burnsides laughed. "I should never wear ties. My wife buys me flowered ones. For that reason. She says if I spill anything on them the spots won't show so much."

Mike tried to join him in the laugh, but the man nauseated him, so it was difficult to see anything funny in the situation.

"Yes." Burnsides finally answered Mike's question. "I sell only to wholesale houses. Except shops like Buckingham's and Campbell's. I sell directly to them my cut stones. They get the first choice. Otherwise I sell to wholesalers. You know my diamonds. I have the best. I am one of the few individual American buyers who are allowed to get in on the best buys from De Beers. You understand how that works?"

Mike nodded. "I know De Beers have a monopoly on the diamond business, on the mining."

"We aren't allowed, the buyers," Burnsides said, "to pick out our diamonds, even see the rough material. It comes in packages. We buy the lot and take what's in it. I have always got very fine rough material."

"How," Mike said, "would a person like myself be able to become a stone man, that is a diamond merchant? Like you."

Burnsides laughed, taking a gold-headed toothpick from his pocket. "You buy from me."

He put the toothpick in his mouth and began to explore the bridgework. Mike had to turn his head away to keep from getting ill.

"You buy from me, diamonds, already cut. I have the best diamond cutters cut for me. Unless you had the capital," he winked a granulated eyelid, "and it would have to be a big capital and you'd have to have the in, too, which would be almost impossible to get." He shook his head. "You buy the cut diamonds from Maxie here. If you want to handle sapphires, rubies, emeralds, gem stones, you buy elsewhere. From other reputable dealers or houses."

"It doesn't sound very encouraging to a man with little capital, does it, Mr. Burnsides?"

Burnsides shrugged, "You have no chance, my boy, to buy raw stuff on the market. It's better to buy the cut stones from me."

He suddenly reached in his pocket and pulling out a white paper, opening it carelessly, his food-stained hands still unwiped, he displayed a small lot of diamonds. "Like these."

They were brilliant cut, blue whites. Their fire was like a sacrificial fire to Mike, beckoning him on, into the furnace, into the melting-pot of desire. He reached out to touch them.

Burnsides' laugh came out like the cackle of a cocky rooster. Quickly he pulled the packet of diamonds toward himself, out of Mike's reach. Almost, it seemed to Mike, as if it were done on purpose, as if he didn't trust Mike.

He folded the paper, closing it. "There are only sixty carats in this package. Some two and three pointers for small rings. Pretty good blue whites though. Around three hundred, four hundred dollars a carat. These will be made into wedding rings. For Campbells, Inc."

"They're beautiful," Mike said.

Burnsides shrugged again. "Nothing. Nothing at all, my friend. Not the finest." He put the paper back in his outside coat pocket.

Mike watched him closely. This man was just asking to be robbed.

"You—you carry the stones—you carry them like that? In your coat pocket? Aren't you—? Well, it seems foolish...."

Mike stopped. Maybe he was talking too much. He looked over at Burnsides. He was waving to a friend in the restaurant, apparently not even listening to Mike. It was a good thing the man wasn't a listener. If he were a listener he wouldn't talk as much. And people who don't listen are the easy ones to fool.

But Burnsides fooled Mike. He suddenly turned back towards him. "Diamond men, like myself, most of us are funny creatures, Mike," he said. "We have our idiosyncrasies. I think after you carry around stuff like this for so long, it becomes routine. You think no more about it than a kid carrying around a collection of worthless jack-knives. I figure this way. If I'm gonna get it I'll get it. I could carry my most expensive stones in a steel case or in a locked leather case, and I do when I have, say, two or three hundred thousand dollars' worth." Mike couldn't keep his eyes from bulging. "Like I'll bring with me in May. But so what? Somebody could crack me on the head at a busy intersection." He looked out of the window nodding toward Thirty-fourth. "Like this. And if it was my unlucky day I'd get it. A friend of mine got it that way. High noon. Busy street. They clunked him over the head with a lead pipe. Robbed him, of course, and got away in the crowd."

"What happened to him?"

"Him? Oh, he recovered. The diamonds were insured."

"Did they—get the guys?"

"I don't know. I never followed the case. The police? You know, smart like the little foxes, all dead." He laughed and looked at his watch. "I gotta get back to the Alton. I got an appointment in twenty minutes."

"You didn't answer my question completely, Mr. Burnsides. How do I start in this business?"

"Oh." Burnsides was lighting a cigar and trying to get his fat body out of the chair at the same time. "I tell you, Mike. When you get ready to move into the wholesale end of it, I'll send you to various houses, get you introduced around. Buckingham's won't like that, will they?" He grinned as though he had a big secret he was dying to share.

"Oh, I don't know. I guess I've done pretty well there."

"They like you, Mike. I've heard 'em talking. The old man, Buckingham, thinks you're a smart fellow. He told me so. College graduate and all that. Good knowledge of stones. Well, we'll see. When you're ready. If that's what you want." He finished the speech on the way to the door.

Mike, tagging him, couldn't keep what was definitely a triumphant smile off his insolent face. Smart, Burnsides? Much smarter than Mr. Buckingham even thinks I am.

"Thanks for the lunch, Mr. Burnsides," he said. "I'll remember this place the next time I want some corned beef."

With the knowledge from Burnsides anent his habits, and gleaned so quickly, so without a struggle, gleaned from a fatuous, stupid, fat fool, Mike felt his plan couldn't fail. Knowing Burnsides stayed at the same hotel on every trip, Mike moved to the Alton three months later, in January.

In February he quit Buckingham's, telling them he was leaving for South America. He got his passport and was ready to go on a moment's notice. He waited out the two and a half months till Burnsides' arrival in the Alton, carefully avoiding anyone from Buckingham's who might recognize him.

On May 11th he was sitting in the lobby of the hotel when he saw

Burnsides enter. He supposed that somewhere on his person or in his luggage were the diamonds he had told him about, $350,000 worth of blue whites, whites, yellows and a few blacks which had been expressly ordered by Buckingham's. Mike had to get to Burnsides before he hit the trade and sold any of the diamonds.

He had made himself thoroughly familiar with the hotel, so when Burnsides registered he found out where his room was, cased the layout, and then waited for his moment.

A few months before he had bought himself a forty-five with no particular intention of using it, but he felt he had to have that added protection.

He would wait until he was sure Burnsides was sleeping, climb the fire escape from his room to Burnsides', enter the window, case his luggage and his clothes for the diamonds, and be out of the room and back in his own room before Burnsides should even awaken.

The actual theft seemed so simple it hardly needed a plan. It was so simple it bothered Mike a little. By hard study and a job he'd hated, selling, by superior psychology he'd come to this point and now it all seemed so easy. Perhaps that was the way with long-planned, well-executed jobs. The actual job was a breeze because of the previous plans. And because of the superior intellect of the planner. Oh yes, and because of a bit of Irish luck, the fact that the guy Mike picked was too loquacious for his own good, and artless, an artless man who made no game of deceiving. So, according to the facts, nothing should have gone wrong with Mike's plans. Absolutely nothing at all!

Burnsides had gone to his room at ten and had apparently gone to bed at once, for the lights in the room had gone out by 10:15. Mike had passed the door and had seen the lights go out. He went down to his own room and waited until eleven. He checked his gun, then began his climb up the fire escape, three floors to Burnsides' room window. The window was open. To reach in and unhook the screen was a cinch.

He could see the big man on the bed, his pajama top unbuttoned, a great expanse of hairy chest and fat stomach heaving with sleep. His snores were so loud that it seemed as though they would be heard in the next room.

Mike climbed in the window, stood, waited. No movement from the bed. There was indication that Burnsides might have taken a sleeping pill. A small box on the night table by the bed, next to it a glass of water. He had told Mike he usually had to take a pill to be able to sleep in a noisy Manhattan hotel.

Mike moved toward the luggage. He would try it first. Then Burnsides' clothes. He might even have them in a secret pocket in his overcoat. But that they would be some place in the room Mike had no doubt.

He picked up an overnight case and opened it. He felt around in it. Nothing. He took out the shirts and underwear and felt around the bottom of the case. Next, two larger suitcases. Then his clothes. He began to get frantic. Nothing anywhere. Maybe the man lied to him. Maybe he *had* left the diamonds at the desk. Maybe they were in the safe now, locked up. Maybe Mike was all kinds of a damned fool, and Burnsides was the Dean of Oxford. Maybe he wrote the book and was just waiting for Mike to open it. He turned and stared at Burnsides. His breathing was still regular. He hadn't moved.

He'd have to start over again with the overnight case. He opened it again. Held it up. Empty. He shook it. The bottom of it seemed uneven now. Something had moved. He played his pencil flash on it. He carried the bag toward the window, into the light. He moved his hand around the edges of the bottom. It was a false bottom. He dug his fingers into the side of it and pulled up the covering. Underneath were the packets of diamonds.

He started to take them out when it seemed as though the devil had blown his destructive breath at the room, into the room. A slight breeze, which had hitherto meant nothing but the calm after the storm, whipped itself into a sudden fury howling into the room. The curtains billowed over towards the dresser, sideswiping a glass pitcher. The water pitcher rolled over to the edge. Mike tried to get to it before it fell off on to the floor, but he was too late. It shattered against the floor with a sound as ominous as a bomb striking. The concussion of the pitcher hitting the floor shook the window in its frame and it crashed shut.

Mike stood immobile, a frozen man iced to the floor. He waited, staring at Burnsides. With the shattering of the pitcher the diamond merchant had merely moaned, turning in his deep sleep. But with the added sound of the window breaking into his sleep-numbed consciousness, causing that moment of awareness, he sat up, a startled expression on his face, as yet incognizant of the real meaning of this intrusion.

He stared towards the window. Mike tried to move into the shadows, but as he did so he hit a chair, sending it smashing against the wall.

Now Burnsides' bulbous eyes snapped open wide, his hand to his throat, constricted with sudden fear. "Who's there?"

Mike stepped into the light. Burnsides, not recognizing Mike, merely seeing a form loom at him dangerously, reached quickly toward the drawer in the night table.

"Don't!" Mike spat it at him between his closed teeth. But it had little effect on the terrified man. There must have been a gun in the drawer and yet the diamond man had indicated to Mike that he never carried a gun.

Mike shot twice. Once in the middle of the stomach because Burnsides moved suddenly, then he hit the target directly in the heart. The man fell back on the bed, sprawled out, his arms dangling on either side, blood spurting forth, enough for the Red Cross and the saving of a life.

Mike had no time to remove the packets of diamonds from the overnight case. He snapped the case shut and moved quickly to the window. He tried to open it. It was stuck fast, a corner of the drape caught in it.

There was only one exit now, the door. He ran to it. Once out in the hall he took his first deep breath. As he ran past the next room the door opened and a man stared out at him.

He darted down the corridors, zigzagging up one and down the other. As he ran, doors behind him started to open. He turned down a dark corridor, flattening himself against the wall. He stayed that way for a few minutes, then he looked behind him. There was a sign, FIRE ESCAPE. He ran toward it. As he turned the corner he bumped headlong into a body. The impact was so great he dropped the case. The person he'd bumped into was stooping over, reaching on the floor at his feet. He kicked his suitcase to one side and waited till the figure straightened up. It was a woman, a woman he'd seen earlier in the hallway. His face was only a few inches from hers. She couldn't fail to recognize him if she were called upon to do so. If he had time he would use another bullet on her. But there was no time. The sound of footsteps coming closer.

The woman herself seemed to be quite frightened. He shoved her against the wall, stooped and picked up the overnight case, turned and ran to the fire escape. He'd have to think about her later on when he was safe in his own room again.

He raced down the fire escape to his own room. In the window. Lights out. He threw the case on the bed, then walked unsteadily toward the dresser. He opened the bottle of Bourbon sitting there and took a big swig.

He sat down on the edge of the bed and lit a cigarette. If the woman identified him they'd start down the fire escape, probably search every room. So what? He'd been in his room in bed for two hours. He'd prove it.

He got up and walked to the window. He closed it and pulled the drape. When he heard them coming was time enough to get out if he felt he should. And maybe they'd never come. The dame looked as though she were running away from something, too. Maybe she was in just as big a hurry to get out. Why should she stop to report him? And for what reason? She hadn't seen him kill anyone.

Yeah, things had been *so* simple. Up until *now*. *Why* had they suddenly gone so wrong? He hadn't meant to kill Burnsides. If the man hadn't reached for that gun ... Why the *hell* had that wind blown up like that so strangely, without the slightest warning? It wasn't blowing now. He pulled the drape back and looked out again. There was no one on the fire escape. Above or below. All was still. In the distance, only the sound of the sirens.

Tonight, he thought, for some evil reason, the wind blew crooked. With sudden anger he pulled the drape over the window and walked toward the leather case lying on the bed.

4

The District Attorney suddenly stopped shuffling the papers on his desk and leaned toward Roger. "Roger Davis?"

Roger nodded. He could hardly keep his eyes open. He had been caught while trying to sneak out of the hotel, arrested and subjected to intense questioning, then thrown into a cell with a wife-beater who had hay fever. The first hour he spent in that cell was the longest hour of his life.

He'd always congratulated himself that he could get out of any predicament. But this was one he saw no way out. He paced the small cell, up and down, just like a condemned man, reviewing his life, reviewing the stupidities as well as the pleasures. What was going to happen to him now? The man who had murdered had stolen 350,000 dollars in diamonds. Did any of them think for one moment that he, Roger Davis, could have stolen them? Yes, they did, or he wouldn't be in this mess. What if, on circumstantial evidence, they proved him guilty? And yet, what circumstantial evidence? What did they have? Only an assumed name he'd used to protect Clara. Only the fact that he was trying to get out of the hotel without being questioned. To protect Clara. And whatever the hell for—? One moment of pleasure. He'd had hours of pleasure with other women and no aftermath. And yet, as he thought about Clara, he realized he loved her, perhaps more than he had other women.

To hell with love! What about himself? Hanged by the neck until dead. He shuddered, thinking about it. No! It wasn't probable. He could prove he had no gun, no diamonds, no knowledge of them, no connections with the dead man. But he must prove it rationally, without emotion. He must be calm about it, intelligent. He must protect Clara's name and his own, of course, in a manly manner, as a gentleman would. Let them know he was not frightened because he was not guilty. But if the going got tough he'd have to give the D.A. Clara's name. He couldn't play hero and get himself hanged. Martyrdom hurts like hell. It was no pleasure to have nails driven through your hands.

By the time he was dragged out of the cell and taken to the District Attorney's office his clothes already looked as though he'd slept in them and they smelled of a sickening disinfectant. Somebody had lifted his good linen handkerchief and he kept wanting to sneeze but didn't dare. There was only one thing he had to remember, to keep calm.

"What's your home address?" the D.A. continued with the questions.
"2130 Linda Street, Westfield, New York?"
"That's right. Apartment D."
"A bank teller in the Westfield Union Bank?"
"Third window as you enter."

Roger looked at the man's clean hands, his well-manicured nails. He quickly hid his own hands. He couldn't get the fingerprinting ink off them and he had no nail file.

"How long have you worked at the bank?"
"Five years."
"Did you ever meet a man by the name of Max Burnsides?"
"No. No." Roger hesitated. "I'm sure he isn't one of my customers."
"Where did you work before that?"
"Farmers National Bank. Dayton, Ohio."
"Were you ever in Baltimore?"
"Maryland?"
"Is there any other?"
Roger smiled. "Ohio—Baltimore, Ohio."
"No, I mean Maryland."
"I've never been to Maryland."
"Max Burnsides lived there."
"Oh."
"Why did you leave Dayton?"

Roger smiled again, wearily, wondering if this man would understand about women. "I was going with a woman and her husband was beginning to object."

He stared at the District Attorney's face, watching carefully for that flicker of humor. It was there, in his hard grey eyes, in his firm mouth now moving toward a smile. He leaned back. Reaching for a pack of Luckies on his desk, he offered Roger one. Roger took it, fumbling for a match he knew he didn't have. The D.A. got up and walked over toward

Roger, holding out a Dunhill desk lighter. Roger looked up, relief on his face.

"Thank you, sir."

This time the smile appeared fully on the D.A.'s face. He was a good-looking man when he smiled. His face could grace any poster for a western movie. The hero with the far horizon eyes, the leathery skin tanned from exposure to the elements, exposure to the elements of sin, also. The grim mouth that could pronounce a death sentence or vow simple words of love, more effective because of their simplicity, their understatement.

The D.A. went back to his desk and sat down. "What do you make at the bank, Roger?"

"Between fifty and fifty-five hundred a year. Fifty-two at the bank, but I have a few stocks that bring in a few hundred."

"Then three hundred and fifty thousand dollars would be very acceptable to you?"

Roger's eyes narrowed. He bit his tongue to keep from being sarcastic. He tried to smile but it was definitely a failure. First you liked this man, then you hated him, then you were wary of him, and he supposed you liked him all over again. "Wouldn't it be to you, too, sir?" he finally answered.

"Why did you try to get out of the hotel with your luggage? Your bill wasn't paid."

"I told the cops I had a friend with me. She has a husband."

"Why did you use an assumed name?"

"Her husband has friends in New York."

Suddenly without warning the D.A. shoved a piece of white tissue paper across his desk toward Roger. "Come here."

Roger arose and walked to the desk. He looked down at the paper. There were diamonds of all cuts and shapes lying on the paper.

"Pick out the diamonds."

Roger's quizzical look caused the D.A. to stare at him intently.

"There are other stones with the diamonds. I want you to pick out what you think are the diamonds in that paper."

Roger didn't hesitate. Why should he? He didn't know the diamonds from the glass. He picked out two or three at random and handed them to the D.A.

The D.A. studied them. "One is a synthetic white sapphire, one a piece of glass and one a titania, which is a manufactured diamond."

"I wouldn't know," Roger said. "I bought one diamond ring in my life. Gave it to the first girl I was ever engaged to. She sold it when we split up."

"Tell me again everything that happened, from the time you and your lady friend heard the shot in the room next door."

Roger sighed. How many times did you have to tell a cop the same thing? He wondered if they ever heard you. "We heard the shot. I ran to the door. I opened it. I saw a man running down the hall. It was only a brief glance. I couldn't describe his face. But he was thin, tall, well built. I would say a fairly young man. He was wearing, I believe, a dark grey suit, a snap-brimmed hat. I think he had something in his hand like an overnight case. But I couldn't be sure."

"Which hand?"

"The one farthest from me, that would be his right one. That's why I wasn't sure. He seemed to shield whatever he was carrying as though he didn't want anyone to see it. I shut the door and turned to—" He almost said Clara. That would have started things popping. He swallowed quickly. "I turned to my friend and told her to get out as fast as possible, that I thought someone had been shot, that she would have to get out before they questioned us. Get out while the crowds were gathering, when she wouldn't be so conspicuous. To go back to her hotel."

"Did you tell her you'd call her later?"

"No. I didn't even think of it. She was almost hysterical with fear. I figured she'd go right back home."

"Where does she live?"

"I—I can't answer that."

The D.A. waved him on.

"Then I started to get dressed. I was in my robe. The phone rang several times while I was getting dressed but I didn't answer it. I figured it was the manager or desk clerk. When I was ready I started for the door. Then I realized I'd forgotten my wallet. I went back to check the dresser where I'd laid it. Before I could leave, the cops had come into the living room and that's about it. You know the rest."

The D.A. nodded. "What would happen if your friend, the lady you're so gallantly shielding, should be made known?"

"Her husband is a very well-known man in the town in which they live. They've been married eighteen years."

"Children?"

"No, but the scandal would no doubt cause him to lose his job. It's a city job. It wouldn't matter about me."

"How would she take it?"

"I don't know. I don't know what her plans are. As for me, I've found it better to live just for the moment. The past can't be recalled. Who would want it recalled? Especially now." He smiled wearily. "The future? We don't know a darned thing about it. So this day, today, that's the only thing that's important."

"Roger ..." The D.A.'s face softened its grim lines. Even his eyes took on a fatherly-like glow. He looked into Roger's anguish. "I've found in my life that there are a hell of a lot of paths. A great many of them lead straight on. Crooked as they might seem, they straighten out if we put a little effort into the work. I'm no philosopher, no Spinoza or Emerson. I'm supposed to be a psychologist. Of sorts. What the hell? I've missed my guess many times. But I do know about comeuppances. You can't beat the rap quite as many times as you think you can. If and when you get out of this, don't start the thing over again. The finger points and having pointed moves on. Or something like that. Anyway the lesson's there. It must be pretty plain to you now."

He stood up. "The stickup and murder have probably been done by a professional. A professional planner, shall we say. He planned the job well, but some kind of natural circumstance, as usual, was against him. I don't think he meant to kill. Circumstance was against you, but I don't think you're a professional planner. I've got a report coming in on you in a few minutes. I'd like to talk to your friend, Madam X in the case, but I know how you feel."

He walked around his desk, in front of it, and stood over Roger. "You're in a real spot this time, Davis. I'm not giving up the thought that you might have done this. You're a natural suspect."

Roger's face clouded over with fear. The D.A. saw his fear and tried to explain.

"Look at our angle. You register at a hotel using an assumed name a few hours before Burnsides and his diamonds appear. A woman whom you refuse to identify comes to your room. She is there just long enough to make her escape after the murder. I know the murderer entered the window from the fire escape and left by the door. That would have been comparatively simple for you, situated as you were. You have nothing in your luggage to indicate the theft. No gloves that apparently were used, no gun and no diamonds. But the woman left carrying an overnight case. She could have the gloves, the gun and the loot. Do you follow me?"

Roger bit his lip, sucking in his breath until it cut into his lungs. "Too well," he said.

"Okay. Your past records, both professionally," and now the D.A.'s eyes softened a bit, "and romantically, point otherwise. But," he shrugged, "today this game of theft, of murder, is played by the oddest people."

He walked to his desk and snapped on the intercom. "Send in Sergeant Monohan."

This meant they were putting him back in his cage. God, he thought, how much more of this? Couldn't the guy see he wasn't a murderer? If the D.A. were really any good at psychology, at analysis, he could see that he was actually yellow. He was scared stiff of guns, knives, implements of torture. He'd fought in no wars and had he been healthy enough to have been drafted he would have no doubt been a conscientious objector. But that really wasn't being yellow. Why did the world call a man who refused to fight yellow? False courage, fighting. Red badge of false courage. No man likes to kill or be killed.

"I'll probably talk to you again in a little while." The D.A. was trying to get through Roger's reverie.

Roger stood up. "Can I have my handkerchief and my nail file? It was a white linen handkerchief."

"Certainly." The D.A. smiled. "I'll see that they're sent to you. Don't stab yourself with the nail file."

Roger stared at him. "You're too much of a psychologist, aren't you," he said, "to believe that."

5

Back home. Back in her ivory tower. Insecure no longer. The bad dream past. And, after all, what is sensuality but a dream and because it always ends in sorrow it is a bad dream.

A protecting arm around her. She turned and looked at John's face, so strong, so sweet in repose. A graciousness about this man. His sleeping lips formed in a smile. She reached over and touched his face with the strong, high cheekbones. It was good. So good. He was good. What is this grave of the senses? Why does it beckon us only to bury us a few minutes later? It looks so inviting. A mirage of ecstasy is actually a pit of quagmire. But, anon, the veil lifts. The mirage dissipates. The flames of illusion die. The ground underneath is solid, firm, good for standing, walking, running, not likely to crack, splitting open, dropping us into that self-dug grave.

A few minutes of pleasure are not worth years of pain. When will this stupid world find that out? Why do we have to find it out through terror?

Healing. She was healed of all that Roger or, rather, that impersonal lust stood for. She was at rest at last.

She turned over and went to sleep again. Her second sleep was more peaceful, refreshing.

When she awoke again it was morning and John had the breakfast on the table. She put on a robe and went downstairs, sitting opposite him studying his face in the morning light. Never a handsome face in the accepted sense, it had now grown handsome, a beatific face. The world should be seeking more of the spiritual. Only in that is there permanent security.

He was reading the morning papers. She had just finished her orange juice. He stopped abruptly and stared over at her. "Clara!"

The tone of his voice told her that terror had not yet ceased for her. Whatever he had seen in the paper concerned her. She did not have to ask him; if she could have spoken, if she could have found words.

"Roger Davis!"

The name exploded from his lips, hitting her between the eyes, a vulnerable spot. She clenched her fist, holding it tight against her shaking thigh.

"He's been arrested. Held for murder!"

Held for murder! Oh, my God! She hadn't even given *that* possibility a thought. That would never have occurred to her. She'd been so sure he would get out without even being questioned, as a witness or anything. When she thought about him at all it was in reference to their affair and the end which she herself had written. Roger was clever, suave was the word. He'd gotten himself out of other scrapes, why not this one? But arrested and held for murder! It was—a fiendish mistake dictated by the devil.

And why should this happen to her again, all this anguish? She was a repentant soul. She'd made her peace with her God. This was a cruel anticlimax.

John was reading from the paper. Roger had been caught while trying to sneak out of the hotel, the refusal to give the name of the woman, the alias he was using, etc., etc. The woman he was protecting. Protecting! Oh, my God! Protecting! The devil is protecting that woman, too, digging his pitchfork deeply into her open wounds. Does martyrdom hurt as badly, Roger?

John looked over at her. She tried to avoid his eyes. She looked away. She looked down. But had she looked back? Roger had told her of Lot's wife who looked back longingly. *She* was turned into a pillar of salt.

"Isn't that awful," John was saying. "Why doesn't the woman make herself known, give Roger an alibi? My heavens, Clara, imagine Roger a murderer! This is insane, a horrible mistake. Circumstantial evidence. I've known Roger, well, you know, dear, for, well, ever since he's been here. You wouldn't believe this, would you, about Roger?"

He looked directly at her when he asked this. This time she couldn't avoid his eyes. Was he a fool? Blind fool? Or did he suspect and was this his way of dealing with it? His eyes held no accusation, no hint of suspicion, only indignation because of Roger's dilemma. If he'd stopped for a moment to add it up. A married woman in New York with Roger for a weekend. Clara in New York at the same time. Clara and Roger who used to play tennis together. Clara who came home early from her weekend, completely unexpected, who came home ill the night of the murder but who recovered very quickly. But frightened so badly now that her legs were numbing, her arms, her mind. She would really be sick if this kept up. Was John waiting for an answer? Or waiting for a confession? Or waiting for her to step forward and give Roger an alibi?

"I think it's awful, too." Her voice was thin, running away in the fresh morning air. "Dreadful. Roger—a—a murderer ..."

He took his eyes away from her frightened face and continued to read. "The murdered man was a diamond merchant." Now a gasp from Clara. "Over a quarter of a million in gems stolen." He whistled. "That's a fortune!"

"A fortune? Roger stole a fortune?"

She began to laugh, softly at first, then her laugh rose, higher and higher, louder and louder, until it became a shout and the shout hysteria and before she realized what was happening a hand was leading her over to the couch. It was John, a patient John, furrowed brow, quizzical face now. He made her lie down. He stood over her towering, a sentinel lighting her way in the awful darkness.

She rubbed her hand across her perspiring forehead. "I'm so upset. Poor Roger. I like him, John. He's our friend. He's—he's honest. You know that he wouldn't—wouldn't—steal—he wouldn't kill! You know that. We must help him." She turned her face toward the back of the couch and prayed. Help him! Help *him?* Help *me!*

"I wish I could help, Clara." John's voice was softer than usual. "But we mustn't let ourselves go like this. Surely when they find out about his reputation here and so forth, they'll release him."

She turned and looked at him. His eyes were still clear of accusation but his face was far from carrying an expression of joy. It was a troubled face. He might be beginning to add it up.

She sat up. "John, forgive me. But I'm not feeling too well anyway. I was thinking, what if that were John, my John. In that horrible predicament. You see, I imagine things. I guess anything would upset me."

"Well, this *is* very upsetting. Upsetting is really too mild a word." His words didn't ring as sincerely as they were meant to. He was looking at his watch as though it were time to leave.

"They couldn't convict him on that kind of circumstantial evidence, could they, John?"

"Actually, I imagine he's just being held for questioning. That's what it probably amounts to but the papers have to play it up, exaggerate." All of a sudden the indignation had gone from his voice. He was reciting as if from rote.

He walked to the door. "Well, I'll be late." He turned, throwing her what seemed like a perfunctory kiss. "I didn't know Roger had a romance, did you? But why not? Except a thing like this might cause him to lose his job."

"If he's released."

"Oh, they'll no doubt release him in a few days. When they find no evidence on him whatsoever. Maybe the bank'll post bond. I don't know. He could raise it from a bondsman. When the woman appears and gives him a better alibi." He sighed. "I suppose the woman has a husband."

Clara stood up. "Wait!"

John, hand on the doorknob, turned, watching her curiously.

She crossed over to him. "I know this woman, John. Roger told me who she was, a wife of a well-known businessman here. He met her when she came to the bank recently."

John's shoulders seemed to relax suddenly. He took a deep breath and came up smiling. Now she was sure he had suspected her.

"If I should go see this woman, plead with her to appear, they wouldn't hold him, would they?"

"Naturally they want to know what the woman knows, too. They want to talk to her. It would be easier for Roger, I'm sure. But let's be rational about it. They know their people, Clara. Very well. This job was a big job, by professionals. Holding Roger is merely routine, I'm sure." He opened the door.

"But you do what you think best. Well, goodbye, dear, I'll be home early today."

She shut the door after him, watching him walk towards the garage. He believed her now. It took so little.

She stood at the window until he backed his car out and turned it around facing town. They lived on the outskirts of Westfield in a small comfortable English cottage. There were no houses near them. John loved solitude but it got pretty lonely at times. This particular morning she knew it was really going to be lonely.

Lonely! Lonely! Lonely? Did John ever *once* realize how lonely she'd been for the ten years they'd lived in this house? No, never once. Never once! She wanted to scream and beat her head against the window. Fate, that stupid word that covers a multitude of sins, indecisions, weaknesses. Lonely—lonely? Afraid! Oh, God, how afraid she was. *Why* had she got into this mess? John, come back! Listen to me! Listen to my heart beating. Listen to your own. You've been so good, so good.

But so thoughtless. John, will I ever be able to talk to you again?

She turned from the window. She had to brace up. She had decisions to make. She had to make them correctly this time.

She crossed to the table, picked up the paper, rereading what John had read to her. Oh, God, what *was* her decision to be? *What* was the step she must take? What must the woman Roger was so gallantly shielding do?

Steady now, Clara. Take it easy. Think it out rationally.

If she did appear at the D.A.'s office there would be a scandal, because the reporters would get hold of it. Her and Roger's short-lived romance would be splashed across the front pages of the world. Everything that she now wanted would be lost. Because of this tragedy, which was fast becoming too real, she knew what she wanted—she wanted her home, her quiet, her peace more than anything or anyone. It takes climaxes and fears, piled so high we can't see over, to make some of us realize the truth.

Yet, despite her selfishness, her desire for self-preservation, how could she sit idly by and allow Roger to assume the entire blame? To be the victim when all she needed to do was make herself known.

Perhaps by phone. If she could speak to the D.A. If he were an understanding man, if he would promise to keep her out of it. Ask him. Go ahead! If I come there, Mr. District Attorney, would it be possible to keep my name out of it?

But that was childish, stupid reasoning. The law was the law. They didn't play Old Maid with children's cards. The D.A. would want to know if she heard anything, if she saw anything, what she surmised. There was the man on the stairs. The same man at the fire escape. She'd have to tell about him. They would question her and question her and finally confuse her and she would drop into the trap and open *her* trap, work her silly mouth overtime. She would tell. And then if he proved to be the murderer and they caught him, she'd have to identify him. No matter how she figured it it would spell finish for her. For John.

She began to pace the room, actually wringing her hands as she'd once seen a woman do in the asylum. With no escape.

She quickly dropped her hands to her sides but continued pacing, the tears now running down her face, streaking her anguish. Closer and closer she got to the phone. She reached out for it, grabbing the receiver without waiting to think any longer in a logical manner. She called long distance, asking for the District Attorney's office in New York City. She was shaking worse than the night of the murder, but she was going to go through with it. If nothing else, she'd always had guts. And they appeared sooner or later. She would see a thing through once it seemed right to her.

She suddenly found herself talking to the D.A.'s secretary, a curt masculine voice. "I'm calling," her voice wavered, "in regard to Roger Davis."

"Roger Davis?"

"The Westfield, New York, man, the man that's being held for questioning in the murder case." What was the matter with the secretary? Couldn't he understand English? "The diamond robbery at the Alton Hotel." Or was he stalling on purpose?

He finally caught on. "Oh, Roger Davis. Oh yes. Yes. He's just been released, madam. If you'd read the papers ..."

"Oh ..." She could scarcely breathe. The secretary seemed to be waiting for some kind of explanation. "I—I haven't seen the late edition. I'm—I'm a relative," she stammered. "Thank you. Thank you very much."

She hung up the phone. The relief was too great. She began to weep again. Finally it was all over. The security she now wanted more than anything else was no longer threatened. And Roger was free again. A man who could walk the streets again with freedom beside him. She could see him, his handsome face when he received the news of his release.

She worried for a moment that the night in jail might have caused him sickness, or he might have been badly bitten by the lice she heard infested most jails.

Then a sharp pain stabbed her in her solar plexus, tightened, running down the middle of her into her groin and through her legs. She was recalling the moments before the murder. She could feel Roger's hands on her body, moving over her. His strong muscles, his hard body next to hers. "Body to body, I die in your desire."

She shuddered and threw her hands to her face. It was all over, this desire. It *is* all over! It *must* be all over! It *has* to be all over!

> "Now at the end when all delight is slain,
> And love's caresses gone where none may go ...
> We feel foreboding and an ancient pain ..."

Stand up. Straighten up. Throw off the heavy weight of desire, and it is heavy. It is ancient and immovable. It bows one down until his forehead touches the dirt of the ground, and not in prayer.

She stood up. She started for the stairs. Oh, God, that this desire were dead. It *is* dead. She would will it so!

Now that the fear was gone, too, she could unpack her bags. Now that

Lot's wife had stopped looking back she could free herself from the frozen tundra, the hard earth, and soar into the heavens of harmony again. She could return to the normal, mundane routines of daily living. She threw back her head and shoulders and straightened up, marching up the stairs like a prisoner with a last-minute reprieve from the death house.

She went into her bedroom. Stooping down she pulled her overnight bag out from under the bed. She lifted it up, placing it on top of the bed. It seemed extremely light. She started to open it, then stopped, her hand in midair. This case was plain black leather and hers was a grain. The locks were different, too. This was not her case. She'd never seen this before. Roger's, of course. God, what irony if she'd got Roger's overnight bag by mistake and that's apparently what she'd done. Or rather, he'd given it to her by mistake.

She pushed her finger against the bent catch. The bag opened, revealing its mysterious interior. There was nothing in it! She gasped with surprise, then she noticed that the case had a false bottom. There was something underneath. She pulled up the covering. There were compartments, ten or twelve of them. In each compartment was a leather folder, a little larger than a billfold. The folders were secured by straps. She unstrapped one of them. Inside were several packets of white papers. She unfolded these.

Lying on their snowy background were hundreds of diamonds!

She opened one leather folder after another. One after another. Square cut diamonds. Brilliant cut. Marquise. Baguettes. One point to thirty carats. Blue white. White. Yellow. Black. A fortune in diamonds!

6

A man, a thief, a murderer, sits with his head in his hands and weeps like any three-year-old child. How could this happen? Is it an emotional instability? The psychiatrist would tell us that all thieves, gamblers, alcoholics, dopers, nymphos, murderers are emotionally unstable. But what normal man wouldn't weep when he sees his entire life's plan torn up before his very eyes? By the stupidest kind of mischance.

Mike Grant had gambled and lost. He could have been a roulette player at Monte Carlo or Las Vegas. He could have been a business man in 1929 during the crash. He could have been a refugee who stares in horror as his home is confiscated, a man at a railroad station watching stunned as his family is dragged down the tracks, beheaded and dumped in front of him. All security gone. False security though most of it is, nevertheless the loser does not understand this. The house built on sand has washed away, but regardless of sand or brick it took a long time to build.

When Mike first discovered the mistake, that he had the wrong suitcase, he was like a wild animal pent up and penned up in a barbed wire enclosure. He swore and wept alternately, pacing, throwing his belongings around the room. Anyone watching might have thought his actions belied his masculinity. A spoiled, angry woman might have acted the way he did, but not a man who is supposed to learn a certain control of his emotions. When he was able to calm himself down, to begin to think rationally, he realized how the suitcases had got mixed. When he and the woman collided, they'd both dropped their cases. In picking them up they'd taken the wrong ones. He knew what the woman looked like who had the case of diamonds. He knew what kind of night gowns she wore, where she purchased her cosmetics that were in the case. There was a Saks tag on the robe. There was a Ronson lighter with the initials C. H., actually the only bona fide clues, if they could be called that. But where would he start to search for this woman? She might still be in the Alton, but he doubted it. She, too, had been trying to make a fast exit from something or someone. The fright was there in her face. By the time she had discovered the mistake she could be on a plane to Tanganyika.

Waiting was fatal, but he *had* to wait. To question the hotel clerks, the bellhops, the waiters, the maids, would arouse suspicion toward him. He must wait until the excitement of the murder died away and then try to find out who owned the initials C. H. and whether she had left a forwarding address. By that time she would have probably sent the diamonds to the police, if she were honest, and she looked honest the brief glance he had had. She had a description of him, too, which would aid the cops. There was absolutely nothing he could do. The only chance he had—if she were registered at the hotel and hadn't left she would have to come through the lobby at some time or other, or if she visited someone at the hotel she would have to come through the lobby. His waiting, his interminable waiting would have to be done in some obscure place where he could watch all doors.

He went into his bathroom and washed up, changing his suit and shirt in case someone had seen him, the man in the room next door to Burnsides, for one. Things had gone so wrong, who the hell knew, he might have been seen by eyes he had no knowledge were there. By the devil's eyes, that was sure.

When he took up his vigil in the lobby it was full of reporters and the morbid seeking their midnight excitement, looking for the pools of blood to drop their pennies in, wishing wells of human sacrifice. He looked into the faces of people who follow fire trucks and ambulances, who stare into the eyes of the unknown dead, white wool pulled over a hard surface, bland, dull-eyed faces, their heads rocking with termites, gutless and unimaginative. Did these people ever gamble? They didn't have the courage. If they did gamble would they lose, too? No! They would be the stupid but lucky ones at the race track who bet once in their lives on that hundred to one shot which, curiously enough, would come in.

He'd seen people like these crowding the lobby now; he'd seen them get up in the middle of the night, no matter how tired they were, get up and, throwing on a grey, spotted robe, rush their work-wracked bodies and small minds down the steps, four at a time, out into the street where the crash occurred, out into the cold, stepping with their moth-eaten house slippers into the glass and gore, watching breathlessly, excitement gnawing at their ulcered vitals as the policemen dragged the broken bodies from under the broken cars. People! How he *really* hated them with their mass reactions of stupidity.

He tried to shake these thoughts, bitter thoughts, caused by his failure. If he got his own thinking all fouled up now, he wouldn't be able to figure out anything. Anyway, he *hadn't* actually failed yet. He didn't intend to fail! Somehow, some way, he would find that woman!

He sat down in a corner of the lobby, behind a plant, where he could watch the exits. The cops were questioning everyone. They might even get around to him, but it wouldn't matter. He was three floors from the murder. He was well known at the hotel and he had a perfect alibi. He'd been in his room until now, which was his usual time to come out, buy a paper, eat a bite at the coffee shop next door, then go back to his room. The bellhops knew his habits.

The paper. He wondered if the night finals had come in. He motioned for the bellhop. "Get me a couple of papers, will you, Joe?" He reached in his pocket for the money.

Joe grinned. "Dija hear about the murder?"

"Yeah." His voice held only casual interest. "I heard about it."

"They caught a guy in the room next door tryin' to sneak out."

"What?"

"Yeah. Arrested him. He was here under an alias."

Mike's heart began to pound so fast that he thought maybe the kid could see it through his coat. "Go get me the papers, Joe." He tried to make his voice sound normal but the excitement crept in, causing his tones to be sharper than usual.

The kid ran over to the stand. He was back in a few minutes with two night finals.

He tipped the boy and started to read. Then he began to smile. Pretty soon his smile was a grin, then a laugh, and if he hadn't stopped himself he would have laughed too loud. Laughed without control as he had cried without control and someone would have wondered.

There it all was. The entire story of the missing diamonds, the murder.

"Roger Davis, a teller in the Union Bank of Westfield, New York, is being held for questioning in the brutal murder of Max Burnsides, diamond merchant, who was shot as he slept in his room in the Alton Hotel. Three hundred and fifty thousand dollars' worth of unset diamonds were stolen from Mr. Burnsides' luggage.

"Davis, who had the room next door to the diamond man, was apprehended while attempting to escape from the hotel. Although he was registered under an alias, Davis, who insists upon his innocence, refuses to explain fully his guilty actions, only that they were the results of trying to shield a woman who was staying in the room with him. The woman, who was not registered at the hotel, apparently made her escape before the police arrived at the scene.

"Davis, refusing to divulge Madam X's name or whereabouts, was immediately arrested," etc.

So Roger Davis of Westfield, New York, a bank teller in a Westfield bank, had a lady in his room, a lady whose name he couldn't reveal (were the initials C. H., Roger?). Those were the initials on the lighter found in the woman's suitcase. Mike's lady at the fire escape was the one, and the one who had the case of diamonds. It had to be. That's why she looked so frightened, she was trying to get out of the hotel before she was identified with Davis. If she came forward now with the diamonds, everything the man, Roger Davis, was trying to do, which was to protect her, would be wrecked. It stood to reason the woman would keep the diamonds until Davis was released. Then the two of them would get together and decide what to do. There was even the greater danger, if she admitted having the diamonds, that Roger Davis and she would be proven guilty beyond that old shadow of a doubt. Circumstantial evidence. The thought of it would frighten her into silence.

Was all this wishful thinking on Mike's part, that both women were the same? Or was it intuition? Or merely adding up the factual clues? Or was he believing they were one and the same because it was the only positive idea he had to hang on to? Whatever it was, his only chance was to believe that C. H., the woman who got his case, was the same one Roger Davis was shielding.

He folded up the papers and placed them on the seat beside him. Now!

Now his waiting was important. He would wait and watch which way the case went. When Davis was released he would follow him to Westfield, New York, because sooner or later he had to contact the woman. If she didn't live in Westfield he would no doubt contact her wherever she was.

Mike would be on the steps of the precinct station when Roger Davis exited, if he exited, and from there on Mr. Davis would never be free of a shadow until he contacted C. H.

The lines were again falling into their proper places. He had obviously been delayed but he had not, as yet, lost. He knew it! He *had* to know it! And maybe, in the end, the delay would prove salutary for him.

He walked through the lobby toward the coffee shop, stopping at the entrance to the restaurant. Wait! He'd left the papers back there on the chair next to where he'd been sitting. If his habits were to remain the same he mustn't let excitement cause him to forget minute but very important details. He always took his papers in the coffee shop with him.

He crossed back through the lobby toward the chair. The papers were gone! He looked around. He saw a man walking toward the desk. He had papers under his arm. Mike was sure they were his because the papers were carelessly folded, rumpled up, as he had left them.

He hurried behind the man. He moved up close, tapping him on the shoulder. The man turned, blinking his ferret-like eyes. He was a fat little man in a mussed trench coat. Unimportant. Seedy looking. Perspiration coursing down his puffy face.

"My papers," Mike said, pointing to the papers under the man's arm. "I left them on the chair over there."

The man looked down at the papers he was carrying. "Oh? Yes, I see!" He handed them over to Mike. "I'm sorry. I thought they were abandoned."

"That's okay. I—I hadn't finished reading them. Thanks."

"I see. I'm sorry."

Mike put the papers under his arm and tipping his hat in acknowledgment he turned and retraced his steps to the coffee shop.

The man had turned toward the desk and as soon as Mike left him he turned around again, watching Mike enter the restaurant; then he stepped to the desk. He smiled at the desk clerk. When he smiled his face lit up, changing its blank expression, becoming bright, alert, intelligent.

"That man," he said, nodding in Mike's direction, "does he live here?"

"Yes, Mr. Dolan," the clerk said. "That's Michael Grant. 316. He's a permanent guest."

"Is 316 an outside room facing the fire escape?"

The clerk nodded.

"So that's Mike Grant," the man said. "I see." He consulted the back of an envelope he took from his pocket. "Can I," he continued, "have the key to 316, Grant's room?"

"Yes, sir." The desk clerk handed him a key. "Mr. Grant has lived here, sir, for about six months. He's been a quiet guest, I can vouch for that."

"I know Mr. Grant's reputation," Dolan said as he pocketed the key to Mike's room. Then he turned and walked swiftly toward the elevators.

7

The knot in the pit of her stomach wouldn't go away. It had been there all day, ever since she found the diamonds. It hurt her to swallow, to breathe. She tried to eat her lunch but it stuck in her throat like balls of cotton. Her mouth felt as though it had been sprayed with alum.

Why was this still happening to her? She had repented enough. She had made her peace with God and with herself. What she had done with Roger, was it a sin so evil that she must continue this retching repentance? People were doing the same thing hourly, by the minute, all over the world. They paid no doubt, in one way or another, but she *had* paid. To the fullest. The last farthing.

Locking the diamonds in her linen closet and hiding the key on the top shelf of the kitchen cabinet was like locking away a guilty conscience. It had to be taken out again and completely destroyed. She had read an article recently in a digest saying that we were the result of what we thought, that everything we thought was reflected in our outward lives. Was she still desiring Roger? Was this restlessness still a part of her? Was it going to be true that she could no longer live in peace with John?

Contrary to Lot's wife, who looked back on her trespasses and was turned into a pillar of salt, she had been turned into a facet of ice. A bright blue-white diamond. Hard. Expensive and dangerous.

It was four o'clock in the afternoon and she had done nothing, absolutely nothing. What was she waiting for? She didn't know. She would have to contact Roger, ask his opinion on what to do. It was four o'clock and John wasn't home yet. That was odd. Did John really suspect her? Perhaps he, too, was waiting for Roger to come home. Oh, God, when and where would it ever end?

It had begun to rain around one o'clock and now the downpour looked like a real deluge. The radio had said to expect storms. Perhaps even a flood. Floods were horrible in this part of the country. The rain ran in rivers down the hills toward the towns. Sometimes the rivers washed out the roads and marooned all of them in the country. She hoped to God that didn't happen now.

If Roger were released that morning he should be home by now. The bank was closed, but she might be able to reach him at his apartment. She went to the phone. Her hand was shaking so she could hardly hold the receiver.

She asked for his number. While the operator was ringing it she had the desire to hang up, to do nothing. To throw the diamonds in the rubbish pile. Did diamonds burn? What good's money when one's heart is in anguish? What good's money when it isn't yours to use? What good's money? The poor are happy. The poor are safe. Who commits suicide? Not the unsuccessful materially. Not the poor. The poor have hope. It's the rich, the well-to-do, the unhappy ingrates. Everything to make them happy and always they want more. More of what? More of trouble? More of anguish? She had had everything and she had wanted more.

She had forgotten she was holding the receiver. Someone was talking. It was Roger.

"Hello—hello ..."

"Roger!"

"Clara!"

"Roger, I must see you as soon as possible." Her voice was unsteady, fearful.

Roger hesitated a moment. "But, Clara, do you think it's safe? After all, you've read the papers. You know what I've been through."

"Don't argue with me, Roger. It's very important."

"But should I come tonight?"

"Tonight? No. No. I guess not. It wouldn't be wise. Tomorrow. Come as soon as you can."

"I'll be there in my lunch hour. What's the matter, Clara? Does John know?"

"It's not that, Roger. It's—it's— Believe me, it's *imperative* that you come. I can't talk anymore. I must hang up."

"I'll be there, Clara." He hung up, too, with somewhat of the same sense of futility that Clara had felt when she discovered the diamonds. What now? Hadn't he been through about enough?

8

Mike didn't believe he'd be questioned by the police. It wasn't wishful thinking. It was not wishing to think. It was the forced blindness of a brash ego.

But insurance companies leave no stones unturned and in this case the stones were worth three hundred and fifty thousand dollars. Even the theft of a few towels from a housewife occasions an investigation paralleled only by a Mr. Holmes and Dr. Watson investigating the headless torso murder of a member of the British Parliament.

Mike was about to check out of the Alton when he had a visitor. He heard the knock on the door and, thinking it was the bellhop for his things, yelled, "Come in."

The man walked in. He was around forty-five. Short and squat. His worn trench coat spanned him like an old girdle spanning the rear of a lackadaisical madam. His face was fat, pudgy. Little rivulets of perspiration formed on his upper lip, on the bridge of his nose. His eyes were black, small, beady and bright, shifting constantly from one face to another, from one spot to another. When he stepped in, Mike was in the bedroom. His eyes took in the entire room in one quick glance. He had catalogued everything. An overnight case on the bed. A larger piece of luggage on the floor, both pieces locked, ready to go. An overcoat, a snap-brim hat, a newspaper on the dresser, open to a follow-up on the robbery. The window in the room leading on to the fire escape, an ashtray piled high with cigarette butts. Camels. Even though he'd seen this room before, he appraised it again, minutely, in the same manner.

Mike walked into the room. He stopped abruptly when he saw the stranger. What was this man doing in his room? Well, go ahead, Mike, ask him. Wait a minute! Where had he seen this man before? Some place recently he'd seen this man ... In the lobby! This was the man who had picked up his newspapers last night.

He stood staring at him. The man looked as though he had got the right room. Why didn't *he* say something? Well, one of them *had* to say something soon. Suddenly Mike knew why he felt as he did—this man smelled like a cop, a private dick.

"What's the matter?" Mike asked it pleasantly. Be pleasant with the cop at first. "You got the wrong room, fellow?" He smiled.

There was no answering smile from the man.

"Michael Grant?"

Mike nodded.

"I'm an insurance investigator. International Casualty Company." He opened his wallet and passed the identification to Mike.

Mike looked at it and handed it back. "What can I do for you?"

"I don't want to detain you. I see you're getting ready to leave."

Mike smiled. He knew that the agent had evidently already ascertained that from the hotel. "That's all right. I'm just driving northeast for a short vacation."

"You worked at Buckingham's Jewelry Store?" He consulted the back of an envelope. "I believe you were there a year in all."

"That's right."

"Did you ever meet a man, a diamond man, by the name of Max Burnsides?"

"I never knew him well but he did come into the store."

"You're aware that he was murdered here in the hotel?"

Mike nodded and gestured toward the paper. "I've been reading about it. Of course, everyone here's been talking about it."

"A man that worked with you at Buckingham's says you were seen with Burnsides several times, that is for lunch and so forth."

"I don't know who the man was that said that," Mike bristled, "but I'll tell you now his eyes are bad. I never knew Burnsides well enough to do anything but nod to him when he came in the store. My business with Buckingham's was selling, not buying. Yes! I *do* have an idea who told you this and if you were any kind of a psychologist you'd know the guy was dying to have his name written down somewhere. Exposed to posterity."

"Never mind that kind of talk, Grant. This is just a routine questioning." The man was eyeing Mike's luggage, his overcoat. Mike's gun was in his suit-coat pocket and thank God he'd put the coat on. There was nothing mysterious except the overnight case with the woman's apparel in it. He figured the guy had a search warrant. Well, it was okay, let him search. It might even be better if he did.

"I thought you had arrested a man," Mike said, pointing to the paper. "A man who had the room next door to the—to Burnsides."

"If you'd read today's paper carefully," the investigator said, "as carefully as you apparently always read papers, you'd see that he'd been released."

"Oh?" Mike simulated surprise. He knew Roger Davis was released. He'd followed him all that morning, finally to Pennsylvania Station, where Roger had taken a train for Westfield. Mike planned to drive there in his car and was on his way when the investigator arrived.

"I'm sorry that I have to do this, Grant." The investigator reached into his pocket for a piece of legal-looking paper, which he tossed on the bed.

Mike knew what it was without looking, a search warrant. He gave it a cursory glance and was about to nod okay when he realized he shouldn't act as if he knew what a warrant was. He leaned over the bed, pretending to read the warrant, pretending to look surprised and indignant.

"I don't get this. You have no reason to suspect me of—of this robbery, any more than you have anyone who worked at Buckingham's, or any other place where this guy sold his stones. I could sue your company for slander."

"Let's leave Buckingham's out of it for the time being. We have reason to suspect everyone in this hotel, since we feel it was an inside job." The man was opening the larger of the two suitcases. He went through it very carefully, putting the things back neatly as though he were a professional packer. Then the overnight case. When he saw what it contained he stopped and looked up.

Mike grinned. "It belongs to my girlfriend," he said.

The man took the things out, carefully laying them on the bed. A silk nightgown, a silk robe, a nylon hair brush, a box of Guerlain's Shalimar powder, a comb, a girdle, a white nylon brassiere, a pair of panties, two linen handkerchiefs, a box of bobby pins, Kleenex, toothpaste, a toothbrush, a pair of nylon hose, leather Daniel Green slippers, a small bottle of Woodhue cologne, a musical clothes brush. The bag was bulging. Mike wondered how the investigator would get everything back. But he had no trouble at all.

"Where does your girl live?"

" Connecticut. Riverside."

"I thought maybe she lived in South America. I understand you have a passport to travel there."

Mike stared at the man, narrowing his eyes thoughtfully. "I got it almost a year ago. I changed my mind about traveling."

"Why did your girlfriend leave her overnight case here?"

"She leaves things here so she'll have them when she comes to New York. Now that I'm leaving, I'm taking her things to her."

The investigator seemed to accept this explanation. He got up from the bed. Mike thought he was moving slowly toward him. The gun! It was in his inside pocket. If the guy frisked him the jig was up.

The man was standing directly in front of him now. Mike needn't have mentally criticized the ugly perspiration coursing down the investigator's red face, because it was pouring down his own now.

Suddenly the man held out his hand. "Sorry, Grant," he said, and he was wanting to shake hands. Mike took hold of his hand. Mike's hand was damp. "But, you know," the man shrugged, "routine."

Mike grinned with relief. "That's okay, detective. It's a good thing I wasn't catching a train."

"Driving?"

Mike nodded.

The investigator turned and walked to the door. When he got to the door he took a card from his pocket and flipped it towards Mike. "Here, my name and where you can get me, in case you hear anything important. Relative to the theft, that is."

The card fell on the floor at Mike's feet. The investigator stared at Mike staring at the card. He was waiting for Mike to pick it up.

Mike leaned over. The gun in his inside pocket began to slip out. He grabbed his breast pocket, holding the gun intact. He was sure it hadn't slipped far enough for the investigator's owl eyes to notice. He straightened up with the card.

"I won't be here much longer," he said, "but I'll keep the card for reference."

The investigator's eyes were bland. If he'd noticed anything peculiar you wouldn't be able to tell by his face.

"So long, Grant," he said, and stepped into the hall.

Mike stood a few minutes, waiting until he was sure the man had turned the corridor; then he hurried to the door and locked it. He took the gun out of his pocket; slipping it into his overcoat pocket; then he sat down a minute. To get his breath. He wiped his forehead with his handkerchief. He looked down at the card in his hand. James Dolan, "private eye." Mr. Dolan was not the sort of man he cared to fraternize with. He tore up the card, tossing it toward the wastebasket.

He looked at his watch. Three o'clock. He wanted to make Westfield by night. These close shaves were doing something to his nerves. It was stage fright and he didn't like it. He stood up and took a deep breath. There, that was better. Wait a minute! The man hadn't searched his room. That was odd. There were dressers and closets and a mattress where something could be hidden. Why hadn't he searched the room? If he really suspected Mike he would certainly realize that perhaps the diamonds were still in the room, hadn't been placed in any baggage, although Mike was ready to leave. Then he remembered. Last night. When he'd come back to his room after having his midnight snack; the moment he'd entered he'd felt something was wrong. But he had thought it was his imagination. His room had been searched last night, that was it! The luggage had been searched then, too. But the gun had been on him.

He ran to the bed. Pulling up the blankets and sheets, he felt along the side of the mattress. His hand went inside and he felt the cotton stuffing. He looked at the slit along the side of the mattress. They'd even cut the mattress to look inside for the diamonds. He remade the bed, slamming the pillows back on it angrily. They had suspected him all along because of that hitch at Buckingham's. Guys in the hotel knew he'd worked for them. As soon as they'd started checking it was easy to find out who all of the hotel guests were. But if they suspected him that strongly why the hell didn't Dolan pick him up now and take him down to headquarters for grilling?

Why had this bloody thing gone so wrong? And yet *had* it? If the case of diamonds had not got switched with the woman's case they would have been in the room and the investigator would have found them. So who knows but what Fate actually played into Mike's hands?

He picked up his overcoat and luggage and walked to the door. He stopped at the door and looked back into the room to see if he'd left anything. He saw something on the bed. He crossed over quickly. It was his grey suede gloves, the gloves he'd used for the stickup. They had been in his overcoat pocket and now they were lying on the bed. *He* didn't put them there. Dolan, the investigator, had left them out like that. Had it been a mistake? Or had he done it on purpose? And for *what* purpose?

Mike picked up the gloves, stuffing them back into his overcoat pocket. Nights during the month of May were sometimes chilly in New York. Everyone wore gloves. To wear gloves was not an oddity.

Sure, the guy had just left them out by mistake. They had nothing on him. Nothing concrete. Absolutely nothing. Or they would have arrested him. Dolan wouldn't let him get away as he was doing.

He shrugged his shoulders. But the shrug was no longer quite as casual as it used to be. He stepped into the hall, shutting the door behind him.

9

It was the suitcase that had cinched it, but it had started a long time ago in his mind. After he had watched their faces through the fence when they were playing tennis. He hadn't meant to watch. He knew they had been playing almost every morning, his wife and his friend Roger, but this particular morning he had had to leave school to go into town to see about something or other and he had driven past the tennis court. It was only a matter of a few minutes, but it doesn't take long for an empire to fall, for that assassin's bullet to hit its mark, for a man to die, to lose at love.

He had arrived at school at nine. His new vice-principal, Mrs. Williams, had told him about the school plumbing. He couldn't get Mr. Orenstadt on the phone so he had driven into the plumbing supply house to pick out the new sinks himself. He never had success leaving important things to be done to other people.

It was a quarter to ten when he drove past the tennis court and saw Roger's car still there. At first he had meant to stop and say hello, but a crazy kid-like thought took hold of him and he had this insane desire to peek through a knothole in the big green wooden fence surrounding the court.

If anyone had seen him, Principal John Harris of the Westfield High School, peeking through that fence, what a story it would have made. But after he had peeked, after he had watched them playing, he forgot about his own posture, his own ridiculousness, embarrassment if he were discovered. They were so happy, Roger and Clara, happy as a couple of high school sophomores. Their faces were younger than they looked when they were with other people. Young, happy faces batting that silly ball back and forth. Thirty-love and forty-love and love! Two young-old people in love. Two people reflecting young love. He knew it then. It only takes one glance. It's a feeling, really. He knew who they were. His wife and his friend. He knew them well. He didn't need to look at them, he could have felt that radiance through the green, wooden fence.

And yet, though he drove away from there with his heart in his body as heavy as lead, he tried to deny what he felt. He had merely seen two people playing an ordinary game of tennis. That's all.

But many times, too many during the day, his mind wandered to that scene and the chill and the cold sweat and the futility blanketed him, bedded him down into a depression, deep, hard to shake. Difficult to extricate oneself from that kind of torment.

Where had he failed? He had loved Clara for years. He thought he was a considerate husband. Their life had been pleasant, perhaps too—what is the word?—too complacent. Had she been restless for a long time? That *he* had failed he knew. Can one love too much? It is possible, of course. That rope we hang around another's neck usually swings our way, choking us to death instead. Bondage! He had never been jealous before. But then she'd given him no reason, before this. It was a heavy load, jealousy. It made a hump of hate on one's back. It's not easy to carry around that kind of weight. A thousand-pound piece of iron would seem less difficult to drag.

For years sex had meant very little to him and, he thought, to Clara, also. After the years, love is supposed to grow into a companionship in which the physical is not too important, especially to women. But it must have been important to Clara. Had he known! Had he been able to fathom! He still felt that way about her, but he was always so tired, and kindly affection seemed more necessary than the physical. But he was evidently wrong. He didn't know women very well. Or his nature was different from most people's. He could so immerse himself in his work that it became an outlet for his natural energy. He had obviously been thoughtless. Clara had never had his powers of concentration nor had she ever been so involved or interested in anything outside of herself as he had been in his nightly writing. A philosopher was writing a book on philosophy and yet he had failed to use it in his own life.

And how had he failed to use it? He could have taken almost any paragraph of his own writing and he could have applied it to his and Clara's life. He could quote pages, paragraphs, sentences from the basic academic text books he was using for reference and he could have applied the enclosed theories to his situation with Clara and he could have arrived, had he made the formulas work, at a happier relationship between them.

Through his works he stated repeatedly that self-condemnation, self-righteousness, self-pity, self-absorption, anything preceded by "self," was merely a form of selfishness. And yet he had been so self-absorbed in his book that he had completely ignored Clara and her possible reactions toward her resultant loneliness.

He had not encouraged her with her painting. In fact, now that he thought about it, he had ridiculed her paintings. "Ridicule," as he so wisely stated in his important tome, "is a form of self-righteousness. We ridicule because we set ourselves up as an authority. And who are we to designate ourselves as an authority? Authority carries power, but power that should be used on expansive knowledge."

Who was he to criticize, to ridicule anyone's painting? He was not a connoisseur, had never studied the critique of painting. For all he knew, with his blinding self-righteousness he might have helped to stultify a primitive, artistic talent latent in Clara.

He had never wanted children and he always considered it fortunate when they discovered Clara couldn't have any. She said it didn't matter. But it *had* mattered. If she'd had children time would not have hung so heavily upon her idle hands. And yet, even though they might have adopted children, the children themselves would have been no excuse for him to hide behind, for his neglect would have still harmed his and Clara's relationship.

Now he was an object of self-pity, *hurt*, which is self-pity, which is selfishness in one of its most subtle forms. You can be hurt only if you're thinking constantly of yourself.

And he was jealous. And what does Webster say about jealousy? "Suspicious; uneasy through fear that another has withdrawn or may withdraw from one the affection of a person he loves—or enjoys some good which he desires to obtain"—a person *he* loves—some good *he* desires—self again. Someone was taking a person *he* loved, enjoying some good *he* desired.

Now he had the delayed opportunity of proving the power and

perfectibility of his theories, his philosophy he'd labored so hard to set down. While giving the pills to others, he had neglected to see if they worked on himself, who needed desperately—a healing.

After the awakening, after the realization Clara was straying, he had courageously tried to deny his hurt, to rise above it. He used the epigrams he knew. He repeated the philosophy that had helped others. He rolled the pink pills around under his tongue. "Sweet are the uses of adversity; which like the toad, ugly and venomous, wears yet a precious jewel in his head—" Even Shakespeare couldn't help him. His hurt went to bed with him at night and sat opposite him in the morning, across from him at breakfast, watching the food form in lumps in his throat.

The day Clara had told him she was going to take a weekend in New York the real portent had passed him by temporarily until he discovered that Roger had gone to New York, too. That was the crisis. That was the night he paced the floor. That was the night he wept for the first time in eighteen or twenty years, recalling vividly wonderful moments he and Clara had had together ... the first time in New York at the French restaurant on 12th in the Village, when they heard their song—what was the name of it? He could remember some of the lyrics—"You'd be so easy to love"—*Easy to Love*, that was it. "So easy to idolize ... all others above ..."

There was the night on the Weehawken Ferry when he proposed and it cost them two dollars to get to Weehawken, New Jersey, and back at a nickel a ride because they didn't get off the boat for two or three hours.

What was the poem?

> *"Oh, the sky was so blue, and the water so bright,*
> *The wind was so soft and the ships were so white*
> *That I wanted to sail and I wanted to fly*
> *And I didn't know why—and I DON'T know why."*

There was the night they decided to fly from New York to Palm Springs, California. It was their third wedding anniversary. Clara had never flown any farther than from New York to Camden. They'd decided on the spur of the moment to take the weekend in Palm Springs. It cost them both a month's salary but they never once regretted it.

He was going to Columbia then, taking his Master's. Clara was working part time in a dress shop. He was also an assistant basketball coach at a Long Island high school. They had moved from Middletown, New York, to New York City for him to get his Master's so that he could teach.

He was gay in those days. He'd noticed himself becoming so sedate, conservative. Why, he didn't even like to watch basketball any longer and he'd been a coach because he loved the game. Of course, he was no longer young, although men older than he seemed to enjoy themselves on trips and so forth. If Clara had suggested his flying to Palm Springs now he would abhor the thought. And yet he had twenty times the money he had when they took the flight.

He'd even forgotten her anniversaries. She must have thought him an awful bore. And he was. No wonder she was interested in someone else. No wonder she'd gone off on a weekend with—on a weekend alone. Or was she alone? Was she with someone? He couldn't stand it. He couldn't stand thinking about it. To visualize her in anyone else's arms was too horrible. Yet he hadn't taken her in his arms for—well—a very long time.

He wondered how he could make up for it. Yet there was no making up. It wasn't a question of making up for it. It was too late. He was too late. This time he'd missed the boat, the flight.

He wanted to call her in New York. Just say anything. Just "Hello, Clara. How are you?" But he didn't really have the chance because, curiously enough, she called him, saying she was ill and was leaving for home, wanting him to meet her at the station.

He was so happy. He was like a little kid whose pal had been away from him for a long time and was just coming back. He could scarcely wait until the last train from New York arrived. She hadn't really been with anyone. This was proof, her coming home already. His fears and jealousy had been unfounded.

Then the bubble burst very quickly when he read the papers the next morning anent Roger's complicity, so-called, in the murder, for he watched Clara's wild-eyed fear, her raw nerves, her calm when she discovered Roger was released. It all added up. And yet, as he had done at the tennis match, he tried to add it up differently, to believe it was imagination, the rankest, vilest kind of suspicion, the warped mental meanderings of a jealous husband. People will do that. And even people with strong wills. Particularly people desperately hanging on to their worn egos.

But the suitcase affair settled it for him.

It was the second day after Clara had returned home. He was looking for his new clothes brush. He remembered that she had asked him if she might take it to New York with her. It was a leather brush that had been given him as one of the presents from the graduating seniors of the year before. It hadn't seemed much of a present to Clara until she heard it play. It played tunes like a music box. The "Jig of the Elves" and

"Les Sylphides." For the less classical it had a third tune, "If You Knew Susie."

"Clara, where is my clothes brush?" That's all he had said as he walked into her bedroom. There was that terror in her eyes again.

"Why, I—I guess I haven't unpacked it yet," she said and started to the closet where her suitcases were kept. Halfway there she stopped suddenly and turned back toward him. "Oh, John, I think I left that in the hotel room. I remember when I packed, the night I took sick, the night I called you, that I couldn't find the brush. Then I got sicker, you know. I hurried my packing. I didn't find the brush. No, I didn't. When I unpacked yesterday I remember saying to myself, 'Clara, you forgot John's good brush.' Oh, I'm so sorry, John. I'll buy you a new one. Or perhaps we could write the hotel. I know the desk clerk, George. I think his name is George. He'll send it if it's still there, and why not? Who would want to steal a clothes brush?"

She said it all so fast and almost in one breath. None of it sounded like Clara. She never talked that fast. She was never that breathless. He knew there was fear in her again, but why? Something about the brush this time, but what could be so upsetting about a clothes brush?

He turned and walked back to his bedroom to finish dressing. "Okay, Clara," he said, "Forget all about it. It'll either show up or I'll get another. No, don't bother to write."

The telephone had rung shortly after that and Clara had gone downstairs to answer it. Again he couldn't contain himself, he had to sneak in her room and look for the overnight case, search through it, not to find the brush any longer, but to try and discover what it was that was making her so fearful. To find what was causing him the added pain of jealousy that seemed to cut into him like a cancerous sore. Intuition can be a hateful, evil thing. Clairvoyance, when used this way. He could see things he hated desperately to look at. He could see the end of things.

He searched through her closet, the floor, on the top shelves. Then in the room, under the bed. In his own bedroom, the same procedure. But no overnight case. Clara's good leather overnight case that he'd bought her on their twelfth wedding anniversary was gone. And yet he could have sworn she brought it home with her. He knew she did. This was a new puzzle to add to the list.

He thought about looking in the linen closet, but that would be a stupid place to put an overnight case.

Should he ask her what happened to it or just wait? Wait! Play the waiting game. Until it appeared again or until he could find it. Maybe she put it in the attic or basement. But why? Her other suitcases, much larger, were in her closet on the floor.

Perhaps she had, by mistake, picked up Roger's case and hidden it, waiting for him to return with hers. It was obvious that Roger had been shielding a woman the night of the murder, so that woman in her terror at escaping would make a mistake such as this.

The more he thought about this the more logical it seemed and the clearer his decision became. He couldn't stand to go through this mental torture one minute longer. Although his philosophy would no doubt eventually help him, the experience he was suffering would really be the open sesame to a greater understanding. And yet he couldn't continue to be foolish and carry the burden so far when all he needed to do to lighten it somewhat was to be sensible. Practical. His work was suffering, too. Never mind his school. It was his writing at night. Nothing must interfere with that. That book had been an ogre causing this rift. But, on the other hand, the work would now occupy him so that his suffering would not be as acute.

He formed the letter, the one he was going to send to the bank that day. He would have one of his pupils drop it off. Roger would receive the letter and come to the house that night and the three of them would bring the situation into the clearing, talk about it in an adult manner and decide on what to do. When one uncovers a thing it is already three-quarters destroyed. And unless this were destroyed in his life, or at least started on its way to obliteration, unless he could grapple with it and win, it would begin to cause a malaise, a sickness. Not only within himself, but he was sure within Clara, too. He must remember her confusion. He must try and be tolerant in spite of or because of his hurt. It must be tearing the insides of her apart, too. She seemed to want to stay with him and yet she wanted someone else. Perhaps her confusion was even worse than his.

Yes! Tolerance. He must make every effort to be tolerant. What was it someone said on the subject? "Intolerance is ignorance matured."

He must pray again. He must ask a Higher Thought than himself for help. Pray. Make the words mean something. He hadn't actually utilized the power of prayer, its obvious healing efficacy, for years. In fact, the more erudite he had imagined himself becoming, the less he gave tribute to a higher intelligence. Perhaps in that lay his *grave* mistake. The coldness of intellectuality was no ungrounded fact. The intellectual places his own intellect above all. Above God.

"... Only love the Lord, and serve Him in truth with all your heart: for consider how great things He hath done for you ..."

The words used to mean something. When he was a child he understood the words. To understand is to believe. To believe is to see the reality. Reality is the real. The real is in the realm of God. But to enter the Kingdom of Heaven one must be as a child again—having a child-like thought, simple, unfettered with human theories and hypocrisies. Heaven is a kind of harmony. He was having enough of hell within his own mind. He didn't need to go elsewhere.

10

The rain? Would it ever stop, Roger wondered. It was beginning to drive him a little mad. Any other time he would have liked it. Its steady greyness. Its soothing aspect. When he was little he used to love the rain. It kept him indoors and sometimes away from school, but the actual reason he liked it was because it gave him an added feeling of security. In mother's and father's home there was security, in his mother's arms, but the rain added to it. It shut off the world, blotted out for the moment any little-boy problems he might have.

But today there was danger in the rain and the wind. It was a cold, driving rain. It hit with superior force. The papers said it would rain like this for days, perhaps harder than it was now. There might be a flood. As he stood behind his teller's cage looking out on to the street, watching the small rivers of water run down the gutters, he was sure that before night there would be flood waters racing down the hills, over the fields on to the highways.

He was back home again. He was safe from his nightmare. He had awakened. The security of work was his again. Soon the stares would begin to cease. Oh, there would be an occasional joke, some of the girls in the bank would titter stupidly as he passed by. But he had been a victim of a huge mistake (some said he could even sue the city of New York), and even though there had been a woman with him in the room on the night of the murder, he was a bachelor and had a right to have whom he pleased in his rooms. No one in the bank seemed to suspect anyone in town, for he'd told those with whom he was friendly that it had been a New York girl.

But the danger for him had not ceased, and that was another reason the rain was making him unhappy and depressed. The real danger was alive and at the moment in the form of a note delivered to him at the bank, a note from John Harris, Clara's husband. He had the note in front of him on the counter. It read:

"Dear Roger,
Happy to know you're back and suffering no more ill effects

from your eventful trip. It's too bad circumstance sometimes weaves its nasty web around us, but I've always felt that if we are guiltless the web is easily broken.

I have something I want to talk over with you and, if possible, tonight. I feel that it is important enough that it can't wait any longer to remain undiscussed. I would like you to come to my house at eight tonight. I have not mentioned this to Clara, but she will be there at the time and will, perhaps, be able to offer a solution.

Yours,
(signed) John Harris"

There was no mistaking the tenor of the note, nor the import. The underlying meaning was there and was, perhaps, the reason for Clara's calling him yesterday. Clara with fear in her voice. John must know!

How the hell was he to handle it? If John divorced Clara, would she expect him to marry her? Did he want to marry her? The scandal would really be something if he suddenly married her. But why start the bridges, then try and cross them before they were finished?

If this were so, it had to be faced. Maybe Clara would be better off away from John. She was no young schoolgirl jail bait. He didn't have to marry her. Nor did he have to stop seeing her if she left John. But meetings like this were no doubt going to be hard on the pride.

He looked at his watch. It was almost noon. He'd promised Clara he would be there by noon. They could talk this thing over and chart their course of action before night, when they faced John.

He left his teller's cage and walked back to the closet where his raincoat and hat were hanging. He put on his coat. He saw several pairs of overshoes in the closet and a pair of goloshes. He wished he'd worn his overshoes. With the rain like it was he was bound to get wet feet and wet feet to him meant a nasty cold.

By the time he'd walked out of the back door of the bank and around to the parking lot and got in his car he was absolutely soaked. The rain was knife-like in its intensity. The sky had really opened up this time. The phrase "wet rain" seemed like an anomaly, but this was a wet rain. He shivered a little before he could get the heater in his car going.

He drove out of the parking lot and past the Starker Hotel, out toward the edge of town where Clara and John lived. As he passed the Starker Hotel, a curtain in a third-floor window parted and a face, shielded from recognition due to the rain, peered out.

The curtain closed quickly and Mike Grant moved away from the window. Grabbing his trench coat and his hat, he started for the door.

By the time he was downstairs, through the lobby and out in the hotel parking lot, Roger was three-quarters of the way through town. But with the sheets of water in the street, the rivers in the gutters, it was slow going for Roger. Before he reached the city limits sign, Mike, in his car, was close behind. Had Roger been aware he was being tailed he probably couldn't have told who it was or what kind of a car the person was driving, for the rain caused such poor visibility.

Roger was within a block of Clara's. There was a small hill ahead. At the bottom of the hill was a perfect pool of muddy water. He knew low places like this could be dangerous with continued rain. But it looked safe enough now. This was a spot where the road had previously been washed out.

He approached the spot carefully, shifted into first and took it slowly. As he was halfway through, a truck coming the other way, down the hill, without lessening its speed, took the puddle like an LST, splashing huge waterfalls high into the air. Roger's windows were up but the water completely covered his car. "Damn fool!" He swore at the driver, who was far from hearing his ineffectual oath.

After letting the water settle, he moved his car forward again, but there was a fearful sputtering and the motor went dead. The truck had obviously splashed enough water into his engine to kill it. He stepped on the starter. Grind after grind. It would not start. It would have to dry out.

It was raining harder and visibility was getting poorer and poorer. He felt the ground underneath begin to give a little. The water was pouring down the hills opposite him. Panic welled within him. He could get out of his car. He could wade to higher ground. But he didn't want to leave his car there to be smashed into bits by another oncoming truck. But if the rains kept up he'd have to leave his car. He hated floods. Water stifled him. This kind of water. Rain could be soothing, but water, rivers of water, were dangerous. Water, out of control, frightened him worse than fire. He always felt helpless in the face of a lot of water, a large body of water like a lake or an ocean. He hated to look at the ocean for that reason. It gave him a feeling of distrust. Any moment it could jump its shores and envelop one, destroy houses, highways, complete cities, inundating the world. Where was Noah? Noah?

"Damn that truck driver!" he swore again, out loud. "Damn inconsiderate humanity. Damn humanity!"

What to do? What to do? He couldn't just sit for ever, waiting for the ark to float by. He tried the starter again. It wasn't going to turn over for pleas or prayers.

Behind him Mike Grant moved up. He saw Roger's dilemma. He

wanted Roger to get wherever he was going as badly as Roger now wanted to get out of the water. Mike could probably get through the low place, push Roger ahead of him, but he'd have to face him. If Roger were the man who'd seen him in the hall next to Burnsides' room Mike's number would be up. And yet he had to make some move, too.

He honked his horn at Roger. Roger rolled down his window and looked back. He didn't recognize Mike, only as a sudden savior. Breathing a great and deep sigh of utter relief he waved to Mike. Mike gunned his motor. Roger put his car into neutral. Mike began to push him slowly through the water and mud. Mike had the heavier car. If he took it carefully he could get Roger out.

It was only a matter of a few minutes but it seemed like an eternity to both men. Mike got Roger's car on dry ground. He kept pushing him until he heard the motor turn over. When Roger finally got the car going he leaned out and waved his thanks.

Mike slowed down to let Roger get farther ahead of him. When he saw him turn into the driveway of a house on top of the hill he pulled over to the side of the road and turned off his motor. He lit a cigarette, taking a deep puff of it, bracing himself; smiling with satisfaction. The cards were falling into their right places again. He would wait until he saw Roger come out and then he would make *his* reconnaissance.

11

"Roger, Roger, please! I told you I don't want this in my life any longer!" Clara tried to pull away from him but he held her more tightly. For ten minutes she'd been arguing with him. She was beginning to get very angry. When he realized that, his pride forced him to release her.

"Roger, it doesn't matter any longer what we want or don't want, that is, personally. What matters is getting out of this mess." Her voice was hard, bitter. For the first time he heard its other than dulcet tones. "You seem to be more concerned with our love than you are with the diamonds. I'm not! The important thing is, what are we going to do about them?"

She pointed to the table where the case of diamonds lay. Roger's shock had been very great at first seeing the stones, but it was true, he seemed to be more concerned with her coolness, her evident decision to cut the affair in midstream.

"I don't know, Clara. I'm upset, sure. With you. With the note from John. The diamonds, curiously enough, seem to be anticlimactic. They're inanimate objects, they can't hurt you."

"No, they can put us in jail, that's all."

"When we decide to get rid of them or, rather, when we decide what to do with them, it will mean a certain finality. You decide to get rid of me, of our love, it's no end for me. It means sleepless nights. It means that awful lump of hurt that lies in the pit of your stomach until everything you eat or drink comes up again. There's no sickness like hurt."

"Unless it's desire, Roger."

"Desire can be consummated."

"Hurt can be freed. You've never been hurt before, have you, Roger?"

"If I never had I wouldn't know how it felt, would I? Yes. Once. When I was young."

"Then you know about Time, the Great Healer."

"But Time the Healer comes so late. This will be worse, Clara. When you're older you're not able to take things so easily."

"On the contrary, Roger, you should have more wisdom, you should be able to take things in your stride. I suppose I do have a feeling left for you. But when I had to, I've been able to close the door. This is a question of closing the door now."

"You're a selfish woman, Clara. The retribution for selfishness is terrible."

"I want John to be happy. Is that selfish?"

"You should have thought of that a long time ago."

"If he knows about us and tells us so tonight, but is still willing to take me back, I'll stay. If he isn't I'll get a quick divorce."

"You haven't given anything of yourself to John in the past, why should he expect it in the future?"

"*What?*"

"Have you ever been interested enough in his book even to—to help him with it?"

"Don't talk about things you don't know anything about!" she shouted at him now. There was vehemence in her voice. "You know nothing about what I've been through in the past!"

"I know more than you think I do," he went on. "You've only given thought to your own pleasures. And when the chance came, through me, to further your selfish desires, you took it, not considering John for a minute."

"Why, you're out of your mind! How dare you talk to me like that? You're the one who led me by the nose. Did *you* think of John? Did you ever think of anyone but yourself? I'll bet not!"

"You aren't through, Clara, with trouble," Roger continued as though she hadn't spoken, "until you're through with selfishness. You can stand here now and throw this in my face, throw our love in my face as though you were tossing a dead fish at a fishmonger. With just about as much animation and interest."

"Look, Roger, let's not be vindictive at this late stage. There are always two sides. No matter what I say, you would think differently. This is juvenile. Grow up, Roger. The pains are terrible but we've *got* to grow up."

"Speak for yourself."

"Don't give me that about one person's selfishness. We're all selfish. That's why the world's in such a horrible mess now. Please, please, Roger, don't act for me. It's better to say things you actually believe, even if they're small, unworthy, rather than play the hero."

She turned from the sudden hurt she saw in his face. Lord, she had to be understanding. He was right. Hurt is a dreadful illness. It can make us dishonest if we're not already.

"I'm sorry, Roger. But my nerves are in a state. I'm sure yours are, too. What *are* we going to do about the diamonds? I've nearly gone mad trying to figure it out."

"We'll contact the D.A. or the police, I suppose."

"We can't. Don't you see the predicament we put ourselves in? We'll be arrested if we're not careful."

"I've been arrested. Remember?"

"We don't know the man, who he was, so we can't ask him to come and get them."

Roger laughed mirthlessly. "Dear Mr. Crook, we have your diamonds. We will leave the loot in a paper parcel at the corner of G Street come next Palm Sunday. Please leave our suitcase when you pick up the sparklers."

"I'm trying to figure it out, Roger, even if you're not." She was getting angry again with his *laissez-faire* attitude. "Your levity doesn't lend itself to this kind of situation. You're acting like a—a sixteen-year-old. God knows I haven't slept a wink thinking about this mess."

"We could keep them, Clara. Go away. To Europe. South America. Mexico. Never come back. It would be so easy. Since no one suspects us. Any longer, that is."

She stared at him closely to detect the continued note of derision in his voice, the sign of humor in his eyes. There didn't seem to be any.

"You really mean what you said, don't you?"

He nodded. "I suppose, in an odd way, I do. That's because I'd do anything to keep you, to keep you from getting away from me."

Now it was Clara's turn to smile and her smile also held sarcasm. "You want me because I don't want to continue with you, Roger. It's that simple. If I still wanted our great love, as you seem to think it was, your enthusiasm for it wouldn't be as intense. These are things I know about you."

Roger's sudden silence was eloquent. He looked at his watch. He'd been there longer than three-quarters of an hour. He had to get back to the bank. He walked toward the windows. Pulling back the drapes, he stood looking out. The rain seemed to be worse now, if that were possible.

"I've got to get back to work, Clara. Tonight, when I come back, I'll have a solution. I'll figure it out. I think maybe driving to some other town, like Camden, or Newark or Hackensack, or I don't know—some place—mailing the diamonds to the D.A.'s office, that's the best thing. Although I suppose the cops can trace them, through the paper they're wrapped in, through the ink the address is written with. If a man's honest there seems to be nothing he can do to escape trouble." He sighed. "Anyhow we'll talk about it tonight."

"Not with John here, surely?"

"Why not? He's smart, isn't he? You think so, don't you? Smarter than I am. Maybe he'll be able to offer a solution."

Clara couldn't visualize talking about her and Roger's affair in front of John and yet it had to be done. John would force it now that he knew. It was so really horrible, the whole thing. There had always been a graciousness about her and John's life together, a respect toward each other. A rule, unwritten of course, but vulgarisms had never been associated with their relationship. Perhaps not because of her righteousness but because of John's.

Roger had his coat on and was standing at the open door before she could take her mind away from the meeting that night. She shuddered and looked at him. A stranger in their midst, the personification of the snake in the garden, and she had eaten of the fruit of the poisoned vine.

He was staring out on to the porch. "If this keeps up, I might not be able to get back."

Her heart picked up the beats. It was a hope, a hope that the rain would keep up and that he couldn't get back, prolonging the agony, of course, but giving her a respite.

"Will you kiss me goodbye, Clara?" He turned and smiled at her. "Just one for the road."

She hesitated. Why in the world should she? It was over. In her own mind it was all over. In her heart it was finished. But looking at Roger's hurt eyes, she saw the mask which the sudden tragedy of love seemed to give his face. A mask of drawn white wool, hanging in its particular man-made void.

She crossed over toward him. She turned her cheek for the farewell kiss, but he grabbed hold of her roughly, swinging her toward him. He put his lips to her, allowing them to push against her mouth, forcing her lips open. She tried to pull away but couldn't. It was all there again. The thrill. Or it hadn't gone far. Really. Perhaps if he hadn't kissed her. Perhaps if she didn't see him she could forget. She was a blind, stupid, arrogant fool, hoping like an old woman hopes for youth, endlessly and without success. The desire was still there. To be close to desire, so close, is to lose one's perspective. Completely.

When he released her she was shaking again as she had done before in his arms in the hotel. She looked at his face, blank no longer. It was wearing the merest suggestion of a triumphant smile. But it was enough, shadowing his handsome mouth. Roger would never give up easily. Between the two of them she knew she was much the stronger because she had never before made a constant, continuous bed companion of desire.

"I'll see you tonight, Clara," he said, and went out with the warrior's winning banner high. Now she hated his masculine ego. She didn't smile or say goodbye. Her voice would have been husky, or bitter. Either way giving him the signal of her downward flight again. "Get out, Roger," she prayed, "get out of my life. Leave me alone. For this I was not born, to lust after the flesh, but after the Spirit."

She turned and walked back to the center of the room. The diamonds still lay in their case on the dining room table. She felt that, as long as they remained in her house, objects of materiality, desire would remain.

She stood in front of them, hating them passionately as one would hate, would delight in destroying the evil idol whose incantations to it, whose prayerful pleas had gone unanswered.

Greed! They were a symbol of Greed. Of greedy women who fought for them to flaunt them. Who slept with ugly men for them. Of grimy men who mined them, who bargained for them, who killed for them to give them to greedy women who paid for them.

She wished to God she could burn them in the furnace. But diamonds, she knew, don't burn.

12

When she first heard the knocking on the door she decided not to answer it. She didn't want to go to the door. Something told her not to go to the door and when she did go and open it and saw him standing there she wished to God she hadn't gone. With all that was left of her sanity she wished that she hadn't. He didn't need to tell her who he was or what he had come for. He had her overnight bag with him and the diamonds were still on the dining room table. She had not yet put them away.

He walked on into her house as though he were an expected guest. He set her bag down and stared around the room. He seemed pleased with the decor and then his eyes discovered the diamonds. He walked over to them, a greedy man at the end of his search. His hands traveled through the case as swiftly as deer darting through the underbrush. Long, thin, artistic, greedy hands.

She found what was once a voice. "If you're counting them, you needn't. They're all there."

He turned around, facing her. He was smiling. "I should give you one at least. For your trouble."

"I don't want any part of them!"

"How fortunate you are, Mrs. Harris!"

"Your coming has solved a very unhappy problem for us. We didn't know what to do with them."

He smiled again. It was a wan smile, as though he were exhausted after his long vigil, his search, as though it were difficult to show emotion.

"You know who I am then?"

"Remember?" she said. "We met before."

"Yeah. You were as scared as I was, I guess."

"Please. Please take them," she pointed to the case of diamonds, "and get out of here."

"First we've got to get something straight, Mrs. Harris."

"Before my husband comes home. Please!"

"How do I know you won't phone the cops as soon as I leave?"

"Police?" She shook her head, gritting her teeth to keep from screaming. "If you *knew* what I've been through you wouldn't say that!"

"You must know there's a reward for any information leading to—" He cut his speech off in mid-air. The look on her surprised face told him she hadn't heard of the reward. He'd read it in the late editions before he left New York.

"Monetary reward," she said, "no matter how much, means no more to me now than—than that box of diamonds. And I loathe every one of them. Could I possibly make myself any clearer?"

He stared at her. "You sound very convincing. But you're still human and turning me in for, say, ten thousand bucks wouldn't be a problem, would it?"

"I told you how I feel. Either you trust me or you don't. To tell you the truth, a few minutes before you came I wouldn't be able to stand up and talk to you like this. But experience seems to make us stronger. By the minute."

He rattled her statements around in his fertile brain wondering if she were just a good actress or really meant what she said. He was rather inclined to believe she meant what she said. There were evidently a few people left that thought like that.

But before he could answer her the phone rang. She, unconsciously, looked to him for direction.

He nodded. "Answer it. If you believe what you just said I can trust you." There was now a glint of humor behind his words, his sly smile.

She walked over to the phone. Although confidence was growing, she still kept one eye on him. She picked up the receiver. "Hello."

"This is Mrs. Williams, Mrs. Harris," the voice on the other end of the phone said. "Mr. Harris wanted me to tell you that he was on his way home. The floods are so terrible that school has been dismissed. He was afraid he wouldn't get home unless he started now. I understand some of the roads are already washed out and they expect more rain. Isn't it awful?" She was excited and said it all in one long hissing breath.

"Thank you, Mrs. Williams. I'm sure John will make it. But thank you just the same. Goodbye."

She hung up. "You'd better leave now," she said, "that is, if you want to make it. The flood's getting worse. School has been dismissed, that is, my husband's school. He's on his way here. Some highways are already washed out. I know what happens when there are floods around here. Six years ago we were completely marooned for three days."

He crossed over to the window and pulled open the drapes. The rain was piling down hard. So hard that they realized, now that they were aware, that the sound was almost deafening. From the house the roads were smooth sheets of glass-like water.

"I don't know which way you're going," she continued, "but if you're going back to Westfield the bridge you passed over, if the rain continues, will be washed out. If you're going on through Havensford there's a creek crossing under a culvert at a very low place in the road. When it fills up and overflows it's impossible for cars to get through."

He turned back into the room. "This is all very lucky for you, isn't it, Mrs. Harris? Because I'll have to leave now if I want to get away safely. But the flood still wouldn't prevent your calling the police. As a matter of fact the flood seems to be on your side, doesn't it?"

"You could cut the phone wires if you feel you can't trust me."

"You could still go to the neighbors. I can't run around chopping down telephone poles."

She looked at him thoughtfully. "You were obviously able to follow us here, Roger Davis and me. You must know the score. You know why I don't want to be involved in this any longer. I've just got out of one mess. I'm fairly secure again. I want to remain that way. I want to try and be happy again. Here with my husband." She paused. He didn't say anything to fill up the pause, so she went on. "You seem quite intelligent. Otherwise I wouldn't talk like this. Otherwise I'd be more frightened than I actually am inside. I'm *sure* you understand."

He still didn't say anything. He turned and walked over to the dining room table and stood looking at the case of diamonds and then he began to work swiftly. He restrapped all of the loose folders and placed them in their rubber bands. He put them in the case, then secured the false bottom and, taking a small key from his pocket, he locked the case. As he went about this activity he suddenly began to talk and, although his back was to her, the import of his words and the small insight into him were not lost.

"I've worked too long on this job to have it fail now. Too many things have already happened. I don't know why I'm going to trust you. I usually don't trust women. I don't trust anyone. Everybody talks too damned much. But I think you've got a basic sincerity. If by chance you and I ever pass again. On some street. In a train. On the deck of a boat," he shrugged. "I guess you won't want to recognize me either."

He crossed over in front of her to the door. She stared after him. This strange, handsome boy. Why was he a thief? A murderer? She could scarcely bring herself to think the word and yet she knew it to be true, even though she hadn't actually seen him kill a man. She stood there looking, almost admiring a killer. Not admiring. Wondering how he could be saved. Wondering why this had happened to good potential material. Good in the intelligent sense. He wasn't a moron by any manner of means.

She almost understood him, too. There was a definite rebellion against what he must feel were unfair conditions. Wasn't that why she had rebelled? Wasn't that why she listened to those inner impulses which had proved to be—wrong?

As if in answer to her thoughts he said, "To live a fairly normal life in this abnormal world perhaps would seem a better way of existing to you. Although it wasn't a better way or you wouldn't have been in New York that night. This is a crazy mixed-up world. Where's its security? It hasn't any. Neither in home nor government. Where's its opportunity? It has none. What we create we tear down again. What we earn we give to crooks," he smiled, "if you'll excuse the expression crooks, *crooks* and politicians. I don't know where one can go to escape it, but at least I have the dough to search for the place."

It all sounded fairly intelligent, analytical in a kind of man-to-man way but, all of a sudden, she saw a strange glint of exhilaration in his eyes as he turned and looked at her. She'd seen it in actors in New York making their exit with a particularly witty or profound exit line, one, of course, they had not written themselves. Then he smiled at her. And she saw a brilliant beauty in the smile, lighting her now darkening thoughts of him. Again she wondered what he would have become if he'd taken the normal, mundane paths. She even wondered what it would be like to love this man. That he needed love, she was sure. She was probably looking at one of the loneliest men in the world. There must have been times when he realized it. There must have been times when he took out the broken mirror and held it to his lonely soul. She knew he was a thief, a murderer, a mean man in search, not of himself, but escape from himself, and yet her heart went out to him. To break down that coldness, that wall of icy self-sufficiency.

As he started out of the door they heard, over the sound of the driving rain, the motor of a car. She ran to the door. It was John chugging up the rainswept road, his old Buick wheezing, pulling with extraordinary capacity. Thank God, he'd made it.

Mike turned to her questioningly.

"Go on," she said. "It's John, my husband. Go, before he sees you."

"He'll see me run to my car."

"I'll tell him you stopped to call about the roads ahead."

He shut the door quickly and bounding off the porch he ran down the front lawn and over to his car. The rain had the right effect, shielding him enough so that John, if ever called upon to do so, would probably never be able to recognize him.

He had some difficulty getting the car started and John, instead of doing what Clara expected him to do, had seen Mike and ran across the lawn to Mike's car.

Clara, standing at the window inside, watched in utter disbelief. Now why did John do that? Why did he have to do that? God knows what would happen to both her and John now. Yet why was she so panicky? John didn't know who the man was and didn't ever have to know.

John banged on the window of Mike's car. Mike lowered the window, glaring out at him.

"Pardon me, sir, but I don't think you can get through. Either to Havensford or back to Westfield. All bridges and roads but one are out."

Mike looked at John strangely, not seeming to comprehend. "I—I just stopped," he nodded toward the house, "to call about the roads."

"I came through the back way," John went on. "Dirt road, you know.

Muddy, but not out when I came through. Wooden bridge over the river. It's the last route left open. What they call the Old High Road. But God knows how long it will remain open. You'd better come back in the house; otherwise you'll be stuck." He looked at his watch. "When I started home they estimated the old wooden bridge would hold about a half hour. The half hour is up. The last time we were marooned here for three days."

"I know. I know. Your wife told me. Okay," Mike sighed, "you better run up and tell her. Tell her why I had to come back."

He rolled up the car window.

John turned, sprinting through the rain up to the house. He was soaking wet but he felt all right, just fine. They were going to have company. He could help out a stranger. It would be more pleasant this way. To be marooned with Clara, knowing about her and Roger, and not being able to tear down the wall. It was better to put the whole thing off for a little while. Roger wouldn't be able to get through, either, so that ordeal would also be postponed.

But Mike was thinking a great deal differently. To him it was a hell of a turn of events. Now. Now when he had the diamonds, when the road ahead was clear? Clear? Muddy and impassable! He felt himself getting angry again. He had to watch that. He couldn't let himself go now. If he got angry, if he lost his temper, uncontrollable as it could be, he was liable to do stupid, nutty things that would really wreck everything.

He locked his car and with his case under his arm he ran toward the house. He saw Clara's strained, uneasy face waiting for him at the door. He smiled at her. He tried to make his smile give her assurance. He didn't want it to be ironic for her. Because he didn't hate her. She had done nothing to him. Only circumstance had been his Nemesis. The elements, God damn them!

He looked at her peering out at him. There was actually something about her that attracted him. He had felt it, even consciously, the minute he'd met her, in her own house. She wasn't a beautiful woman in the way he was used to thinking of beautiful women. But there was something deep about her. There was something deeper than beauty, sex, in the attraction he felt. He didn't like to think of it as a mother-son deal, because it wasn't exactly; she wasn't that old. And yet he had never known a mother.

He stopped on the porch a moment to take off his wet trench coat, his hat rimmed with water. He laid them across a chair on the porch. He didn't want Clara to think he was not well bred.

Clara, watching him, didn't smile, because she wasn't happy. But, under more normal circumstances, she would have smiled. A few minutes ago when he walked into her house the first time, he hadn't taken off his wet coat and hat. As a matter of fact he'd worn his hat in the house.

She opened the door and he walked into her house again. This time as a guest.

13

James Dolan, investigator for the International Casualty Company, put a call through from his room in the Starker Hotel in Westfield to his main office in New York City. He needed help. After talking to Mike Grant in his room in the Alton he had followed him from New York City to Westfield.

He had enough on Mike to pick him up. Although it was all circumstantial evidence, that old bromide, still the fabric covered pretty well despite a few holes.

But more important than arresting a man who was, to Dolan & Co., a natural suspect, was finding the diamonds. Dolan worked for an insurance company which was interested in finding the insured.

From studying Mike's apparent activities, from the time he went to work at Buckingham's to and through the murder, his investigation of Mike's room, his meeting with him and the attendant suspicions, Dolan had a pretty good idea of the kind of person he was dealing with—a man who, no doubt, would be difficult to break down. He also figured Mike had an accomplice. If so, the accomplice and the diamonds were probably together, wherever they were.

From the night of the murder to the time Mike left the Alton, got in his car and headed for Westfield, Dolan tailed him. Besides searching his room thoroughly, he had searched his car, his clothes.

He knew he had deposited no packages, no case, nothing anywhere that would point to his hiding evidence. The finding of the woman's case in his room suggested to Dolan that Mike had switched cases with someone.

When Dolan followed Mike following Roger Davis to Penn Station, Dolan was pretty sure, despite Davis's release, that he was an accomplice. The unknown woman in the Davis case was apparently the Madame X who took the diamonds off Mike. That made one more suspect, one more accomplice.

By the time Dolan had reached Westfield his conclusions were fairly well formed. Roger Davis and Mike Grant and Madam X had engineered the robbery. The woman had gone to Westfield with the case of diamonds. Davis had not meant to allow himself to be caught and questioned but a mistake in timing had evidently occurred. Because of the mistake Mike Grant had had to hide out in the Alton until the woman reached Westfield or until Davis was released.

The three of them were, at this moment, in Westfield splitting the take and waiting until their opportunity came to skip the country.

There were large holes in the fabric of this theory, Dolan knew that. What was Roger's and the woman's motive in being in the room next to the victim when Mike was allocated to do the dirty work? They weren't necessary there and it seemed it was an extraordinary, even stupid risk they took. Why did the woman leave her overnight case with Mike? Why didn't she take it with her? It must have been her case because Dolan, as soon as he started checking, found out she arrived in Westfield carrying a case which was the one that evidently held the diamonds.

Dolan figured that maybe Roger Davis was the brains of the foray, had planned the entire scheme. Yet Mike could have carried it out alone.

These were all points that would be cleared later, of course, when they were arrested and began to talk. The pertinent thing, it had been a theft pulled by a team and that team and their booty were in Westfield. At the house of Clara Harris, who Dolan discovered was the unknown woman.

But to apprehend them was going to require help, not only from the Westfield Police, but from the elements, because Dolan was marooned in Westfield in the Starker Hotel until the storm cleared, which had been predicted to be at least three days, and he was very bitter about it. He had them all in one corner, a ten-thousand-dollar reward in the offing, and now he was boarded up in an antiquated, smelly hotel for three days. It was frustrating. But then, on the credit side of the ledger, none of the trio at Harris's could move either.

While he waited he could do some further checking on the new element—what might prove to be the fourth member, Clara Harris's husband, John Harris.

To anyone but a cop it would seem, and Dolan knew this, that John Harris, Principal of the Westfield High School, highly thought of, much-loved citizen in Westfield, with what was told him was an unassailable honor, could not be, by the wildest stretch of a detective's deducing powers, a criminal. But this didn't bother Dolan. He knew that there was always only one step to take, the first. And sometimes a guy took it when he was eight, eighteen or eighty. All depending on the personal circumstances at the time, the weakening of a hitherto exemplary character. He could have recounted, if anyone cared to listen, innumerable cases to substantiate the above. There was the accountant in Los Angeles who, after working eighteen, twenty years' honest routine, no black marks against his character, had suddenly defied convention and stolen from his employer one hundred and fifty thousand dollars in negotiable securities, and had, using his right name, calmly taken a plane to New York, where the authorities just as calmly waited for him.

There was the seventy-five-year-old lady who held up several banks, depositing her loot in the paper sack that held her gun. There was—*ad infinitum*. John Harris was only another human being to Dolan, and human beings, he had proved repeatedly, were not as yet immortals.

He was also going to check with the small air strip in Westfield and if a plane could take off, if there was an open field near Harris's house where it could land, he would land near the Harris's house before any of its inmates had a chance to escape. Either way, by plane, if feasible, and he doubted it, or by road block, it was now just a matter of waiting until the rain let up, until the road was cleared.

14

Panic began to choke Roger. He wasn't an extraordinarily brave man. He really wasn't brave at all. If he'd admit it, life had always frightened him. He'd been in personal predicaments, yes, with women and husbands of these women, but most of his courage was a smart-aleckness, a derring-do. Had he been called upon to fight a duel he would have had to lose the lady or lose his life. Now, sitting marooned in his car again, this time in water up to the floorboards, he was as frightened as a child on a rock in the middle of an angry ocean, for he'd almost made it back to Westfield when at the last low place in the road he had sealed his doom. Or rather, the elements had sealed it for him.

Every place he looked there was water. There seemed to be no way out unless he abandoned the car and waded, struggling through muddy water, on foot, to higher ground. It might mean he'd lose his car to the elements and that he himself would develop a good case of flu. The last time he had had the flu he'd almost died. It's rough to be alone and ill. Either to be ill or to be alone is bad enough, but to be ill and alone, then the loneliness is suicidal, that is, if one is not too ill, already in a coma. Futility is a horrible hangover to this kind of malaise.

As he sat, trying to figure out his next move in this game of man against nature, his past did not review itself before his watery eyes as it had done that night in jail. He was not interested now in what he had been, what he had done, should have been or should have done. Only in what was going to happen to him from this minute on. He would wade through the water as he'd done before and if he were lucky this time he would get through. He had heard of people drowning in a few feet of treacherous undertow. He would pull himself up the hill and over to the farmhouse he'd just passed. There, if the lines were not down, he would call Clara. He couldn't go forward. He could see that the roads ahead were getting worse. Perhaps he could get back to Clara's. Perhaps when John got home he could come after him. Three antagonistic personalities marooned together, or at least three involved personalities; throw in the rain, the depression, the closeness of no escape and you have good, fine ingredients for drama—tragedy. He wondered what would develop.

And then toss in a lapful of stolen diamonds. Nothing anyone could think of could be more exciting fare. And yet diagnose the persons involved, none of whom was a terribly exciting or exotic being reflecting unusual drama. Each one heretofore had been just the ordinary everyday citizen involved only in mundane routines and occasional pleasures, until someone decided to steal some diamonds.

The diamonds! Thinking of the diamonds suddenly gave him a strange sort of delight. Let's search that, he thought. Clara, he knew, wanted the diamonds out of her life as soon as possible. John would hate the materiality for which they stood. But he, Roger, was beginning, regardless of his depressing state at the moment, to toy with an idea. If he took the diamonds himself, told Clara he was sending them to New York anonymously, or even taking them to deposit on the steps of some subway or any public place for that matter, he could actually do what the murderer evidently planned on doing. He could leave the country. Alone. He knew Clara wouldn't go with him. Anyhow it was better to go alone. Leave of absence from the bank and all that. Naturally he'd never come back. Could he get away with it? Men had got away with more dangerous plans. There was the Brink's robbery, for one. This would be solace for his hurt.

He looked down at his feet. His ankles were covered with water. His car gave a sudden lurch, then there was a squashing, sinking sensation as he felt the car settling itself into a deeper place. He had to get out at once or he'd never make it. He pushed open the door. Even though he knew the water was only a couple of feet deep, the muggy, swirling wet mess had a new and dreadful effect upon him, causing that tightness in his throat again, only worse, constricting, shutting off his breath. He stepped down gingerly, into the water. It dragged around his feet and legs menacingly. It was being carried down from the hills. It was deceiving. It had force.

Holding his overcoat around him tightly he began to wade toward higher ground in the rear of his car. It was a laborious process. He kept slipping, fighting the water. Once he went down on his right knee. His entire coat and suit were ruined. And he was soaked, chilled to that so-called marrow, beginning to feel ill from fear and the thought of what the consequences would be.

He finally pulled himself up the hill on to the muddy, swishy ground. Slipping and twisting, he eventually got a solid foothold. It was getting darker, which meant a new storm. The rain would be coming down harder, obliterating the landscape, and with the fog that was creeping in ready to blot out his future destiny. He must hurry. The farmhouse was ahead, to the right. He had to make it before the new storm struck.

It was getting dark enough for lights. He was at the peak of the hill when he saw the farmhouse lights go on. He made his wet, weary way through the field toward the house. He was not a praying man nor one who sought protection from a Supreme Being, but he found himself saying the only prayer he remembered from his childhood, "I thank thee, Father, all wise, all loving servant. Amen." It didn't relieve his weariness but it *was* a form of gratitude.

15

She looked over at John's face. She could see the hurt in it and was afraid, more so than she'd ever been. If he knew to whom he was talking so animatedly. If Mike Grant, whose name she now knew, should tell what he knew about her and Roger ...

The dinner she'd prepared under duress (duress caused by her own thoughts) had gone off surprisingly well for the two men. They seemed to like each other. Mike was quite bright. He was able to hold his own with John conversationally. John obviously welcomed the stranger's visit. She also felt that Mike was beginning to be grateful for a hideaway for a few days. This would no doubt throw the police off his trail if they suspected him. Of this, of course, she could not be cognizant.

But what about her and John? That was the imperative question. How was their problem going to end?

She served the coffee, and as the two men talked, this time about fishing, she studied Mike. Now that fear of him was abated for the time being she saw his face in a still different light. He was still handsome, physically, but now she saw animation, what seemed a solid intelligence, sanity, all these qualities making his charm a great deal more potent. Talking as he was with John, anent the ordinary pleasures of ordinary living, she realized she was listening to and looking at one of the most attractive men she had ever met in her life. Why hadn't he taken a less precarious path? The women who could have loved this man. Or had they? She doubted if he'd ever let anyone love him, know him well enough to love him. His eyes when they turned upon the diamonds were bright with greed, but so cold and hard that any woman who loved him, when he turned those eyes upon her with a cold, "I've come to say goodbye" look, would have been frozen into immobility.

When she finished her third cup of coffee, a normal routine for her since she was a heavy coffee drinker, the conversation of the two men had turned into the political stream. This man who seemed so bitter about many things was more on the right side of the road than the left. He was no gangster, she must remember that, nor a man that felt revengeful toward the world. He was an independent, a hybrid, a highly attractive *gentilhomme* with the mark of the beast across his forehead.

She knew she was beginning to settle down for the moment into a comfortable rut of security, false though it might turn out to be. "How," she thought, "could this man ever do us harm? He perhaps killed in self-defense, but even though it isn't condoned, it was, in the light of his character, understandable." Yes, this evening *was* going more smoothly than she could have ever dreamed. Roger wasn't there and would no doubt be unable to make it. Mike was proving an outlet for both John and her and, curiously enough, an entertaining one, and the fear was lessening, was very close to the disappearing point.

But this was her last comfortable thought, if it may be called that, before things began to happen with the rapidity of machine gun fire. John suddenly asked her to make them a highball. As she arose to go into the kitchen the thought came to her that music might be appropriate for their after-dinner drinks. What kind of music, she wondered, would Mike Grant like?

She was at the phonograph, turning it on. "What kind of music would you like to hear, Mr. Grant?"

"Liszt. Anything from Liszt." He said it quickly, without hesitation. "'Liebestraum', the old hat. Or Schumann, one of his fantasy pieces. 'Opus 12'. Rubinstein does that well. Or Richard Strauss. Have you 'Death in Transfiguration,' 'Salome'?"

She hadn't quite expected this kind of taste in his music. She figured he might ask for a Strauss waltz, Johann, that is, or even light opera, more of the operetta order. Most likely swing. Jive. But he'd asked for two of her favorites. "Salome" and "Death in Transfiguration."

"You're surprised at my taste in music, aren't you?"

She smiled, acknowledging his clairvoyance.

"I played by ear," he continued, "when I was a kid. I took a few lessons, later. Then got bored. But for some reason, even when I was little, my tastes ran to the classical. I guess because my grandmother's old victrola only played the classics. She always said if you put a jazz record on it wouldn't start."

Clara and John both laughed. This was the first real display of humor in Mike that Clara had noted. She decided she'd play "Til Eulenspiegel." It was gay and he would like that in his present mood, then she'd play "Salome" and "Death in Transfiguration" for him. She eagerly put the record on the machine, then started for the kitchen again.

She'd just got to the kitchen door when she heard the car drive up. They'd all heard it at the same time. They looked at each other, surprise, disbelief on all three faces. Their allied thoughts, "Who could get through tonight?"

John arose quickly and crossed over to the window. He pulled back the drapes and peered out. "It looks like Jack Parsons's truck. He's pulling into the driveway." He turned toward Mike. "He's from down the road some way."

Mike got up and joined John at the window. "Did he have to cross one of the bridges?"

John shook his head. "No, he's just a few miles down. That big truck would take care of some deep puddles. But he'd better not flirt too long with this storm."

"I wonder what he wants," Clara said.

John went to the door and opened it, but instead of Jack Parsons walking up on to the porch it was Roger, a disheveled, wet, sick-looking Roger. John took hold of him and pulled him inside. "My God, man, what happened to you?"

"I'm ill, John. I got stuck. I left my car and waded to Parsons's house. He brought me here." They could hear Parsons pulling out of the driveway. John tried to call to him but Roger shook his head. "He's got to get back before he's stuck, too." He started to sneeze violently. John hurried him over to a chair out of the draught while Clara shut the door.

Clara looked over at Mike. His face had clouded over like another and more threatening thunderstorm.

"Good Lord, Clara," John said, "this man is really ill. We must take him upstairs and put him to bed."

"Thanks, John." Roger's voice was so weak he could scarcely be heard.

Clara stared at Roger now. Regardless of his illness she almost hated him for coming back. It seemed the old war debts were continuing to pile up.

John was helping Roger up when Mike spoke. "I haven't met this man," he said.

Although Clara thought she detected undertones of sarcasm, Mike's attitude was one that suggested that both she and John had made a breach of Emily Post.

"This is a stranded tourist, too, Roger," she said. "Mike Grant, Roger Davis."

Mike tried a smile that didn't get any place and Roger was too weary to do anything but nod.

"Fix him a hot toddy, Clara, while I put him to bed," John said.

There was utter gratitude on Roger's white face. "I always get sick," he said, "when I get my feet wet."

They started up the stairs, John and Roger, Clara staring at Mike watching them. Now Mike's face seemed to be absolutely diffused with a strange sort of inner satisfaction.

The truth of it was that his perverted mind actually relished this turn of events, even though it posed another problem for him if Roger found out who he was. But it was Mike's game, really. He had them all where he wanted them. If anything untoward happened concerning him he could expose them all to each other. The reason might not appear whereby he desired to tangle up their lives more than they were already, but he was the magician to do it if proved necessary.

After the two men reached the upstairs landing Clara turned toward Mike. The two of them looked at each other, the irony of the situation quite apparent on both their faces. She shook her head as if the movement would clear her depressing thoughts.

"The Comedy of Errors is progressing."

"Don't let it bother you—Clara." It was the first time he'd used her given name. He rolled it around again, "Clara. Do you mind?"

"What?"

"I can't keep calling you Mrs. Harris. We're now too intimate a group for that."

She sighed, turning toward the kitchen again. "It doesn't matter. As long as this thing comes to some sort of an end soon."

"It's the rain," he said facetiously. "It always makes one depressed." He laughed at the bromide. But without acknowledging she had even heard him she went into the kitchen to mix the delayed drinks.

He watched her walk into the kitchen. He liked the way she walked, smooth with easy grace. He liked the way she looked, wholesome. New England grimness about her face but it was handsome, well formed, strong even in its weakness, promising much. If she really loved he was sure she gave much. How much, he wondered, had she given to Davis.

Davis looked to him like a silly weakling, a small-town Beau Brummell.

If she *really* loved, her heavy-lidded eyes would slumber, lying half-closed, bedded in their desire. Maybe he should have continued his journalism. Maybe he should be a writer now and write a poem to Clara.

If she weren't careful, with a few drinks he might think too much about her. If *he* weren't careful.

16

After Clara had provided Mike with his drink she excused herself and went upstairs with the hot toddy for Roger. John had fixed Roger in bed in the spare bedroom. He'd filled him with quinine and covered him with the electric blanket. She looked at the two men and wondered what each one secretly felt in his heart. That part of their minds were on her was not deft analysis, but what does a man really feel in his heart, that part that he does not, with impunity, bare to all. And in John's case, not even to the one closest to him.

She handed Roger the hot toddy. John raised him up on the pillows.

"Thanks, Clara." Roger said it with a hurt, doglike bewilderment.

For a fleeting second she wondered if he were as ill as he seemed to be and then she quickly put the idiotic thought right out of her mind, idiotic in face of real illness. She must remember, to the patient illness is his cross. She had never been ill very much in her life and there was, at times, creeping into her obvious sympathy a note of impatience.

"You're both swell," Roger said when he finished the toddy. "I don't deserve it." He turned his face to the wall as though he were hiding a stray tear. The effort was sincere but it had its dramatic effect.

"Nonsense, Roger," John said. "We can't have you here sick. We like our guests active. After all, we need a fourth for canasta, if we're going to be marooned here." He laughed, but Clara, knowing John and his attempts at wit, felt this one was a real dud and she knew John knew it.

She wanted to go back downstairs; the situation was embarrassing for her. John said he'd sit with Roger for a while until he felt that his fear was lessening and then he'd come on back downstairs and help her with the dishes.

She walked out of the room without looking back at either man. She couldn't look at Roger's pleading, fearful face now that he confronted a personal disaster in the form of influenza, and she didn't dare look into John's face, search for either that accusing or hurt look.

But had she searched John's thoughts she would have been surprised at what she would have discovered. He wasn't thinking much about her and his hurt. He was actually concerned about Roger. But throughout the thoughts of his concern was the recurring question. Were these two, Roger and Clara, really interested in each other? And if so, and he was positive in his own mind it was so, why were their attitudes now so seemingly indifferent? Roger's mayhap because he was ill. But Clara had thrown ice at Roger. She had even seemed to resent his presence. John could feel the resentment.

What a strange woman, his wife. He didn't really know her at all. Or do any of us ever really know anyone? Perhaps we know people like Roger, the extroverts. But the introverts are always unpredictable.

He didn't think Clara was acting for his benefit because that's one thing she really didn't do, put on a mask to greet each new idea. But then again, who knows? Desire will make a hitherto honest soul flirt with vile dishonesties.

When Clara arrived back downstairs she saw that Mike had fixed himself another drink. She studied the bottle. It looked as though it were down more than two drinks.

She left the kitchen and walked into the living room. He had helped himself to the cards in the drawer in the library table and was sitting playing solitaire. When he looked up at her she saw that his eyes were beginning to blur. I wonder, she thought, if he's the type who doesn't hold his liquor well. There was something about him now, a cockiness that hadn't been as apparent before.

As if in answer to her thoughts he said, "I imagine your husband is an excellent nurse," and his voice seemed to hold a slight touch of sarcasm.

"Yes, as a matter of fact, he is."

"You're so worried about Roger," he went on in the same tone and now the sarcasm was obvious, "but not worried at all about what I might do to all of you."

Her face must have shown him the surprise, the disbelief, as though what he'd said shouldn't have come from him.

"Don't look so surprised. Do you *really* think I trust you?" He laughed. "Supposing you decide to tell Roger who I am. I don't trust him at all. The minute he knew there was a reward for me, sick or not, he'd swim to the nearest police station. I know his type."

"You're very smart, aren't you?"

"Yeah. I am. Now, I know your husband's type, too. He'd turn me in because of principle. That beautiful word that covers a multitude of little self-righteous motives."

"But why are you talking like this? They don't ever need know who you are. When the rain stops you can leave. It'll be just like it was going to be before. You'll leave and—and the whole thing ends there. Leaves with you. God willing!"

"Silent as a tomb. Right, Mrs. Harris?"

"What?"

"Well, I guess it's possible." He swallowed what was left of the drink and set the glass down.

Liquor was bringing out the mean streak. She was right. He would be tough to handle if he got too drunk. Was there a way she could prevent it?

"I've done pretty well so far, haven't I?" she asked. "I mean in concealing who you are."

"Could I have another drink?"

"If you think you can hold it."

"Aw now, Clara. Don't let the mother instinct run away with you." He crossed over to where he'd placed the ice and filled his glass, then started for the kitchen. "I've never been not able to hold it. That's a double negative, isn't it?"

She followed him to the kitchen door. He was teasing now, so why not take advantage of this opening. She had to stop him. "I've read that only two things will give a thief away. Drinking too much. And women."

He had already filled his glass. He turned and stared at her, his eyes narrowing until they almost disappeared into his head. Then he threw back his head and laughed. Forced or not, it was a relief.

"I'm sorry, Mrs. Harris. My vulnerability is only human. But don't hope too much."

He'd caught on to her at once. He was like a bright, highly-bred animal, a dog, interbred too much. Bright as—as—as a diamond. But unpredictable. He crossed in front of her and walked back into the living room. He was beginning to sway a bit. She knew that when he finished the drink he had he'd really be tight.

He watched her walk into the room, too. But he wasn't thinking about her condition as she was about his. Through his half-shut eyes he was appraising her again, as though she were on the market. Legs firm. Breasts the same. Broad shoulders. Good for carrying burdens. Narrow hips. The athletic type. The kind that always attracted him. As long as they were chic and feminine and not masculine. He hated that kind of masculinity he'd often run into at schools for girls. All brawn and some brain, but nothing for a man. He used to get some of them for blind dates. He delighted in teasing them about their athletic prowess and their dubious femininity. He really liked Clara Harris. Now he knew. He wanted her. Regardless of unpleasant consequences. But he'd see to it there wouldn't be any. Tonight, *he* was the power.

"You're very attractive," he said. "You attract me more than any woman I've met in years."

"Don't talk like that!" She snapped at him, sharply. "I told you what happens when certain people drink too much."

"Come here!"

"I said don't talk like that to me!"

He got up quickly and before she could stop him he'd crossed over to her. She began to back up toward the kitchen door.

"You're attracted to me, too," he said, "and you know it. I knew it during dinner. Let me tell you something, Clara, when a woman's frustrated, when she wants sex with a guy, just because the affair turns out wrong doesn't change her mind. Another guy will do just as well."

"You're talking like a guttersnipe," she said.

"Look who's calling who names. A guttersnipe? Just because I mentioned the word sex. Don't be mid-Victorian, Mrs. Harris."

He was moving closer to her. She backed against a table. He caught her wrist and pulled her toward him. She struggled but it was no use. He held her close to him, gripping her in arms of steel.

"Don't make a scene! I've got the ace in this deal and I don't mind playing it!"

He forced her head back, holding her that way while he kissed her.

She was frightened but she didn't dare show it verbally. He was right, he *did* have the ace. God knows how he would play it, but there was everyone to think of now, not just herself. She tried pushing him back with her body but he held her more closely.

This man was not the charming reprobate she tried to force herself to believe. With a few drinks he was showing exactly what he was, an unbalanced mentality, a neurotic, one who could probably love one moment and kill the next.

Without warning, which she realized now was natural with him, he shoved her away from him and walked unsteadily toward the whisky bottle which he'd brought in and set on the table.

"Why don't you come with me?" he said. "Your life wouldn't be dull any longer."

He poured himself another drink, then turned round facing her. His eyes were bloodshot and his face was flushed.

He started toward her again. This time in her terror she turned to run and tripped over the rug, falling to the floor. She tried to get up before he got to her, but she was too late. He leaned over her. She started to crawl away from him but he grabbed her by the arm, pulling her to her feet.

"Don't do that again," he said. "Don't try and get away from me! There isn't any place you can run to!"

His nails were digging into her arms. It was so painful that she couldn't stand it.

"Please. Please leave me alone! Why do you hurt me like this? Your nails are hurting me!"

"Because I want something right now. When I want something I get it, too. I don't like obstacles thrown in my way."

He put his face close to hers. She could smell the heavy liquor odor on his breath and it nauseated her.

She knew that no matter what she said he would have his way. She had only one chance to get away without causing any more noise that John might hear.

She pulled back suddenly and with her free arm she managed to get a good swing. She swung her arm toward him, slapping him in the face so hard that he was forced to release her other arm.

"I wouldn't walk across the street with you," she said. "I'd kill myself first!"

She watched his face turn red and then blow up hard and angry. There was that second in which she thought he was going to calm down as he'd done once before. Laugh or turn away, for the time being hiding his anger. Instead he rushed her so fast that she couldn't get away. He caught her by the arms, pinning them behind her. She stared at his maniacal expression. He looked as though he would kill her.

She heard John coming down the stairs but she had no time to warn him.

John hesitated on the stairs a brief second, trying to understand the dreadful picture he suddenly saw before him; then he roared at Mike. He was like a stuck bull. She had never seen him as angry before.

Mike dropped her arms and turned just as John leaped at him.

In that split second she saw Mike's hand go toward his pocket.

"For God's sake don't, John!" she screamed. "He'll kill you!"

John's blow got Mike on the nose. He fell to the floor but caught himself on one knee. He shook his head, bewildered. The punch had stunned him badly.

She ran over to John to stop him. "He'll kill you, John! I know! He'll kill you!"

Mike got up slowly, trying to get his bearings.

"What the hell do you mean? What were you trying to do to Clara?" John began to shout. It wasn't like him to take the offensive.

"Please, John, let *me* explain." She pleaded with him to keep quiet.

"I'd toss you out now, out of the house, if there wasn't a flood! I've got a half mind to do it anyway!"

It was as though Mike wasn't listening, as though Clara and John were playing the scene alone. He was dabbing at the blood on his nose with his handkerchief. His actions were as deliberate and slow now as they had been frenetic before.

He finally looked up and over at John. "Forget it, Harris," he said and his voice was like ice. "I'm sure your wife doesn't mind as much as you do."

John swung at him again but Mike was expecting it, had actually asked for it, had set it up. He caught this blow on his arm. When he countered, hitting John, he hit him low, in the stomach, doubling him up. He folded like a dead eel, slithering to the floor.

Pushing Clara out of the way Mike leaned over and pulled John up, dragging him toward a couch. He rolled him on to the couch. John sprawled on his face, a ludicrous position for a man of seeming dignity. It hurt worse than the blow.

Clara had followed Mike to the couch. She was crying now.

"You're worse than an animal." She doubled up her fist at him. "If I had the strength I'd—I'd almost—"

"If you had the strength!" Mike sneered.

She leaned over the couch to help John.

"Leave him alone! He's all right. Just got the wind knocked out of him." John was trying to straighten himself up. "He ought to know what a faithful wife he's got. Why don't you tell him about you and Davis instead of slobbering all over him?"

"You stupid fool!" She straightened up and walked over to him now, braver now that she'd seen him hurt, braver now that she realized he was not infallible. "Do you want to give yourself away, too?"

"What the hell do I care? I told you before, I hold the ace. Don't I? What do I care?"

"Just as I thought," she said. "You're talking too much. You'll see. Don't any of you know when to keep quiet? If you'd behaved there wouldn't be any problem. Now. You'll see."

"Who is this man, Clara?"

The words didn't come from John, who was now sitting up searching the couch for his glasses. The voice came from the direction of the stairs.

Both Mike and Clara turned round. Roger, white-faced and tense, stood on the stairway, staring down at them.

Clara looked over at Mike.

"Go ahead," he said. "Tell him, if he's so damned dumb he can't figure it out for himself."

"He—he came after the diamonds," she said haltingly. "He followed you from New York."

"The man you saw in the hall?" She nodded. Roger could hardly believe it. How did the man get here? How did he find out about the diamonds? Now that he was here what was he going to do to all of them?

John, who had missed none of the conversation, had found his glasses and was now trying to get up on his feet.

"You remember, Davis," Mike sneered. "You saw me in the hall. Next door. When you and Clara were having your little rendezvous."

John got to his feet. He couldn't take any more. Whether it was true or not, and now he finally knew, he couldn't stand to have a stranger washing their linen for them.

"Okay, Grant," he said. "If you're talking for my benefit you might as well stop. I know about it. Have known for a long time. You're not telling me anything I don't know."

Clara was watching John, an incredulous look on her face. He knew all of the time. They hadn't fooled him for a minute? She felt like dying. If only the floor *would* open up and she could drop into the void.

She looked over at Roger for his reaction. He was as stunned as she, and despite the pallor of his face there now appeared a vivid pink color, moving up from his neck, spreading the embarrassment over his entire face. This time, she thought, Roger had not been so clever. He had been found out by a man not nearly as sophisticated as Roger, himself, liked to appear.

"I don't think you know the entire story, Harris," Mike said. "You might as well know it now, don't you think so, Clara? The diamond deal was mine. I stole the diamonds. Your wife's and my cases got mixed. In the hall. When we were both trying to beat it from the hotel. She got the diamonds. I would have turned up the world to find her. But I didn't have to. It turned out to be comparatively simple."

"And now *you* have the diamonds," John said, "and us, too. Therefore the only thing of concern to us now should be saving our lives. Isn't that right?" He said it matter-of-factly, turning to Roger and Clara for confirmation.

But he didn't feel matter-of-fact about it. It was taking all of the intestinal fortitude he could muster to keep from either shouting his hurt for all to hear, or blasting his anger for all to witness. He didn't know which he felt the more keenly, hurt or indignation.

Clara was as surprised at John's sudden calm as she'd been before, at his fury toward Mike. She'd never seen John hit highs and lows like this. She'd never seen him angry, or as in command of an embarrassing situation as he was now. He usually shied from the unpleasant and shunned the violent. She looked over at Roger, again. His flush of embarrassment had gone and in place of it there seemed to be an apprehension as he watched and listened to John, as though he were turning to him now, to get them out of this predicament.

"Let's forget the personal angle," John went on. "For my part I'd like to forget it. Forever. The point is, Grant, what are you going to do about us? When the time comes for you to leave? When the storm is over?"

Without answering, Mike crossed over to an end table and took a cigarette from a box on the table. The three of them waited while he fumbled around in his pocket looking for a match.

"There are some matches on the table," John said.

He gave John a look that was meant to wither him. He found a match in his own pocket, lighting his cigarette with it. He took a deep puff of the cigarette, letting them wait a few more tense moments.

He was really fighting his temper. He was angry at Clara. At her stupid husband, at her jerk of a lover. At himself for going on the make for her. He would have liked to have screamed and beaten his head against the wall. He would have liked to have lined them all up, watched them while they played Russian roulette, dropping like dead flies at his feet. He would have liked to have started running, the diamonds under his arm, running and never stopping until he reached safety, that never, never Isle of Utopia. But he knew that he had to keep control of himself in order to win the last hand.

Roger, weak from his recent fever, had to sit down, but it didn't relieve his tenseness.

Clara stood stiffly, waiting for the fireworks. She felt that she alone knew Mike's unpredictable temperament. He might decide suddenly to turn on all of them, killing them without a chance for escape.

Only John still seemed calm. There was now a deadly calm about him, his impassive face showing no emotion whatsoever. It was as though what was happening around him now was of very little import. But his mind was working fast, building his defense, building defenses for all of them, searching for a way out of their dilemma.

He looked over at Clara, who was watching Mike. He knew her inner turmoil. He looked at the sick face Roger was presenting. He was no good to anyone now. That left only himself. He had to be the strong one.

"It would be a ridiculous thing," he said, "to kill all of us, if that's what you're planning. That would be four murders, including what was his name—? Burnsides. You'd never get away with it."

"Never," Mike said, "is a long time, Harris. Consider the domestic triangle." He nodded toward Clara and Roger. "Irate husband kills wife's lover, then turns gun on wife and himself. A perfect setup for me.

Staging the scene would be simple."

"It looks good, Grant, on the surface. Since you apparently figure no one knows you're here. But I don't think you want to kill us. In fact, I don't think you're really a killer. At heart, that is."

"I'll kill anyone who stands in my way now! I've worked too damned hard on this thing. Things have gone wrong, sure, but I'm gonna leave here with those diamonds! If I have to kill again to do it!"

"I think most people would kill when they're backed against a wall, when they see there's no other way out! But you'd be foolish to take another chance. They got the bullets out of Burnsides' body. They'd find the bullets that killed us were from the same gun."

"So what? They haven't traced the gun and if they do, they'll find it was a stolen gun. I bought it at a hot shop, where they sell stolen guns. They don't know who the hell the murderer is. So what gives with the bullets? Nothing."

"You don't think you're suspected at all?" John said.

"No!"

"Maybe the cops are in Westfield now, just waiting for the roads to open."

"Why *should* they be?"

"You followed Roger here. They might have followed you."

"I told you," Mike began to raise his voice, "they don't suspect me!"

"That's a lot of diamonds for an insurance company not to do a complete investigation. Didn't a detective question any of the hotel guests?"

"How should I know?"

"You sold jewelry at one time, didn't you? That's what you told us at dinner. You'd be a natural suspect then, living in the hotel and so forth."

"Lay off me, will you?" Mike shouted now.

Clara saw the uncontrollable anger welling up in him again. She was afraid John had gone too far.

"Weren't you questioned at all?"

"They don't suspect me! How many times do I have to tell you!"

"That's funny," John said, "when one edition of the paper I read said all of the hotel guests were questioned."

"That's right." Roger suddenly spoke up. "The District Attorney told me they figured it was an inside job, someone living in the hotel."

Mike swung around angrily, facing Roger. "What *else* did the D.A. tell you?"

Roger shook his head. "Nothing. Nothing at all. Except they knew it was a job by a professional. A professional planner, that is."

"What the hell does that mean? Everybody makes plans."

Roger looked over at John. He was making motions to him that meant something. What was it he wanted him to say?

John was trying a little mesmerism on Roger. Couldn't he be of some use? Couldn't he see what he was trying to do, put the fear of God in Mike. Think, Roger, think!

"Did the District Attorney say anything about the investigation by the insurance company?" John asked Roger.

"What?" Roger stared at him.

John nodded to him again as though he wanted him to confirm his remark, although it wasn't so. Then it seeped into his tired mind. John wanted him, as he was doing, to keep baiting Mike until they got him so nervous he might break down.

"Oh, yeah," Roger said. "He told me that the insurance company would leave no stone unturned. If they had a suspect they'd trail him for the next ten years until they found the diamonds." He took a deep breath after his fabrication, then he looked over at John. There was a slight smile on his face and it was one of satisfaction. He'd evidently said the right thing. At last he'd done something right. Although it was an infinitesimal thing, it would put him in a better light as far as John was concerned. And sick as he was he still felt like a damned fool, in John's eyes.

Mike looked from Roger to John. Dolan! If this were true, what Davis had just said, Dolan must have tailed him.

"Weren't you questioned at all, Grant? Before you left the hotel?" John started it all over again. He knew he'd have to be careful, but this was gambling. Gambling with big stakes, with people's lives. The biggest stakes. Although he had never gambled in his life, he had to do it now, but play it very close to the chest. "Didn't they question you, Grant?"

"Yes! Yes, goddamn it! I *was* questioned! By some jerky private eye. An insurance investigator! That's a laugh. A stupid jerk, if I ever saw one. He discovered he had nothing on me. He even apologized for searching my suitcases."

"Searching you?"

"That's right. He searched my room and didn't find a damn thing."

"Did he know about your work at the jewelry store?"

"I suppose."

"Did he question you about ever meeting Burnsides?"

"I don't remember!" Mike was getting angry again. "All I know is he didn't suspect me!"

John smiled with superior knowledge. "It's amazing to me, Grant, how you engineered this, then missed completely the psychological follow up.

Yes, it's an amazing thing about people—intelligent people, too. They've got it all figured out, all, that is, except the one thing that'll trip them up."

"What?"

"By now the insurance company, the cops, the D.A.'s office, they know everything about you. If you ever saw Burnsides, met him outside the store. If you ever talked to him about diamonds. They know, by now, every move you made, before and up to the murder. I'll go even farther; I'll make a bet with you. I'll bet they followed you clear to Westfield and they're sitting in town now waiting until the roads are clear."

Mike's eyes narrowed. He was listening carefully. John had called the shots awfully close. Maybe he was calling them too close for comfort. But he would have known if he were being tailed. He would have discerned the tail. What did he mean "missed psychologically"? It was true he hadn't figured he'd be questioned. But he hadn't planned on remaining in the hotel long enough to be questioned. Except for the diamonds being lost he wouldn't have been. Or would he? How the hell could he have missed so completely? The cops were stupid but, as Harris said, insurance companies very seldom missed. Why the devil hadn't he figured on the insurance company? Their damned private investigators, ugly little men who hid under bedclothes, in mattresses, drapes, behind old newspapers.

"What was the investigator's name?" John said. "Do you remember?"

"Yeah. Dolan. James Dolan."

John walked towards the phone.

"What're you gonna do?"

"Call the Starker Hotel. See if a James Dolan is registered there."

"You're nuts!"

"I don't think so."

Roger and Clara, absorbed with the sudden turn of events, watched John closely. Both of them were offering up fervent prayers that John's deduction, his intuition, would pay off.

Roger was secretly wishing he could show up as well as John was doing against a crook, a murderer of seeming intelligence. Whenever anyone, like the D.A., started to question him he became almost subservient, remaining always the little clerk on the high stool. If he could break out with something startling now maybe Clara might think of him differently instead of the way she seemed to be. Every time he looked at her his flesh crawled. She gave him the fish eye, of a dead fish. She looked as though she hated him. Could he help it because he got stuck and stranded and sick and had to come to her house for help? How did he know Mike Grant was there? How could a woman love one moment and hate the next? Feel something toward someone on Wednesday and on Thursday feel nothing but repulsion. God, if he were anyone but who he was, a person who loved life, he'd wish he were dead.

John dialed operator, asking for the hotel number. It took him a while to get through. Mike never took his eyes off John. He waited, seeming not even to breathe.

The desk clerk at the hotel finally said hello.

"This is John Harris, Jimmy. I wonder if you've got a James Dolan registered there." John glanced over at Mike, who was now moving toward him, an expression of incredulity shading his cagey face.

"Yes, Mr. Harris," the clerk said, "he's across the street eating right now."

There was a triumphant smile on John's face. Roger and Clara knew he had hit the bull's eye.

"Will you repeat that?" John said. He held the receiver for Mike to listen.

"Mr. James Dolan is across the street at the restaurant right now. Shall I give him a message?"

"Yes." John took the receiver from the stunned Mike. "Tell him that John Harris called. To call me as soon as he comes in. What? Oh, is that right? Well, glad to hear it. Thanks, Jimmy."

Mike, with the snort of a mad bull, pulled the phone away from John. He hung up the receiver and then with an angry heave he pulled the phone out of the wall, throwing it at John's feet.

"That little jerk! How the hell could he have tailed me and I not know it!"

John smiled. "It isn't easy to win, Grant. Failure comes much more readily."

"Shut up!" Mike turned and walked towards the front window. He pulled back the drapes and looked out. The rain was lessening but it looked just as bad out as it had before. He might as well take a chance on getting through a ring of fire.

"You can leave now," John said.

Mike swung around toward him. "What do you mean, leave now? Go out in that mess and get stuck?"

"No," John answered him quietly. "If you leave now you can get through. Jimmy, the desk clerk at the hotel, just told me the back road was open. That's what he said before you grabbed the phone. They just got the news. It'll take you through to Havensford from here. But Dolan still can't get through to us, yet."

"I don't believe you."

John turned toward Roger and Clara. "Didn't you hear me say to

Jimmy, 'Oh, is that right? Glad to hear it'?"

Clara nodded.

"That's when he told me about the road."

"Where do I go from Havensford?"

"If the road's open from Havensford, and it apparently is, you can circle around, back to New York City."

"I don't know the roads. You said the back road was a dirt road. It would be muddy. I might get stuck. Or lost. Is this a trick, Harris?"

"If you hadn't pulled the phone out I'd prove it to you. You can wait till dawn if you want to take that chance. You would have faster going." John shrugged. "The back road is treacherous. But as long as it's open. Of course, it's up to you. If you wait Dolan may get through to us. If you leave now you might get lost."

Mike turned and walked back to the window. He stood looking out, trying to decide what to do. If the road were open, and he was inclined to believe Harris, he might as well wait a couple more hours, take that chance on the light aiding him, rather than go along a treacherous road that was, as far as he was concerned, uncharted. He turned from the window.

"Go on upstairs. All of you!" he commanded them. "I'll do my own deciding."

John crossed over to Roger. "Come on, Roger. I'll get you back in bed first."

Roger allowed himself to be helped up. After all, he was sick and he felt a relapse coming on.

John and Roger started toward the stairs, Clara following. She looked back at Mike's troubled face and there was another fleeting moment of sympathy for this man of the handsome face and the mixed-up emotions, the warped mentality.

As the three of them reached the upstairs landing Mike called to them. They stopped and looked down.

"I've decided," he said, "to wait until it's light. I want every one of you to go to bed. Don't come back down here. And don't even come down when you hear me leaving." He pointed to the couch. "I'm going to sit here until dawn, so don't try anything."

"Don't worry about us, Grant. We're happy to know it's all over."

"It's not all over yet, Harris. And any minute I can change my mind. I've got nothing to lose now. And everything to gain."

They looked at each other, realizing the same thing, that they'd never be able to take a fear-free breath until this man was out of the house.

"If you need anything, Roger," John said, "just tap on the wall."

"No," Clara said. "He might hear you."

"He's not going to frighten me into letting Roger get sick again and not helping him."

"Thanks, John. I'll be okay." Roger nodded and walked into the back bedroom.

John and Clara went into her bedroom. They were silent until they were both ready for bed. Clara sighed with relief when she looked at the beckoning bed. Although there was still a fear of Mike and his unpredictability, the fear was beginning to recede again and the exhaustion she felt seemed to be foremost. She was glad that she had twin beds in her room. She wouldn't have to experience the embarrassment of being too close to John, now that he knew everything.

Just before John turned out the light he broke the silence. "That isn't true about the Havensford road," he said. "Being open."

Clara sat up in bed staring at him, surprise on her face.

"No. Jimmy at the hotel didn't say that. He told me his wife was going to have another baby and I said, 'Is that right, Jimmy? Well, glad to hear it.' I faked it, the road business. When he tries to get through this morning he'll be marooned. In the meantime, after he leaves, I'll get down the road to Parsons's and call Dolan at the hotel."

She smiled wearily and John turned out the light. "The battle of wits," she said, "is on your side."

Of all three men, she thought; Roger, the suave, now as helpless as a woman. Mike, handsome and hateful and really stupid. John, the smart one, the thinker. And she'd given him up for a cheap substitute.

Mike, sitting alone in the darkness, started back to review his last few days. And try as he would he could only lay the blame for everything that had gone wrong on one thing, on the elements—if the wind hadn't blown up suddenly and the resultant fiasco awakened Burnsides there would have been no reason to kill him. The theft wouldn't have been discovered until the next morning and Mike would have had plenty of time to make his getaway. Without the noise of the shots, the murder, there would have been no bumping into Clara and the loss of the diamonds.

So the elements had tricked him. Not as Harris put it, his lack of psychological preparation, whatever the hell that was, not his lack of insight or foresight as far as the insurance company was concerned, not his rashness in killing Burnsides, nor his emotional instability—none of this was to blame. The weakness lay with the gods, Fate, circumstance. He had been a victim of circumstance. Even the flood, even after all the rest—if there hadn't been a flood he'd be gone.

But come high water or another hell, in some manner, he was going to win. He knew it. He had to know it! To keep knowing it!

17

The call from John Harris was given to Dolan when he went back to the hotel. Jimmy, the desk clerk, handed him the written message.

Dolan looked up from the surprising message.

"John Harris? Is this Clara Harris's husband?"

Jimmy nodded.

"How long ago did he call?"

"Just about ten or fifteen minutes ago."

"Get him for me on the phone, immediately. I'll take the call in my room."

"Yes, sir." Jimmy turned to the switchboard while Dolan hurried up the stairs to his room.

He waited and, instead of Harris, it was Jimmy the clerk's voice.

"The operator says Mr. Harris's line is out of order, Mr. Dolan."

"Are the lines down because of the storm?"

"No, sir," the clerk said. "I asked her and she said that it was only Mr. Harris's phone that was out of order."

"Thank you." Dolan hung up more puzzled than ever.

He began to try and add it up. In the first place, how did Harris know Dolan was at the hotel? And in the second place, why would he call unless it were a call for help?

He started back to review the facts in the case. Assuming that Roger Davis were an innocent victim and was merely shielding Clara Harris; and that she, Clara, knew something about the theft, the murder; that she saw either the killer or the actual killing. If so, the murderer, in this case Grant, knew that she could identify him and had tailed Davis to her house.

But the case of diamonds, where were they?

He started over again. Supposing the suitcase with the woman's things in it was Clara Harris's and Grant had got it by mistake in some way. If the mistake had also involved Clara getting the case of diamonds, then there would be a double motive for Grant tracking her down.

Now the call from Harris for help from Grant, who might at this moment be threatening all of them and had evidently cut the phone wires.

There was, also, another possibility, that only John Harris was innocent and was desperately trying to call for help; to tell what he knew about the trio.

This was really one for the books, but Dolan had had plenty of cases as screwy. The strange, coincidental elements that go to make up life—detectives should know them better than anyone.

18

When Roger went upstairs he knew exactly what he was going to do. He was going to search John's room (the back bedroom where he was to sleep) for John's car keys. They might be in his overcoat pocket. Roger had seen John's overcoat hanging in the closet. Or they might be in John's coat or pants pocket. If the latter, he would either have to wait until John and Clara were asleep to search in their room or abandon his scheme.

When he found the keys he was going to make his preparations to get away, take John's car out of the garage, push it down the driveway on to the highway, and head it toward the back road which John said was open.

He had two reasons for daring this. He wasn't going to stay in that house all night. He had a strange foreboding that Mike Grant was going to kill all of them. And even if he didn't, he saw which way the wind was blowing. He and Clara would never be together again. She'd either stay with John, depending upon how John felt, or she'd divorce and probably leave town, leaving Roger and all of the tragic picture behind. The future, no matter how he figured it, didn't include him any longer.

And more importantly, he wanted the ten-thousand-dollar reward. He needed it. He *had* to have it. Then all that he'd gone through for one moment of pleasure would be worth it. He could use the money to assuage his hurt pride. He could use it better than John or Clara or some stupid cop. If he invested part of it right he could live for a few years without working. The few thousand plus his bank account would give him a nice long vacation, a thing greatly needed at this moment.

After he found John's keys he would wait an hour or so. Mike would fall asleep, maybe. He'd had enough to drink to make him drowsy. He couldn't keep awake five hours till dawn. It wasn't human. Anyway there would be a way to get out of the house.

The more he thought about it the better he felt. He was actually getting over his cold. Having important work to do is a form of medicine and more potent than any pills.

He could hear John and Clara getting into bed. When he heard their light go out, he got up and went to the closet. He opened the door. Besides John's overcoat there was a raincoat hanging next to it. John must have worn the raincoat over his overcoat. The raincoat was still slightly damp.

He searched the pockets of the raincoat, then the overcoat. No keys of any kind. How stupid of him. The keys wouldn't be in his outside coat pocket. Where did he put his own keys? In his pants pocket. Or when he hung up his clothes he took out the keys, wallet and so forth, and put them on the dresser.

He'd have to search John and Clara's room.

He slipped out of the pajamas John had given him to wear and put on an old suit of John's, since his own was still wet, then he put John's robe back on, sat down on the edge of the bed and lit a cigarette. He'd give them all half an hour anyway, to get to sleep.

19

Roger woke with a start. He'd fallen to sleep himself. The cigarette he'd been smoking had burned itself out in the ashtray. He sat up and looked at his watch. He had slept over an hour. He walked to the hall door. Opening it a crack, he stood and listened. Only the sound of John's snoring. The sound of the snoring and the sound of the rain. He stepped into the hall. Easing slowly past Clara's bedroom door, he arrived at the head of the stairs. He peered down into the darkness. He could see Mike's outline on the couch, his arm dangling over the back. By the way his arm hung there, limply, Roger was sure Mike was asleep. He turned toward Clara's door when he heard the sudden movement downstairs. He turned back.

Mike had jumped up and was standing at the bottom of the stairs. "Who's up?" He peered up the stairs. "Come here. In the light. So I can see you!"

Roger, cursing under his breath, moved into the light.

"I was coming from the bathroom," he said.

"Okay." Roger saw that Mike was holding a gun on him. "Get back in your room. The next time you have to go to the can, tell me first."

"All right, sir." Roger sneered, but Mike was unable to see the disrespect on his face.

Roger turned and went back into his room. Damn it! He'd have to wait another damned half hour! Until Mike settled down again. He stood next to the wall, listening for movement from Clara and John. Apparently they had slept through it. Everybody but Mike, God damn him, was exhausted from their ordeal.

While he was waiting he'd have to figure out another way of escaping from the house. He'd have to make a rope of bedclothes and ease himself down into the backyard.

He began to pull the covers from the bed. He worked furiously now, against time, for time would bring the daylight and everything he was gambling on would be lost.

When he had the rope of bedclothes tied and dangling out of the window he looked again at his watch. He had been working a half hour. He went to the door again and listened. This time he wouldn't dare Fate and walk to the head of the stairs. He'd go right to John and Clara's room and try to find the keys.

If either Clara or John woke up he'd have to take a chance on telling them he was on his way to the bathroom again and had opened the wrong door.

He began to get a mounting thrill from his nefarious activities. This was the most daring, the bravest thing he'd ever done in his whole routine-dulled life, broken only by his various romances. This was what a daring man would do, a soldier, or a spy, or a hunted man, a condemned man staking all on his escape. This would make up for every suffering moment he'd had when he saw others before him waving their banners of the brave, bowing to the adulations of the cheering public.

This would really make him front-page news, in the hero's way. He could visualize the papers now: "Westfield Man Hero," "Westfield Man, Roger Davis, Saves Trio from Killer." "Roger Davis, Bank Teller, recipient of ten-thousand-dollar reward for aiding in capture of murderer."

He got to Clara's door. He stood and listened. No sound from within. He opened the door slowly, easing himself into the room. He looked over at John and Clara. John was sleeping on his face, the pillow over his head. Clara was on her side, one arm flung outside the covers. Her posture told him that she was so exhausted it would probably take a lot to awaken her.

He moved over to the dresser. He reached up, his hand moving quietly over the top. Suddenly he came in contact with something cold. The keys! Yes, the keys! His hot hand folded over them. He squeezed them tightly to keep them from jangling. He pulled his closed fist back. Back. Now his body. Moving slowly back from the dresser toward the door, watching the beds for any sudden movement.

Now he was within inches of the door. He kept backing toward it. Reaching around behind him he opened the door wider. He continued backing, into the hall. Just a few inches farther and he would be out, and could shut the door again.

When Mike shot, the first bullet ricocheted off the door frame and past Roger's head.

Roger, panic on his white face, turned toward the sound of the gun.

Mike shot again, this time straight at him, through his chest. He stumbled forward, falling to the floor. He almost got up on his feet again as Mike shot the third time. His body stiffened in mid-air. He whirled around like a marionette, falling toward the stairway. His body rolled to the edge of the stairs and then started its terrifying descent to the bottom.

Mike had shot from the back bedroom doorway, where he had been standing while Roger was in John and Clara's room. He had heard Roger in the hall and had slipped up the stairs, quietly waiting for him in the doorway. The door to the bedroom was open. The wind and rain were coming through the open window, next to where Roger had pushed the bed with his bedclothes rope tied to the bedpost, the other end dangling out of the window like a white flag of surrender.

With the sound of the first shot John was up and at the door. He quickly saw what was happening. Clara began to scream. He shut the door and crossed over to her, taking her in his arms, trying to quiet her.

When the firing ceased he went to the door again. Opening it cautiously, he peered into the hall. He saw the finish of Roger's descent down the stairs. Mike, as though he were in a daze, was standing at the top of the stairs watching Roger's battered body come to rest at the bottom.

John ran into the hall, brushing past Mike, and down the stairs. When he reached Roger he saw that he was dead, his hand clutching a set of keys. He prised open his fist. They were Clara's house keys.

Mike had come down the stairs, too, and was standing by him. "He was trying to get away," he said. "I was in his room. A rope was tied to the bed. He was trying to get away."

"These are Clara's house keys."

"He was in your room. I told her, I told Clara that if he knew about the reward for me—he must have known about it—he'd swim to the nearest police station to turn me in. I was right."

John looked up the stairs. Clara was standing at the top landing now, clutching her robe around her, her eyes popping out of her head with fear, her terrified face staring down at John.

"Your keys, Clara." John held them up. "He must have thought he was taking my car keys."

"I had to kill him. Don't you understand? He was trying to get away."

Dead? Roger dead? Clara couldn't believe it. Roger dead! That's what he said. That's what Mike had said. He said "I had to kill him. He was trying to get away."

"John," she called faintly, "is—is Roger dead?"

"Yes, Clara." He turned to Mike. "Go upstairs," he said, "and get a sheet so I can cover him up."

Mike nodded meekly. He seemed to be glad someone else was taking charge. As he started up the stairs he felt ill, weak, sick to his stomach. His head began to hurt like hell. His head was in a vice. If he could remove his head everything would be all right. He used to have these headaches when he was a little boy, after anger. He used to think his head would explode. Now, every step he took shook him as though he were made of jelly. Was he? Was he made of jelly? With a head in a vice?

Clara saw Mike coming upstairs. She turned from him. To her, he wasn't a man made of jelly. He was a leper lunging at her. She fled back to her own room. She shut and locked the door and then she began to break, her nerves finally giving way. Roger dead? Why? *Why* did he have to die? He loved living so much—so much ... She began to pace up and down the room, clutching her hands, releasing them, clutching them again so tightly that if she were aware of the pain she would have ceased. The back of her neck! A pressure. A pressure was forming at the base of her skull. Her neck was stiffening. She felt hot all over. Her heart was beating so fast she thought she was going to die. She began to moan, the moans turning into sobs. *Roger!* Roger dead? Oh, my God! We'll be next. John! He'll kill John. And if he does what will happen to me? He'll attack me. Kill me. *Why*, oh, why, God, *why* has this happened to me? I was willing to give up Roger. I *did* give him up. I'm even willing to give John up to make my peace with God. Please help me!

What did miserable sinners do? They knelt on their knees and besought long and humbly. She flung herself down by the bed. She grasped her nervous hands together in an attitude of prayer. Her hands were shaking so she could scarcely hold up her arms. She began to pray, her sobs quieting, becoming more regular in their rhythm. "Dear God," she whispered, "if there is a God of Mercy, help me now. Help John and me. Help us!"

She put her head down on the bed and closed her eyes. She was so tired, so awfully tired. Wouldn't there ever be a surcease, a chance for rest? Roger—Roger! Oh, God!

John had to cover Roger's body. Mike couldn't help him. He had got so ill that he went to the bathroom and vomited. He had killed Burnsides in what could be termed cold blood, but he hadn't remained to look at the body. He hated blood. He couldn't look at blood. Cruel and calculating as he was, as he envisioned himself, he couldn't look at blood. John knew that if he hadn't lied about the road being open Roger would have never attempted his ill-fated scheme. And yet he also knew that circumstance had been against Roger. From the beginning. Whether anyone else believed it or not, he believed there was a law of retribution and that it had just taken care of Roger.

20

Clara and John were sitting in the living room on straight-backed chairs which Mike had brought in from the dining room. He had forced them to sit that way the better part of an hour.

Roger's body, now covered by the sheet, was still where it had fallen. The crisis had passed for Clara, but she was so sick from fear and exhaustion, from the terror she'd gone through, that she could scarcely sit up, yet she knew she didn't dare move. Both she and John were prepared for the worst, but neither wanted to precipitate it in any way.

Ever since the killing, Mike, gun in hand, had been pacing up and down in the room, lighting one cigarette after another. He had got over his sickness but he was unnerved and he knew it. Yet he was trying desperately not to telegraph his inner emotions to John and Clara. Every so often he would consult his watch, then stop by the window and peer out, as if by doing so he could force the dawn to come sooner.

But that he was almost as upset as Clara and John was obvious to John. He knew that Mike was suffering now with an inner frustration, an inner guilt, as though he had not wanted to kill Roger, as though he regretted it, wished he could have prevented it.

John watched him closely, wondering if he dare speak to him. Soon his curiosity got the better of his fear.

"You wonder," he said quietly, "why this turned out so badly, don't you?"

Mike, stopping abruptly, turned toward John. "What did you say?"

"You wonder," John repeated, "how this could have turned into such an utter failure."

"How *what* could have turned into failure? Who's failed?"

"You have," John said.

"Why do you say that?"

"You didn't mean to kill Roger."

"He was trying to get away. I had to kill him. I had to."

"Basically, Grant, you're not a killer. I told you that before."

"Okay. You're so smart, writing a book on philosophy. *You* tell me about myself. Why don't you think I'm a killer?"

"You don't want to hear the truth."

"Go ahead, now that you've started it."

John looked over at Clara. He saw she was still standing up under the terrific strain, but how much more could she take? Could he take? If he could only keep this maniac interested until he could figure out what move to make next, or until dawn, when he hoped to God he would leave.

"I said go ahead, Harris! Are you gonna talk or just sit there?"

"All right, Grant. You asked for it. To begin with, killing Burnsides unnerved you. From that time on you've made wrong decisions, let yourself go, talked too much and so forth.

"There are many types of killers. There's an 'I could kill that guy' type who someday gets an inflamed emotion—his wife cheats on him—his best friend steals from him—somebody merely calls him a name—and he suddenly finds, in that moment of seeing red, that he is an actual killer. That's not your type. You've got angry here two or three times but you haven't killed at those moments.

"There's the cold-blooded killer, whose ego is his God. He'll kill anything that stands in his way. He has no conscience at all. We've stood in your way but you haven't killed us yet, that is, Clara and myself.

"There's the maniac killer, the quirk with the idiosyncrasy, the peeping Tom, the rapist, the so-called vampire. You're not in any of these categories. You've killed because you were afraid—self-preservation. You killed Burnsides probably because you were afraid he'd kill you. You killed Roger because you were afraid he'd get away, turn you in. And maybe you thought he was going to kill you."

He saw Mike's eyes shift meaningfully. What he was saying was hitting at the target.

"And you're in this mess," he went on, "because of your fear. But that's not all. I don't think you're a genuine criminal type either. Not even the petty thief type. This is your first job. You've bungled it. You're an egoist. You're not quite balanced right, emotionally. But who is? But you chose the wrong profession.

"You're not exactly afraid of dying. You're afraid of not getting away. Of not being able to do all the wonderful things you've planned. Yet you feel, despite all that's happened, you *will* get away. You have the idea that you're indestructible, which comes with youth and inflated ego. You would have been better off if you could have found a rich woman and married her or had become a gigolo—"

Mike had been listening intently to John's analysis of him as though he were standing awed before an oil portrait of himself, painted by a master painter. But during the last few words his eyes shifted again, this time towards the door. John caught the movement and looked over at Clara. She, too, was staring at the front door.

"What's the matter?" John said.

"Didn't you hear that?" Mike said. "I heard a knock on the door."

"So did I," Clara said.

They listened. In a few minutes it came again. This time John heard it. It was a knock. There was no doubt about it.

Mike crossed to the window. Cautiously pulling the drape, he looked out.

Clara and John waited tensely.

Mike turned back, his expression puzzled. "There's no car out there. I can't see anyone at the door."

He'd no sooner said this than there was another knock. This time Mike stiffened as though he'd heard a ghost whisper.

"Why don't you answer the door?" John said.

Mike glared at him. "*You* open it!"

John got up slowly. He walked across the floor, passing in front of Mike. He stopped at the door. Mike moved over, standing a few feet behind John, holding the gun on his back. Fear began to gnaw at Clara again. She started to shake all over, as though she had the ague.

John opened the door wide, flinging it back, proclaiming his courage, though his heart, too, was beating rapidly.

There was no one at the door. No one in front. No one anywhere. Mike leaped ahead of him and outside.

Clara had risen by now and was standing in the doorway beside John.

As Mike came back into the room Clara and John moved to their prisoners' chairs again.

"It must have been a branch of a tree," he said, "hitting the door."

"There are no branches near enough to the house," John said.

Mike turned round to shut the door. He was just reaching out his hand to fasten the night latch when they heard the voice.

"Drop your gun, Grant!" The voice came from somewhere inside the house. Mike swung around quickly, firing toward the darkened dining room. The shot was wild. Clara began to scream. John ran over to her, pulling her back against the wall.

The first fire from the man's gun dropped Mike, and James Dolan stepped into the light. He had come in the back, through the kitchen door, and had been standing in the dining room, in the shadows.

As Dolan walked toward the living room the knocking began again. Clara and John, still standing, their backs against the wall, watched Dolan cross the living room to the front door. He opened the door and a policeman, with drawn gun, stepped into the room.

John realized what had happened then. The cop had been doing the knocking and then disappearing, to distract Mike while the other man entered the back.

The cop nodded to Dolan and then stooped down to examine Mike's body.

Dolan turned to John. "You're John Harris?"

John nodded.

"You called me at the Starker Hotel. I'm James Dolan."

John looked at him, amazed. "How did you get through?"

"The back road's open. Clear to Westfield now."

"What?"

"It's been open for a couple of hours but it's slow going."

"Roger *could* have made it then, Clara, if he could have got away."

Dolan looked from one to the other, then he suddenly spotted Roger's covered body at the foot of the stairs. He walked over to it, pulling back the sheet. "Roger Davis?"

"Yes," John said. "He was trying to get out to get help when Grant caught him."

"Please," Clara said. "Please, John, ask him if I can—can go and lie down. I don't think I can stand it any longer."

Dolan looked over at Clara. "Are you Mrs. Harris?"

"Yes," John said, "this is my wife, Mrs. Harris."

"Was that your suitcase Grant got by mistake?"

She nodded.

"Clara got his case," John interposed quickly. "He followed Roger here. He was holding us here, trying to get away by dawn."

"Now that the road's cleared I'll need you both in Westfield. At the station. For questioning."

"We understand," John said. "And the diamonds. They're here. Where are they, Clara?"

"I don't know … I don't know. I think they're in the linen closet. He took the key to the linen closet. It's probably in his pocket. Please, please don't ask me any more questions now."

"I'm sorry, Mrs. Harris," Dolan said.

The cop knelt down beside Mike's body and started through his pockets.

"The thing that puzzles me," Dolan turned to John, "is how you knew my name. How you knew I was at the hotel."

"Grant told me your name. I bet him that you'd followed him here. As you can see, I won my bet."

Dolan looked down at Mike's body. "They don't know when to shut up, do they?"

"Could I take my wife upstairs, Dolan? She's pretty sick, exhausted. It's been a terrible ordeal for us."

"Yes. I'm sorry, Mrs. Harris. I know it's been rough on all of you, but I'm here to find things out, you know." He looked at his watch. "It's after 4 a.m. We won't need you until this afternoon. By then I hope the roads will be even better."

John helped Clara toward the stairs. When they came to Roger's body she stopped, shuddering violently. She looked at John and the tears began to course down her cheeks. "I don't think I can stand it, John. Help me."

He leaned over and picked her up, carrying her up on to the landing, away from Roger's body. He set her down on the steps. She was able to make it the rest of the way upstairs, although her legs were heavy as lead and it seemed every step she took was like pulling her feet out of quicksand.

She stopped on the upstairs landing, turning to John. "What's going to happen to us, John? That's the important thing now."

"They won't hold us, Clara. They know."

"No, I mean you and me."

He smiled gently. "I'm no good without you, Clara."

"You mean you want me to stay?"

"Only if you want to. We'll go away. I'll resign. We'll go away. Italy, maybe. France."

"We can't."

"We have to go away. Start over again."

"I guess you could finish your book anywhere, couldn't you? I can help you. I can really help you now, John."

He took her by the arm, leading her to the door of her room. He leaned down and kissed her on the cheek. "You lie down for a while. Then this afternoon, tonight, it'll be all over."

She looked at him quizzically, doubt still in her eyes. "You don't—hate me, John?"

"You don't ask people you hate to stay with you. I can see things more clearly, too. Part of the burden belongs to me."

She smiled, accepting his sudden humility.

He opened the bedroom door for her. "I'll go on back downstairs. If you need me, call."

"I'm afraid."

"No, you're not afraid, now. It's all over, Clara. You've always had courage. Remember, you used to say, 'I can shut the door, John, on anything unpleasant.' Shut the door now, Clara. Black it out."

He caught her hand as she started in the room, drawing her close to him. He kissed her. She began to cry again. He released her and she walked slowly into the room. The sun was trying to break through the clouds. The dawn was rising. She could see it through the windows. She crossed the room and stood looking out on to and into the new day.

What was that Bible verse? "... All days are not the same and some come that can be called miraculous ..."

Was this one of those days the verse had reference to—? Was this a new day? A rebirth? One does not have to die to be reborn. Rebirth goes on hourly, all through life. One has only to be willing to accept the change.

She was willing, oh God. She was ready—to be reborn, to change her old self for a new one—with more courage, more understanding—greater love, more desire for the things of the soul—.

Peace—quietude of spirit—appreciation of true principles—

—John!

THE END

You've seen the movie, now read the book...

FILM NOIR CLASSICS

Jay Dratler · **The Pitfall** · $14.95
An adulterous liaison puts the life of family man in jeopardy.
Filmed in 1948 with Dick Powell, Lizbeth Scott, Jane Wyatt and Raymond Burr.
"Taut, uneasy, downbeat and unputdownable."
—Paul Burke, *CrimeTime*

Marty Holland · **Fallen Angel** · $15.95
A con man drifter tries to pull a grift on a naïve young woman with a large inheritance, but becomes involved with another woman.
Filmed in 1945 with Dana Andrews, Alice Faye and Linda Darnell.
"If you like movement, just watch Marty Holland step on the gas."
—*Liverpool Echo*

Lois Eby & John C. Fleming · **The Velvet Fleece** · $15.95
It's up to Rick to get the fix in by conning a rich widow, but can he pull it off with his boss' girlfriend hot on his heels?
Filmed as *Larceny* in 1948 with John Payne, Joan Caulfield, Dan Duryea and Shelley Winters.
"...pack[s] a punch inside its fleece-lined velvet glove."—Curtis Evans

Stark House Press, 1315 H Street, Eureka, CA 95501
greg@starkhousepress.com / www.StarkHousePress.com
Available from your local bookstore, or order direct via our website.

www.ingramcontent.com/pod-product-compliance
Lightning Source LLC
LaVergne TN
LVHW021804060526
838201LV00058B/3229